SONG OF BLOOD & STONE

EARTHSINGER
CHRONICLES
BOOK 1

L. PENELOPE

HEARTSPELL

Heartspell Media, LLC
www.heartspell.com

Cover design by James T. Egan of Bookfly Design
Interior book design by reflection:digital

Penelope, L.
    Song of Blood & Stone / L. Penelope - 1st ed.
    ISBN: 978-0-9909228-0-3
    1. Fantasy — Romance. — Fiction. I. Title

Printed in the United States of America.

First Edition: January 2015
This Edition: June 2015

10 9 8 7 6 5 4 3 2 1

For my father,
who wanted me to live a happy life

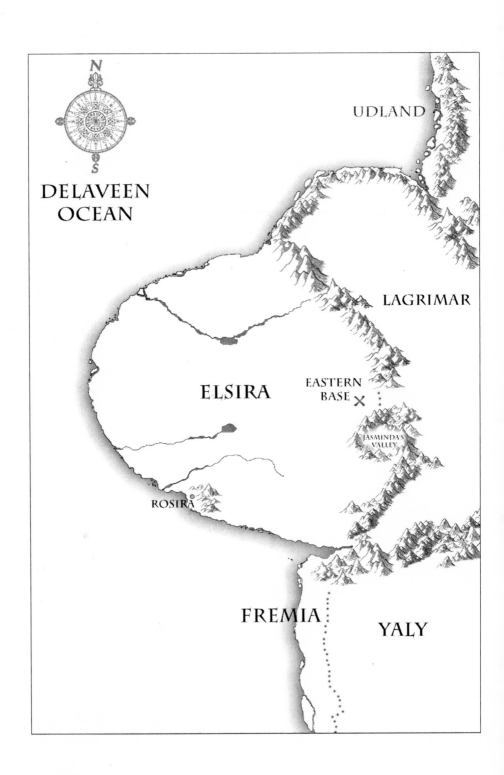

CHAPTER ONE

NOT FOR THE first time, Jasminda wished for invisibility. Sadly, it was not one of her gifts. To the best of her knowledge, Earthsong couldn't be used for such a thing. She wished she could ask Papa about it, along with his recipe for sweet turnip bread, a clearer understanding of the plumbing he'd installed in the cabin, and how he'd managed to walk through this town for nearly twenty years with a smile on his face.

Do what you think you can't, he always said. So she raised her chin a notch higher, ignoring the heads that turned as she passed and the stares that followed her down the street.

It wasn't exactly a smile, but it would have to do.

The bell on the door of the post station tinkled obscenely when she entered. Postwoman Mineeve emerged from the back with a smile on her face. It promptly fell when she saw her customer.

"Just one moment," she said curtly before disappearing behind the curtain again.

One moment became many, and Jasminda kept a restless eye on the wall clock, her fingers drumming an impatient rhythm in time with every tick. The front door sang out again, admitting an elderly woman who gasped at the sight of Jasminda.

"Don't worry, I'm not contagious." Jasminda crossed her arms as the woman kept her distance all the same, her back pressed against the wall as if being confronted by a wild animal and not a nineteen-year-old girl.

Jasminda smiled bitterly before closing her eyes and focusing on the well of power within her. By itself, her Song was nothing but raw potential, a match waiting for a strike. But when the rush of Earthsong swept over her, the match caught fire, burning bright.

She opened her eyes, the flame inside as hot as her temper. Extending her arms, she scrutinized the deep, rich tone of her skin, so different than everyone else in the town, than just about everyone in the entire country of Elsira. The energy rippling through her gave her a deeper connection to her body. She became even more aware of her skin, how it knit together over muscle and bones. Silently, she sang a spell to shift its color to match the wilted, less vibrant shade of the astonished woman in front of her.

"Better?"

The woman made a sound like a cat struggling with a hairball and reached back, grabbing at the doorknob several times before she was successful.

"*Grol* witch," she muttered, wrenching the door open and fleeing, the bell overhead singing its good-bye.

Jasminda released her hold on the power. Her skin changed back to its natural hue. She hugged her hand to her chest and sank back against the counter. Using Earthsong left her invigorated, but she had to be shrewd. There was no telling what she might meet on the journey home, and she didn't want to be depleted.

Her skin color and Earthsinging abilities had come from Papa, hallmarks of his native land of Lagrimar. Her citizenship in this country had come from her Elsiran mother who'd been gone so long the memories of her kind eyes and gentle touch had dwindled to almost nothing. Jasminda's heart ached a constant pulse of longing. Mama, gone these eight years. Papa and the twins gone these past two.

She blinked back tears as Mineeve finally returned, a parcel wrapped in brown paper in her arms. The woman dropped the package heavily on the counter. Jasminda scowled, though there was nothing fragile inside, merely her monthly delivery of books, a favorite escape from the drudgery and loneliness of farm life.

"You been scaring off my customers again?" Mineeve asked, not attempting to hide her hostility. Jasminda's spine straightened, and she redoubled her desire to get through the afternoon and back to the safety of her quiet home as quickly as possible. A storm was brewing over the mountains. A bad one, and she couldn't risk being caught crossing when it struck.

Without a word, she placed her payment on the counter, scooped up the package, and headed for the door.

"Oy," Mineeve called, and Jasminda turned back. "You forgot this." She waved a letter in the air. One look was all it took to confirm that it was one that Jasminda had sent herself weeks before, RETURN TO SENDER scrawled across the front in elegant script. This letter—and all the others she'd sent over the past two years—had been returned, unopened, after traveling much farther than Jasminda ever had. All the way to Elsira's capital city of Rosira on the western coast. She had no doubt that the handwriting on the front belonged to her maternal grandmother. After all, the woman had spent the past twenty years denying Jasminda's existence.

"Keep it," she said through gritted teeth.

"Maybe you should send a telegram," Mineeve said under her breath as she ripped up the letter and tossed it in the wastebasket. Jasminda left the post station cursing the merry bell that ushered her exit.

The area around the row of shops was quiet. It was only an hour before most of the merchants would pack up and leave for the day, and she had one stop left to make.

The blacksmith shop was at the end of the row. She entered the warm building and placed her package on the counter. Smith Bindeen turned from his forge and smiled at her. Against her wishes, her heart unclenched. Bindeen had been the closest thing to a friend Papa had made in town and was the only one who didn't make her feel like a five-legged dog.

"Jasminda, it's been a while."

"As long as I can make it," she said, smiling sadly. She gave him her order, and he gathered the supplies she needed: nails, an axe head, shotgun shells, door hinges.

"Haven't seen a winter this mild in a little while. Think it'll last?" he asked.

She relaxed a fraction at his kind manner. "Bad storm's hitting the mountain tonight. Don't think it'll reach town, but best be careful."

"How bad d'ya reckon it'll be?" He avoided her eyes as he spoke.

"As bad as two years ago." She kept her voice steady but clenched her hands into fists. Forced back the memory of searching the mountain paths for Papa and her brothers. Of never finding any trace of them.

Bindeen pursed his lips and packaged her purchases.

"That'll be fifty pieces."

Jasminda frowned. She was used to being cheated by the other merchants and avoided them whenever she could, preferring to order through the catalogs what she couldn't make herself. That way she just had to pick up the packages from Mineeve. But she'd always trusted Bindeen.

"I'm not tryin' to cheat ya, young miss. The price of everything's gone up. Taxes, too, especially on what comes imported in. It's the best price I can give."

She searched the man's face and found him sincere. Using Earthsong would have confirmed his intentions, letting her feel the truth in his heart, but she didn't bother, instead counting out the money and placing it in his hand.

"If ya have any of that magic cream of yours, ya can make some of this back, eh?" He flexed his empty hand, gnarled with arthritis.

"It's not magic—just goat's milk and herbs." She fished around in her bag and dug out a jar, handing it to him and pocketing the money he gave back to her.

"Works like that magic of yours is all I know."

"You're not afraid of Earthsong like everyone else. Why?"

Bindeen shrugged. "I fought in the Sixth Breach. I've seen the power of those *grol* witches." Jasminda flinched at the epithet, but Bindeen didn't notice. "I been in sandstorms in the middle of a wheat field, pelted with rocks and hail and fire. It's a blessed mercy it can't be used to kill directly. Even so, that Earthsong of yours . . . There's plenty of reason to fear it. But I've also seen your father put a man's bone back in its socket and heal it up good as new without ever touching him."

He smiled and patted his hip. "This joint he fixed is the only one on me that doesn't ache." He sobered and looked down. "Most folks hate easy and love hard. Should be the other way around, I reckon."

"Maybe so," she said, placing her newest packages into her overstuffed bag. "Thank you. May She bless your dreams."

"And yours, as well." He bowed his head with the farewell as Jasminda left the shop.

The sun was hours away from setting, though the journey home would take her much of the night. Even leaving now she'd have to cross the steep mountain paths in the dark. When she was younger and her family would go into town to trade, they would break up the long walk by camping in a little grassy area halfway up the mountain. These days, she opted for a faster turnaround. The entire trip from door slam to door slam was almost twenty-four hours. It left her sore and tired but kept the time she spent away from home to a minimum. Had the bit of her axe not been worn to a nub, she wouldn't have risked a trip so close to the storm at all.

The skies remained deceptively clear as she hurried along the street. Not so much as a cloud marred the blue overhead. Horses and carts rumbled down the tightly packed dirt road, just like any other day, except today, right in front of the city hall sat a sparkling, hulking automobile.

Dazzling chrome and black steel glinted in the sunlight, and a throng of townsfolk gathered around it, speaking in hushed voices. Jasminda tried not to stare. These autos were common in the cities from what she'd read, and she'd seen pictures, but way out here on the edge of nowhere, a real, live automobile had never graced the streets before. The mayor stood next to it, pride of ownership coming off him like steam.

A small boy and girl were among those stroking the metal, their mouths open in awe. A tall man had even set up a camera on a wooden tripod in the middle of the street.

"Photographs! Two pieces!" he shouted, and the crowd tittered with excitement. The two children pulled at their mother's skirt, begging for a photograph.

Jasminda paused, her gaze glued to the family. Farmers, by the looks of them. The young mother held a baby and smiled lovingly down at her other two children. The father kept an arm around his wife protectively. They were the first to take their photo with the vehicle, and the anticipation in the air was thick as butter as the flash popped and crackled.

Jasminda had a photo of her own family at home on the mantle. It was taken at the traveling carnival that had set up a few kilometres outside of town the summer her brothers had turned six. She had been eight and witnessed the intense negotiation by her mother to get the photographer to even allow "a pair of *grols*"—Jasminda and her father—to sit for the photo.

At the time, Jasminda had still thought of having a family of her own someday. She'd noticed the stares and whispers that followed them whenever they left their home, of course. She and Papa looked different than everyone else and could use Earthsong, while Mama and the twins looked Elsiran and had no magic. Two parents from two different lands. But the long war between Elsira and Lagrimar had still been an abstract concept back then. The hatred was something she'd learned later. She had still dreamed of meeting her fairy-tale prince who would take her away from the goats and the chickens of her valley to somewhere new and spectacular. Not until she'd become a teenager had that dream died forever and she'd accepted she would always be alone.

The children's laughter across the street brought Jasminda back to the present. They pleaded and begged for another photo as the parents corralled them away to make way for the next in line.

"Let's hear it run," someone said, and a chorus of agreement rang out. Jasminda pivoted to leave; though she was curious about the auto, mistrustful gazes had already turned her way. She'd made it only about a metre when an earsplitting *bang* sounded.

Several things happened at the same time. White smoke shot from the back of the vehicle into the gathered crowd. A horse tied just behind the auto reacted to the noise, rearing on its hind legs. The little girl stumbled backward, out of her father's grip and directly into the path of the horse's front legs as they came crashing down.

A sickening crunch of bone echoed in Jasminda's ears. Screaming, shouting, chaos all around became a fog hovering on the edge of her senses. She kneeled down next to the child, not remembering having crossed the street. Not having made a conscious decision at all. Tears streamed down her face as she did what came naturally to her.

With a deep breath, she reached out to Earthsong. The first moments of tapping into that infinite sea of life energy were like drowning. Even the small trickle flowing through her was overwhelming. The combined life force of every living thing pulsing in her veins made her sensitive to the raging emotions around her—shock and grief, pain and sorrow. Blocking them out, she focused only on the girl, who gasped desperately for breath through a crushed rib cage, a bone piercing her lungs. Jasminda's Song was not nearly as strong as her father's had been—he would have been able to erase every injury, making the child as good as new—but she could ensure that the girl would survive.

Life energy flowed into Jasminda, and she focused it into the child. Though she didn't know the names of all the internal organs, she could sense their damage and sang a spell to route the healing energy to them. She restored the lungs and stanched the flow of blood that had been leaking internally. The broken bones would have to be set, but at least the child would live long enough to have that done. She let the connection to Earthsong slip away, and she swayed on her knees, completely tapped out. It would be many hours before she would be able to use her Song again.

The fog around her mind lifted as she became aware of her surroundings. The girl lay on the ground, crying but breathing normally. Her leg stuck out at an awkward angle, but she blinked through watery eyes and called for her mama.

"What have you done, witch?" an older woman said. Dozens of faces stared at her, most in horror and fear.

Bindeen appeared beside Jasminda and helped her to stand. "Can't you see she's helped the child?" he said. She wobbled a bit before finding her footing, grateful for the blacksmith's strong arm to lean on.

The girl's mother sobbed, cradling her daughter's head in her lap. "We don't want any of that witchcraft here. Why don't you go back to where you came from?"

A few people in the crowd stood, heads bowed, repeating out loud the Promise of the Queen Who Sleeps, a prayer of protection. Others pegged Jasminda with hard glares and accusatory expressions.

The town physician pushed his way through and kneeled in the spot Jasminda had vacated. The girl's father met Jasminda's eyes, his expression grateful. He nodded once but his acknowledgment did little to lessen the sting of the rejection surrounding her. His wife continued to cry, stroking the girl's hair. As the physician performed his examination, the mother looked up at Jasminda and screamed, "Get her away!"

Jasminda stumbled back, pulling away from Bindeen's grip. She retrieved her bag, which lay abandoned on the other side of the street. Bindeen moved to follow her, but she waved him off. Her body was weary from the use of Earthsong, but even wearier was her heart. It ached with renewed pain. She hadn't thought these people could still hurt her.

Shouldering her bag, she pushed through her exhaustion, focusing on one step and then the next. The journey ahead was long, and she had no more time to waste.

THE GIRL LOOMING above Jack looked like a mirage. She'd marched directly to his hiding place behind a cluster of coarse shrubbery and stood, peering down, head cocked at an angle. He went to stand, years of breeding kicking in, his muscle memory offended at the idea of not standing in the presence of a lady, but apparently, his muscles had forgotten the bullet currently lodged within them. And the girl was Lagrimari—not strictly a lady, but a woman nonetheless—and a beautiful one, he noticed as he squinted into the dying light. Wild, midnight curls floated carelessly around her head and piercing dark eyes regarded him. Her smooth skin was a confectioner's delight. His stomach growled. When was the last time he'd eaten?

Her presence meant he was still on the Lagrimari side of the mountain range bordering the two lands and had yet to cross the other, more powerful barrier keeping him from his home of Elsira: the Mantle.

The girl frowned down at him, taking in his bedraggled appearance. From his position lying on the ground, he tried his best to smooth his ripped uniform, the green fatigues of the Lagrimari army. Her confusion was apparent. Jack was obviously Elsiran; aside from his skin tone, the ginger hair and honey-colored eyes were a dead giveaway. And yet he wore the uniform of his enemy.

"Please don't be scared," he said in Lagrimari. Her brows rose toward her hairline as she scanned his prone and bloodied body. Well, that *was* rather a ridiculous thing to say. "I only meant that I mean you no harm. I . . ." He struggled with how to explain himself.

There were two possibilities. She could be a nationalist who would turn him in to the squad of soldiers currently combing the mountain for him, perhaps to gain favor with the government, or she could be like so many Lagrimari citizens, beaten down by the war with no real loyalty to their dictator or his thugs. If she was the former, he was already dead, so he took a chance with the truth.

"You see, I was undercover, spying from within the Lagrimari army. But now there are men looking for me, they're not far, but—" He paused to take a breath; the effort of speaking was draining. He suspected he had several cracked or broken ribs in addition to the gunshot wound. His vision swam, and the girl turned into two. Two beautiful girls. If these were his last moments before traveling to the World After, then perhaps he was not as unlucky as he'd always thought.

He blinked rapidly and took another strained breath. His mission was not complete; he could not die yet. "Can you help me? Please. I've got to get back to Elsira."

She stole an anxious glance skyward before kneeling next to him. Her cool hand moved to his forehead. The simple touch was soothing and a wave of tension rolled off him.

"You must be delirious." Her voice was rich, deeper than he'd expected. It eased the harsh consonants of the Lagrimari language, for the first time making it sound like something he could imagine being pleasant to listen to. She carefully worked at the remaining buttons of his shirt, pulling the fabric apart to reveal his ruined chest. Her expression was appraising as she viewed the damage then sat back on her haunches, pensive.

"It probably looks worse than it is," he said.

"I doubt that."

Jack's chuckle sounded deranged to his own ears, so it was no surprise that the girl looked at him askance. He winced—laughing was a bad idea at this point—and struggled for breath again. "The soldiers . . . they're after me. I have to get back through the Mantle."

"Shh," she said, digging into her bag. "Hush all that foolishness; you're not in your right mind. Though I'll admit, you speak Lagrimari very well. I'm not sure what happened to you, but you should save your strength."

She retrieved a jar filled with a sweet-smelling substance and began spreading it over his wounds. The constant, throbbing pain eased a notch making it easier for him to breathe.

"What is that?"

"Just a balm. Helps with burns, cuts. Can't do any more for you right now, but you can't stay here. Storm's coming."

He laid his head back on the ground, closing his eyes to savor the slight reduction in pain. "A quick rest and I'll be back on my way. Need to keep moving, though. Need to get back."

She shook her head. "Back through the Mantle?" Her voice was skeptical.

He nodded.

"And away from the Lagrimari soldiers chasing you?"

"Yes." Her palm met his forehead again. She thought he was delusional. He wished he was. Wished the last few weeks had been nothing but the imaginings of an impaired mind.

"The Seventh Breach ended almost five years ago." Her voice flowed over him, as cool and comforting as the balm she'd used. "We've had peace since then. No way to cross the Mantle from either side."

He shook his head, aggravating the hole in his upper chest, inches from his heart where an inconvenient bit of metal was still lodged. "There are ways."

A crunch of boots in the distance set him on alert. He grabbed the girl's wrist to halt her while he listened. The soldiers were near.

He opened his eyes and looked into her startled ones. "Shh, they're coming."

Her head darted from side to side and he could see the moment she realized that someone was indeed coming. Jack couldn't let her be found helping him. Having seen firsthand what these men were capable of, he couldn't let her be found by them at all. The Lagrimari army was filled with men unfit even for Elsira's prisons. This girl had been kind, a trait his people didn't believe the Lagrimari even possessed, but he knew better and felt the need to protect her. He wrestled himself to a sitting position, ignoring the daggers of pain impaling him with every movement, but her strong arms prevented him from standing.

"Hide here, and I'll draw them away," he whispered and motioned for her to crouch down. "They will find me anyway, but it's best they don't see you." She frowned, looking back toward the sound of approaching footsteps.

As he agonizingly made his way to his hands and knees, the pain flared hot, threatening to blind him. With a tug on her arm, he pulled her behind the shrubbery and half crawled, half dragged himself back onto the narrow, rocky path. Her head stuck up over the grouping of rocks and shrubs, and he motioned for her to get down as he put a little distance between them.

The footfalls grew closer and he turned to face them, not wanting to draw any attention to the girl hiding only a few metres away.

Six Lagrimari men appeared from around the bend in the path. The sergeant spotted him, and a hard smile spread across the man's narrow face. Jack only had time to feel a small amount of satisfaction at the purple bruise around the sergeant's eye before a kick to his midsection stole his breath and his consciousness.

THE FIRST SNOWFLAKES began to fall as Jasminda crept down the mountain. She followed the lantern light of the men who'd dragged away the unconscious Elsiran, staying a dozen metres behind. While she'd thought his tale fantastical, there was no doubting the six Lagrimari soldiers who'd appeared, or their viciousness toward him. She'd winced as they'd continued to strike him, long after he'd passed out.

He was an odd one, surely—his manner, his clothing, his perfect Lagrimari speech and accent. She'd never heard of an Elsiran who could speak the language. Even her mama had never been able to master it. And with his talk of crossing the Mantle, of course she'd thought him deranged. The magical border between the two lands followed the mountain range. The Mantle had stood for five hundred years and had only been breached seven times, each resulting in months or years of war.

Her papa had come over during the Sixth Breach. He'd been one of the soldiers stuck in Elsira as prisoners of war when the gap in the Mantle closed. After their release from prison, they'd been unable to obtain citizenship or find jobs, so the Lagrimari had formed settlements, shantytowns really, and eked out a meager living with the help of the Sisterhood. But Papa had met Mama and built a life with her. He never talked much of home or said anything about wanting to go back.

Jasminda had asked him about it, over and over, always afraid that as soon as the chance came, he would disappear into the mysterious country of his birth. He would reassure her that he wasn't going anywhere—sometimes with a chuckle, sometimes with an exasperated sigh, and occasionally with a haunted look in his eye that made her stop the questions.

The Seventh Breach took place the summer of her fifteenth year. The fighting had ended before her family even heard about it, isolated as their valley home was. Jasminda was glad they didn't find out until the breach had closed. She believed Papa's words that he would never leave her—believed them until two years ago when he'd been proved a liar.

But now her own two eyes bore witness of Lagrimari soldiers on her mountain. The odd Elsiran had been convinced he was still in Lagrimar. That meant he'd crossed the Mantle without even knowing it. Was this the start of another breach war, or something else entirely?

The snow fell steadily as the men wandered down the mountain. They took paths that led nowhere, then would double back and end up bickering about how whichever of them who was supposed to be leading the way was stupider than a *fergot zinteroch*, whatever that was. They used Lagrimari words Papa had never taught her.

The temperature seemed to drop another few degrees as they quarreled, and she pulled her coat tighter. A whispered prayer to the Queen Who Sleeps left her lips, asking for protection during the storm. Following the men had been an impulse, one born of guilt. If she had believed the odd Elsiran, could she have helped him avoid the men? There was little she could do for him now, not until her Song restored itself, but she was unable to walk away and leave him to his fate.

It made no sense; he was nobody to her. Just another Elsiran. Except . . . He had not stared at her or been cruel. He had, in fact, shielded her from those men, put himself in their path so they would not find her. Why would he do such a thing?

More than curiosity motivated her, more than guilt. What more she could not say, but she followed the soldiers for hours as the storm began in earnest, pelting her with cold. The direct route she'd planned to take would have had her home and warm in bed by now, but she did not change course, even as the men took wrong turn after wrong turn. Dawn poked its head over the jagged peaks, and with its arrival came the crowing of a rooster. The soldiers stopped short at a fork in the path. Jasminda knew that crow all too well.

The men conferred for a moment and chose to follow the crowing. The mountain made the sound seem closer than it really was, but the sign of civilization could not be mistaken. Emotion battled within her, relief to be headed out of the storm and alarm that these strangers were now on a path that led only one place.

Her home.

The Elsiran had regained his senses by now, and instead of being dragged behind the men like a sack of beets, he stumbled along, his hands tied in front of him. The men climbed down the mountain, leaving the storm behind bit by bit. The snow and ice would grow worse over the next few days, but it would stay at the higher elevations. The valley where her home lay would remain lush and green, protected from the harsh weather either by the mountains surrounding it, or some lingering spell of Papa's, or perhaps a little of both. But there would be no way out. These men would be trapped in an area that was only a two-hour walk from end to end. They would find her cabin; there was no way to avoid it.

She doubled back and took a shortcut she usually avoided, though it had been a favorite of her brothers. It involved a very steep climb, required scaling several large boulders, and brought her far too near one of the caves that peppered the mountain. She ignored the yawning black opening and focused on beating the men to her cabin.

Awake now for over twenty-four hours, she pushed herself far beyond exhaustion. Snow made the rocks slippery, and she lost her footing and slid down an embankment, skinning her hands and forearms. She picked herself up, ignoring the injury, and raced to her cabin, confident she had at least twenty minutes before the soldiers arrived.

She hurried to the barn, where she found the goats already awake, agitated and jittery, no doubt because of the storm. They were like her, craving peace and quiet. Any interruption to their routine or change in the weather troubled the sensitive creatures. She checked their food then barred the outer barn door to keep them from wandering.

Her next stop was the cabin, where she set down her bag and retrieved her shotgun. She carried a pistol with her on trips to town, but the shotgun was her favorite. It was almost an antique but shot straight and true. She loaded it with the shells she'd purchased the day before, then sat on the porch steps. Waiting.

Do what you think you can't. She'd wanted to stop going to town, hide in the valley, and never hear *grol* spat at her with hatred or contempt again. But he wouldn't let her. And now, even if she had somewhere else to go, she wouldn't have left. This was her home. The only thing she had in the world. She would face anything to protect it.

It wasn't long before the telltale clomp of boots announced the men. She hadn't gotten a good look at them in the dark, but the cool, morning light revealed dirty uniforms and even dirtier faces. All except for their leader, a man of skin and bone, his narrow face overshadowed by both a giant, curling mustache and a blackened eye. He was clean and well-groomed, hair parted and shining with pomade.

She stood as they approached, shotgun dangling almost casually from the crook of her arm. The Elsiran, barely standing, was held upright by a soldier.

The leader spoke first. "Pleasant morning to you, miss. I am Tensyn ol-Trador, Honorable Sergeant of His Majesty the True Father's royal army. My men and I are in need of food and shelter. We must speak with your father or husband." His voice was high and nasally, like a human rat.

"This is *my* home."

His eyebrows shot up, and he glanced back at his men, his mouth twisting into what perhaps was meant to be a smile. "You are alone?"

"I want no trouble here," she responded. The Elsiran's head popped up, he frowned and squinted at her, his bruised face freezing once he recognized her. Astonishment and sorrow settled across his features, and his shoulders slumped.

Her Song had regenerated over the many hours of travel, but she struggled to catch hold of Earthsong while keeping her attention on the men before her. The power skittered out of her grasp.

"We have been caught in the mountains by the storm and cannot make it to the capital until it passes. We are tasked with transporting this spy to face the True Father's judgment."

"An Elsiran spy? In your uniform?"

"Yes, he had been spelled to look like one of us. I witnessed it wear off with my own eyes, miss. There are traitorous souls infecting our land, working with our enemies. The Singer responsible for this spell is soon to meet the World After, I think. But that is a matter for the True Father to sort out."

The soldier holding the Elsiran kicked at his legs, causing him to crumple, face-first, to the ground. His upper body heaved as he drew in jagged breaths, but he did not cry out. Jasminda held her breath, keeping her face rigid to hide her horror. The prisoner rolled awkwardly to his knees, then slowly struggled back to his feet. The soldiers beside him snickered as he wobbled before finding his balance. His head shot up defiantly.

Her breath escaped in a rush. The man she'd met the day before on the mountain had been somewhat peculiar, but also gentle. Even with the uniform, he'd struck her as a painter or poet who had fallen upon thieves or been mauled by an animal. She hadn't truly believed him to be a soldier. But now, the sharp lines of his face had turned savage. With his sculpted cheekbones, decisive chin, and that cold power in his eyes, she wondered how these soldiers ever thought they had him cowed. How could she have thought him anything but a warrior?

She forced her gaze back to the sergeant who looked at her expectantly. He'd been speaking, but she hadn't been paying attention. "Excuse me?"

"May we shelter here?" His tobacco-stained smile sent a cold chill rolling through her.

"You and your men may stay in the barn. I will bring you food and water."

A collective grumble arose from the other soldiers. Sergeant Tensyn's grin fell away. "The barn? You must be joking?"

"The cabin is quite small, as I'm sure you can see. Plus, I am not in the habit of inviting strange men into my home."

He took a step closer to the porch, bringing his eyes level with her chest. Though his gaze reached her face quickly, she did not miss the route it took. "Miss . . . ?"

She clenched her jaw. "Jasminda ul-Sarifor."

"Miss Jasminda. As the True Father says, it is your duty to aid his representatives to the best of your ability. I'm afraid the barn will not do. For the prisoner, perhaps, but my men have been marching for days with little food or rest." His eyes narrowed. "We have already learned there are traitors among us. Would not a loyal citizen answer the call of our great leader?"

As she had suspected, these men also believed they were in Lagrimar. If they thought her Elsiran they would likely kill her. She gritted her teeth, closed her eyes briefly, and finally connected to Earthsong. With the energy pulsing into her, she could sense emotion and mood. It was not her strongest skill by far, but these men were easy to read.

Danger rolled off them, impatience, barely reined in malice. And determination. She would not be able to keep them out. Her best chance was to go along with their assumption of her loyalty, be vigilant, and bide her time. Though she knew little of her father's land, being a Lagrimari may save her life, so that is what she would be.

She released her connection, adjusted her shotgun in her hands, all while glaring at the sergeant. "You may wait here for the storm to pass, but listen to me clearly. I will kill any man who touches me."

He swallowed. The others shifted where they stood. Finally, Sergeant Tensyn bowed. "I give you my word on the True Father that none of my men will harm you in any way. Food and shelter are all we ask."

Her raw palms burned from gripping the metal of the gun, and her heart stuttered in her chest. The Elsiran looked on, an apology written on his face. She was sorry, as well.

"Well, come in then."

CHAPTER TWO

IT WAS NOT in Jack's nature to despair. He'd been through his share of hardships in his twenty-two years—well, less than most but more than some, he suspected. The Seventh Breach in particular came to mind. Ninety-nine days of misery that had felt like a thousand. But even then, he'd been full of righteous rage, which had kept him from sinking into the depression so many of his men had succumbed to.

There was a desolation that sank into the hearts of people who'd lived through war. He saw it in the old-timers who fought in the tail end of the Fifth Breach, a war that lasted seventy years. But he'd also seen it in the faces of Lagrimari children in the villages the squad had passed through on his spy mission. Before his bloody disguise had worn off.

Now, a kind of melancholy he was not used to threatened to overtake him. He was back where he'd started—captured—and worse, the girl he'd tried to protect had been hauled into this mess. But he couldn't allow himself to sink too far. Giving up was also not in his nature, not while there was breath in his body.

He wasn't sure how many breaths he had left, though. Each one was more difficult than the last. He'd been trained to work through pain, to put it in a box in his mind, then put that box into another box until he had as many boxes as he needed to keep moving, keep fighting. He had lost count of his boxes, and they'd long stopped helping. Pain was all he knew, but even that meant he was still alive and still had a chance to escape.

The brute to his left, a lout called Ginko, squeezed a brawny hand over Jack's arm and pulled him forward, toward the girl's quaint cabin, which sat under the shade of several tall trees. A barn stood off to the side with a chicken coop beyond it. Rows and rows of carefully tended plants stretched out on either side of the house, interrupted every so often by thickets of trees.

Jack had never been inside a Lagrimari home before and found himself surprised at its warmth and coziness. He had imagined they would all look like the dilapidated shacks of the POW settlements, but this was a proper home for a family. Quilts covered overstuffed couches and chairs. Colorful rugs hugged the floor, though they were currently being sullied by the mud tracked in on the soldiers' boots. The mantelpiece featured children's drawings, woodcarvings, a cuckoo clock, and a photograph of several people that he couldn't make out from this distance.

The girl, Jasminda, pointed out two bedrooms and a washroom on the main floor for the men to use. Just beyond the living room was the entrance to the kitchen, through which a squat woodstove was visible. A staircase in the living room led to a closed door that she indicated belonged to her. When he looked back to the mantle, the photo had been turned facedown.

"And what of communications, Miss Jasminda?" Sergeant Tensyn asked. "Our radio equipment is badly damaged, and we've had no contact with our regiment."

She held herself erect with a fearsome expression as she turned to answer. "No electricity. No radio or cables."

"And telegrams?"

She shrugged. "In town. On the other side of the mountain." She waved a hand vaguely in a circle then closed her eyes as if pained. Tensyn looked ready to continue his questioning when she broke in. "Sergeant, you hope to bring the spy in alive, yes?" She had not looked at Jack since that moment of recognition outside, and she did not glance at him now, yet he felt her attention on him all the same.

His whole body began to grow warmer, lighter. The odd sensation of Earthsong pulsated through him. He had only experienced it once before, when Darvyn had cast the spell to change Jack's appearance before leading him through the crack in the Mantle into Lagrimar. The touch of magic stroked him intimately, like a brush of fingers across his skin. The soft vibration cascaded over his entire body, leaving him feeling weightless. Finally, the pain could fit in a box. He gasped, pulling in a deep breath, and fought the desire to fall to his knees with relief.

"There is a reward for the return of this man," Tensyn said. "Alive."

Jasminda wrinkled her nose. "He stinks of infection. Why has he not been healed?"

Fear speared Jack at her words. He'd seen many a man die of untreated infection from more minor wounds than his.

"All of my men have already given tribute to the True Father."

"And their Songs have not returned?"

Tensyn's expression sharpened, and Jack's own brow furrowed at her question. "Tributes are irreversible, as I'm sure you know, Miss Jasminda. Once your Song is gone, it cannot be returned."

All of the men were looking at her now, but her expression did not change. Her eyes flashed for a moment—perhaps with fear or anger—but it was gone so quickly Jack could not be sure.

"I had heard sometimes they did, that is all. This man will die in days if the infection continues." She turned abruptly and stalked into the kitchen.

It was she who used Earthsong on him. Was it possible she was more than just a sympathetic Lagrimari? Her ignorance of the True Father's tributes could mean she was a Keeper of the Promise like Darvyn. They often stayed in isolated places like this, free from the dictator's edicts.

"Can you keep him alive?" Tensyn asked.

"Yes." Her voice was clipped.

A cautious hope welled within Jack.

She slammed a basket of fruit on the kitchen table and retrieved more food from the pantry, still clutching her shotgun. The other soldiers, except for Tensyn and Ginko, sat and began eating without ceremony. Jasminda grabbed a bowl, filled it with water, and gathered towels and a knife.

"Back porch," she said curtly. "The floors in here are already filthy."

"My apologies, miss," Tensyn said with a genteel bow. "I'll have my men be more careful with the state of your home."

The sergeant motioned to Ginko, who pushed Jack forward. His injuries screamed, but he remained silent. Jasminda's lips pursed and she spun around, leading the way out the back to the porch. She motioned to the top step with her chin. Jack was pushed down until he sprawled across the stairs, gasping for breath.

"Untie him," she said, staring at his lashed wrists. "I need to check his wounds."

Ginko pulled a knife from his boot to cut the rope. The sharp edges of the pain had been bound by whatever spell she'd sung a few moments before, but the weakness in his limbs couldn't be ignored. The lack of food and water, the days of walking and hiding, had all left him teetering on the edge of his endurance. She too had deep circles under her eyes, and he wondered what she'd been doing up on the mountain.

As she settled next to him, his awareness of her pulsed like an extra sense. She smelled of cool mountain air, pine, and something light and feminine that he couldn't place. He closed his eyes and inhaled her nearness, allowing it to soothe and calm him. He imagined himself far away, in the barracks he'd called home since childhood or maybe even farther away, floating on his back in the Delaveen Ocean, the sun warming his face.

The vision faded when her fingertips grazed his forehead.

"Does that hurt?" she whispered, her voice gentle. He opened his eyes to find her closer than he'd expected. Unable to find his voice, he shook his head.

"Take that off," she said, pointing to his shirt. He had the absurd desire to chuckle. How many times had he longed to hear a woman ordering him to take off his shirt? What he'd felt of her touch so far had been very soft . . . She must be soft all over. He'd never imagined a Lagrimari girl could be so lovely. The coils of her hair called to his fingertips and—

Tensyn's oily voice broke through Jack's musings. "Has your tribute day been scheduled?" He and Ginko stood in the doorway behind him, and Jack hated having anyone at his back. That kind of sloppiness had literally been beaten out of him. He blamed the pain and the fatigue.

His bruised fingers faltered on the tiny buttons as he shrugged awkwardly out of his shirt. Once again, she assessed his injuries impassively, though he suspected things were quite a bit worse than yesterday when she'd seen him.

"No," she said, answering Tensyn.

"And your family?"

"Dead." The unexpressive mask of her face slipped for an instant, and he glimpsed a cavernous well of grief in her eyes.

"May they find serenity in the World After," Tensyn intoned.

Jasminda repeated the blessing. Jack's eyes met hers briefly before she looked away. "Lie back," she told him.

She dipped a cloth in the water and ran it across his chest, cleaning away the blood and grime. He suppressed a groan at the incredible coolness of the water on his skin, relishing in it until she stopped suddenly. He craned his neck down to see what had caught her attention. The bullet wound was far worse today, the skin black with infection, blood and pus seeping out.

The screen door slammed. He looked up to find the two of them on the porch alone.

"What is your name?" She pitched her voice low, speaking directly into his ear in perfect Elsiran as she continued cleaning his chest.

He took hold of her wrist, stilling her hand. Even the former POWs spoke only a broken version of Elsiran. How had she been able to learn it when no one in Lagrimar spoke the language? She shook free of his grip and continued cleaning his chest and face. Inside, the soldiers chortled, ensuring they would not be overheard.

"Jack," he whispered, scanning her face desperately. "Are you a Keeper of the Promise?"

She frowned, darting a look at the door. "No. I don't know what that is."

"How can you—"

"This is not Lagrimar." The door opened again, and Ginko emerged, taking a stance with his arms folded while he chewed on a stick of jerky.

Jasminda switched back to Lagrimari, speaking quietly. "I need to cut away the dead flesh from the wound. Otherwise the infection will kill you."

He nodded faintly, still trying to process her last words. If they weren't in Lagrimar, that meant they had all passed through the Mantle without knowing it. He'd been on home soil the whole time. That must be why she'd acted as if he were deranged.

Escape was so close. The despair threatening to pull him under faded away like mist in the sun.

"My Earthsong is not strong. I can't both stop the bleeding and dull the pain."

He met her worried gaze and smiled, though the action reopened one of the cuts on his lip. She frowned, giving him that look that meant she thought he was delirious again. Perhaps he was.

"The only way to the other side is through it," he said. She blinked, staring at him blankly before the corners of her mouth rose a tiny fraction. He hadn't seen her smile yet, and even this hint of one lightened him. She closed her eyes, and soon the warm buzz of Earthsong poured into him like a fizzy cola. He opened the largest box he could to tuck away the pain and imagined Jasminda's smile.

JASMINDA LAY AWAKE in bed, straining to hear any movement in the house. Had she slept at all? She couldn't be sure. Dull moonlight filtered in through Mama's frilly curtains. It was several hours to dawn, so she must have dozed a little. Her last full night of sleep had been days ago, before she left for town and this nightmare began. Exhaustion hollowed her bones. Her Earthsong had been depleted again by helping Jack. She'd wanted to keep some in reserve to better monitor the soldiers, but the Elsiran's wounds were severe. Though her Song was too weak to effect a complete healing, the infected flesh was gone, and he would live another day.

Her muscles tensed and she held her breath, listening. Was that the creak of a floorboard? Gripping the shotgun she'd taken to bed in one hand, she reached under her pillow for her father's hunting knife. Another, smaller blade was already strapped to her thigh.

She rose, seized with the desire to check on Jack. The men had left him tied to the porch, saying even the barn was too good for the likes of him. She wrapped herself in a robe, hiding the shotgun in its folds, and slipped down the stairs. Snores rumbled from behind the doors of both bedrooms. Pushing down the anger at having strangers around her parents' and brothers' possessions, she crept through the kitchen to peer out the window.

Jack lay on his back shivering, hands bound in front of him, feet tied to the porch railing. She doubled back to the main room to grab a quilt, then went out and draped his shuddering body. He didn't appear conscious, but when she began to move away, he grabbed her hand through the blanket.

"Thank you," he said in Elsiran. She cast a glance into the quiet shadows hugging the porch.

"They didn't feed you, did they? You must be hungry," she whispered, drawing the quilt closer around his neck.

"Mmm," he groaned, leaning his cheek against her hand. His skin was cold and clammy, face drawn and gaunt, and yet she could not pull away. She brushed his forehead and ran her fingers through his short hair. He did not flinch from her touch, but sank into it. His hair was like the soft bristles of a brush, his expression serene as she stroked his head. The fierceness in his face had once again been replaced by a soulful calm.

Such a contradiction, this Elsiran. Neither her skin nor her magic frightened him, yet he had more reason than most to hate Lagrimari. Of course, she wasn't Lagrimari, but she wasn't truly Elsiran, either. She forced herself to pull away.

"I'll be right back."

"I'll be here," he said, a small smile playing on his lips.

She rooted around the dark pantry to produce a tin of jerky and some dried fruit. She returned to give him a few strips of jerky, then pulled up a loose board in the floor where she could hide the food.

"You can get to this when no one's looking. You'll need to build up your strength."

"We are truly in Elsira?" His accent was lilting and formal, and it put her in mind of her mama's, a good deal more refined than those of the townsfolk.

"We are."

His forehead crinkled in confusion. "But you are Lagrimari?"

"My papa was a settler; Mama was Elsiran. She was in the Sisterhood. That's how they met."

"I've never heard of such a pairing."

Jasminda shook her head, expression grim. "She fell pregnant, and her family disowned her. Papa found this place and built a home for them."

She stroked the board beneath her feet, cut and nailed with her father's two hands, a structure that proclaimed a love that never should have been. That even now, twenty years later, was not accepted.

"We're so far out, the Prince Regent doesn't even send tax collectors. He must not know we exist." She ducked her head, unable to stop thinking of her family in the plural. Their lives were etched into the walls and the floors; even the smell of the air brought them back to her. She clenched her jaw to keep the emotion at bay.

Jack laid his hand on hers, and her skin tingled at the contact. The intensity in his expression dissolved her creeping sorrow, bringing instead a pang of yearning. She did not touch people. She barely even spoke to people. She was either here alone with no one but the animals as audience, or in town armoring herself against the cutting stares. The tingle in her hand turned into a warm heat that threatened to spread. With great effort, she pulled away from the impossible temptation of his body.

"How far is it to—"

He paused as a floorboard inside the house groaned under the weight of heavy footsteps. Jasminda froze as another floorboard creaked. She grabbed her shotgun, scooted away, and crept down the steps into the yard. The moonlight cast heavy shadows on the yard and she crouched beside a cherry tree, holding her breath.

Two soldiers darkened the doorway. They stepped onto the porch. One nudged Jack with his foot, and Jack moaned, pretending to be asleep. The men chuckled to themselves and leaned over him.

"You're sure the sergeant is out?" one of the men said. Ginko, she thought his name was.

"Thank the Father for thick walls and a soft bed. He sleeps like he's in his mother's arms," the second man said. Based on the outline of his large, misshapen head, Jasminda thought this was the one called Fahl. He'd eaten the last of the boiled eggs earlier, before she'd even had one.

Fahl squatted down and ran his hand across Jack's body. The action took an impossibly long time, and Jasminda's stomach hollowed. When he moved to loosen his own belt, she fought back a gasp. They were going to whip Jack.

"The bitch is upstairs. Are you sure you wouldn't rather . . ." Ginko said.

"I'm thinking the sergeant has her in his sights. Besides, she looks like she's got a mean scratch. No. I'll make sure this one won't make a peep, and who's to care what state he's left in? What Tensyn don't know won't hurt him."

The two snickered, and Ginko scratched his meaty head, looking back toward the house.

Understanding dawned on Jasminda like a blow to the face. She had worried for herself, expected trouble from these men seeking *her* out in the middle of the night, but she'd never considered Jack's vulnerability. Never considered how depraved these men might actually be. She could not sit by and allow him to be violated, though she was not sure what could be done to stop it.

They'd said the sergeant wouldn't approve. Maybe if she woke him, he would stop this. But she couldn't be sure, and going into his room at night could put her in the same predicament. She gripped her shaking hands and prayed to the Queen Who Sleeps for a solution.

The soft bleat of a doe rang out from the barn. The storm on the mountains was still making the goats uneasy. An idea took hold. What she needed was a distraction, and quickly.

Jasminda crouched, setting her shotgun down at the base of the tree, and felt around for a stone or branch. After finding a good-sized rock, she threw it with all her might. It sailed across the yard to hit the chicken coop. Once the men turned toward the sound, she raced around the front of the house, taking the long way to the barn.

The first distraction bought her a minute, but now she needed something larger to really draw the men away. She slid open the well-oiled barn door. Instead of nestling on the floor sleeping, many of the goats were awake and stumbling around, agitated. She hoped that, for once, the stubborn animals wouldn't need much cajoling. Luckily for her, the buck was eager to be out of doors and the does were of a mind to follow him. Grabbing the shovel, she nudged the herd along, increasing the pressure on their backsides until they bleated in disapproval.

The goats operated almost as a hive mind—when one was upset, they all were—so Jasminda continued poking and prodding at them, pushing them from the barn. Their discontent grew louder. Whines and cries pierced the night air. She'd often cursed the herd's fickle temperament, but tonight it was a blessing.

She couldn't see the back porch from where she stood, but an oil lamp flickered on inside the house. The goats' racket would keep the soldiers awake, and Ginko and Fahl wouldn't have the opportunity to hurt Jack.

She slipped into the garden shadows as the front door opened and the smallest soldier, Wargi, stumbled out. The sergeant's voice carried over the yowls of the animals as he barked orders. The remaining two soldiers, Pymsyn and Unar, followed Wargi out to investigate what had spooked the goats.

She stifled a laugh at the way the men floundered, chasing after the scattering herd. They wouldn't get much sleep trying to track down each animal. If they asked her in the morning, she'd say she slept through it. She'd been listening to them her whole life, after all.

When she returned to the backyard, she retrieved her shotgun and found Jack as she'd left him. He opened his eyes and the moonlight made them sparkle. She knelt and pulled the blanket down from his chin to check him out, not sure what she was even looking for.

"Are you all right?"

"What did you do?"

She shrugged. "A distraction. Have they . . . harmed you?" She grimaced at the foolishness of her question. "Further, I mean."

He shook his head, his face a mask. Warrior Jack was back.

"But they will . . . when they can," she admitted aloud, the braying cries still echoing in the distance.

She gathered up the hem of her robe and nightgown, and reached for the band holding the knife in place around her thigh. His eyes widened, and her face grew hot as she hurried to remove the blade and put her gown back in place. After prying open the same loose floorboard as before, she hid the knife beside the tin of food.

As she laid the board back in place, his hand covered hers. "Thank you."

She flexed her fingers under his palm, ignoring the tingles sparking on her skin again. "I'm sorry I didn't believe you yesterday."

"You thought I was mad." His mouth quirked. He must have been in a great deal of pain, but it hardly showed. Perhaps he was a warrior jester—fierce one moment, jovial the next.

"I still might."

He snorted a laugh, then winced.

Guilt tightened her chest. "I'm sorry. You shouldn't laugh."

"I'd rather laugh than cry. Wouldn't you?"

She couldn't even remember the last time she had something to laugh about.

Jasminda sat back on her heels. "Is this a new breach?"

He sobered. "Not yet, but soon. There are cracks in the Mantle. Places where people can slip through, either knowingly or accidentally. But a breach is coming. The Lagrimari think they've found a way to tear it down permanently."

"Permanently?"

He nodded. "The True Father has never been able to cross during a breach, not while any part of the Mantle is intact. But without it . . ."

"Without it, he could cross. What would that mean?"

His grip on her hand tightened. "The end of Elsira."

The True Father was the most powerful Earthsinger alive. He had ruled Lagrimar for five hundred years, stealing more and more of his peoples' magic through the "tributes" to keep him alive and in power. But it had never been enough. Each breach had been an attempt for him to expand his influence.

Though her relationship with the land and its people was tenuous at best, Elsira was her home. She had no connection to its government; the Prince Regent, his laws, and the structures of society had never applied to her. But she couldn't believe her isolated home would be forever immune to the fall of the country. "Could nothing stop it?"

"Are you a follower of the Queen?" he asked.

"Yes."

"If She were awoken, they say Her power is great enough to stop the True Father."

"Do you believe that?"

His expression turned guarded. "I don't know. She has never visited my dreams. I've prayed to Her many times without response."

"Papa dreamed of Her when he was younger," she admitted. Both of her parents had been devout followers of the Queen Who Sleeps, the long-absent ruler of Elsira. A visit from Her was a blessing, as She dispensed Her wisdom through dreams. But those dreams were exceedingly rare; few people ever received them.

"Is there no hope then? She has slept for hundreds of years; there's little chance She will awaken now."

Jack shrugged. "We can fight. We can prepare. There is always hope." He closed his eyes and took a deep breath. "But I must get back to alert the others. Lagrimar is already amassing their forces; the breach is likely only days away."

A cloud passed over the moon darkening the porch.

"You can't cross the mountain before the storm dies." She released his hand and laid it down gently. So much of his body was still cracked and bruised. "It is too dangerous, and your wounds must heal more. I will do what I can to help you. I promise." She rose and moved to the door. "Now get some sleep."

She started to go inside, then turned back for one last look and found his gaze on her. The two sides she'd seen before—soulful Jack and warrior Jack—merged before her, giving a complete picture for the first time. She took in a jagged breath as a renewed surge of longing crashed into her.

I promise, she mouthed, and closed the door behind her.

SLEEP WAS IMPOSSIBLE, so Jasminda had spent the quiet, predawn hours in the garden picking herbs by lamplight. Her morning chores went by quickly. The goats, safely back where they belonged, had been milked and were now grazing, and the eggs were collected before even one of the soldiers awoke. She made a modest breakfast—so many mouths were taking a toll on her food stores—but she was sure to set aside a bowl for Jack.

The six soldiers crowded around the table, devouring what she put in front of them. Their favorite pastime seemed to be making fun of the youngest and smallest: bespectacled Wargi.

"This one is more coddled than an Elsiran brat," Pymsyn said through a mouthful of eggs. "Came into the army straight from his mother's skirts, he did."

"Thinks he's better than the rest of us because he's not harem-born," said Fahl. "Just because your mam didn't have to spread her legs for the True Father doesn't make you top shit."

"And doesn't make your mam any less of a whore than ours," Ginko grunted. The table erupted in laughter.

Jasminda paid close attention to the men as she washed the dishes, not wanting to make any mistakes to cast suspicion on her Lagrimari identity. But she knew next to nothing of life in that land. Her father had been tight-lipped, and it wasn't as if any of her books had information on their culture or practices. Aside from the breaches into Elsira over the years and very limited trade with Yaly, their neighbor to the east, Lagrimar was cut off from the rest of the world. Mountains surrounded the country on all sides, with only a small flat area a few hundred metres wide on the Elsiran border, where all the breaches had occurred.

As the men continued to mock Wargi, the young soldier just smiled and laughed, appearing to take it all in stride. But his eyes remained tense, and Jasminda almost felt sorry for the boy. His round face hadn't yet lost its baby fat; he couldn't be older than sixteen.

Soon enough, the sergeant called the table to order, issuing instructions for the men to split into pairs to explore the valley and monitor the progress of the storm. All the soldiers except Wargi and Tensyn himself headed out.

The sergeant turned his attention to Jasminda. "Is there anything my men can help you with, Miss Jasminda?" His stained smile verged on lecherous. She swallowed the bile that rose and forced herself to smile back.

"No, sir. Dishes are almost done. Once the spy gets his rations, I'll be back to my chores."

"Wargi, finish the dishes for the lady, then throw some crusts at that vermin outside," he barked as he walked away.

Wargi stood and gently removed the dishrag from her hand.

"Thank you," she whispered to him. He looked embarrassed and began tackling the pots in the sink.

"Come, rest your feet a moment, dear girl," Tensyn said.

She could think of no way to refuse and keep her cover, and so took the seat offered, cringing as Tensyn slid uncomfortably close to her.

"Beauty such as yours should never have to look upon that filthy Elsiran. Wargi, find a bag to cover the pig's head with."

"Yes, sir."

Jasminda shot a quick glance toward the porch but couldn't see Jack from her position. Tensyn launched into a long and meandering tale of his valor during the Seventh Breach, of the vast number of Elsirans he'd killed and the accolades he'd received from the True Father. Every so often, he would twirl the tips of his mustache and pause to check her reaction. She'd never thought herself a good actress, but she strove to appear impressed.

He finished his story, and she bobbed her head enthusiastically, eyes wide as saucers to portray her awe. He then gave a great yawn and announced he was off for a nap. Jasminda slumped in her chair, exhausted, and noticed Wargi had slipped away at some point. She stood to retrieve the extra food she'd set aside for Jack before heading out to the porch.

He sat propped against the railing, looking like a discarded scarecrow with the sack covering his head. She knelt before him and removed the bag. He blinked at her, then frowned.

"I was rather enjoying the privacy."

She bounced the sack in her hand. "I can put it back if you like."

He yawned, stretching his shoulders as far as he could with his arms tied. His shirt was still open, and she watched the muscles of his chest bunch and flex. Though he was bruised and scarred, she couldn't draw her eyes away.

Silence stretched between them, and she realized he hadn't missed her stare. Her cheeks grew warm and she ducked her head, pushing the bowl of mashed turnips toward him. He picked it up and awkwardly shoveled the food into his mouth with his bound hands, then turned to her with raised eyebrows and a grimace.

"Those are the herbs," she said. "They're bitter, but they'll help you heal." She would have to wait until later in the afternoon to use any more Earthsong.

A clattering inside drew her attention, and she slipped back through the door.

In the main room, Wargi knelt in front of the large oak cabinet, the contents of which were lined up on the floor. Spread before her were the memories she kept locked away. Her mother's quilts, toy trucks whittled and painted by her father's hand, the twins' hiking boots, their sketch pads, tiny tin soldiers. When they'd first gone, she'd opened the cabinet several times a day to touch something of theirs, to remind herself that though she was alone now, she hadn't always been.

"What are you doing?" she demanded.

The boy turned around, his eyes wide behind his spectacles. "S-sergeant said to make an inventory."

"An inventory? Of what?"

"Everything, miss."

"For what purpose?"

Wargi stared at her, one of the seven bottles of gin her father had purchased shortly after her birth shook in his hands.

"Put that down before you drop it," she snapped. He placed the bottle down next to the others.

She spun on her heel and marched into her parents' bedroom. Wargi scrambled to follow her. Tensyn lay across the bed, a cloth covering his eyes. He startled when the door crashed against the wall and sat up, moving a hand to the empty holster at his hip. His revolver sat on the dresser, just out of reach.

"Sir, your men have no right to paw through my family's belongings."

Tensyn blinked slowly. His normally perfect hair was lopsided from the pillow. His mustache was slightly askew to match.

"Miss Jasminda. It is imperative that we take all the necessary security precautions during our stay here."

"Including snooping through my things?"

"It is standard procedure and should cause little problem if you have nothing to hide." He rose, taking a moment to stop in front of the mirror and pat his hair back into place. He smiled that repellant smile, then led them back into the main room.

"Seven bottles of gin?" His eyebrows rose.

"The dowry my father prepared."

He bent to inspect a bottle. "Where did your father acquire this? I've never seen this labeling before."

The brand was Elsiran. Jasminda's mind raced to come up with an explanation. How would an Elsiran product be purchased in Lagrimar? "I was an infant when he bought them, so I can't be sure. Perhaps it was bounty from his time in the Sixth Breach."

After scrutinizing the bottle for a few more moments, he finally set it down. The tension in her shoulders unwound just a notch. "I'm sure you realize that a dowry is an old-fashioned concept, Miss Jasminda. The True Father frowns upon such indulgences and archaic traditions. All nonessentials must be paid as tribute to the True Father or his representatives. This is a difficult time for my men, and if there's something here that can make them more comfortable, I'm obliged to provide it. I'm sure you must understand my position." His voice oozed false sincerity.

She crossed her arms in front of her chest. "So that gives you license to steal what you wish?"

"As you have not given your tribute yet, this is the least you can do."

Jasminda froze at the accusation in his voice. He ran a finger across the items on the ground, marking them with his scent like a cat. Anger bubbled up inside her with no outlet. How dare he so much as breathe on her family's belongings? Moreover, her home was no doubt filled with items unavailable in Lagrimar. This ruse of hers was in jeopardy.

Something had to be done about the soldiers, and soon.

She backed away from the men as they conferred about the quality of her brothers' boots. Praying to the Queen Who Sleeps for the patience she so often lacked, she went out the back door.

Jack was licking the last of his breakfast from the bowl but paused, mid-chew at her appearance. She tried to tamp down her rage, but by the look on his face, she wasn't doing a very good job. She kneeled next to him, glaring back at the house.

"From now on, eat only food that comes directly from me," she whispered in Elsiran. "Understand?"

His forehead crinkled in confusion, but he nodded.

"Only from my hands. And be vigilant."

———

THE MORNING PASSED slowly for a man tied to a porch with nothing to occupy him. Jack invented names for each of the chickens pecking away in the fenced-off yard and developed stories for them. Margritt had spent half an hour bickering with her sister-in-law, Heleneve, over whose eggs were larger. Then he listed all of the presidents of Yaly in descending order, and all of the Elsiran Prince Regents in alphabetical order. Anything to keep his mind from the fears that circled, fears of the deluge of death and destruction that would accompany another war, and his current inability to stop it.

He also strove to bar his thoughts from the other force demanding entry into his mind: Jasminda. The feel of her hand in his, the curve where her neck met her shoulder, the hint of collarbone above the fraying fabric of her dress. Even the scent that filled his nostrils whenever she was near. What was it about her that captivated him so? Less than a month ago, he'd attended an officer's ball and danced with a dozen pretty socialites. None of them had affected him nearly as much.

Perhaps it was his captivity. Perhaps being close to death made his fingers long to lose themselves in the twisting coils of her hair. But perhaps it was just that she was unlike any woman he'd ever known. The giggling debutantes of the city, cinched and beaded to perfection, were lovely to look at, but Jack sensed a bottomless well inside Jasminda that made him want to know more, to sink into the pools of her eyes and linger.

He let out a breath of frustration. The attraction was inconvenient. So was being tied to the bloody porch. The blade under the floorboard called to him. *Freedom*. He could cut the ropes and head for home. But how long would he last in the storm? It was better to bide his time and trust Jasminda to keep her promise.

Time was precious and steadily running out, though. He had witnessed the Lagrimari brigade gathering a dozen kilometres from the border. Whispers of the True Father's rapidly increasing strength had spread through the army like a plague. Word was, tributes were being taken from whole towns at a time. Not just adults but children, infants even, were being drained of their Songs to feed the god-king's unquenchable thirst for power. Darvyn had warned him as much, but Jack hadn't believed the former POW. How could *he* have known, having been trapped inside Elsira since the last breach?

But Darvyn knew a great deal, including the location of the crack in the Mantle. He'd led Jack through that place where the magic had weakened in order to personally gather the proof his Elsiran government would not accept from a Lagrimari. The two had agreed to meet in a fortnight to return to Elsira, but Darvyn's spell had worn off early, and Jack had been exposed, shot, and forced on the run before the appointed date. He rubbed his chest wondering, not for the first time, what had happened to the young man.

The open kitchen window carried a low conversation between his captors to his ear.

"How do you not know where she's gone? Didn't I tell you to keep closer watch on her?" Sergeant Tensyn said. Jack perked up.

"Y-yes, sir. But you said to be secretive about it; I can't follow her everywhere without her knowing." The timid voice must have been from the boy, Wargi. The soldier was only a handful of years younger than himself, but Jack had been in the army since early childhood, training for his role.

"I don't want excuses, ensign. I want results. There's something about this place that isn't quite right. Too many strange objects and labels."

"We are on the outskirts, sir. People here live differently than in the towns."

"Nothing in Lagrimar is *that* different. When was the last time you saw real honey?"

"I-I can't say that I've ever seen it, sir."

"Not since the last breach, that's for sure." Tensyn may have been a popinjay, but he was not stupid. Jasminda's instincts to pretend to be Lagrimari had been good, but Jack sensed the gambit would not last much longer.

"Keep an eye on her," the sergeant snapped.

"Yes, sir."

Their footsteps faded into the house, leaving Jack on edge.

HOURS LATER, JASMINDA reappeared through the copse of trees behind the back garden, a full basket on her arm. Her dark eyes flashed as she scanned the area, always alert. The sight of her ignited him as a gentle breeze ruffled through her mass of curls. She would have made an excellent soldier, if such things were possible. Her beauty was raw and pure, and a torrent of desire he had no business feeling rose inside him.

As she passed, he reached out, wanting to warn her of the sergeant's suspicions, but she shook her head slightly, and the man in question appeared at the doorway. Jack closed his eyes, feigning sleep.

"Pleasant evening, Miss Jasminda. I hope your day was enjoyable." The sergeant's obsequious voice made Jack's skin crawl. Jasminda merely grunted. It didn't sound unladylike coming from her, though. Jack cracked his eyes to find her trying to get past Tensyn, whose angular form efficiently blocked the doorway.

"And may I ask where you've been off to?"

Jack couldn't see her face, but the tension in her shoulders indicated her displeasure with the inquiry.

"Needed to restock. Eight eat far more than one."

Tensyn peered into the basket, its top protectively covered by her arm. "And what do you have there?"

After a moment's pause, in which Jack could feel the waves of irritation pulsing from her, she moved her arm to show him. "Wild greens and herbs. Potatoes and berries. Potatoes aren't quite ripe. The herbs should cover the bitterness." She stayed rigid as Tensyn inspected the basket's contents, poking and prodding at the vegetables.

When the leaves of the greens came into view, he nearly gasped, but caught himself and clamped his jaw shut. The sergeant did not appear to see anything amiss in her haul. Just as Jack was beginning to exhale the long-held breath, Tensyn's body brushed against Jasminda's. Jack clenched his hands into fists until she shifted the basket, cutting off any further bodily contact.

"If you'll excuse me, Sergeant." She motioned toward the kitchen, and Tensyn finally stepped aside.

Jack snapped his eyes shut when the man's attention moved to the floor in the corner where he lay. When the footsteps retreated into the house, he sat up, mind racing. He'd only seen the edge of one leaf, but that was enough. Every child in Elsira learned to identify and avoid ruaba leaf. The plant was so poisonous it was illegal, sold only on the black market. A quick killer, it caused a rapid, deadly fever in the victim within fifteen minutes of ingestion. A fever that grew hot and fast, causing death within the hour.

Jasminda's plan was clear enough, and while Jack admired her strength of spirit and quick mind, he thought it too risky. If any of the men recognized the plant or chose not to eat it for some reason, there would be trouble.

The smells of her cooking soon wafted through the window, causing his stomach to rumble. The other soldiers were arriving back from their missions, and Jack slumped down as one tromped past and slammed himself in the old outhouse. The main cabin had a single washroom that was always in demand.

Pymsyn approached the outhouse next and banged on the door, receiving a grumbled curse from inside. "How long are you going to stay in there, mate?"

Jack couldn't hear the response, but Pymsyn shrugged and moved to the nearest tree to piss. The stream was seemingly endless; he must have drunk a gallon of water. Just as he finally finished, the outhouse door opened and Unar came out, buckling his belt. The two men shared the thick build the Lagrimari were known for.

"I'm starving, mate. When do you reckon dinner will be?"

Pymsyn shrugged. "Smells good, though. You on first or second round?"

"First." Unar clapped the other man on the back heartily. "And you?"

"Second," Pymsyn said, annoyed. "The sergeant's gone bonkers, hasn't he? Making us split dinner shifts as if that little chit were putting something in our food."

"Aye, paranoid as the True Father, he is. But what officer you've met ain't? What with spies and traitors running around willy-nilly? But for a spark the bale wouldn't burn, you know."

"Easy for you to say. You get to eat first."

The men's voices were lost as they rounded the house again. Jack scrambled to his feet. His ropes were long enough to allow him limited movement on the porch. He crouched under the kitchen window and peered in to find Jasminda chopping and adding vegetables to a boiling pot on the stove. Wargi sat at the table, surveilling her openly. A handful of ruaba disappeared into the bubbling pot. Squatting down again, he ran through the possibilities in his head.

If her plan moved forward, the first wave of soldiers would eat and fall sick, leaving her open to the accusations from the second wave. They would kill her quickly, or worse—the thought hit him like a blow to the gut—kill her slowly.

He had to warn her. But how?

He rose to the window again. A few of the men filed into the kitchen and sat expectantly around the table. Jasminda looked up and met Jack's eyes but managed to hide her shock at his appearance. He shook his head meaningfully. Unable to raise his hands high enough to point at the pot, he tried using his head to motion downward, but she merely crinkled her forehead in confusion.

"That smells good now, doesn't it?" Unar said from inside.

"Feck off, mate," Pymsyn shouted from the outer room. Unar grinned and stared at Jasminda's backside as she bent to retrieve something from the oven. Jack gritted his teeth and tried to catch her eye again, but she refused to look to the window.

"Stewed greens," she sang out with false cheer, while her face contorted in barely contained rage. "Ready in a minute."

Wargi passed out the plates and straightened the silverware. Jasminda pulled down a stack of bowls from the cupboard and stirred the greens again, readying to serve them.

Jack was out of time. He had to do something.

"Shining brightly, coast to hill,
Her beauty waning never.
Elsira lives on by our will.
Elsira is forever."

All chatter inside the house stopped as Jack's voice rang out, singing the Elsiran National Anthem in his native tongue. He'd stepped away from the window and could no longer see inside but guessed his outburst would have the desired effect. He rushed into the second verse, modifying the original lyrics to suit his need, knowing the soldiers would not understand the words.

"They're ordered to eat in two shifts.
You must not give them poison.
Or they'll discover what you've done.
Find a way to destroy it."

The last words were barely out before Ginko and Pymsyn rushed onto the porch, fists swinging. They cursed his traitorous soul for having the nerve to sing his foul anthem and pummeled him to the floor. Their anger was real, but the severity of the blows paled in comparison to what he'd suffered when he'd first been discovered. A few days of rest and relaxation had turned the men soft.

"Is that all you've got?" Jack wheezed out in Lagrimari as the two stepped back. Then a foot to his midsection stole his breath. A kick to the head stole his consciousness.

HE WOKE TO the murmur of Earthsong ebbing away his pain. Night had fallen, and the call of birds kept time with the pounding in his head. A cool hand slid across his forehead and he pressed into the touch.

"I was right. You *are* mad." Her voice was as soft as her skin, and he moaned slightly at the way both refreshed him.

He rolled to his back and took a deep breath. It was too dark to see her face, especially with one of his eyes nearly swollen shut, but her presence, here and alive, soothed him.

"What happened to the greens?" he said. His lower lip was numb, making it hard to speak.

"I accidentally emptied a bottle of vinegar into them." Her silhouette shrugged. "They had to make do with the potatoes."

He exhaled, releasing tension from his entire aching body.

"Thank you," she said. Her hands moved, her two tiny ones holding one of his in their grasp.

"The men?" he whispered.

She sighed. "They discovered my father's gin. They're three noses into the still."

He struggled up to a sitting position. Even with her healing treatment, he still felt every one of the blows he'd received.

"You're a mess," she said, and began wiping at his face with a rag. "Your rib's broken again."

"Nothing too serious, then." He was able to fill his lungs with enough air to keep breathing—that was enough. "It was a good effort . . . the poison."

"Not good enough. Sometimes I wish Earthsong could be used to . . ." She shook her head.

Jack shuddered. "We would have been wiped out a long time ago if Earthsong could kill. But . . . I've never understood . . . If you can see into the body in order to heal, why can't you . . ."

"Kill?" She shrugged, staring down at her hands. "Earthsong is pure life. Trying to cause harm in that way is like trying to swim up a waterfall. The energy doesn't flow in that direction."

Jack remained quiet, peering at the mountains. "How much longer will the storm last, do you think?"

A shifting of clouds revealed the moonlight, illuminating her pensive expression. "Another twenty-four hours or so."

The glow of her skin made him lose his train of thought. She peered at him, concern clouding her face.

"I need to get back home," he said.

She nodded. "Let me wrap your ribs." She produced a bandage from the pocket of her dress and leaned toward him. Her fingers slid underneath his shirt, and he shivered at her touch. He focused on her scent enveloping him and bit back a wince as pain speared him with every pass of her hands around his abdomen. "The only way to the other side is through it." She repeated his words back to him with a wink.

When she'd finished, he closed his eyes and leaned his head back against the railing. "I wish I could go through the mountain."

"You're still in no shape to travel."

His lids flew open as he focused on the words she didn't say. "*Is* there a way through the mountain? Darvyn mentioned tunnels in the north—does this range have them as well?"

She busied herself folding and refolding the rag she'd used on his face, not meeting his eyes.

"Jasminda." He reached for her, stilling her hands. The contact shot through him just as strong as the hope her hesitation had inspired. "Please. You know what's at stake."

Her eyes softened for a moment as she threaded her fingers through his. His pain faded to the background as he watched her mouth move, beginning to form words, then thinking better of it.

"Sleep with the knife tonight. Nothing can be done until tomorrow."

"Please—"

A crash sounded within the house, and the door slammed open. Jack drew back. Jasminda stood suddenly. The loss of contact burned his palms. Her expression held no trace of guilt, but a swaying, inebriated Tensyn narrowed his eyes at the both of them.

"You!" He pointed a shaking finger at Jack and lurched forward.

"Sergeant," Jasminda said, injecting meekness into her voice. It sounded foreign and wrong on her tongue. "The spy's injuries are not life threatening. He will live to meet the True Father's justice. However"—she used her body to block Tensyn's view of Jack—"another beating may kill him, and then Lagrimar would be deprived of the knowledge he holds."

Tensyn's hand went to his mustache, and he twirled the end, raking his gaze over Jasminda.

"Come," she said, grabbing hold of his arm and turning him back toward the door. Jack leaned forward, unsure what he was going to do but unwilling to see her making nice with the man. She kicked his ankle gently before leading Tensyn away. "I think there's a berry tart waiting for you. Wouldn't that be nice?"

She spoke to the sergeant as she would a child, and Jack couldn't make out the man's slurred response. This time anger replaced the pain coursing through him. He was leaving tomorrow, and he was going to make bloody well sure Jasminda was safe, even if it meant taking her with him.

———

JASMINDA'S SLEEP WAS heavy with forbidden dreams. Moving versions of the pictures in the magazines she'd found long ago under her brothers' mattresses. While she'd been ordering endless books from mail-order catalogs, the twins had been interested in a different sort of literature.

Her shock at the discovery had quickly turned to fascination at the pages of nude and proud women displaying themselves unselfconsciously. Teasingly hiding a breast behind a hand or shielding the apex of their legs with clever positioning. But some of the pictures, the ones burned into her mind, were of couples, men and women draped over one another, body parts aligning in ways that caused moisture to pool between her legs and her imagination to soar.

In the dream, the pages came alive, but she and Jack were the models. His lips glanced over hers in a soft caress. Flashes of sensation assaulted her as she chased the constantly changing visions, unable to hold on to one for long. His lithe body stretched out over her own. Her hands ran across his muscular chest, smooth skin warming her fingertips. Gripped in his powerful arms, she wrapped her legs around him, melting into his touch.

The dream died to the sound of tinkling wind chimes—the makeshift alarm she'd hung on her door. She came awake instantly, bypassing the bulk of the shotgun to grab for the knife she'd hidden under her pillow. This time she did not need Earthsong to sense ill intentions.

A figure loomed above her in the dark, and a beefy hand covered her mouth, stifling her scream. Fahl towered over her, reeking of gin. He was strong and had an iron grip on her face, pushing her back into the pillow. The hand holding her knife was stuck underneath her head, and Fahl's other hand felt roughly for her nightgown and grabbed at the hem.

Jasminda kicked out, struggling, fighting with all her might, but Fahl was huge and heavy as he lay on top of her, fully immobilizing her. He eased up enough to continue pushing up her nightgown and then pawed at her thighs as she tried to clench them together.

The shotgun rolled off the bed, hitting the floor. Fahl chuckled when he saw it, launching a blast of alcohol-infused air into her face.

"Keep fighting, sweetheart," he said. "It's been months since I had any, and I don't mind working for it a little."

Jasminda stilled, unwilling to give this man anything he wanted. She hunted for an escape.

He fumbled with his trousers, pulling and tearing at them until his squiggly, limp penis emerged. He made a sound of disgust, then started stroking himself while pinning her down, one hand still over her mouth. Jasminda strained to see what was going on down there—and thanked the Queen he wasn't making much progress.

Her plan with the ruaba leaf had been abandoned, but the terryroot was doing its job. Odorless and tasteless, her herb dictionary listed its use for "wives wanting some peace from their husbands." Her mother had laughed heartily when a young Jasminda asked what that meant, telling the girl that she would find out when she was older. Since the soldiers had arrived, Jasminda had been liberally dosing their food with the herb.

Growling in frustration, Fahl kneeled up over her, angrily pulling on himself. Without his weight on top of her, Jasminda could now move her arm but didn't know if she would be quick enough with the knife. The moment of indecision cost her when he stood suddenly, grabbing her by the hair and arm. She winced from the pain as he forced her down the stairs. Her side pressed against his giant chest, immobilizing her arm, but allowing just enough reach for her to slide the knife into her pocket.

"Ginko!" he whispered loudly. "Mate, where are you?"

An answering groan sounded from the living room. The door to one of the bedrooms hung open, revealing another soldier sprawled on the floor inside. Fahl pressed her onto the couch next to a groggy and very drunk Ginko.

"I've brought you a present, mate," Fahl said. His pants were still sagging and his flaccid penis hung out shamelessly.

"Eh?" Ginko replied, peeling open his eyes. When he noticed Jasminda, his demeanor changed. "What about the sergeant?" he slurred.

"Fucker can't hold his liquor." Fahl grinned evilly, showing off his blackened, stinking teeth. "He'll never know, and when he comes 'round, we can just say she run off."

His grip loosened for a moment, and Jasminda tore free with a shout, lunging off the couch toward the kitchen, jumping over furniture in her way.

But Fahl and Ginko surprised her with their speed, catching up to her quickly and slamming her down on the kitchen table. She pulled the knife from her pocket and swiped out, slicing through a fleshy arm. A corresponding yowl rang out from whichever of them she cut.

She screamed a war cry and lashed out again, but a hand pinned her arm like a vise before the knife met its target. A blow to her face rattled her senses before her legs were pinned, as well. She kicked and flailed with all her strength, but it felt like immovable rocks held her in place.

Ginko clutched her legs, nudging her nightgown up. Near her head, Fahl still pulled at himself futilely.

"Perhaps this will go better if I stuff it down your throat," he said, releasing her arms to grab her hair and tilt her head back toward him. His grip was tight enough to make her vision blur, but she focused on her newly freed hands. A little closer and she'd be able to reach the two sensitive sacks behind his drooping manhood. She would rip off whatever she touched and bite off anything that came near her lips.

As Fahl drew closer and Ginko's hands slid toward her panties, the back door crashed open. All movement stilled. Through watery eyes, she saw Jack standing in the doorway, the knife she'd hidden for him in his hand, his restraints dangling from one wrist. He leaped across the room and tackled Fahl, plunging the knife deep into the man's belly. Ginko sprang away.

Jasminda crawled off the table and dropped to the ground. She blinked, clearing her vision, and rose to see Jack duck Ginko's wide punch. The swing threw the soldier off-balance. He wobbled until Jack landed a vicious, crunching kick. Ginko crumpled, hitting his head with a loud *crack* on the kitchen counter before falling to the floor. Blood pooled around his head and he stared upward, unseeing.

Fahl, knife still lodged in his belly, had been leaning against the opposite counter, but when Ginko fell, he rushed Jack with a new burst of strength. He grasped Jack in a bear hug and wrapped his hands around Jack's throat, squeezing. Jasminda screamed and ran toward the hulking man, climbing on his back. The fingers of one hand sunk deep into his greasy hair as she pulled back his head, then in one swift motion slit the man's throat with the other, just as she'd do with a goat.

She jumped back and he fell, blood spurting everywhere, covering Jack with its spray. Heaving for breath, she barely registered a new presence in the room until it was gone.

"Wargi!" she said, taking off after him. Jack followed on her heels as she entered her parents' old bedroom.

Wargi stood over the sergeant's prone body, sprawled across her parents' bed. His eyes, wide and wild, focused on the bloody knife in her grip. He shook with fear and made little hiccupping sounds. This boy was too young to have been in combat. Had he seen a man die before?

The weight of what she'd done hit her. She'd just killed a man. Wargi looked ready to vomit, and Jasminda felt the same. She released the knife from her shaking hand. It clattered to the floor, and she eased toward the boy, trying to appear as nonthreatening as she could while covered in blood.

"You know they were monsters, right?" she whispered.

Wargi's gaze darted from the sergeant's barely moving form, to Jasminda, to the doorway behind her, where she could feel Jack's presence.

For all the blood and death that had just taken place, the house was eerily quiet, its hush broken occasionally by soft snores from the passed-out soldiers in the room next door. The dowry liquor was a powerful blend. She wondered idly if the dead soldiers had made sure the others drank more, to ensure there would be no interruptions.

"Wargi, I . . . I don't want to hurt you. Just . . . just let him leave." She motioned toward Jack. "You were on patrol by yourself, right? You could say you were far away when this happened."

The young soldier's eyes glazed over for a moment as he seemed to consider what Jasminda was saying. The furrow of his brow as he thought reminded her so much of her brothers. His shoulders slumped, and she was close to inhaling in relief when he focused on Jack again and narrowed his eyes. His back straightened, expression hardened. Jasminda sank into herself when he moved to the sergeant and began to shake him.

Jack stepped around her, pointing his knife at Wargi. "Sit down," he said, his voice a forceful command. Covered in blood, he looked every bit the warrior he was. Wargi backed up a step, the moment of bravado gone, then collapsed onto the ground. The sergeant groaned and shifted, rolling over on the bed and rubbing his face.

"Jasminda, gather their weapons," Jack said.

She scanned the room and found two service revolvers on the dresser. She checked the chambers, pulled back the hammers, then handed one to Jack. The men had arrived with rifles, as well, but had spent what little ammunition they had firing at birds in the valley earlier.

Tensyn sat up, bleary-eyed. Long moments passed before he processed what was before him. He sputtered, his face contorting in rage as Jasminda aimed the gun at him.

"Traitors." The word was laced with venom.

Holding the gun steady, Jasminda cast a glance to Jack. "What now?"

He pointed to Tensyn. "On the ground." The sergeant complied with a sneer.

Jasminda backed up to the corner so she could see both Jack and the door to the room.

With remarkable efficiency, Jack stripped the bedsheets, ripping them into ribbons as Tensyn seethed and spat curses.

"Are you going to make this difficult?" Jack said, kneeling and pulling the sergeant's hands behind his back. He was securing the man's wrists with the strips of cloth when suddenly Tensyn gave a shriek, shot to his feet, and ran directly at Jasminda. His wild, desperate look froze her in place, her finger hovering on the trigger.

Two shots rang out in the small room, and Tensyn's body jerked before he fell, crashing into the dresser against the wall. Jack lowered his smoking weapon, his eyes never leaving hers.

"Are you all right?"

She nodded, dropping her arm to her side, then looked over Jack's shoulder in shock.

Tensyn's fall had knocked the items off the dresser, including the two oil lamps lighting the room. Flames quickly licked up the spilled oil and raced along the wooden legs of the dresser, engulfing Tensyn's clothing and flesh.

Jasminda stared at the flames as they flew up the walls unreasonably fast.

"Jasminda!" Jack shouted. She blinked, unable to think, her feet locked in place. He wrapped an arm around her and pulled her into the living room.

Wargi coughed and sputtered, crawling out behind them. Jack pulled the door shut and stuffed the quilt from the couch in the crack at the bottom of the doorframe.

"Do you have a fire suppressor?"

His words scrambled in her head. "A what?"

"No, I suppose you wouldn't, all the way out here. We don't have much time. I'll gather some food. Save what you can." He dashed into the kitchen, leaving her staring at the door, still not believing what lay on the other side.

A coughing fit caused by the acrid smoke filling her lungs shook her from her stupor. Her house was burning. Her home. The only thing she had left.

She raced upstairs and pulled on a dress and her boots. Tossed items blindly into a sack. Some part of her was still in her parents' bedroom, watching the flames consume the walls. She stared at the bag in her hands, not remembering how it got there, not knowing what was inside but only that the tightness in her chest was not just smoke, it was the mouth of an endless river, a wash of despair sweeping her away.

She found herself in the living room again, standing in front of the cabinets. Had she run down the stairs? Is that why she was struggling to breathe?

No . . .

Everything here was precious. Sooty fingers skimmed each shelf, committing the feel of each object to memory. Her chest contracted. Was that her heart shrinking away to nothing?

Jack appeared next to her, carrying the basket stuffed with what remained of the once-full pantry. "Give that to me," he said and snatched the sack from her. She stared at her empty hands for a moment, then to Jack, and felt grounded by the firmness of his expression. His uniform was tattered and bloody. She pulled out a set of her brothers' clothes from the cabinet and tossed them at him. "Put these on. They should fit—the boys were tall for their age."

Flames reached out from under her parents' door, the quilt having been eaten away. In mere minutes there would be nothing left of her life.

"Jasminda."

She turned to find Jack changed and ready to go. He'd even pulled on Papa's old coat, the one the three children had saved up for over the course of a year in order to replace. Papa had been wearing the new one the last time she saw him.

Tears formed and her throat began to close up. Jack said her name again. "We have to go."

She nodded mutely and allowed him to take her hand and pull her from the house.

On the front yard, Wargi dragged Pymsyn's body, laying him next to the motionless form of Unar.

Jasminda dropped to her knees as a loud crash sounded. Part of the ceiling had collapsed. Something broke inside of her. Somewhere close-by, a voice wailed in agony. Jack wrapped his arms around her and pressed her into his chest until she realized the screaming was coming from her.

He whispered something she couldn't hear above her own cries. Gasping, she worked to pull herself together, clutching at the coat Jack wore that had long since lost her father's smell. Finally, she was able to breathe steadily. His arms were a cage of safety around her, but she still felt like her chest had cracked open and everything inside was leaking out.

"This is all I have. I have nothing else."

He held her tighter and rocked her gently, but she found no solace in his arms.

THE ADRENALINE SURGE fueling Jack was beginning to wane. Each injury pulsed again with renewed strength. He released Jasminda gently, leaving her staring almost catatonically at the house. Wargi hovered over the two remaining soldiers he'd laid out on the ground. Neither man appeared to be breathing. With great effort, Jack knelt and felt for a pulse on each. Scared eyes regarded him from behind round spectacles. Jack shook his head, and the boy's mouth quivered.

"Head east," Jack said. "Go home. Find the path you took to get here. Do you remember the red rocks?"

Wargi nodded and stumbled away into the darkness. Jack hoped the boy would be able to find his way back through the Mantle, but he'd done all he could. He turned to Jasminda, but she was gone. A rush of panic swept over him. She was so distraught, at first he feared she may have run back into the burning house, the way husbands to the north in Udland threw themselves on the funeral pyres of their dead wives. He quickly discarded that idea; she was devastated, yes, but far too strong of spirit for that.

He found her in the barn, standing over the goats that slept on the floor, nestled together in groups of threes and fours. The barn was far enough away from the house that he did not think it would catch fire.

He sagged against the doorframe, every ache and pain making itself known. When he would have collapsed indecorously into a heap, a sickening smell assaulted his nostrils.

"Where is that perfume coming from?" Jasminda asked, glancing around.

"Sweet Sovereign's slumber," he said under his breath. "Cover your nose and mouth! Quick!"

Jasminda's brow furrowed, but his frantic words had the desired effect. She wrapped a scarf over the lower half of her face as Jack pulled a rag down from a peg and did the same. The rag smelled strongly of kerosene, but he ignored it.

"What's wrong?" she asked as he pulled her away from the barn.

"Palmsalt."

She froze, her eyes wide, then turned and ran back toward the barn.

"Jasminda!"

"The goats," she called over her shoulder. Jack rushed after her.

The dead soldiers must have had palmsalt in quite a large quantity among their things, and it was now burning and spreading through the air. The possibility had never crossed Jack's mind. This was technically peacetime and the substance had only one use. The mineral was mined in Lagrimar and found alongside their iron deposits. Once ground into a powder, it was added to grenades and bombs that, when ignited, created a cloying, sweet aroma that many found pleasant. Right up until their lungs shut down.

The gas would spread quickly, and if they breathed much more of it, they would soon be dead. As would the goats Jasminda was shoving noisily out of the barn and into the night.

"We need to go," he said, grabbing her arm. She gave one of the little beasts a kick to the backside, then nodded and followed him out.

He tried to inhale as little as possible, but breathing was a sad necessity. His movements were far slower than he would've liked, and the wind was changing, the breeze bringing more of the gas their way.

He limped along, matching her swift pace as best he could down a path through the expansive gardens. She dashed off to retrieve a thick branch from beneath a tree and handed it to him. He accepted the walking stick gratefully. His shoulder and abdomen were ablaze with pain, each breath a struggle. But each breath no longer held the nauseating mix of oil and palmsalt.

They had walked nearly a thousand metres. "I think we are clear of the gas," he said.

She shook her head in disagreement. "I'm singing a barrier for us, just around our heads. The palmsalt is spreading through the valley. Bloody wind. We'll have to get to higher ground."

He hadn't felt the telltale murmur of Earthsong. Then again, she wasn't directly affecting his body. The mountain was clearly still in the throes of the storm, thick clouds churning out snow at higher elevations. He silently prayed to the Queen Who Sleeps for protection on the journey.

"Will the goats fare well?" he asked.

"They're quick. And too stubborn to die." Her voice cracked, belying her stony countenance. Earlier tears had dried, streaking her cheeks—her red-rimmed eyes had turned cold and determined. A bruise marred the side of her face, but it looked like war paint, further accentuating her competence.

She held a shotgun in one hand and a lantern in the other, with the sack containing the items saved from the house draped across her back. Though he'd protested, she would not let him carry anything, giving a pointed look to his limping legs when he had tried to insist.

"I'm not an invalid."

Her arched eyebrow contradicted him. "Focus on staying upright, and I'll do the rest."

She winced a bit from some injury she wouldn't acknowledge, but overall, she was in far better shape than he. Common sense told him she was right to insist, but his pride stung.

"Are we going through the tunnels?" he asked as they neared the path that would take them into the maelstrom.

"We'll see." She pursed her lips, avoiding his gaze. She was hiding something, some additional anxiety she refused to let him in on. He received only silence in answer to his questions, so he saved his breath for the moment.

As they walked, the moon peeked out from the overhead clouds, brightening the way out of the valley and up the path leading into the mountains. Though the valley was calm, the storm still raging ahead worried him. As the path rose, the temperature fell drastically and the ground changed from grassy, to dirt covered, to snow covered. Each torturous step brought not only a deepening of the snow but an increase in his pain.

Jasminda led the way, the light from her lantern reflecting off the snow, now knee-deep but swallowed up by the surrounding darkness. He leaned heavily on the walking stick as each step became more difficult than the last. Pausing to catch his breath, a coughing fit struck him, leaving red splatters on the pristine white.

When he straightened, he found her staring at the blood on the ground. Almost immediately, the warm hum of Earthsong rippled through him.

"Save it," he advised. "I'm all right."

She scowled. "You are not all right. You are worse than when you arrived. Stop being such a fool." The buzz of Earthsong continued for a few moments before she turned and stomped away.

For hours, they battled the storm, their progress arduous. Strong gusts of wind blew against them, sometimes knocking them on their backs and forcing them to stop until the gale calmed some. Icy blasts whipped through Jack's coat, freezing his fingers until he could no longer grip the walking stick and had to leave it behind.

"Let's stop here for a moment," Jasminda shouted, pointing to a notch in the rock wall just big enough for two people. Underneath the rocky overhang, the snow stood only ankle high, and the sidewalls protected them from the worst of the wind. They crouched down together, shaking from the cold. She took his hands in hers and rubbed, bringing some feeling back into them. In the flickering lantern light, worry etched a frown on her face.

Jack rallied, drawing whatever inner strength he could into his depleted limbs. A small hum of Earthsong tickled at his wounds, but he could sense her weakening. He cracked his knuckles and tried to fashion his frozen face into a grin.

"Now's not the time to grow lazy." He wasn't sure she could understand him over the chattering of his teeth, but she nodded and they stood. At a groaning rumble overhead, they looked up. Something large shifted and slid. He moved forward to see what was happening, but she grabbed him by his coat and pulled him back. Her eyes were huge circles of fear as everything around them started to shake.

With a violent *boom*, an avalanche of snow slid down the mountain, obliterating the path that they were on. The motion pushed them back against the wall as sheets of snow and ice crumbled away and slid off the mountain in front of them. Beneath their feet, the ground convulsed, knocking them off-balance. Jack fell forward into the rioting rush of snow.

Where he'd expected his hands to hit the ground, they hit nothing. He reached out frantically, grasping for purchase as his weightless body plummeted into the darkness blanketed by the cold wet pressure all around him.

CHAPTER THREE

"JACK!" THE RUSH of the avalanche swallowed Jasminda's scream. Desperate fingers came away empty as he disappeared beneath a gush of snow and ice. She reached for Earthsong, opening herself too quickly and not able to control the flow of energy. Her heart stuttered. It was as if the ground beneath her own feet had just fallen away.

She tried again, this time connecting, drawing a stream of power inside her, but she was so weak there was little she could do with it. She stared at the sudden drop-off where the path had been moments before. The shotgun and the lantern had fallen with Jack, leaving her only the dim glow of ambient moonlight to see by as it reflected off the whiteness all around her.

The crush of snow from above tapered off, then stopped. She fell to her knees, leaning over the edge, panic and anguish blinding her as much as the storm. Nothing but snow was visible in any direction.

She called his name again into the black.

Was this how Papa's and the twins' last moments had been? This mountain had already taken so much from her, and now it had claimed Jack, as well. She sank down farther, allowing the cold to leach away what little feeling she had left in her feet and legs. What was left to fight for? What was left at all? Despair choked her, cutting off her oxygen, silencing her sobs.

Look up.

The thought appeared in her mind as clear as a voice, though the night was silent save for the wailing wind. She obeyed, peering up toward the blustering clouds. Like water swirling around an open drain, the falling snow overhead swam in a spiral with a patch of clear sky in its middle, directly over her head. The snow ceased and starlight twinkled down on her. A sound from over the cliff's edge pulled her attention back down. A soft, glowing light approached her, floating upward as if on wings. She rose on trembling legs, unable to look away from the eerie brightness. As it drew nearer, Jasminda recognized the outline of her lantern. Rising along with it was an unconscious Jack.

The soft buzz of Earthsong surrounded her, lifting her off her feet, as well. Her head whipped around, searching out the mysterious Singer, but nothing pierced the weak lantern light. She grabbed Jack's motionless hand and pulled him into her arms as they floated straight up. Having him back calmed her enough that she could take a breath and reach again for her own connection to Earthsong.

The energy moving them was benevolent. She could never have sung a spell strong enough to lift two adults into the air, but at least she could sense that the powerful, unknown Singer had no ill intentions. Her relief was short-lived. As she stretched her reach further, she brushed against the awareness of several others nearby. She could feel their presence but all other emotion was blocked. Tension tightened her belly once again.

The avalanche had destroyed much of the physical path. The spell carried them to where it began again, farther up the mountain, and set them down on a patch of snowy ground. The space was protected from the storm by a sort of bubble, similar to the one she'd made to protect them from the palmsalt, but this one was much larger and stronger. While she couldn't see anyone, she felt people close-by.

Jack stirred, pulling her attention away from their surroundings. She brushed snow off his face and let out an anxious breath when he blinked his eyes.

"Welcome back," she said.

"Delighted to be here." He frowned. Flexed his arms and legs.

She crawled closer, anxious. "What's wrong? Are you hurt?"

A brilliant smile spread across his face. He shook his head. "Not at all."

She studied his energy and found his wounds completely healed. Bones sound, blood stanched, the hole above his heart had not even left so much as a scar from what she could tell.

The darkness around them moved and shadows broke away from the rock wall, stepping into the weak circle of light. Two men and two women, all Lagrimari and armed with rifles, came forward. Jasminda scrambled back, her hand diving into her coat pocket where she'd stored her pistol. Jack too produced a revolver—the sergeant's—holding it at his side. The Lagrimari weren't pointing their weapons but held them at the ready. They weren't soldiers; they wore no uniforms. Their clothes were made from tough, gritty-looking material similar to burlap. The men and women themselves seemed tough and gritty, as well. Jasminda tensed as the group regarded them with hard gazes.

Footsteps crunched in the snow behind the Lagrimari. A small head appeared and pushed its way to the center.

"I told you to go back to the cave," one of the women spit out as a little boy pulled away from her grasp. The woman's face was badly scarred on one side with jagged lines. The boy was around six or seven with a shock of black hair and round cheeks. He smiled brightly revealing two missing front teeth.

Jasminda pointed her pistol to the ground, peering at the boy.

"Well, hello there," Jack said in Lagrimari. "Are you the welcome wagon?"

The boy beamed at Jack, who smiled back uncertainly. Jasminda watched the exchange, confused. What exactly was going on?

"He's an incorrigible child," the scarred woman spat.

"He is only trying to counteract your pigheadedness, Rozyl," another voice said from the darkness. An old woman stepped into the light, her face leathered and wrinkled. She was gray-haired and stooped, and wore a ragged coat of matted fur. "It's too cold out here for all this bother. Pssht. Put those away." She waved her hand, and the armed men and women strapped their rifles to their backs and retreated into the shadows. Rozyl was the last to do so—she scowled at Jasminda before she went.

"Come, children. Come inside where it's warm." The old woman placed a hand on the boy's shoulder. "Thank you, Osar. We wouldn't want our guests to feel unwelcome."

"Who . . . who are you?" Jasminda asked.

"I am Gerda ul-Tahlyro. This little one is Osar, always trying to do good deeds." She smiled down at the child, who seemed a bit abashed.

Jasminda could only stare at the boy. "That was his spell?"

"Oh yes. He's the strongest of us all."

"They don't need to know that," Rozyl growled from somewhere in the darkness.

"Osar has already said these two are safe. What reason have we not to trust them?"

"I don't trust anyone." Footsteps crunched away. The cave entrance must be there, hidden in the darkness. When the last footsteps disappeared, Jasminda stood, taking Jack's offered hand.

He was peering at Gerda, his brows drawn. Jasminda expected him to say something, but when he didn't, she offered her hands to Gerda, palms out in greeting. "I'm Jasminda ul-Sarifor, and this is Jack . . ." She waited for him to provide his surname, but he remained silent.

Gerda squinted at her outstretched hands. Jasminda blinked rapidly, unsure of her mistake. Though she'd never actually had anyone greet her properly in Elsira, she hadn't thought this Lagrimari woman would shrink from her touch.

"In Lagrimar, they greet one another by bringing a hand to the forehead," Jack said, reaching for Gerda's right hand and bringing it up to touch his head. Jasminda swallowed and dropped her hands, heat rising in her neck and cheeks.

"Sarifor, you say?" Gerda said, cocking her head to the side. "Any relation to Dansig ol-Sarifor?"

The world fell away for an instant as an image of Papa's smiling face crossed her vision. She blinked past it and forced herself to breathe. "You knew my father?"

Gerda nodded. "Long ago." She turned and disappeared into the shadows. "Come along now. There's a warm fire inside."

Utterly shaken, Jasminda moved to grab the bag and lantern, but Jack's quick fingers plucked them away first. He chuckled at her exasperation, but the expression did not reach his eyes.

"What do you think?" she whispered.

He watched the storm blustering just on the edge of their little invisible wall of protection. "I'll go first," he said, then grabbed hold of her hand and charged ahead.

She was glad for his hand in hers. The mountain caves and tunnels frightened her. They had been strictly off-limits growing up, and even her intrepid brothers had listened to Papa's words and stayed away. Only half a dozen cave openings lined the mountain path, and her family passed them countless times on their way to and from town. But they had never ventured in. Something about the gaping openings sent off danger signals. On a primal level, they felt like places to be avoided.

Though Jack had been expecting them to use the tunnels to shortcut the storm, she'd had no real intention of doing so. Her plan, such as it was, had been to hope the storm abated early or, if it didn't, wait it out at the mouth of one of the caves. Once he stepped inside one, he would no doubt feel the danger and agree that waiting and going over the mountain was the best option

But he did not shudder the way she did as they entered. He gave no evidence that his skin was crawling with the oppressive atmosphere in the darkened cave. With each step, the temperature grew steadily warmer, but cold goose bumps abraded her skin.

A short tunnel opened to a huge chamber many stories high. The interior was wholly unexpected; instead of the rough surface of rock, the walls and floor were glassy and smooth, but not slippery. It was as if they had been blown in the forge of a glassmaker. They reflected the lamplight, illuminating the entire space. She ran her fingertips across the strange rock, then jerked them back as if stung. There had been no pain, but she struggled to calm her rioting belly. Her breath pulsed in short gasps.

Jack turned, concern on his face. He pulled her closer, wrapping an arm fully around her. "What's wrong?"

"You don't feel that? The *wrongness* of this place? It's like . . ." The lifeless eyes of the man she'd killed swam into her vision. The cave smelled of pungent earth and stale air, but underneath it all, she smelled blood. She considered connecting to Earthsong to explore the foreboding, but the idea caused a ripple of nausea to overwhelm her. That same instinct screaming the danger of the caves told her that this was not a place for magic. For the first time ever, the thought of using Earthsong filled her with dread.

"We can just wait here for the storm to end," Jack said, his warm breath on her ear pulling her back from the edge of panic. She focused on him, his arm around her, the strength in his body now that he was no longer in pain. He was a solid thing to hold on to, and she leaned into his sturdy chest. "I think these Lagrimari are Keepers of the Promise. Rebels against the True Father."

Her breathing eased, allowing his words to sink in. "They've crossed the Mantle . . . How? Why?"

He shook his head. "Perhaps they knew of the cracks. As to why . . ."

Off to the right, another tunnel was lit by a flickering fire. Voices buzzed from within. Jack grew quiet as they approached and paused at the entry to the small cave. A well-tended fire roared in the center, sleeping packs spiraling out from it. A handful of careworn women, each huddled with a small child or two, looked up at her. Osar sat with a slightly older girl near the fire. Rozyl and the others from outside stood grouped together in the corner, hovering over Gerda who sat on the ground with two other elders.

"Come," Gerda called, her voice cracked. "No use skulking about in the corridors."

Jasminda surveyed the two-dozen Lagrimari and approached. She had never seen so many people who looked like her in the same place. But each face she peered into held a sort of quiet desperation, a somberness that hinted at a life of struggle. Except for Rozyl's. She merely glared. Jasminda set her jaw and glared back, unsure as to the source of the hostility. The woman's gaze dropped to Jack's arm around her shoulder, and Jasminda tensed. He was the only Elsiran here.

"Have a seat," Gerda said.

Jasminda eyed the ground suspiciously but had little choice unless she wanted to stand for the foreseeable future. They settled on the ground in front of the elders, but Jack kept his body turned to the side, continually scanning the room. Rozyl and her crew moved a few metres away.

"This is Turwig ol-Matigor and Lyngar ol-Grimor." Gerda pointed to the old men.

"You are Keepers of the Promise?" Jack asked with a sidelong glance.

"We are," Gerda said. Rozyl groaned.

"Did you know my father, as well?" Jasminda asked the men. A look passed between them that she couldn't decipher.

"It was many years ago, child. I can hardly recall," said Turwig, whose kind face held a grandfatherly quality.

The one called Lyngar had deep lines etched into his face, his perpetual scowl making her wonder if he was related to Rozyl. "I can. He was a scoundrel. He abandoned his regiment. Unforgivable!"

Jasminda tensed and focused on the unpleasant man. "He was captured in the Sixth Breach. A prisoner of war." She forced the words out through clenched teeth.

"Is that what he told you?" Lyngar snorted. Gerda shot him a murderous glare, and he looked away, not exactly chastened, more like he'd grown bored with the conversation.

"He journeyed to the World After two years ago along with my brothers . . . to join my mother, who was Elsiran." She said the last as a challenge, to see how he would react. Lyngar's head whipped toward her before his gaze shot to Jack.

"So that is why you cavort with them."

Jasminda moved to stand, wishing she could throttle the old man or, at the very least, get away from him. Jack's hand on her arm stilled her, and she sat stewing in rage. The fire was either far too hot or her blood was boiling.

"Why have you brought these people across the Mantle?" Jack said, motioning to the women and children in the center of the room.

"It will fall soon," Gerda said simply.

"Yes, and the Elsiran side will be no safer than Lagrimar if the True Father makes it across."

Gerda and the old men shared another meaning-laden glance. Rozyl stalked up, towering over the seated group. Her face was taut as she stared at Gerda, pleading silently. Whatever was going on, it was obvious Rozyl did not want Jasminda or Jack to know about it.

Gerda held up a hand to wave Rozyl off. "Life in Lagrimar has become unbearable. That is why we've come. To seek better lives for these young ones."

"Better lives like those in the settlements?" Jasminda scoffed. "There are no better lives for those who look like us here. Those who can sing. There will be no welcoming party for you. In fact, I would be surprised if they don't send you right back the way you came."

"They would not do that." Jack's voice was grim. "It is the Prince Regent's duty to protect all within the borders of Elsira. He is honor bound."

Jack had not suffered the stares and cutting remarks. The bad trades and cheating merchants. The young mother screaming. The insult *grol witch* uttered over and over.

Jasminda reached out for Gerda's gnarled hand. "I do not think it will be a good place for the children. I do not think they will be safe there." From the corner of her eye, she saw Jack's jaw tighten, but he stayed quiet.

"You have never been to Lagrimar, have you, girl?" Gerda said.

Jasminda shook her head.

"Of course not, for you seem to believe they were safe back there." Her voice was kind but stern. Admonishing her ignorance. Jasminda turned toward the gaunt and hollow expressions of the mothers, the wordless appeals in the eyes of the children. They clung to each other like lifelines in a raging storm.

Rozyl's voice broke the silence. "Do you know what awaits these children? Slavery. It's either the mines, the tribute camps, the harems, or the army." She ticked the list off with her fingers. "In the mines, at least you get to keep your Song. Though you exhaust it every day chipping away at bits of rock, pulling precious jewels from the mountain, and filling your lungs with dust. The tribute camps are for the boys to have their Songs sucked away, then be sentenced to hard labor for the rest of their lives. Girls go to the harems to 'bless' the Father with sons for his army."

"And the daughters?" she whispered.

"They never leave the harems," Rozyl said, staring coldly.

Jasminda's stomach churned violently.

"He . . ." Jack sputtered. "With his own daughters?"

"All the True Father's children are sterile," Lyngar hissed. "Not that it is any less disgusting."

"The suffering is immense," Gerda said. "There are many who cannot bear it. That is why we left."

Jasminda brought her hands to cover her face, not wanting these people to see her cry, especially not after what they had all been through. She'd had no idea how terrible Lagrimar actually was. Her stomach churned as nausea threatened again.

"How do you know about the Keepers, boy?" Turwig asked Jack.

Beside her, Jack swallowed and cleared his throat. "After the Seventh Breach, I was stationed at the Eastern Base—"

"You're a soldier?" Rozyl asked, her voice an octave higher than before. She rolled her eyes and pounded the wall of the cave.

Jack waited out her mini-tantrum before continuing. "When we transferred the POWs to the settlement, as per the terms of the treaty, I met a young man called Darvyn." More than one person in the cave sucked in a breath. "You know him?"

Gerda silenced everyone with a glance. "Go on."

A wariness crept into Jack's expression. "We used to talk. We became friendly. He let me practice my Lagrimari with him. One day, a few months later, I went to the settlement, and he was gone. Disappeared. I called for a search, thinking something must have happened to him, but we found nothing."

Jasminda listened, impressed that he had even tried to find a missing settler. It was more than most Elsirans would have done.

"Then, just over three weeks ago, he returned and called for me at the base. He wouldn't tell me where he'd been, just that the Mantle was going to be destroyed and Elsira needed to be warned. I contacted the Council and the Prince Regent, but they wouldn't take the word of a Lagrimari settler. But I believed him."

Jack scrubbed a hand down his face, his eyes growing faraway. His voice dropped as he told of the spell Darvyn had cast to make him appear Lagrimari, of hiding within Tensyn's squad and discovering the terrible truth. "Not just cracks, not just a breach—the entire Mantle will fall. Soon. And the True Father will be unleashed on us all."

Jasminda shivered. The faces of the Lagrimari were pensive.

"And the boy's spell, just . . . failed?" Turwig asked. The old man had leaned forward, intent on every word of Jack's story.

Jack nodded, his shoulders sagging with weariness. He needed to rest after the journey and the healing.

"The boy must be dead," Lyngar said matter-of-factly.

"Or so badly injured he could not maintain the spell." Gerda placed a comforting hand on Turwig as the man shuddered.

Jasminda wondered who he was to them. "You know this Darvyn?" she asked.

Turwig nodded. "Since he was a small child."

Lyngar's face was perpetually twisted, as if everything smelled bad to him. "You've got your proof now, boy. What will you do with it?"

"Make them listen. Prepare to fight," Jack said.

Lyngar appeared dubious.

"You should rest, now," Gerda said, echoing Jasminda's thoughts. "You're welcome to our fire—"

"No," Rozyl broke in. "I don't care how strong Osar's Song is. They'll sleep in one of the adjacent caves." Her suspicion bored into Jasminda.

"Rozyl—"

"It's fine, Gerda. We don't want to be any trouble," Jasminda said.

"We keep our weapons," said Jack.

Rozyl sneered. "As will we."

Jasminda was tired of the attitude. They'd done nothing to this woman, to any of them, to cause such distrust. Perhaps living in Lagrimar made one overly cautious, but the bitterness was undeserved.

Exhaustion seeped deep into her bones, as well. She would take sleep any way she could get it. Jack led the way back to the outer cave and to a smaller cavern a hundred metres away. It was cooler than the refugees' camp, and Jasminda missed the warmth of the fire. The heat had dampened the anxiety of being inside the mountain, but now it was back full force, tightening her chest and constricting her airways. She focused on her breathing as Jack checked every inch of the cavern until he appeared satisfied it met his standards.

They hadn't brought blankets or sleeping packs in their haste to escape the fire so they curled up on the ground next to each other, using the lumpy sack as a pillow.

The evasiveness of the Lagrimari, the lies told about her father, and

Rozyl's bitter hostility filled her mind.

"Why do you think they've really come?" Jasminda whispered. Jack lay with an arm behind his head. In the dim light, she could barely make out his profile.

"The women and children likely are seeking a better life."

Jasminda sighed. "I guess better is relative."

"But the Keepers," he said, shaking his head slightly. "Whatever their true purpose, at least we have the same goal. I hope we will be able to fight against the True Father together."

Jack's hope and determination were fueling him. He had something to fight for.

All she had now were ashes where a whole life used to be.

She closed her eyes and stopped just short of praying not to wake up again.

JACK'S ARMS WERE wrapped around something warm and soft. As he opened his eyes, any hint of drowsiness fled as a spark tickled behind his ribs. Jasminda lay curled on her side, her back pressed against his chest. Her head was tucked just under his chin, and his heart sped as he watched the rise and fall of her gentle breaths.

He brushed her hair back, letting his fingers get caught in its tangled softness. Her scent was enticing, soothing, and he lay for a moment breathing it in. Once again, thoughts inappropriate to their current situation stole into his mind. The curve of her buttocks grazed his groin, and he inched backward so as not to scandalize her with his growing erection. The floor of a cave was a location even more devoid of romance than the army barracks, and yet he had a hard time reining in his mind.

Light footsteps echoed outside the cave entrance. He removed an arm from around Jasminda and palmed the pistol he'd left within easy reach, keeping it down by his side. Though he had trusted Darvyn, he could not be completely certain that *these* enemies of his enemy were, in fact, his friends. Especially not when the Lagrimari they'd met yesterday were Keepers in more ways than one. They may be followers of the Queen and wish to see her promise of return kept, but they held secrets, as well.

Lantern light brightened the entrance as a curly head appeared—a head much lower than he'd expected. Osar stood gripping the lantern shakily. Jack released his weapon. The boy's huge eyes glittered, and he beckoned Jack forward with one hand.

"Jasminda." He shook her gently, not letting go of her shoulder as she rolled over and stretched. "We have a visitor." He nodded in the child's direction, and Jasminda sat up yawning.

Osar motioned again for them to follow before disappearing down the hall. They gathered their things and joined the others in the larger cave. The fire had been put out, lanterns had been lit, and most people were packed and ready to go. The armed Keepers and elders stood in the center, and Gerda's quiet tones carried over Rozyl's hard voice and wild gesticulations.

"I know that was the plan, but it's just not possible now," Rozyl said.

Gerda shook her head. "We follow the course. That is what we agreed on."

"That was before we discovered no one can sing in these blasted caves."

"What's going on?" Jack asked.

Rozyl rolled her eyes but, surprisingly, answered him. "I sent out scouts to determine the way through this maze of tunnels, but not one of us can use Earthsong in here. For some reason, the mountain seems to be blocking us."

Jasminda came up next to him, a frown marring her face. "That doesn't make sense."

"Of course it doesn't. And it also makes no sense to travel down a tunnel we can't feel or see the ending of. We could be lost inside this mountain for years if we take the wrong track. We must wait out the storm and take the path up top."

"No." Gerda's voice was calm but her expression immobile.

"The instructions were clear," Turwig said. The old man would not meet Jack's eye, and he wondered if Turwig blamed him for whatever may have happened to Darvyn. "We must go through."

"And how do you suppose we do that?" Rozyl asked.

"Try again," said Turwig.

Rozyl's face twisted, and she pushed past them, deliberately knocking into Jasminda. She wobbled but caught herself by slamming her palms on a knee-high boulder jutting out of the ground.

"Watch yourself," Jack bit out to Rozyl's retreating back. The woman grumbled out what must have been a Lagrimari curse he hadn't heard before. He turned to Jasminda as she righted herself and brushed off her hands.

A fissure marred the polished surface of the boulder. It had sliced her palm, embedding a sliver of rock in her skin. Jack grabbed her hand to inspect the damage.

"It's nothing," she said, pulling away. His arm felt heavy, his hand strangely empty as she refused his help. But it *was* nothing. The bruise on her cheek was far worse, and she hadn't even complained about it or bothered to heal it.

He clenched his fists and forced his feet to stay rooted, to not follow after the unpleasant Rozyl and give her a piece of his mind. He'd expected to see a mirror of his emotions in Jasminda. The murderous expression she'd had the night before as they'd disparaged her father had made Jack oddly proud of her. But now, her skin was ashen and she looked haunted.

"Wh-what happens when you try to sing?" Her voice was weak, breathy and light, not the full-bodied, sensual tone he'd grown used to in just these few days. Concern furrowed his brow.

Turwig spoke up. "They say their Song calls out but nothing's there to answer it. Like the world has disappeared. Try it yourself if you like, child."

Jasminda shot Jack a worried glance, then closed her eyes. Long, dark lashes brushed her cheeks and her face slackened. But instead of taking on the dreamy quality she'd worn when healing him, her face contorted in pain. Her scream tore through the air, endless and chilling. It froze his heart, but his arms reached out of their own accord to catch her when she collapsed.

THE BEATING OF drums thunders along the walls, pulsing and jittering, almost louder than the pounding of my chest. The thrum thrum thrum beats in time to the chants of my name, called over and over again until it echoes deep in the recesses of every tunnel, every crack and crevice in the mountain.

It was my name Oval's deep voice called at the Choosing.

It is a great honor to be chosen.

So as I kneel on my hands and knees while Mother shears the hair from my scalp, why do I feel such betrayal?

She wraps me in the ceremonial coverings. Chatters on about how proud she is and what this will mean for the little ones, the sisters and brothers I will never see again. The one I will never meet still lodged in her belly.

My sacrifice will protect them from the dangers threatening our caves. Our family will be held in high esteem.

I am scrubbed raw in the hot springs. My newly uncovered head is tender and aching. Blood comes away on my fingers when I rub at my baldness.

Mother pierces me with a glance. You must not waste it, she says, eyes darting around to make sure no one else has seen.

Once your blood is chosen, it no longer belongs to you.

The drums and chanting only grow louder as I follow my family to the gathering. I wish my aching head would pound hard enough to tear it from my body.

Not *my* body. Not anymore.

Oval is there, his eyes pale with age, leached of the fiery color they held in his youth. My eyes will never lighten another shade. My skin will never grow loose and gather in bunches, showing proof of my wisdom. I will be fourteen summers forevermore.

The chanting is frenzied now, the noise unbearable.

I am laid on the smooth stone altar. It vibrates beneath my skin. Mother does not shed so much as a tear for me. Her smile cracks me in two. I am not her daughter.

Not anymore.

I am everyone's daughter now. I belong to the Folk, to the caves, to the drums.

When the blade comes, I do not close my eyes. The pounding in my chest fades as the sharpened stone pierces my flesh.

My blood belongs to them all now.

JASMINDA CLUTCHED AT her chest, pulling at the neck of her dress only to find her skin smooth and unmarred. Her breath came in shallow bursts. Her vision swam. There was no knife plunging between her breasts. No warm blood fleeing her body. No odd, chanting crowd watching, enraptured.

When her eyes focused, an anxious face filled her view. Fire-lit eyes regarded her and a familiar scent filled her nostrils. A man's arms surrounded her. This was safety. Comfort. She knew him, though she couldn't quite recall how. His face relaxed as she stared up at him, hypnotized by the color of his eyes. Voices spoke nearby, but she did not recognize the language.

"What happened?" she said.

He frowned. "I should ask you that. You collapsed. Why are you speaking Elsiran?"

She did not understand his question but caught sight of her hands. Held them up in front of her face. They were back to their normal hue, not the sickly, almost colorless gray they'd been before. "I died."

"I can assure you, you did not," he said, his mouth turned down at the edges. He brushed her hair from her forehead, then sat back as she struggled up to a sitting position.

"No, not me. I was someone else."

"Someone who died?"

"Yes." Her body was heavier now than it had been. Larger and thicker.

"What is she saying?" an aged voice called out in the strange language. She was surprised that she could now understand it. She looked up into a disapproving face that was both familiar and not. People were gathered around her, concern in their eyes, but the only one she recognized was the man. His name danced just at the edge of her memory.

"The mountain demanded my blood." She repeated the words in the language the old man had spoken, testing it out on her tongue. It tasted wrong somehow, as though the syllables didn't fit together properly.

"Did she hit her head?" a woman said.

"Give her some space."

"Try to sing again, child."

"No! That's what got her in this state to begin with."

The voices went back and forth. She couldn't hold on to them. Her vision swam again, but she didn't want to go back to that other place, the place where she was just a sacrificed girl, only worth the weight of her blood.

Something pulsed inside her, something demanding attention. She closed her eyes to focus, and it grew with her observation. Surprised, she opened her eyes again. The man watched her intently. She reached out a hand to him, and he did not hesitate to take it. She focused once more on that little pulse inside her. It swelled, unfurling itself like the wings of a bird and taking flight toward some larger rhythm. The rhythm scared her, but it was also beautiful. She plunged into it and let it consume her, leaving her in a darkness far greater than the one behind her eyelids.

"SHE'S COMING OUT of it."

"Again."

Swimming to the surface this time was easy.

She opened her eyes to Jack's fraught face. "Did you die again?"

"No," she said, this time in Lagrimari. How could she not have understood the language before? She sat up, putting herself just out of reach of the cradle Jack's arms provided. Embarrassment tinged her cheeks.

"You're not going to pass out again?" he asked. His touch calmed some of the mortification. His palm against the back of her neck was a balm. She longed to lean into it, but the ground was cold and hard beneath her, and she was self-conscious about what had just happened.

She'd never fallen unconscious from singing before. And to have it happen not once but twice? The elders hovered over her, and she rose on shaky legs.

"Are you all right?"

"Can you understand us?"

"What happened?"

Jack kept a stabilizing hand at the small of her back. A tiny point of contact, but one that anchored her. "I saw— No, I was— I was one of the Cavefolk. I'd been chosen to be sacrificed to the mountain."

While the others looked at her dubiously, Jack frowned. "The Cavefolk practiced human sacrifice? And you were there, you say?"

She nodded. "I wasn't me, though. I was a girl being led up to the altar. A girl they killed." She shuddered, thinking back to the vision. "Mostly I just remember the feelings. The betrayal. The anger. The fear. They were using my blood for magic, a protection spell."

"The Cavefolk had magic? Earthsong?" Jack's voice was incredulous.

"No, something else. Something darker. When I was . . . there . . . my Song was silent. The magic needed the sacrifice."

Everyone in the cave fell quiet. Jack appeared lost in thought. Gerda and Turwig gave her piteous looks that said they didn't quite believe her. She wasn't mad; she knew what she'd seen.

The Cavefolk were among the original inhabitants of Elsira, from a time before recorded history. Just a few tools and skeletons had survived to tell their story. Her books had not included much about them other than the fact they dwelled in the mountains. Elsira had been a harsh and unforgiving terrain, a rocky desert that barely supported life. Before they mysteriously died out, the Cavefolk and the nomadic clans eked out a meager existence. And then the Founders arrived—the Lord and Lady from some distant, unknown place—who transformed Elsira into the lush, beautiful land it was today.

They and their descendants ruled for millennia, years of peace and bounty. The Queen Who Sleeps was last in their line, but She was betrayed by the True Father and cast into a deep sleep. Her last act was to create the Mantle, protecting Her people from the worst of the True Father's power.

The fate of the Founders and the Cavefolk was lost to history. Jasminda had long been fascinated by the mystery, as had many scholars. She'd ordered and read every book on the subject she could get her hands on, but the secrets of the ancients remained hidden.

She kneaded her forehead, searching her memory for anything that would bring what she'd seen into focus. Why that vision? Why her?

"As long as you're all right," Gerda said, patting her arm.

"Can you sing, child?" Turwig asked, his brow drawn low over his eyes.

She drew in a shaky breath. Though part of her was afraid to try again, another, bigger part was curious as to what would happen this time. The foreboding she'd felt when first entering the cave was still there, but curiosity won out over the fear. She opened herself once more to Earthsong. The normally strong pull of the power was near overwhelming; the tide tried to pull her under, harder than ever before.

"I feel untethered. I can barely hold on."

"Can you lead us through the tunnels or not, girl?" Lyngar snapped. Jack shot a warning glance in the old man's direction, but Jasminda saw it as if from far away.

Her attention was on her awareness of the cave, the tunnels beyond, and the mountain surrounding them. Ghosts of the ancient inhabitants brushed the edge of her senses. There was power in this mountain, but it hummed with a different pattern than Earthsong.

Still, a thread of life wove through this place. Insects and creatures too small to see, and mosslike vegetation that needed no light. She pulled the energy inside her, and it formed a path, though faint, that led through to the other side of the mountain.

She let the power slide away. "I can sense the route, but it's long. I'm not sure I'll be able to stay connected and sing for the whole journey, though."

"Of course the feeble halfling is the one we must follow," Rozyl said from her position against the wall. Jack's breathing turned heavy as he glared, lighting a spark of satisfaction within Jasminda at his reaction.

"Perhaps she can link with someone," Turwig suggested.

Rozyl gave him a look that could shear the shell off a beetle. "Why can she sing and no one else? What is wrong with her? I'm not linking with her." Jasminda flinched internally at the bite in the woman's voice, though she had no desire to link with Rozyl either.

"What's linking?" Jack asked.

Gerda patiently began to explain. "It's when two Earthsingers share their connection. They—"

"It's when one Singer gives control of their entire Song to another to do with as they please," Rozyl interjected. "And *that* is not going to happen."

"It's a sharing of power," Gerda continued, "but only one Singer can be in control. It must be done voluntarily, of the giver's free will. If we still had our Songs, we would do it."

"Speak for yourself," Lyngar spat, and Jasminda tensed. She had linked with Papa when she was young and still learning. He'd shown her how to control her power through the link, but she could not imagine linking with a stranger. To do so was to become extremely vulnerable to another. It was like letting someone into her soul.

The elders and Rozyl bickered over what to do. The four armed Keepers were the only adults who had not been forced to give their Songs in tribute to the True Father. Jasminda shuddered to imagine life without her Song; it was a part of her, weak though it was.

A small hand slipped into her own. Osar's round face beamed up at her. She squeezed his hand, and he leaned in, resting his head against her leg.

"You would link with me, wouldn't you?" she asked, smoothing down his hair. "You're not afraid?" He shook his head, then offered her his other hand, which was closed in a fist.

"What do you have there?"

He unfurled tiny fingers to reveal a shoot of green with delicate white petals sparking out of it.

"Where did you get this?" she asked, incredulous, picking up the tiny flower. It could not have grown in the cave, and with the snow outside it was doubtful he'd brought it in with him. Yet here it was. Something beautiful and impossible in the midst of the bleakness. "Thank you."

Silence descended. Jasminda looked up to find the others staring at her and the blossom in her hand. She straightened her shoulders, looking at Rozyl and Lyngar as she spoke. "Osar will link with me."

Rozyl narrowed her eyes. Lyngar merely turned toward the exit, speaking over his shoulder. "Fine. Let's get going. We've wasted far too much time as it is."

JACK KEPT TO the rear of the party as they made their way through the tunnels. He did not like to be so far from Jasminda, who led the group with Osar at her side, but he also did not trust Rozyl or the other armed Keepers at his back. They seemed to feel the same about him, which left him walking side-by-side with a tall Lagrimari woman, Rozyl's second-in-command, who never said a word to him.

On the whole, they were not a talkative bunch. The only sounds they made were footsteps echoing against the oddly smooth cave walls and the soft babbling of the youngest of the children. They did not dawdle, either, deftly navigating the twisting path, which edged steeply downward, leveled off, then dipped low again.

They took no breaks, and not even the smaller children walking on their own complained. Nor did the elders, who were remarkably spry for their ages. Strips of some unidentifiable food source, gray and brittle, were passed around and eaten while they walked. Hours passed like this, the silence companionable but complete.

Jack focused on the back of Jasminda's head, keeping her in sight at all times. Whatever reaction she'd had in the cave did not recur, but he was uneasy all the same. No one had any idea what had happened to her or why she was the only one who could sing inside the mountain.

Her vision of the Cavefolk was disturbing, as well. Barbaric practices like human sacrifice were said to still be performed in Udland, their northern neighbors, but the thought of such things taking place in his land, even in ancient times, was unsettling. Jasminda had been so deeply shaken, he hadn't questioned her tale for an instant. After having his entire body rendered unrecognizable to the point where his own mother would not have identified him, his threshold for belief in the unbelievable had nearly vanished.

Not that his own mother was likely to recognize him anyway. He'd been only a child the last time he saw her.

The woman next to him glanced over sharply before going back to ignoring him. He gave her a brilliant smile and tipped an imaginary hat.

Slowly, the air began to change. The pathway leveled off again, and fresh, clean air filtered in. It was the way he'd always thought a mountain would smell. They extinguished their lanterns when light glowed softly up ahead. Over the thump of their footsteps, water trickled, insects whirred, birds called.

Home.

The tunnel ended abruptly, leaving them at the edge of a huge cavern, much like the one they'd entered on the other side with some key differences. Sunlight streamed in through openings in the rock far overhead. Before them stretched a vast forest; trees and vines and greenery filled the cave. A narrow and somewhat hidden path led down to the forest floor. Just beyond it, a stream of water flowed gently down, vanishing below. The view stole his breath.

The group formed a queue as the path was only wide enough for one. Jasminda disappeared from view first. Not being able to see her made his palms itch. He was returning to civilization and, with it, all of his duties and responsibilities. With no home and family, Jasminda was now listed among those responsibilities, but he was glad of it. He hadn't yet figured out what to do about her, though. Could he find her a farm near the Eastern Base? Possibly. But that would be too dangerous with a breach imminent. Could he keep her safe in the city, far away from the fighting? And then not see her for months or longer . . . The possibilities raced through his mind. All of them included seeing her again. As often as he could manage. Was that even something she would want?

She had stolen into his life—his very complicated life—and he was in no hurry for her to leave. But the war on the horizon would make everything immeasurably harder. Anti-Lagrimari sentiments would kick into effect once again, and her Elsiran blood would not protect her from the ire of the people who saw only her skin. He could tell from the way she spoke, the haunted look in her eye when the refugees discussed Elsira, that it never had.

The cold daylight of early afternoon greeted them at the end of the path, and they left the mountain behind, stepping back onto familiar territory.

But all was not well.

Acrid smoke assaulted his nostrils. The Keeper beside him clutched at her chest and sank to her knees. Alarmed, Jack searched out the other armed Keepers, all of whom looked equally affected. Their faraway expressions indicated they were using Earthsong.

Anxious murmurs rippled through the Lagrimari. He offered aid to the collapsed woman, but she brushed him off. Unease gripped him as he rushed to Jasminda's side.

Seeing her eyes well with tears, he grabbed hold of her shoulder. "What's happened?"

She shook her head and pointed through the thicket of trees. Just a few hundred metres away stood the Lagrimari settlement of Baalingrove, where he'd first met Darvyn.

Or at least that was where it used to stand. Thick smoke now billowed from that direction, and Jack's gut filled with lead.

"I can feel them dying," Jasminda whispered, looking toward the smoke in horror.

HE TRIED TO convince the elders to stay behind, near the caves, to let him and the armed Keepers investigate, but they wouldn't be persuaded.

"We go together," Gerda told him simply, and would say no more.

"People are dying. There is danger near," he said.

Turwig patted his arm. "There is danger everywhere, son. Who's to say it won't find us here, as well?"

With a shake of his head, Jack led the way, two of the Keepers at his sides, their rifles drawn. An armed Lagrimari on Elsiran land would be trouble, but his warnings fell on deaf ears. He did have authority here, though these people did not know it, and the fact that he had no idea what they were dealing with set him on edge. Pistol drawn, he exited the thicket for his first glimpse of what remained of the settlement.

He had last been to Baalingrove only a few weeks before. As always, he'd been struck by the living conditions of the settlers: makeshift wooden shacks with leaky tin roofs, tiny patches of garden, no running water, no electricity. The men survived mainly due to the kindness of the Sisterhood, a charity comprised of devoted followers of the Queen, who provided food and supplies. Neither the Prince Regent nor the Council saw fit to do any more, and the Elsirans as a whole preferred to pretend the settlers didn't exist.

If he'd been a betting man, he would have wagered the place couldn't look worse than it had when he'd left, but he would have lost. Now, charred husks replaced the shacks. Gardens lay scorched with the white crystals of what he guessed to be salt coating the barren earth. More than one blackened body lay smoldering in the dirt. He looked back at the children, wishing they weren't seeing this, but the mothers made no move to hide the eyes of the young ones. They took in the gruesome sight without comment.

"What happened here?" Jasminda said from just behind him.

He had only an inkling, but before he could respond, angry voices rent the air, shouting in Elsiran. He couldn't make out the words but recognized the heavy borderlander accent. Gunshots rang out.

"For Sovereign's sake, get the children back!" he hissed.

He shared a glance with Rozyl, who pursed her lips and made a hand signal to one of her crew. The man peeled off and helped direct the mothers and children to squat behind the wall of a mostly intact shack.

Jack and the armed Keepers remained on the main path, along with Jasminda and the elders.

"Go with them," he told Jasminda. She merely rolled her eyes and cocked her pistol.

The voices came from the edge of the settlement, on the other side of a grouping of smoldering lean-tos. As they approached, gunfire continued to pop and the shouting grew louder. Jack saw movement from the corner of his eye; a Lagrimari woman was huddled with two children behind the wreckage of a building. She was not part of the group that came through the mountain with him. Her eyes grew wide when she saw him, confusion crossing her features as she took in his companions.

Rozyl bent to speak with her. "What happened here?"

"There was some trouble in the town, I think. A girl went missing. Her father got it in his head that one of the settlers took her, and a mob of farmers came here to search." The woman's eyes kept darting to Jack. He took a few steps back, aware that, to her, he must look like one of the men who attacked this place.

"Are you injured? You should try to get to safety." Rozyl's voice was softer and kinder than he'd heard it before.

"My boy's back there. He wanted to fight with the men. I can't leave him." She pointed toward the battle.

"Not even for the safety of these little ones?" Jasminda said. The solemn faces of two boys, each under five, stared up at them.

"We made it out together. I won't lose one of them now."

Jack's heart stung for the woman. "Are you a refugee?" he asked. She shrank back at his voice, her face twisted in fear. Her gaze, full of questions, shot to Rozyl.

"He's—" Rozyl looked back at Jack and shrugged "—with us."

The mother's expression was still rigid with suspicion. "We crossed with ten others three days ago, but I don't know what became of them once the fighting started."

Jack broke away to investigate, only dimly aware of the others trailing behind him. A turn in the road revealed a makeshift barricade erected out of pieces of tin, planks and boards, wheels, furniture, and other miscellaneous items. It was flimsy but blocked the mouth of the dirt road.

A half dozen Lagrimari crouched behind the barrier. Two were armed with hunting rifles, the others with pitchforks, machetes, and one man even held a sword. A boy of about twelve was among their number. He must have been the woman's son. Their backs were to Jack as they focused on the scene in front of them.

A small band of Elsiran farmers was currently being pelted with icicles and dirt clods. They used their rifles to try to bat away the projectiles, every so often getting a shot off in the direction of the settlers. Jack hung back, letting the elders and the armed Keepers go on ahead of him; he didn't want to be mistaken for a farmer.

The way the boy knelt among the older men, looking slightly off to the side, his body alert but unmoving, made Jack believe it was he who was singing the spell to attack the farmers. The Elsirans were penned in a tight group. Any time one of them tried to break out of it toward the settlers, a chunk of mud or an icicle would hit him in the face, knocking him back. Two of them did manage to peel off and run away, back down the road toward the town.

The settlers cheered, and one of the men finally noticed Rozyl and her group advancing on the barricade with their rifles drawn. The Keepers took up positions and began firing on the farmers. The ice-and-mud attack stopped as the boy looked up, startled. This gave the farmers a chance to dive for cover among the nearby trees. They began to return fire.

The armed settlers must have been out of ammunition, for they didn't fire, but Rozyl and her team were methodical, efficiently finding their targets and hitting them as man after man fell.

He felt no sympathy for the farmers, though they were his countrymen.

There had been incidents such as these over the years, when tensions between citizens and settlers had bubbled over, but this was the most destruction he'd yet seen.

Jasminda came to crouch at his side. "I convinced the woman and her children to wait with the others."

The woman's son was staring up in awe as the Keepers made short work of the remaining farmers. Those who hadn't been shot were now beating a quick retreat. Would they go to lick their wounds or try to gather reinforcements and retaliate?

"There were nearly one hundred men who lived here," Jack mused. "I knew many of them."

"Now there are five." Jasminda's voice was husky and thick.

He looked at her and wanted to apologize, though he'd had no hand in it—this was bigger than both of them. But he wished he could make up for the ignorance of his people, for the hatred and fear. He opened his mouth, but no words came out. There was really nothing he could say.

Through the gaps in the trees lining the road ahead, thick wheels kicked up clouds of dust. When the vehicle approached, Jack's tension flared, then quickly fled. An open-topped four-wheeler drove up bearing four Elsiran soldiers. On its heels were two transports, a dozen men to each if they were following protocol. Sure enough, twenty-four men hopped out of the trucks and dispersed strategically, forming a perimeter around the settlement. The soldiers in the four-wheeler exited, guns drawn, and advanced on the barrier.

Jack stood ready to greet his men. Before he'd taken more than two steps, the soldiers opened fire. They gave no warning, no orders or instructions, just began shooting. Those at the barrier dove for cover, and Jack stood, dumbfounded, until Jasminda pulled him down again.

What in Sovereign's name?

"Can you do the thing with the ice and mud?" he asked her. The idea of firing upon his own men was something he could not fathom at the moment, and he didn't want the other Lagrimari to do so, either. He needed a distraction.

"I think so," Jasminda said, and closed her eyes.

The firing stopped as a cloud of dust and dirt rose, blinding the soldiers.

Jack ran to the barricade, passing the shocked Lagrimari gathered there, and hurdled across it, into the dust storm.

"All right, Jasminda," he called, breathing into the lapel of his coat. When the dust cleared, he stood face-to-face, pistol drawn on the lead officer, a captain Jack recognized, but had never personally spoken to before. From the corner of his eye, he saw the soldiers nearby train their weapons on him.

"Hold your fire!" the captain shouted, a dazed look coming over him.

"Do you know who I am?" Jack said through clenched teeth.

"Y-yes, sir."

"Who am I then?" he pressed.

"Commander Alliaseen."

Soldiers nearby gasped in shock.

"I-I have to ask for your identification code, sir."

"Ylisum two five three zero nine." Jack squeezed his hand around the butt of the pistol still pointed at the captain's head, anger vibrating through his every fiber. "Verified?"

"Verified." A moment was all it took for the demeanor of the other soldiers to change radically. The guns were put away swiftly, and the men all stood at attention. Jack lowered his weapon, as well, and tried to control his breathing.

"Commander, I am Captain Daveen Pillos. We had heard you'd been lost."

"I was found, Captain." Jack took in another steadying breath and unclamped his jaw by sheer will. "On whose order were you firing upon these settlers?"

Pillos's gaze darted to the barricade and back. "No one's order, sir. We were engaging combatants."

"When you engaged these combatants, were they firing upon you?"

A tic jumped in the captain's jaw. "No, sir. But reports said they had attacked some civilians."

"Under the rules of engagement, under what conditions is it permissible to fire upon residents of your own country when you are not under immediate threat of harm?"

Pillos blinked rapidly as if trying to recall.

Jack exhaled in exasperation. "Has martial law been declared, Captain?"

"No, sir."

"Then am I correct in stating there are no conditions under which it is permissible to fire upon residents of your own country when you are not under immediate threat of harm?"

"Y-yes, sir. But, sir . . . they are settlers."

Jack took a step back and raised his voice so that all present could hear. "Yes, Captain. These are settlers. And as of the Treaty of the Seventh Breach, they have non-enemy status in Elsira. Unless they directly provoke you and are not, as in this case, merely defending themselves against attack, it is our sworn duty as defenders of Elsira to protect them, as well. Is it not?"

"Yes, sir."

Jack took a deep breath, exhausted from the display of leadership. Pillos was doubtless no different than most of his men, than most of Elsira if he could stand to believe such a thing.

"See if anyone needs medical attention and gather their weapons. But for Sovereign's sake, don't shoot anyone. And I need your radio, Captain. It's urgent."

"Yes, sir. This way." He gave the order then led Jack to the four-wheeler. He hopped into the driver's seat and picked up the earpiece and transmitter, speaking his identification code into the microphone.

"Connect me to the palace immediately." The line was staticky while the call was patched through.

"Jack?" a voice warbled down the line.

"Usher? Is that you?"

"Oh, Jack," the man exhaled in obvious relief. "Thank the Queen you're alive!"

"Usher, I'm not sure how you got on this line, but I have urgent business. I need to speak to—"

"Jack." The old man's voice cracked, weighed down with misery. "It's Alariq. Your brother is dead."

CHAPTER FOUR

JASMINDA'S GAZE TRACKED Jack as he dealt with the soldiers. After the initial incident, the men's sudden change in attitude and obvious deference toward him piqued her curiosity. He only had to say a few words and they would hop into action.

He directed several soldiers over to ask, somewhat hesitantly, for the weapons of the Lagrimari. The settlers understood the commands and translated for the others. Rozyl had scowled but added her rifle to the pile.

Once the guns had all been put away, the other refugees were brought out from their hiding places, including nearly a dozen people she hadn't seen before who'd hidden in the trees just beyond the settlement. They all gathered, seated behind the remains of the makeshift barrier, still wanting some distance between themselves and the Elsirans.

Gerda sat next to Jasminda as she followed Jack giving commands and instructing his men.

"You watch him very closely," Gerda said. "Do you think he will disappear?"

Jasminda pulled her gaze away. "I'd almost forgotten he was one of them." Her heart tied itself in a knot. He'd been so different, so kind, but now, standing in a huddle of other Elsirans, it was difficult to pick him out from the group. The idea of finding warmth and comfort from his presence seemed foreign.

What had she expected? She knew that he was on a mission. He'd risked his life to gain information, and now he had to put it to use. Just because she'd grown to think of him as a possibility, perhaps even as a friend, did not mean he felt the same. She was an ally; they had united against a common foe, and now that he was back on home territory, she was on her own again.

One of the settlers, a grizzled barrel of a man, stood and began inspecting the damage to the nearby shacks.

"What are you doing there?" Lyngar asked. He sat a metre away, snacking on the strange jerky the Lagrimari had brought with them.

"There are sound boards here. Much can be salvaged."

"You're going to rebuild?" The old man's voice dripped with condescension.

"Aye," said the settler.

Rozyl approached from her position nearest the barrier. "Have you any family back home?"

The settler pulled free an unburned length of tin and started a pile at the edge of the road. "I was born in the harems and grew up in the army. No family. This has been home these twenty years. Besides, with so many of you lot coming here, we'll need to rebuild."

The man's tone was matter-of-fact and his logic sound. Where *would* the refugees live? Jasminda was certain the dilapidated settlements were not the salvation they had in mind when they'd started the journey. She certainly could not see herself living here. She wanted nothing more than to go back to her quiet life, her garden, and her goats and to put this whole desperate experience behind her. But the cabin was nothing but cinders now.

Sitting up straighter, she looked with new eyes at the destruction around her. The first settler had been joined by several others, all picking through the smoking remains to find bits that could be reused. If they could rebuild this place, could she not rebuild her cabin? Papa had built the whole thing by himself. It would take her far longer—she was not as strong physically or with Earthsong—but if she took regular breaks, she could sing the heavier logs into place. It would not be the same, but it would be hers.

The palmsalt would have completely dispersed within a few days, and the mountain storm was over. It would likely be a three-day journey over the mountain and then she could be home again.

She looked at the forlorn people gathered around her. "What will you do now that you're here?" she asked Gerda.

"We are here only by Her guidance. There is a plan in place that we must follow."

Jasminda frowned. She hadn't known the Lagrimari were religious. "You follow the Queen? Is that . . . allowed in Lagrimar?"

"Oh no. The only religion allowed is reverence of the True Father. But She graces the dreams of some, and there are many who believe in secret."

Jasminda nodded. "What *is* the plan?"

Gerda's gaze was sharp and clear. It felt like the woman was peering deep into her soul. "It unfolds daily."

Jasminda sat back and exhaled. The woman preferred to speak in riddles. Offering her valley to the refugees had crossed her mind, but she doubted that was a part of the Queen's plan. Jasminda was still an outsider, even among people who looked like her.

She turned again to Jack. He sat in the smaller of the vehicles staring out into space. His face was drawn and troubled. She wanted to go to him, ask what was wrong, offer comfort, but she had no idea if it would be welcome.

Another vehicle rumbled down the road, a sort of motorized covered wagon. Larger than both the auto she'd seen in town and the army vehicle, it pulled to a stop and seven women emerged. Each wore identical blue robes trimmed in gold with her hair tied in a topknot.

"Who are they?" Gerda asked.

"The Sisterhood," Jasminda said. "Devotees of the Queen. They feed the poor and aid the settlers."

The Sisters unloaded crates from the back of their wagon. Several soldiers came to assist.

Jasminda was torn. Jack had exited the vehicle and rallied somewhat, his back was straight, shoulders back, but she could still tell something was wrong. She started to reach out to him with Earthsong, but then thought better of it. If she was leaving, best that she break the ties now. Her imagination had run wild before; there had never been any possibility of something between the two of them. Especially not with him an important soldier and her— What was she? Just a goat farmer. An outcast. It would be better if he didn't know her.

She stood and stretched her legs. Most of the others were now helping in the salvage project. She didn't want to have to explain herself or say any good-byes. Especially not to Jack. It was cowardly, she knew, but whatever hopes she'd harbored were best buried deep and never acknowledged again. She could slip away and, very soon, no one would remember she'd been there at all.

Jasminda took a few steps back, away from the others. Everyone's focus was either on the salvage or the newcomers, the Sisters, approaching with crates of food. Turning to head back toward the mountain, she nearly bumped into Osar. He looked up at her with disapproval, his lips pressed tight. She faltered.

Crouching next to him, she took his little hand in hers. "You'll be all right. Somehow." He continued to glare at her. "I don't belong here. I know you can't understand that, but it's true." He shook his head. "It's not true?" He shook his head again, and Jasminda chuckled. "Why don't you talk, Osar? You seem to have a lot of opinions."

The vibration of Earthsong hit her like the clanging of a bell.

Words lie. Songs don't.

His Song was so sure and strong, she'd nearly forgotten how powerful he was. She could hear his thoughts in her head as clearly as if he'd spoken them aloud.

Look up.

The same words as after the avalanche, when Osar had saved Jack. Again she obeyed, squinting into the sun until it was blocked by a figure standing over them. One of the Sisters held out two paper sacks.

"Food," the woman said in Elsiran, miming eating with one of her hands.

Jasminda stood and took the offered sack, unable to pull her gaze away. The woman before her was the spitting image of Mama. Golden auburn hair, topaz-colored eyes, a straight nose peppered with freckles. The only thing that kept Jasminda from crying out and running into the woman's arms were the burn scars across her left cheek and jaw.

At Jasminda's continued stare, the Sister touched her face briefly and ducked her head. She bowed slightly then hurried away.

"Oh, no, I wasn't—" Jasminda said to her retreating back. With a glance at Osar, who was excitedly investigating the contents of the bag, Jasminda took off after the Sister. The woman was already retrieving more sacks from a crate and passing them out.

"This one's empty," she called out. Her voice was higher than Mama's, lighter and breathier. Jasminda almost didn't trust her memories. There was no way two people could look so similar.

"Sister Vanesse, could you lend a hand?" another Sister called from near the vehicles. The scarred Sister hurried off, leaving Jasminda gaping after her.

Vanesse. She knew that name. Her mother had spoken it often enough. Jasminda had even tried addressing her letters to Vanesse Zinadeel when those to her grandmother kept being returned unopened. But her mother's sister had not responded, either.

Aunt Vanesse.

Her only proof was a first name and a face nearly identical to her mother's.

"Are you going to eat that?" a young girl asked, looking hungrily at the forgotten lunch in Jasminda's hand.

"No, go ahead," she said, handing it off, unable to take her eyes off a face she never thought she'd see again.

SHE DIDN'T KNOW how long she stood there, staring blindly, but the approach of more army-brown vehicles, a bus, and several trucks brought her back to the present. Soldiers rounded up the refugees and settlers, and directed them toward the bus.

"They wish us to sleep at the Eastern Base tonight," she overheard a settler telling the others. "The Sisterhood has set up a place for the refugees near Rosira. We will travel there tomorrow."

The settlers grumbled among themselves about whether or not to leave, in the end deciding to accompany the women and children and ensure their safety. Jasminda too was torn. Home beckoned, but curiosity and anger warred within her. Only metres away stood a blood relative, one she'd never met and who'd shown no interest in her. And in Rosira, lived her mother's mother. A woman Jasminda had begged for help when she'd been left alone at seventeen. This was her chance to get answers. To meet her grandmother, look in her eye, and ask how she could be so callous to her own kin, how she could ignore her daughter and granddaughter for years.

Jasminda was tired of being ignored and being looked at with scorn and derision. She wanted both of these women to know who she was, to know what kind of man her father had been, how strong and smart her brothers had been. She would stand up and give a reckoning of her family. It was the least she could do for their memories.

Jasminda scanned the area. The Sisters were packing their supplies back into their wagon. There was still some small chance this Sister wasn't her aunt, and even if she was, if she approached now, Vanesse may warn her grandmother and she'd never get the chance to confront the woman as her heart now demanded. Jasminda would wait for the right moment.

A soldier waved Jasminda toward the queue forming to board the bus. Staying meant she was little more than a settler or refugee. She searched the area for Jack but he was nowhere to be found. An emptiness took hold inside her, but she stepped onto the bus warily when it was her turn. A clean break was best, wasn't it? The engine thundered to life, and she chose an open seat at the back. Just before the driver closed the doors, Jack slipped aboard, his brow furrowed.

She held her breath as his gaze searched the seats until he found her. "What are you doing?"

She searched for words, but her mouth was too dry to speak.

He moved down the aisle toward her and extended his arm. "Come." Her hand found his of its own accord. She could not control her longing for his touch, for his nearness. No matter how hard she tried to ignore it, her hand in his caused a riot of sensation to shoot through her entire body. The fact that he'd sought her out dissolved the emptiness. Perhaps she needn't make a clean break after all. Perhaps Jack could help. She took his proffered hand, allowing him to lead her off the bus and over to the group of men standing near the other vehicles.

"Captain," he said, though he pitched his voice loud enough for all the soldiers to hear. "This woman is a citizen, born in Elsira, and shall be treated as such. She is not a refugee."

The man before him stood at attention. "Yes, sir. I apologize, sir. I did not realize."

Jack nodded once, then led Jasminda to an armored truck, helping her into the rear seat. She darted a glance back to the bus.

"Are we going to the base, as well?" she asked.

He leaned his forehead against the doorframe and sighed heavily. "Yes." His whole demeanor had changed. Gone were even the hints of the man she'd once confused for an artist. He was all warrior now . . . and a weary one.

"You are in charge of these men?" She didn't know much about military ranks, but High Commander sounded awfully important.

"Yes," he said simply.

Her heart grew heavy. Though he stood next to her, suddenly he seemed very far away. "You are very young."

"I started early. Practically at birth. And my family is very... well connected." There was no pride in his voice.

"The men respect you. It isn't false regard in their eyes. You must be very good."

He shrugged and looked away as though uncomfortable with this topic of conversation. She changed tacks.

"What happened earlier? You seemed distressed. Is it the breach?"

He looked over his shoulder. The captain and another man stood nearby. Jack switched to Lagrimari. "No, but I will tell you later."

She eyed the other soldiers and nodded.

"Later then," she said, placing a hand on his. Gasping at the thoughtless familiarity, she immediately tried to pull her hand back, but he kept hold and squeezed her fingers before letting go. His eyes crinkled in a tired smile, then he turned and walked off.

Voices carried from the other side of the truck. "Looks like the commander has himself a new pet."

Someone snorted. "A *grol* bitch to fetch the paper and eat the table scraps."

The soldiers cackled, their voices fading as they walked away. She clenched her hand into a fist and settled back against the truck's hard seat.

THE THIN, ARMY-ISSUED cot was almost comfortable. After arriving at the base, Jasminda had been given a space in a corner of a small supply building where she could sleep. The Lagrimari had been assigned a barracks building for the night, but Jack insisted she be kept separate. She appreciated his efforts to continually remind his men of her citizenship, but she felt uneasy alone in a strange place. Jack had showed her the space and then been called away again. She'd sat there for the past half hour reading the various labels on the boxes and listening to the sounds of the base beyond the walls.

The door creaked open. Jasminda scrambled to the edge of the cot and retrieved her knife from her thigh. She reached for Earthsong, but the energy slipped from her grasp. Agitation wormed its way into every part of her. She would have to be far calmer in order to control her Song.

"Jasminda. It's me."

She relaxed as Jack's head came into view from behind a stack of boxes. His eyes lingered on her legs as she set her skirt back into place. Her face grew hot.

He pulled a box close to her cot and sat, looking around the tiny space. "How do you like the accommodations?"

"It's no cave floor, but it will serve."

Exhaustion tarnished his face, but she couldn't keep her eyes from him. He was so beautiful. She struggled to push the thought away, but then he reached for her hand, interlocking their fingers, and she lost the battle. Her breath caught in her chest as she delighted in the feel of his skin.

"Are you all right?" she whispered.

"I've been worse."

"And you've been better?"

He seemed enraptured by their joined hands. He stroked her skin with his thumb. "How is it that your skin is so soft?"

"It's the balm." She shrugged as a shiver raced through her. "Will you tell me what happened?"

"My brother . . . is dead." His voice was even and measured. He spoke the words like they were just another fact of the day. The sun rose. The rain fell. His brother died. Jasminda's heart seized.

Her mouth hung open as she struggled to find the words to say. "I-I'm sorry. I'm so sorry, Jack."

He stared off into the distance. "He was piloting his airship and ran into a thunderstorm. The craft crashed. He was thrown through the window." With a shake of his head, he turned to her. She trembled at the intensity in his eyes. "I haven't told you all you need to know about me."

In fact, she knew very little. He'd proven himself kind and honorable. He protected her and cared for others more than himself. In this strange place, he was the only thing that made her feel safe, no matter how hard she tried to deny it. But he obviously came from a rich and influential family. His brother *owned* an airship. She wanted to know him better, if such a thing were possible. Wanted to so much it hurt.

"Will you tell me?"

"I want to, but let us wait until tomorrow, if that is all right. It is not something I want to think about now. Worries on top of worries."

She smiled sadly, a tendril of unease creeping its way through her. "Of course."

They sat in silence for a while as she tried not to allow her fears to get the better of her. What exactly did she expect of him? No matter what his secrets were, he was a high-ranking Elsiran military leader and she a *grol* witch. What else did she need to know?

But there he was in front of her, his pain so clear. She longed to be able to soothe him.

"Was he your only family?" she asked softly.

He shook his head. "My mother lives in Fremia now."

"Has she been told?"

"She's in seclusion. But we are half brothers. Were . . . His mother is long passed. He and I were never close. We didn't see eye to eye, but . . ."

"But he was kin."

Jack nodded. "Kin. And now it falls to me."

He stroked each of her knuckles and massaged the delicate skin between her fingers.

"What falls to you?"

"I—" He dropped his head. Shook it. "It is late. You should rest."

"Tomorrow then." She let her hand slip from his.

Neither of them moved.

"Jack, what do you see when you look at me?"

He gazed at her questioningly.

"Your men . . . they see me as the enemy. How is it you don't?"

"You're not the enemy. Did someone say something to you?" Anger sparked behind his eyes, and she grasped his arm.

"No, no. Just . . . they think it."

"Does Earthsong tell you that?"

She shook her head. "I can just tell."

"You're safe here, I promise."

She wanted to believe him, but she'd never let her guard down. Elsira may be a beloved homeland to him, but for her, it was just as foreign as Lagrimar. She lay down on the cot, pulling the thin blanket up over her. He slid off the box and onto the ground, stretching out beside her.

Jasminda sat up so fast the room spun. "You're going to sleep here?"

"I made you a promise, and I plan to keep it." He settled back, hands behind his head. The bottom of his new, freshly pressed army-issued shirt rose, revealing a thin strip of skin on his abdomen.

"You don't need to do that. You can't sleep on the ground!"

"I've been doing it for the past few weeks. Another night won't hurt anything."

"But you have a whole set of rooms here. With comfortable beds, I'm sure."

He pinned her with his gaze. "I won't let anything happen to you." His face softened. "Besides, this is better than sleeping standing up, which I've done a time or two. I wouldn't recommend it."

She lay on her side, facing him. Her finger traced a random pattern on the thin pillow, her thoughts delving into forbidden territory. His breath rose and fell slowly and could not take her eyes off the muscles of his stomach. The thin strip of hair disappearing into his pants. If he insisted on staying here, she couldn't stop him. But it would not do for him to sleep on the ground.

Perhaps . . .

"You could probably fit on the cot." She held her breath, waiting for his reaction.

Without a word, he stood and slid in next to her. There was just enough room for both of them to lay on their sides. His body warmed her back. His arm curled around her waist. She gathered her hair to one side so it would not be in his face, closed her eyes, and leaned further into his embrace.

The stress and uncertainty of the past days melted away as she settled in his arms. She'd woken up like this today. She wouldn't mind waking like this every day. Aghast at the thought, she froze, not even allowing a breath to escape.

"What's wrong?" Jack whispered into her neck.

"Nothing. Nothing's wrong." She pulled his hand tight against her stomach, both excited and afraid of her feelings. His breath on her neck was her only warning before his lips brushed the skin there. She shuddered as goose bumps prickled her flesh. He kissed her again.

"Jack," she whispered.

His only response was another kiss, closer to where her neck met her shoulder.

"I haven't ever . . . I mean, I want—"

"What do you want, Jasminda?" he said, running his lips across her skin.

She was afraid to say it out loud. While her head knew Papa's dowry was little more than wishful thinking on his part, her heart longed for a family of her own, a husband, or even a lover. Though the embers of these secret longings had grown cold during her years of solitude, they'd never fully been extinguished.

Jack nudged the fabric of her dress aside to press a kiss to her shoulder. "Tell me. I'll give you anything I can."

She burned from his kisses, each touch of his lips a forbidden desire made real. She turned to face him but kept her gaze at his chest. He wiped the tears that had started to fall and tenderly kissed each cheek.

"Some things are not for me." She forced herself to look him in the eye. Her fingers hovered over his lips until she found the strength to trace them. The full bow of his bottom lip called to her. "You aren't for me."

"So why is it that I can't stop thinking about you?"

She drew closer, transfixed by his mouth. One taste—that's all she would allow herself. One kiss just to know what it was like. Her lips met his, and a spark of electricity flooded her. The soft press and sheer strength of him made her dizzy. His heat radiated through her whole body as his fingers threaded through her hair, pulling them together. When his tongue prodded her gently, she opened, giving him entry.

She lost herself in his kiss, drawn under by the insistent waves that warmed her belly and gave rise to a host of butterflies.

When they broke apart, both breathing heavily, he captured her hand in his and pressed a kiss to her palm. Their foreheads met, and he stroked her cheek. Sliding an arm beneath her, he rolled them so he was on his back with her on top of him. He rested his hands on her lower back, and she longed to feel them everywhere, moving across her body, cooling her heated flesh.

He kissed her again, and she wiggled on top of him, wanting to burrow herself under his skin. Her thigh brushed against something rigid and she froze. Jack turned his head to the side and exhaled a breath.

"Please don't move." His voice was tightly controlled, his breathing ragged.

She stifled a giggle and rubbed her thigh against his erection again. Jack gave a mock roar, and in one movement, he swapped their positions and hovered over her on shaky arms. His eyes were intense, cloaked in desire, and she reached up to kiss him. She stroked his jaw, then slid her hand down his chest to his belly, stopping at his belt. His dark gaze was a plea. She moved downward, barely grazing his erection before he trapped her hand in his and placed it next to her head. He grabbed her other hand in a preemptive strike and shook his head. He kissed her once more, hard, before rising from the cot. She rolled to face him as he settled on the ground again.

"You can come back. I'll be good. I promise."

"I don't want to make you an oath-breaker. And I will make no such promises." His gaze stoked the fire within her, and she fell back on the thin mattress, a swirl of directionless desire.

"Tonight, we should sleep," he said. "I do not want to do something that you will regret."

"Would *you* regret it?"

He reached for her hand and drew it to his lips. "No. But it is not my virtue we are speaking of." He kept her hand in his as he stretched out on the ground.

Her virtue. She'd feared it would be intact until the day she died. That she would never meet a man who desired her. But she had felt Jack's desire, had seen it in his eyes. Could there be some kind of future that included her and Jack as lovers? The stories from the magazines were full of clandestine meetings and secret trysts. Marriage, children—those dreams of normalcy were closed to her. From the day she was born, her life had never been normal, but perhaps she could create the life she wanted, even if it was unusual. Perhaps she could create it with Jack.

"They found her."

Jack looked up from the papers on his desk. "Found who?"

His assistant, Benn, stood just outside the office, his hand gripping the edge of the doorframe. "The farm girl, the one the mob was looking for. Turns out she ran off with her beau."

Jack dropped his pen and sat back heavily in his chair, letting out a curse. "Has the magistrate identified everyone involved?"

Benn stepped into the room and closed the door. "He claims to be having a difficult time. None of the men are talking."

Jack stood abruptly, toppling his chair. "They killed ninety men. *Innocent* men. If the magistrate is unable to do his job and find those responsible, I'll find someone who can. Tell him that."

Benn nodded. "What else is troubling you?"

"Is that not enough?" Jack snorted.

His assistant eyed the mess on Jack's desk, which was usually kept in pristine neatness.

"The Council." Jack shook his head and shuffled the papers in front of him. "The Sisterhood doesn't have the resources to care for all the arriving refugees. Another group came over the mountain just this morning, twenty kilometres north of here. We will have to help with their care, but the Council is refusing to respond to my cables."

"Perhaps after the coronation—"

"Yes, I'll have to wait until then," he interrupted. "We'll need additional funds for the troop buildup here, and they're just not bloody listening." He turned to the low window that looked out over the squat buildings of the base. "A bunch of old bureaucrats sticking their heads in the sand."

"In a day's time, they'll have to listen to you." Benn came to stand by him, offering his presence as support. He was a good man, one Jack trusted, who had been with him for close to three years, traveling from base to base without complaint. He had a young family of his own back in Rosira that he probably didn't see often enough.

"In a day's time, any freedom I had will be gone." He held back a sigh. Responsibility beckoned, but every step that brought him closer to the capital took him farther from Jasminda. He would give anything to stop time and spend an eternity the way he had last night, even if it did mean sleeping on the ground. But the city would swallow him up as it had his mother, to the point where she'd had to escape to another country to find any peace. After tomorrow, he was unlikely to have even a moment to himself, much less one to spare to lie in Jasminda's arms.

What he couldn't tell her last night, what he didn't want to think about was that once they arrived in Rosira, his life would not be his own. His duties would overwhelm his entire life. He would see her settled somewhere safe, make sure she was taken care of, but anything more was only wishful thinking.

"How do you stand being so far away from them?" Jack's voice was thick as he tried to swallow his emotion.

"Ella and the baby?" A smile crept onto Benn's face. "She writes every day. Told me just yesterday she's having a phone line put in. It will cost a fortune, but it will be worth it to hear her voice more often."

Jack closed his eyes for a moment, remembering Jasminda's sleep-coarsened voice wishing him well as he'd left her that morning. He rubbed the back of his neck, a bit stiff from his night on the ground.

"What we do here keeps them safe," Benn continued. "I could have joined my father on the docks back home and seen them every day, but then I wouldn't be sure . . . I wouldn't know I was doing everything I could to protect them."

Jack inhaled deeply and let out a frustrated breath. "I don't want to go back there."

Benn looked up, chagrined. "I didn't mean—"

"No, I know. Duty calls me to Rosira, so I must go. But I want to be sure, too. I don't want to leave . . . those I care for unprotected, either."

"But you won't. You have much more power than a dockworker."

Jack leaned a hand against the glass. It was still early, the base just beginning to come to life. "Wouldn't it be simpler though if that's all I was?"

Benn's brows drew low, and he was quiet for a moment. "Duty is a hard thing," he said, "but it's the measure of a man. How you respond to its call is what the world will remember. If they remember you at all." He clapped a hand on Jack's shoulder. "*You* they will remember, my friend."

Jasminda's face stole into his vision, blocking out all else. He didn't want to be remembered in the history books; he only wanted to live in a world where he could exist inside her kisses, breathe in only air scented with her fragrance. Where position, class, duty, and race were not things that could keep people apart.

He sighed and turned back to his office.

This was not that world.

THE CALM BLUE day died with a blood red sunset that faded to black during the long journey from the eastern border of Elsira to the capital city on the western coast. It was a journey Jasminda had never imagined she'd make. For security purposes, Jack rode in an armored vehicle, which couldn't legally transport civilians. He'd woken her with a kiss before disappearing into his work, and she had only seen him briefly that morning before the caravan of trucks and buses left the base.

She had a vehicle to herself, though her driver's eyes would flick back and forth to the rearview mirror, shooting cold, suspicious glances at her. She didn't waver, meeting his gaze each time until he looked away. He was no doubt wondering why he was chauffeuring around a Lagrimari-looking Elsiran girl.

The rolling hills and dense forests of Elsira's picture-perfect countryside sped past. Only occasionally did they pass a small village; most of the population lived on the coast. As night fell, dusty, unpaved roads eventually gave way to wider, paved highways, illuminated by electric lights and full of vehicles of all shapes and sizes.

Jasminda sucked in a breath when she got her first glimpse of Rosira from the crest of a hill. The city swept up and away from the ocean like a gentle wave. Lights sparkled from thousands upon thousands of houses, which from this distance gave the impression of being stacked on top of one another, but as they drew closer, were really etched in layers going up the steep hillside.

There were no skyscrapers or especially tall buildings like in the pictures she'd seen of the megacities of Yaly and other countries. The main industry here was commerce, and docks stretched the entire length of the coastline with an assortment of vessels anchored there like great beasts asleep in their pens.

Before reaching the city limits, her truck turned onto a rough path cut into the dirt, and they drove another half kilometre or so before stopping. A miniature city lay before them, made up of orderly rows of white tents with oil lanterns strung up on poles to form the perimeter.

Jasminda's driver parked the truck and got out, but she stayed put, not wanting to be mistaken for a refugee again. There was nothing overtly frightening about the camp; it was quiet and seemed clean. Still, she felt equal parts glad she would not have to stay here and guilty for being glad.

She reached for her connection to Earthsong, then dropped it quickly, immediately overwhelmed by the dense press of so many energies. How could anyone use magic in a place so heavily populated as this? Did Lagrimar have cities, and if so, how were the residents able to cope?

Word of the refugees' arrival must have spread quickly, for soon people emerged from the tents to curiously gape at the caravan. They were almost all women, children, and elderly folk. All with dark hair and dark eyes, sturdily built with skin the hue of her own.

Jasminda loved her skin as much as she hated it. These people were beautiful, and they made her miss Papa even more. But she shrank lower in her seat, not wanting to be singled out. Though she spoke the same language, she could not relate to the bleak hopelessness coming off them in waves. Even from the children. The past two years had been lonely without her family, but she'd been surrounded by memories of them every moment. The house her father built with his own hands, her mother's quilts, her brothers' tools. And the poor goats . . . She hoped they were safe and hadn't scattered too far. She'd had a happy life before the sadness, but these people had a permanent melancholy etched into them.

The bus emptied and the new refugees were swallowed into the crowd. Jasminda spotted the gray heads of Gerda, Turwig, and Lyngar, along with other elders. Only Gerda turned towards her and gave a nod good-bye before being swept away by the others.

Soon after, the driver returned and the vehicles were back on the road, traveling a serpentine path through the city. Jack had assured her he would find lodging for her, though he hadn't mentioned where. She suspected the Sisterhood had a dormitory of some kind where she could stay. If so, perhaps she could discover more about the woman she suspected was her aunt.

The steep road through the densely packed buildings turned back on itself several times, dizzying Jasminda. After half a dozen twists and turns, the truck approached a gilded gate guarded by soldiers wearing black uniforms with gold trim and fringed epaulets. The gates swung open revealing a brightly lit, curving drive that ascended even higher.

The Royal Palace of Elsira loomed in front of them, white stones gleaming under the illumination of a shocking quantity of electric lights. The pictures in her textbooks did not do it justice. Columned porches ran along the first floor with a seemingly endless number of arched windows just beyond. Carved into the stone above each window were images of the Founders, the magical Lord and Lady in various poses showing how they'd transformed Elsira.

Somewhere within this building lay the sleeping body of their descendent, the Queen herself, protected by the Prince Regent who was to rule in Her stead until She awoke and returned to power. Seeing it in person, Jasminda was transfixed. Though there was no longer any magic in Elsira, the palace seemed to give off its own energy and spoke to her in an unfamiliar way.

Once again, the driver exited the vehicle and Jasminda remained, hoping that whatever business Jack had here would be quick. The trip had been exhausting, and she wanted nothing more than to fall into whatever bed she was assigned. The door she leaned against jerked open and there stood Jack, holding out his hand.

She stared at it uncomprehendingly. "Can I not wait here for you?"

"You would prefer to sleep in the truck?" The corner of his mouth quirked, shattering his grim expression.

She looked from him to the palace and back again. A knowing smile crept up Jack's face.

"When you said you'd find lodging for me, I didn't think . . . Jack, I can't sleep in the *palace*."

"Whyever not?" He crossed his arms and leaned against the truck.

"Because I'm a goat farmer. Palaces are for royalty. The Prince Regent cannot possibly allow someone like me here."

"Trust me, it's all right. Many officials and dignitaries live in the palace. A whole wing is devoted to ranking officers and their families. Honestly, it's more like an inn than a proper palace these days."

"But—"

"I'm well acquainted with whom the Prince Regent allows under his roof." A flicker of pain crossed his face, and he took a deep breath. "Jasminda —"

"Commander!" an insistent voice bellowed from across the driveway.

"One moment, General," Jack responded while his eyes pleaded with her. She accepted his offered palm, gripping it as she stepped from the vehicle and approached the palace.

A battalion of servants greeted them inside the entry. Jack announced her as an honored guest and conferred with a matronly woman who must have been in charge of things. Two maids whisked her away before she could even thank Jack or say good night, let alone find out what he had wanted to tell her. Hopefully it was whatever he'd said she needed to know about him. Her heart burned to know his secrets, even as part of her was glad she didn't.

She barely registered the dazzling hallways of the palace, the opulent room she was led to, the plush carpeting, detailed tapestries, or hand-carved furniture. She saw only the bed, canopied and enormous, and then the backs of her eyelids as she sank into the extravagant mattress.

———

A KNOCK AT the door brought Jasminda fully awake. She garbled a greeting and a tiny maid, not yet out of her teens, appeared with reams of fabric in her arms.

"Have a nice rest, miss?" the girl said in a crisp city accent. Jasminda tried to prop herself on her elbows but gave up after a few moments and collapsed back down.

"I've never slept better," she said, mostly to the pillow.

The girl chuckled, then flitted around the room, opening the curtains. Late-afternoon sunshine filtered in.

"It's time to bathe and change, miss. The Prince Regent has requested you for dinner."

She startled into wakefulness. Was she to be the main course? Neither the servants last night nor this girl reacted to her Lagrimari appearance, but Jasminda remained on her guard. Why could the prince want to dine with her? Jack must have set it up, though after enduring the suspicious glares of the soldiers, she could not imagine the prince would be more welcoming to her than they had been. However, it stood to reason that Jack would be in attendance, as well; he was the reason she was staying there, after all. Her excitement at being near him again grew as she followed the maid into the gold-trimmed bathroom.

Marble floors and walls greeted her. She gaped at the ivory-handled sinks with hot water flowing from the taps and marveled at the modern efficiency of a water closet with a seat that warmed her bottom. Papa had devised a plan for plumbing in the cabin, using some spell she suspected, but water still needed to be heated on the stove.

The bathtub, however, proved to be a stumbling block. The little maid was adamant about bathing her. Jasminda protested that she could very well bathe herself—she wasn't a child—but finally gave in to the girl's steely determination.

At least a bucketful of dirt disappeared down the drain. Her hair was washed and doused with a sweet-smelling concoction. Nadal—for if another woman was to see her naked, Jasminda should at least know her name—

carefully combed Jasminda's thick, tightly coiled locks free of snags in front of the fire, drying it as much as possible. Then she helped her into a complicated dress she wasn't sure she'd be able to get out of again. At a gentle tap on the shoulder, Jasminda turned to face the full-length mirror in the dressing room.

She gasped at the vision in front of her. Shiny, golden fabric flowed around her body, hugging her curves and making her appear, for the first time, like she was worthy of staying in the palace. Her hair was even tamed into a cascade of thick waves.

"You are a miracle worker," she praised Nadal, who blushed.

Nadal searched the pocket of her apron and pulled out a tiny oval mirror on a gold chain. "Where would you like it, miss?"

Jasminda gaped. "Who is it for?" Mourning mirrors like the one Nadal held were worn after the death of a loved one. It was said those in the World After could peer through the mirrors and say their final good-byes to the living. After her mother died, she'd worn one around her neck for a year. When her father and brothers died, she hadn't had the heart.

"You haven't heard?" Nadal's hushed voice filled with wonder. "I'd thought since you arrived with . . . Miss, the Prince Regent has gone to the World After."

Jasminda took the mirror from the girl, gripping it lightly, and shook her head. "When did this happen? And how could he have invited me for dinner?"

"They made the announcement this morning, but he could have been dead for days. They never proclaim the death of a royal until his heir has been sworn in. Fear of attack during the changeover or some such. I heard from a girl who works in the prince's wing that she'd seen His Grace last week, Seconday. But she's just a duster, and she didn't see him that often." The torrent of words seemed to take something out of the girl, and she dropped her chin, staring at the floor as if embarrassed to have spoken at all.

"So the new prince invited me?" Cold dread made her skin go clammy. The air in the room suddenly grew thin, as if Jasminda stood at the peak of a mountain. Jack had wanted to tell her something that night at the base, and again before they'd entered the palace...

She shook her head, unwilling to believe such a thing. He was a warrior, and perhaps a poet. He was almost certainly not a . . . She couldn't even attach the word to him. An image of his face slightly twisted in one of his grim smiles filled her vision. He would have told her something so monumental.

"Is this dinner special in some way? Is it in honor of the prince?"

Nadal shook her head. "It is just dinner. The changeover is seamless. Outside, the people will mourn and most here will wear the mirrors for a week or so, but the business of the palace never stops, not even for death."

Jasminda sucked in a breath and fastened the gold chain around her neck. It fit snugly at the base of her throat. Not quite tight enough to choke her.

"It's time, miss," Nadal said.

Jasminda steeled her nerves and ignored the questions battling for dominance in her mind. They exited the rooms, and Nadal led her to the top of a grand staircase where a black-clad butler ushered her down and through a maze of hallways to a grand dining room. The grandeur of the palace was a blur, the empty feeling in her bones stealing most of her attention.

"Jasminda ul-Sarifor." A hush descended over the vast room as her name was announced by a silver-haired attendant. Every head swiveled in her direction, and she froze under the weight of expectation in the air. The sense of foreboding remained, but she tilted her chin a few notches higher and stepped farther into the hall. Yet another butler appeared at her elbow, a kindly faced man who, despite his Elsiran appearance, reminded her of Papa.

"Miss Jasminda, this way, please," he said, and led her deeper into the dining room. She followed his straight back, walking carefully in her delicate gold slippers. A four-piece string ensemble sat in the corner playing muted orchestral music. Three enormous U-shaped tables took up the majority of the room, with seating around the sides and a wide space for the servants to come and go in the middle. The end of the center table faced a slightly raised dais on which stood a smaller table. She surmised that must be where the Prince Regent sat. The space was magnificent—more carvings of the Lord and Lady adorned the tops of each window and the ceiling was a grid of carved stone. Around each table sat several dozen people, all watching her.

Conversations restarted, but their stares drilled into her as the butler led her to a setting only two metres away from the dais.

She was seated next to a posh woman in an elaborate, feathered hat, her snakelike figure poured into a silken black sheath dress. Directly across from Jasminda, an old man with a hearing cone pressed to one ear and thick spectacles leaned toward the man to his right, complaining loudly of the noise. Each wore a mourning mirror. The most ostentatious display was from an older gentleman farther down the table whose mirror was affixed to his eye patch.

Jasminda fought the urge to squirm as the gazes of so many in the room raked over her, not bothering to hide their inquisitiveness. Her glass was filled by a passing waiter, and she grabbed at it, gulping greedily to soothe the sudden ache in her throat. The hall quieted again, and Jasminda turned to see what had captured everyone's attention this time.

A hidden door built into the wall behind the dais had opened. A group of guards in the fancy black uniforms emerged, then flanked the door. Chairs groaned across the floor as everyone at the tables stood, almost as one. Jasminda raced to catch up.

The same man who announced her stepped forward and cleared his throat. "Jaqros Edvard Alliaseen, High Commander of the Royal Army, First Duke of Cavill, and Prince Regent of Elsira."

The servant slid away, and Jasminda's heart dissolved into a pool of liquid at her feet. Directly in front of her, in full regalia, stood Jack.

CHAPTER FIVE

SHE HAD THOUGHT him beautiful in dirty fatigues and covered in bruises and blood, but in his royal uniform and freshly trimmed hair, he was nothing short of divine. The spark of hope she'd held inside, the one she'd foolishly allowed to grow into a tiny flame, flickered then snuffed itself out completely.

Jack—*Prince* Jack—sat stiffly at the raised table mere steps away from her. His face was a rigid mask. He looked straight ahead, acknowledging no one.

The head butler was speaking again, making announcements about the dinner, the soup, the ingredients, but Jasminda's attention was wholly focused on the man in front of her.

Gone was the ragged creature she'd discovered on the mountain and thought mad, the bruised and bloodied soldier who had sacrificed himself to try to protect a woman he didn't know. A woman who could have been his enemy. When did he become this statue sitting before her, neither warrior nor poet, but prince?

The coronation must have happened as soon as he'd arrived in the palace, but even more than the shock at his new position, she couldn't believe how his whole nature seemed to have transformed. The light in his eyes that had withstood capture, gunshot, and beatings was now dimmed.

The kindly butler approached and cleared his throat politely, placing his hands on her chair. She pulled her attention away from Jack to find that she was the only one still standing. As every eye in the room, except Jack's, bored into her, she took her seat as gracefully as possible, smoothing her dress and thanking the butler in a trembling voice as he slid in her chair.

Her hands shook. She flattened them on the table, imprinting the grooves of the wood onto her palm. Anger flared hot for a moment, then melted just as suddenly into despair. Neither emotion would help her. She was lost in an unforgiving sea. There was no way to escape the glares from around the room, and the one person who had given her comfort during these past days of upheaval was now a stranger to her.

Tears threatened, and she used every trick she could to hold them back, resorting to digging her nails into the inside of her elbow until she could focus on the external pain a little more than the internal.

The first course began, and chatter resumed around the room. The soup set before her was completely foreign. The stunning silverware of her place setting offered four spoons. Jasminda took a deep breath and clasped her hands together, darting glances around the table. The woman next to her had already chosen a spoon, and Jasminda couldn't see from her position which one it had been.

She didn't want to make a misstep. Jack had invited her here, whatever his reasons were, whoever he was now, and she was determined to get through this meal with as much dignity as she could muster. She buried her shock and dismay, replacing it with determination. If she was the only *grol* these snooty city folk ever encountered, she wasn't going to give them any more fuel for their fire of scorn.

Jack filled her peripheral vision, but she refused to look at him again. He cleared his throat, then did so again a few moments later. A waiter hurried to tend to his water glass, but he brushed the man aside. The third time he cleared his throat she snapped her head toward him, narrowing her eyes and clenching her jaw against the swarm of emotion rising inside her.

He slowly drew his hand down and selected the second spoon from the left, all the time staring down at his bowl. At her place setting, she chose the same spoon. The woman next to her tilted her bowl toward her body, then shoveled the spoon in the opposite direction before bringing it to her mouth.

Jasminda glanced back at Jack as he slowly, slowly ate his soup in the same way. She copied his movements, happy to get something in her stomach. She had slept all day and hadn't eaten anything since the day before. Dinner went on like this, course after course. She would be presented with some new obstacle—bread, salad, three entrées—and Jack would model the behavior for her.

The Prince Regent—she vowed to stop being so familiar with him, even in her head—did not speak to anyone during dinner, and this appeared to be taken as normal by those present. It made her feel better that she would not have to talk to him. Just hearing his voice would make it that much harder to mend the gaping hole inside her.

Blessedly, after what felt like hours, dinner finally ended. The last dessert dishes were cleared away by the staff, and the various characters at the table patted their bellies obnoxiously. Jasminda had never eaten so much food at one time in her life. Guiltily, she thought of the refugees. What rations had they been provided? Her meal sank like lead in her stomach.

The company rose from the table and, just when she thought there would be a reprieve from the unrelenting pressure of the evening, the butlers ushered everyone into a huge adjoining sitting room. Small groups split off and clustered around settees or card tables, chatting amiably. Jack was nowhere to be seen. Jasminda stood alone next to the massive fireplace, enduring the uncomfortable heat.

Glances sent her way ranged from mere curiosity to outright contempt. Her back remained straight and head high, but inside, she was wilting.

A girl about her age approached the other end of the fireplace, setting a glass on the mantle. She stood for a moment peering at the flames before approaching Jasminda. Slender and beautiful, she wore a peach-and-gold dress that made her skin appear to glow. Amber eyes the color of her hair appraised Jasminda, not unkindly.

"These things are positively awful."

Jasminda stared at her, unsure of the girl's intentions.

"I'm Lizvette." She held out her hands.

"Jasminda," she responded, placing her palms to Lizvette's and pressing gently.

"Welcome. I'm told you're responsible for saving the life of our new prince." Lizvette's friendly smile seemed genuine, but Jasminda did not dare attempt a connection to Earthsong to determine her true intentions. She scanned the room to find they had attracted a great deal of attention.

"I did save him once, or perhaps twice. But I cannot take credit for the last time."

"Our Jack, always getting into trouble." Lizvette smiled sadly.

"You are . . . friends with the Prince Regent?"

Her smile changed, though Jasminda could not determine precisely what was different about it. It was bleaker, perhaps. "I was betrothed to his brother."

"May he find serenity in the World After," Jasminda responded, bowing her head. Lizvette repeated the blessing. Jasminda considered the girl's dress more closely. What she'd initially thought was shiny gold beading were actually dozens of mirrors embroidered into the material. A conspicuous show of grief that seemed at odds with Lizvette's unassuming manner.

There were not enough mirrors in the world to adequately represent everything Jasminda mourned. So many lives gone, so many could-have-beens. She'd thought she'd gained something after all of that loss—a chance at a kind of happiness she hadn't imagined possible. Now that was gone, too.

An exceptionally tall young man stalked toward them, his face contorted in indignation. She could read his intention quite clearly without Earthsong and took a step backward. Lizvette followed Jasminda's gaze and turned to face him. He took hold of Lizvette's elbow and leaned down to whisper loudly in her ear.

"What do you think you're doing?"

"I'm greeting our visitor, Zavros. She is the Prince Regent's guest. Jasminda, this is my cousin—"

"It's time to go, Lizvette. You're keeping your father waiting."

She smiled apologetically at Jasminda. "It was lovely meeting you. I'm sure we'll be seeing each other again soon. May She bless your dreams."

Jasminda repeated the farewell and stood rigidly as Lizvette was towed away to a card table in the back. The blazing fire had grown unbearable, and the perimeter around her was a quarantine zone. What a surprise not to be the belle of the ball. With a final glance about the room, in which she refused to admit she was searching for Jack, she slipped out the door.

Thick silence draped the empty hallway; each direction stretched on identically. She had absolutely no idea how to get back to her rooms. With no orientation or memory of the route she'd taken to get to the dining room, she took a few tentative steps to the left before a voice halted her progress.

"Leaving?"

She turned to find Jack standing behind her, regal and gorgeous. He was so close, but now untouchable. She hardened her features, not looking directly at him, not wanting to give away the storm of emotions fighting for dominance within her. Her fists clenched and opened as her body stiffened with tension. Traitorous tears welled; she blinked them back.

"I'm not sure if I should bow or curtsy or what," she said, gripping her hands in front of her to stop their movement.

"I am sorry I didn't tell you," he said, voice pitched low. "I wanted to. I should have. It's inexcusable, I just . . ."

She longed to hear an excuse that would satisfy her and return things to the way they were. No words came. He shook his head and rubbed at his chest, just below his collarbone where his bullet wound had been.

"Jasminda." He stepped closer, and she took a step back.

"That wound was healed. Does it still bother you?"

He dropped his hand to his side and drew even closer, backing her against the wall. She stared at the carpet, but he tilted her face up with a finger on her chin. Wanting to numb herself to the feeling of his skin on hers, she refused to meet his eyes and focused instead on his chest, covered in rich-looking fabric with brightly colored insignias on his uniform. He released her chin, but she stubbornly continued avoiding his face.

"Jasminda," he repeated. Her name on his lips was more than she could bear. "If I could change who I am, I'd do it in a heartbeat. You deserved the truth. I owed you that much."

"You can have no debt to me. I helped a captive soldier, not a prince." As much as she tried to avoid it, she was drawn to him. Perhaps this was the last time she'd be this close to him. The tears escaped; she could not stop them. "Now if you'll excuse me, Your Grace, I have urgent business in my room that needs attending to. Pleasant evening."

She slid out of the cage of his body and gave a wobbly curtsy before picking up her beautiful skirt and running. When one hallway ended, she picked another at random. She had no idea where she was going, but she'd rather be lost in the palace for a thousand years than see Prince Jack again.

Blinded by her tears, she finally stopped in a blue hallway full of mirrors. She leaned against a little table but refused to look at her face, ashamed of her reaction to him. He could no longer be Jack. He could no longer be her hope. He could be nothing to her at all.

"ONE OF THE maids escorted her to her chambers," Usher said, entering the dimly lit space. Jack paused mid-step from where he'd been pacing the floor of his sitting room, only half listening to the evening news.

"Thank you, Usher. Make sure she has a servant assigned to her at all times so she doesn't become lost again."

The old man nodded.

"But don't let her know that I ordered it. I don't think she would like that."

To his credit, Usher didn't even raise an eyebrow. The valet had been with Jack's family since before he was born. The old man's kindly face was a warmer, more familiar sight than his own father's had been. Jack switched off the radiophonic, silencing the newsreader mid-sentence, then fell into an armchair in front of the fireplace. He could not begrudge Jasminda her anger and pain. It had been inexcusable for him to keep the truth from her.

But each chance he'd had to tell her—that night at the base, or the morning before they'd left for Rosira when he could have found a quiet place to explain—he'd avoided it. Reality was coming faster than he had wanted, and he'd been certain he could outpace it.

But one of the reasons he'd always hated the palace was that his time was not his own here. Even more so now that he was the bloody Prince Regent. His return had been chaotic, with the secret coronation last night and then a flurry of briefings. The bulk of the armed forces had been ordered to the eastern border in preparation for the breach, which could come any day. And a troop buildup such as this required the Council to approve the additional funds, but they had refused to meet until tomorrow.

Aside from the pending disaster with Lagrimar, he'd had calls with the leaders of their allies, Fremia and Yaly, letters to read and sign, introductions to staff and security personnel to make. He'd hardly looked up when he was being called for dinner, and then it was too late.

He'd been a fool, and worse, a cowardly one. His desire to put off any change to the way she saw him had won out over his good sense, and Jasminda had suffered. The weight of the crown threatened to press him down into the earth.

He'd never wanted to be the prince as a child, never envied his brother for being born a decade earlier. He hadn't even wanted the title he'd been born to, High Commander of the Royal Army, but he'd had little choice and been shipped away at eight years old to begin his training. Eventually, he grew used to military life, but the world of the palace remained as foreign as ever. All the politics and backstabbing, coddling and smiling were just not a part of who he was. He hadn't wanted to admit to Jasminda what he didn't like to think of himself: he would now be chained to position and ceremony for the rest of his life.

But her expression as she'd stood in the dining hall, the devastation marring her beautiful face, made him feel like a villain. It gutted him. The guilt and shame weighed more than the crown.

Somehow, he could not keep the women in his life from hating him.

"Has word been sent to my mother?"

"Yes, sir. But it may be some time before she receives the message."

The last he'd heard, his mother was cloistered in a jungle sanctuary, hours from the nearest Fremian city. "She finally has her wish—her son is the Prince Regent. Too late to do her any good."

The little he'd heard of the news report earlier had confirmed his fears that his coronation was being met with more than a few misgivings. His mother's defection to Fremia, Elsira's southern neighbor, twelve years earlier had cast a long shadow, especially on her only son.

"I only hope she's found peace," Usher said.

Jack hoped so, as well. He stared at the crackling fire until the flames burned themselves into his vision. His fingers picked at the fringe on his jacket, unraveling one of the threads, and he tapped an impatient rhythm on his knee.

"Say what you must," he said, after the silence had grown more oppressive than companionable.

Usher's bushy gray eyebrows rose. "What makes you think I have something to say?"

"Twenty-two years of knowing you, old man. And I suspect I won't like whatever it is, so spit it out."

"I believe I said everything I had to say before you left on your foolhardy mission."

Jack raked a hand through his hair. "Protecting Elsira is my only mission, and I would do anything, even sacrifice myself, to see that happen. The opportunity was once in a lifetime, too great to miss."

"The opportunity for the army's High Commander to go undercover in enemy territory? It is unheard of."

"I was the only one for it. The only Elsiran to speak their blasted language well enough to blend in with them. If I hadn't gone and verified what they were planning, we would have had no chance. At least now we're ready for the fight."

"You paid a heavy cost for that information, young sir."

Jack absently rubbed the place on his chest where the bullet had pierced his flesh. The pain had been gone for days but now there was a phantom ache. He must have been imagining it. "I don't regret accepting the mission."

"And being captured?" Usher's voice was soft, without a hint of censure, but a pinprick of guilt stabbed at Jack.

The fire crackled and jumped, flames leaping upward. The vibrancy of the fire reminded him of her, on the porch with her shotgun, of the blade she kept strapped to her leg. Fearsome beauty. The pain in his chest shifted and grew. It lay mere inches from his heart.

"Being captured nearly killed me. But it also brought me a wonderful gift."

He slumped down in his chair. When had he come to care so much for her? She had been a bright light at the end of a tunnel of pain and desperation, but what Jack felt was not merely due to the debt he owed her for saving him, not just for her kindness toward him. She was strong, with a sharp mind, passionate, and brave. So unlike the giggling, gossiping society girls who had vied for his affection for so many years. Jasminda slit a man's throat and kept her wits about her, for Sovereign's sake; she had a warrior's heart.

Usher steepled his fingers below his chin. "This gift you speak of, is it the kind worth keeping?"

Jack looked up sharply.

"Is it the kind that you would regret allowing to slip through your fingers?" the old man said.

"She is angry and hurt. I was, if not dishonest, at least not forthcoming. She has every right—"

"You do not balk at walking across enemy lines and pretending to be one of them, at great peril, I might add, yet you quiver with fear at one young woman."

"I'm not quivering in fear," Jack scoffed.

"I believe I see a quiver, young sir. Just there." Usher extended his finger, waggling it about, pointing at most of Jack's body.

A smile edged its way across Jack's face. "The Queen Who Sleeps must have a sense of humor to send you to look after me."

"That She must," Usher said.

Jack regarded the fire for another moment before jumping from his seat, what he must do now suddenly clear. "And I thank Her every day for that," he said, kissing Usher on the forehead.

He raced out of the room and down the corridor, flying up the stairs to the great alarm of several passing servants. Jasminda's rooms in the guest wing were on the other side of the palace. He wished she were closer, though visiting her rooms, wherever they were and especially at this hour, was unseemly and could put her reputation in jeopardy. Based on the chilly reception she'd received from the gathered aristocracy at dinner, however, her current reputation was no great asset.

Jack had been caught in the dining hall after dinner by Minister Stevenot, who had profusely dispatched his condolences. Over his shoulder, through the cracked door to the adjoining parlor, he'd watched, heartsick, as Jasminda stood alone, an island in an unfriendly sea. He'd been on his way to her when Lizvette approached Jasminda, and her kindness filled him with gratitude.

As if conjured by his thoughts, Lizvette now appeared on the staircase above him in the grand hall.

"Your Grace," she said, curtseying, an amused smile playing upon her lips.

He climbed up to the landing beside her. "You know, you must try to keep a straight face when you say that."

She nodded, her eyes alight. "I shall keep that in mind." Her expression sobered, and she laid a hand on his arm. "I haven't gotten a chance to tell you how sorry I am for the loss of your brother."

"No, I'm sorry I haven't been to see you. And for your loss. Not only a husband gone, but you were to be the princess."

Her lips pressed to a thin line. "Yes, well, Mother and Father are inconsolable." Her voice was light, but shadows danced in her eyes.

He and Lizvette had raced around the palace as children, under the disapproving eyes of their parents. Her father was a close friend and advisor to his, and still retained a place on the Council. She and his brother had been engaged for two years and were to be married in just a few weeks.

"And you?" Jack asked, craning his neck down to look her in the eye.

"It happened so fast." She dipped her head and ran her fingers across the mirrors embedded in her gown, avoiding his gaze. "Alariq did love his gadgets, though. He would probably have lived in that airship if he could have." She managed a weak smile. "I can't imagine what was going through his mind, piloting through that kind of storm."

"Nor I. He was always so reasonable. I just hope I'm up to the task of filling his shoes."

"You are. Of course you are. You will be a wonderful prince." She finally met his eyes, beaming up at him, though her smile overflowed with sadness. She took hold of his hand and squeezed. He hoped she was holding up well, despite appearing so tired. Dark circles under her eyes were starting to show through her makeup.

"I don't want to keep you," he said, pulling away. She held on a moment longer before releasing him.

"Whatever are you doing on this end of the palace?"

He shifted on his feet, his gaze involuntarily drawn toward the hall leading to Jasminda's room.

Lizvette looked, then frowned slightly. She sighed. "Are you . . . *with* her?"

"I owe her an apology. One that is overdue."

Lizvette took a step back. "The whole palace is talking. They're watching her. Wondering."

"I don't have time for Rosiran busybodies." Indignation shaded his voice.

"Jack, she will be trouble for you."

His protective instincts kicked in. Jasminda was not anyone else's concern. She belonged here, had more right than most who called the palace home.

The worry in Lizvette's face cut through his rising ire. His anger was not for her. "May She bless your dreams, Vette."

"And yours as well, Your Grace."

He walked away, his skin prickling with the sensation of being watched until he turned the corner.

HE STOOD OUTSIDE Jasminda's door, gathering his courage before knocking rapidly. His breathing grew shallow as the seconds ticked by. Would she not answer? When the door finally opened, he schooled his features, attempting to hide his wonder. She was radiant in the outfit she'd worn at dinner. The gorgeous golden dress highlighted the color of her skin and made him want to feel its softness. Her hair was tamed somewhat, but still wild, gorgeous and free, like her. But her eyes were red-rimmed from crying.

That phantom ache above his heart flared again. He rubbed at it unconsciously. She studied his movement, worry creasing her forehead. He swallowed the lump in his throat and bowed low, causing her to take a step back.

"Excuse me, my lady, but you inquired as to the completeness of my healing. I . . . I fear I may have reinjured myself and wondered if you would be so kind as to inspect it for me."

She tilted her head up at him, her brow furrowed. He was afraid she would shut the door in his face at so flimsy an excuse. Instead, she took another step back, allowing him entry. She turned on her heel and headed to the fireplace where a chair had been dragged over quite close to the flames.

"Are the palace physicians not up to the task, Your Grace?" She motioned to the chair, and he sank into it.

"They are the best in the land."

"I cannot sing here. There are too many people. But I can take a look." The bag she'd brought from home lay on the floor, and she crouched, retrieving her jar of balm. She approached him, her focus solely on the spot beneath his clothes where the wound had been. When her eyes finally met his, something passed between them, but she firmed her mouth into a frown. "That will have to come off," she said, motioning to his covered chest.

He unbuttoned his coat and laid it aside, then undid his dress shirt and slid out of it. Her focus never left his chest the entire time. When he'd disrobed enough, she knelt down in front of him, one hand resting on his thigh, the other gently prodding the newly healed skin.

"What makes you think you've reinjured yourself?" she said, voice full of accusation. "Your Grace," she added, yanking her fingers away.

"Because it hurts. Just here." He retrieved her hand, holding it in place against his heart. "And don't call me that. I'm still Jack."

Her lips trembled, and the pools of her eyes swam with tears. "No, you're not just Jack anymore. You never were."

She again tried to draw her hand away, but he held on tight, grasping the other, as well, and bringing them up to meet. He stroked her silken skin and lifted her joined hands to his lips, kissing each softly then placing a palm on each side of his face.

"I'm sorry, Jasminda." He squeezed his eyes shut, unable to take the pain evident on her face.

"What are you sorry for?"

"For not telling you. For being unable to be just Jack for you. Trust me, I never wanted any of this."

"Why not?"

"My elder brother was groomed to rule. I was never as smart or accomplished as he. Never as good at all of this." He waved around the lavish room. "Most of my childhood was spent in barracks, training for the army. I don't believe I'll ever feel like a prince, not on the inside. I should have told you . . . I just couldn't bear to."

Her thumbs skimmed his cheeks, and she slid out of his grasp to brush his forehead, his chin. A finger grazed his lips causing him to shudder.

She kept hold of his face but rose from the ground and sat on his knee, leaning her forehead to meet his. He wrapped his arms around her waist and held her tight, never wanting to let go.

"I don't know what to do with you," she whispered, stroking his face, her lips a hairsbreadth from his own. "I cannot keep you, but I cannot turn you away."

Jack nudged her head up and drank her in. When her gaze dropped to his lips, he leaned forward, capturing her mouth with his. They kissed tentatively at first. He allowed her to explore, touching her lips softly to his, then with more pressure. Eventually, she tilted her head and opened for him. He caressed her tongue, his control nearly slipping when she groaned into his mouth.

She gripped the back of his head tighter, her mouth hungrily attacking his. Her taste was so sweet, the scent of her slowly driving him crazy. He pulled away, but she leaned in, not letting him go.

"Last night I— Perhaps we should slow down," he said, shifting her in his lap, moving her away from his rapidly growing erection. His desire for her was intense, but she would likely need time to trust him. He couldn't push. It was enough that she was in his arms again.

Her chest heaved, thrusting her breasts up seductively as she sat atop him, eyes still closed, kiss-swollen lips slightly apart. "Slow down?"

"Yes, darling. I may be a prince, but I'm only human." That night at the base he'd lain awake, convinced every nerve ending in his body was connected to the place where their hands had touched. Now, she was so much closer and he was having an even harder time holding himself back. "I don't want you to feel pressured."

She dragged her hands through his hair, igniting sparks of pleasure that rolled down his spine.

"I want you to be certain . . ." He sucked in a breath as she ran her fingers down his chest, then up again. She ducked her head and kissed his collarbone. He did not trust himself for much longer.

"Jasminda," he groaned.

She shifted her knee ever so slightly, rubbing against his straining cock.

"Yes?" she smiled wickedly, her mouth edging closer to his nipple.

"You're killing me."

"Then let it be a warm death," she said, hiking up her skirt so that she could fully straddle him.

SITTING ON HIS lap, she delighted in his unmistakable desire for her as it settled between her legs. A blast of pleasure assaulted her as she brushed against his hardness. She should be appalled at her forwardness. The rich, city girls he was used to were probably far more demure. Even prettied up in a fine gown after a fancy bath, Jasminda would never be like them. But he had come to her. He wanted her. It was not possible, and yet here he was.

Jack's skin burned hot beneath her hands. The contrast of hard and soft made her fingers long to stroke him everywhere.

He stilled her hands. "Jasminda, are you certain?" The heat in his eyes was tempered with concern.

She nodded. "I would like to have this with you." Unspoken was the reality that this could well be her only chance. He could be her lover. Perhaps not the way she'd imagined, perhaps not even for more than this one night, but if that was all she had, then she would take it. Leave the teasing flirtations to the girls bred for such. Jasminda far preferred the women in the magazines, unashamed of their bodies and the pleasures they could wring from them. She would take this night with this man, this prince, and hold it close in her memory forever.

"You have done this before, I would imagine." She laughed at his sheepish expression. "Handsome soldiers are not the lonely sort." She pressed a kiss to his forehead, nose, and lips, then brought his hand to her breast and trapped it under hers. "You can show me."

"But I've . . . I don't want you to think . . ." He shook his head. "It was different before."

She sat back, dropping his hand, her skin rapidly cooling. "Am I so different?"

"You are. In every way."

Her mind raced as doubts swarmed. She drew away and moved to stand, but he wrapped his arms around her.

"Jasminda, don't mistake me. You are like nothing I ever thought possible. You are like no one else I have ever met. And I am glad of it. You are remarkable."

She did not want to feel the joy his words inspired, the resurgence of hope within her. Nothing had changed. He was still a prince and she a farm girl with the wrong skin color. Tonight was just a night. But as his arms tightened, pressing her against him, her heart threatened to revolt.

He kissed the shell of her ear, her jaw, her chin. "I will show you, if you will show me."

"Show you what?" she whispered as his tongue tickled her neck.

"Your secrets."

"I haven't any secrets."

He focused on her other ear, tugging on her lobe with his teeth. She shivered, the tiny motion sending a spark all the way to her toes.

"Your body begs to differ." He stood, lifting her easily. After she settled on her feet, he leaned in for another endless kiss. Molten longing pooled between her legs.

"There is sylfimweed in the kitchens, I trust?" she asked.

"I should think so with the number soldiers I reprimand for being found sneaking out of storerooms with maids." He placed a hand on her belly. The thought of having his child was not something she could entertain in the moment. Yet another fanciful idea to quell. She would go to the kitchens in the morning to obtain the herb.

Jack frowned as he pressed against her stomach. Thinking of half-breed bastards, no doubt. Before she could reassure him that she had no such designs, he kneeled and placed a kiss over her navel through her dress. She froze. He reached down to the hem of her dress, then slid his hands underneath to caress her ankles and legs. Her breath hitched. She needed the damnable dress off. Now.

Fumbling with the strap wrapped around her bosom, she found the end and gave it a strong tug, causing most of it to unravel. Jack watched with rapt attention as the dress loosened and eventually gave way, leaving her top half bare and only a thin silken slip covering her bottom half.

Hot with undiluted desire, his eyes traveled up her body to meet hers. Never breaking their locked stare, she walked backward to the four-poster bed overtaking the room and sat facing Jack. He still kneeled by the fireplace, staring at her. What would it take to snap him out of it? Inspiration struck, and she ran a hand over her breast, mimicking one of the women from the magazine. Jack's soft gaze snapped to attention, and he stalked over to the bed.

She crawled back until she hit the pillows, then lay down, her legs barely spread apart. Jack prowled in her direction like a cat ready to pounce. He grasped one leg, tugging it to the side, mirrored the movement with the other leg, and then crawled between them.

A shiver rippled through her as he caressed her legs, hands sliding under her slip, running up her thighs, pulling the material up to her waist.

"No knife?" He sounded disappointed.

"It didn't match the dress."

The silky scrap of underwear Nadal had provided for her was all the protection she had from his thumbs as they ran up and down her opening. He kissed her once there, through the fabric, before moving his tongue up her stomach to circle her navel. The anticipation of feeling him inside her swelled.

He worshipped her body with his tongue, pressing kisses every place he could reach. Hands on the curves of her bottom, he spread her legs wider, settling his weight between them. When he finally reached her breasts, Jasminda feared she was in danger of passing out from all the sensations. Kneading a breast while his tongue went to work on the nipple, circling and sucking on it, he then moved to the rounded flesh to kiss and caress. His other hand rubbed her through her panties, creating a wet spot where her juices overflowed.

Jasminda arched up, wanting more but at the same time longing to touch him, too. She freed her arms from her sides and slid her hands down his back, digging her nails into his flesh when he did something particularly delightful with his tongue or fingers.

The panties had to come off. Jack's head popped up, focused on the material sliding down her legs before she kicked them away. She reached for the front of his trousers but stopped, perplexed at how to undo them.

He grinned and showed her the buckles and buttons, easing them off along with his drawers. Kneeling above her, completely naked, he cradled his thick penis in his hand. She sat up, enthralled with the sight of him. She reached out for it, stroking his length. His eyes closed on a hissed breath. Jasminda loved learning him, changing the pressure and monitoring his reaction as she squeezed and caressed.

With a low rumble in his throat, he pulled away and came to rest on top of her, bringing his face close to hers. He was settled at her entrance but made no move to go further. Just cupped her face and kissed her silly once again. She wrapped her legs around him, urging him to keep going, go all the way. She just wanted more of him, all of him inside her the way she'd dreamed.

He eased a hand between their bodies and stroked her, sliding silkily through her wetness. He continued, probing deeper, and she tried to widen her legs even more. Finally, one finger worked its way inside her. She bucked and wriggled beneath him, wanting more, and he chuckled softly before inserting another finger and working them in and out of her, sliding deliciously.

She moaned when his thumb circled her most sensitive area. He kissed and caressed her, creating an amazing buildup of longing and desire. She teetered on the precipice, overwhelmed by what was coming when he pulled out his hand.

Gasping at the loss, she looked up at him, wide-eyed. He positioned himself once again at her entrance, his expression seeking approval.

"Jack," she cried. "Please."

With the permission granted, he eased himself into her. A sharp, stinging sensation accompanied the feeling of being stretched wide. She strained as he pushed further inside her and focused on his face inches from her own. The discomfort was expected, and tempered in large part by her excitement.

Their pelvises met, and she curled her legs tight around his waist.

"Are you all right?" he whispered.

She kissed him in response. "What happens now?"

"Now I start moving, but I want to be sure not to hurt you."

She wriggled against him, delighted by the fullness of his invasion of her body. Jack grimaced, the tension of not moving evident in the veins bulging in his forehead and neck.

"You're not hurting me," she said and kissed him again. He slid out of her a bit then plunged back in, then did it again with a gentle movement, a rocking in and out of her, creating a sweet friction between them. She raised her hips to meet his strokes, and when their pelvises met again, the impact roused the little nub at the top of her mound. Jasminda gasped.

Jack voiced unintelligible, impassioned sounds, as well, his arms straining as he kept the majority of his weight off her. Their dual rhythms harmonized as they moved together.

She ran her hands down his back and even lower, squeezing each cheek of his buttocks in time with his strokes, wanting to push him even deeper inside her, wanting to hold all of him with her body. When he sped up his pace, she matched him, and the wave built up again. It rose, rose, rose, until she didn't think anything could ever be better.

Then it broke, a dam shattering, and she came completely apart, nothing but pleasure rushing through her unbridled. She screamed but wasn't aware of it until the rawness in her throat brought her back to reality and the crest that felt like it had lasted a lifetime slowly faded away.

Her breath came in short bursts, and Jack, on top of her, was doing little better. His face was flushed and sweat dripped from his hair down to his chin. He gave her a look of pure tenderness and peppered her face with more kisses. He remained inside of her, still pleasant, even as his swell reduced. When he moved to get off her, she clutched him to her more firmly.

"No, not yet."

He rolled them onto their sides, still intertwined, still one. Jasminda wiped the sweat from his brow and kissed him everywhere she could reach.

"Jack."

"Yes, my darling?" he said, breathless.

"Just . . . Jack," she said and smiled. He brought her even closer, kissing her until they both had to stop to catch their breaths again. She locked her legs tighter around him, determined to imprint this moment not just in her memory but into her skin, her bones, her soul, and her Song. When she left, it would be all she had to remember him by.

"IT MAY BE easier if . . ." Jack trailed off. Jasminda lifted her head from his chest, not liking the tone of his voice. Somewhere, a clock struck midnight.

"If what?"

He stroked a hand across her jaw. "I don't want them to make your life here miserable. There will be questions, speculation . . . gossip." Worried eyes searched her face.

The tiny light that had flickered to life in the center of her chest after their lovemaking faltered. But she'd known. When he'd showed up at her door, she'd known. When she'd let him in, and when she'd chosen to go down this path, she knew where it would lead and where it would not.

"So what would be easier?" The question fell from her lips on a whisper. She must not have done enough to mask her feelings for he pulled her closer, tightening his grip around her and pressing her into his chest.

"If we remain discreet." His voice wavered. That tiny wobble stole the strength from her growing hurt. It was not exactly a rejection, but the reality was clear. He could never truly be hers.

She remembered the feeling of the vision in the cave, the girl whose eyes she'd looked through. That girl had lost herself when she'd been chosen as a sacrifice. She'd belonged to the people, as did Jack, and the people were fickle masters.

"You are right," she said to his chest, then pressed a kiss there to show she bore no ill will about the state of affairs. She did not. If her heart broke the tiniest bit, it was only because she had allowed it to grow weak and sentimental. That would never do.

She sat up, pulling herself out of the cage of safety his arms provided. "This is no one's business but ours. We don't ever have to speak of it again, if you'd prefer."

"No, that's not what I . . ." He reached for her and she pulled away, turning to sit on the edge of the bed with her back to him.

"You should probably go. You will be missed if you leave it until morning." She wished she had something to cover herself with. There were robes in the great wardrobe hulking in the corner of the room. She'd peeked in it earlier. All she had to do was walk over there and retrieve one, but she did not trust her shaky legs.

Tears formed in the corners of her eyes, but she pushed them back. She tried to force that same will into her legs to push her to stand, but just as she thought she'd found the strength, nimble hands enfolded her waist, sliding her across the bed. Jack turned her over until she was on her back with him straddling her, his face inches from her own.

He kissed her. She closed her eyes involuntarily and lost herself in it. Even if by some miracle she found someone to kiss again, it would never be like this.

"If you want me to tell the world I will," he said. "I will call for a press conference on the steps of the palace and shout your name from every roof and balcony." He placed kisses down her jaw and neck, pausing to nuzzle the crook of her neck and inhale deeply.

She threaded her fingers through his hair, so short now there was barely anything to hold on to, and pulled his head up so she could peer into his eyes. "Don't be ridiculous."

"I don't want you to think that I . . . that I care what anyone else thinks. I just don't want it to be harder for you than it has to be."

"All right." A quiet acceptance of an unavoidable fact. "What have you said about my presence here?"

He settled onto his elbows, still on top of her, and her core warmed at the press of him against her.

"You are my honored guest. You saved my life and lost your home in the process. There may even be a medal involved."

She matched his smile, battling the sadness that kept creeping in from the corners. The clock struck the quarter hour.

"You really should go and get some sleep," she said, smoothing a finger across his brow. "Can you discreetly get back to your rooms?"

He sighed, rising to a knee. "I can use the back passageways. There are hidden corridors throughout the palace too narrow for the servants to bother with. I used to hide in them as a child." He reached for her. "How I wish I could stay beside you the whole night."

She did not give voice to all the things she wished that would never be.

He stood, finally, retrieving his scattered clothing and dressing. Jasminda admired each of his body parts as they were hidden from her view. Now that he was no longer naked, her mind cleared enough to remember her plans.

"Might an honored guest of the Prince Regent get a ride down the mountain?"

His brow furrowed. "Certainly. I'll have Usher, my valet, assign you a driver. Where do you want to go?"

She wasn't sure she wanted to share with him the real reason she'd come to Rosira. It felt too personal, the wound far closer to the surface than she'd thought. But there was no point in hiding it; her driver would no doubt reveal her destination if questioned.

"My mother's family is here. I want to see them."

Jack paused his fumbling with the buttons of his sleeves. He stood across the room and nodded once, simply, with a look just as intimate as what they'd shared that night. She'd expected questions, for him to perhaps scoff at her errand or even rail against her family's abandonment. But his look said he understood the whirling emotion wrestling within her. That he knew how hard this was for her and why she had to do it.

She glimpsed a well of pain inside him she had never seen before, one that tugged at her in a new way. And it made it all the more difficult when he kissed her good-bye and walked out the door.

CHAPTER SIX

THE ADDRESS JASMINDA had been writing to for the past two years was a fifteen-minute drive from the palace. Situated in an obviously well-to-do neighborhood, it sat midway up the steep incline of Rosira's skyline. Two stories of butter-colored stucco, topped with a red-tiled roof, loomed over her. Bushes trimmed in perfect spheres decorated the tiny front yard. The breeze off the ocean rippled her hair as she exited the backseat of the town car Jack's valet had provided for her.

A gated driveway led to a small carriage house in the back. She wasn't prepared for the grandeur. The house was nowhere near the scope of the palace, but it was a far cry from the cabin she'd grown up in. Even the windows were ornate, rectangular at the bottom but arched at the top. How could Mama have lived here? Had she felt as stifled as Jasminda did simply looking at the home's exterior? Or had she secretly longed for this life from her place in exile on the borderlands?

Jasminda stood before the massive, double wooden doors and ran her fingertips over the brass door knocker before raising it and rapping three times. While waiting for a response, she struggled to figure out what to say. No words had come to her in the days since she'd first thought of confronting her grandmother. Perhaps the words would find her tongue once the two were face-to-face.

The door opened, revealing a white-haired woman, not strict or severe in appearance as Jasminda had imagined, but plump and inviting with Mama's golden eyes. Those eyes widened as they took in Jasminda from head to toe.

She tugged self-consciously at her dress. Nadal had arrived that morning with a stunning array of clothing for her to choose from, hemlines ranging from a respectable mid-calf to an eyebrow-raising above-the-knee. Beading, sequins, and tassels adorned the collection. But she had chosen the simplest frock, cream-colored and stylishly loose-fitting, with a waistline that grazed her hips. Now she wished she'd selected something fancier, something that screamed, *I'm staying in the palace and am the very close acquaintance of the Prince Regent.*

Her grandmother's gaze flicked to the shining auto parked in front, with the uniformed driver in place, then back to Jasminda in confusion.

Jasminda notched her head higher. "Olivesse Zinadeel?" she said.

"Yes?" Her grandmother's voice was reedy, nothing like the rich tones of Mama's.

"I'm Jasminda. Emi's daughter."

All the color drained from the old woman's face, and she did another full body scan of Jasminda. Searching for similarities? There weren't many to see on the outside. Everything that made Jasminda like her mother was on the inside. Her love of gardening and making things grow. Her thirst for knowledge and hunger for books. But she liked to think she was more practical than Mama had been, not as much of a romantic. Still, when her grandmother snapped her mouth shut and shook her head, pain cleaved her heart in two.

Olivesse's color came back, and she winced as if pained by something. She took a step back.

"Please don't come here again. I . . . I don't have anything for you." She took another step back and shut the door.

Jasminda swayed on her feet. For just a moment, heartache swelled, but then her anger rushed in full force. She banged on the knocker again, rhythmically, for so long her arm began to hurt. When that produced no results, she started hammering away at the door with her fists until they were raw and pulpy.

She cradled her arms to her chest and turned to see the driver in the front seat watching her curiously. Hitching up her chin, she turned back to the house, walking backward a bit to peer in the windows. They were all covered by curtains, offering no glimpse inside.

"I'll be right back," she told the driver before taking the path to the driveway. Beyond the house, the gravel drive slanted down quite steeply and ended in a quaint carriage house. The main house had a small backyard with a well-tended garden, each row completely free of weeds and labeled with little white wooden stakes.

She stood trying to imagine her mother here learning to garden from that woman inside, who was the storybook picture of what a grandmother should be, except, of course, for ignoring her grandchild. The windows in the back of the house were all shuttered or draped except for the glass doors leading to the garden.

Jasminda approached cautiously and peered inside. Dark hardwood floors were visible beneath finely woven rugs. Heavy, expensive-looking furniture sat atop them in rich colors and brocades. Her shoulders sagged as she took in what she could from her limited view. She did not bang on the door to request entry. She could break the glass and storm in, but the determination she'd felt moments before fled, leaving only sadness.

A creak sounded as the iron gate opened. Jasminda crouched beside a bush as a door slammed and then an auto pulled up to the carriage house. The driver emerged, a rather slim and short fellow with a black suit and hat, and opened the door for the passenger in the back. Jasminda's breath caught. The woman coming out of the car was the scarred Sister who had aided the refugees at Baalingrove. It was indeed her Aunt Vanesse.

Vanesse looked back toward the house, and Jasminda held her breath, trying to remain motionless and unobserved. With a final anxious glance, Vanesse followed the driver into the carriage house using the side door. Jasminda peered behind her and darted to the side of the small structure. The door was closed, but a small window was uncovered.

Vanesse was not dressed in the robes of the Sisterhood today. Instead, she wore a knee-length skirt and silk blouse with a stylish fitted hat on her head. She removed her hat, placing it on a cluttered table. The driver had his back to Jasminda, but when he removed his hat, she froze and her breath hitched. The small man was really a woman, who shook out her shoulder-length locks and turned toward Vanesse.

With another furtive glance over her shoulder, Vanesse approached the driver, cupping the woman's face in her hands and leaning in to kiss her. Jasminda dropped her eyes, guilty for spying on such an intimate stolen moment.

Jack invaded her mind, then—his lips against hers, his body pressed close, the hope that they would not be discovered. All the trouble that would bring.

This house, the wealth—Mama's family obviously had a privileged place in society. What did they say about their long-lost eldest daughter? Jasminda knew better than to think they'd told the truth about Mama's marriage to a settler and her half-breed children. They had probably killed her off in their lives long before her actual death. Maybe what her grandmother had slammed the door on wasn't a real relationship with her flesh and blood kin but just a ghost. Jasminda felt like a ghost spying on her aunt from the shadows.

It seemed these sisters were alike in many ways. Was loving another woman so different from loving a Lagrimari? Both were taboo. And Jasminda was beginning to realize you couldn't choose who you loved.

The house where her mama had grown up looked different to her now. So many secrets, so many falsehoods and betrayals. Jasminda had wanted to make them see her, but did they even see themselves? She'd thought making her family acknowledge the lives of her brothers and her father was what she wanted, but now she just wanted to protect those memories and hold them close to her like armor. Not have them sullied by the cold eyes of a woman who had no regard for her.

She crept back around the house and climbed into the auto.

"Back to the palace, please. There isn't anything for me here."

As the Council of Regents meeting bled into its fourth hour, Jack longed for nothing more than to be back in Jasminda's arms. Her touch still shivered across his skin, and he could swear her scent suffused the air. If he did nothing else but listen to her soft breaths until the day he died, he would not consider it a wasted life.

The reality of the Council Room and the petty squabbling among a group of grown men was cold water thrown on his reverie. His temper flared at the intrusion. The Minister of Finance and the Minister of the Interior bickered like an old married couple and could be counted upon never to agree with each other. Even in a circumstance as dire as imminent war.

Alariq would have been able to follow this miserable meeting quite adeptly, and known just what to say to bring the petty quarreling to an end. It was, after all, what his brother had trained for his whole life. Military training had done nothing to dull Jack's edges into a tool of political usefulness. His manner was ill-appreciated by the men. Minister Stevenot of the Interior sputtered like a flooded engine when Jack interrupted him.

"I do not want to hear another word about the allowable roof colors in East Rosira. They can paint them pink with blue dots for all I care!" Jack slammed his hand on the table; several of the old men jumped. "How much longer must we go on discussing this ridiculous minutiae? Objections to the fabric of the shipbuilder's guild's new uniforms? Reshodding the mounts of the dock guard? None of this will matter in mere days when the Mantle comes down, yet you all refuse to seriously discuss the most pressing issue."

The faces around the table resembled fish, wide-eyed with their mouths opening and closing mutely.

"Your Grace," Pugeros, the Minister of Finance, said, his face taking on a fatherly quality that held more than a little condescension. "Lagrimar has given no indication they plan to attack. And it has only been five years since the last breach. They have always needed far longer than that to build the dark magic needed to cross the Mantle."

"Why would they warn us of an attack? I have seen their preparations, Minister. *I* am warning you. And the time between the breaches has grown shorter and shorter. They are finding new ways to use their *dark magic*, as you call it. We need to inform the people, especially those near the border. Perhaps even evacuate."

"That would be extreme, Your Grace," Stevenot said. "We do not want to alarm the populace and cause a panic. Our superior technology and skilled army will easily defeat their witchcraft as we have done in the past."

Red stained Jack's vision. "Easily?" he said through clenched teeth. No one in this room aside from him had ever seen combat.

"The last breach was barely even three months long." Stevenot turned away as if he'd made his point. As if three months in the trenches was merely an extended vacation. These men hadn't the faintest clue.

War. The exact cause of the conflict all those years ago was lost to history. Its absence conspicuous since such careful records existed from that point on. Each breach was a devastation. Early on, the Lagrimari use of Earthsong resulted in heavy Elsiran losses. They, in turn, had responded with innovation, better weapons, more artful strategies, but by no means did that guarantee their victory.

"Have you forgotten the Iron War? The Princeling's Scourge?" Jack looked around the room. "Many of you were alive when they destroyed the citadel, killing thousands of civilians in the borderlands. Ignoring this will not make it go away."

"The farmers will not leave," the Minister of Agriculture said, shrugging his shoulders. "They would much rather die on their land."

"Then may they find serenity in the World After." Jack leaned back. "There are thousands of borderlanders that can and must be saved. This threat cannot be taken lightly. The Lagrimari have found some new way to weaken the Mantle. There are more and more cracks appearing, and in a matter of days, it *will* fall. We will defend our lands as we always have, but we've never faced the True Father on Elsiran soil before."

The men blinked stupidly in response. Jack kneaded the bridge of his nose. "Is it necessary to invoke Prince's Right to make you take this seriously?"

Voices around the table exploded.

"You will do no such thing!"

"Preposterous!"

"How dare you!"

Minister Nirall's voice cut through the din. "The Council serves at the pleasure of the Prince Regent. In times of war, it is fully within his right to dissolve this Council if and when—" Shouts and censure drowned him out.

Lizvette's father, Meeqal Nirall, was Jack's favorite Council member, a former professor and the Minister of Education and Innovation, he was most often the voice of compassion and reason.

"Listen," Nirall said, his voice rising over the others. "We must not let it get to that point. Let us hear him out."

"Thank you," Jack said.

The man nodded.

"If we evacuate the borderlanders, where will they go? How will we feed them?" the Minister of Agriculture cut in.

"Yes, these *refugees*"—Pugeros spat the word out like he would a rotten bite of food—"are already straining the Principality's coffers. With this year's abominable harvest and the increase on import tariffs out of Yaly, we are already facing difficult financial waters. The latest debacle with the King of Raun means an even more dire situation for our economy. If we reduce the refugee rations, or refuse them entry entirely, we would be in a better position to care for our own people."

"There is international precedent," Stevenot said. "We are under no obligation to burden ourselves with their care."

"This is not a financial question, but a moral one," said Nirall. "They are fleeing a brutal dictator. We must treat them the same way we'd treat our own women and children. There are enough resources to care for them all."

"Minister Nirall." The low timbre of Zavros Calladeen's voice resonated as he addressed his uncle formally. Calladeen, the youngest on the Council save Jack, owed his position as Minister of Foreign Affairs not to his uncle's influence but to his own keen intelligence, politicking, and ruthless ambition. "I've seen this camp, and much as I would like to feel sorry for these refugees, I am moved by something less like pity and more like suspicion to see them crossing our borders in such increasing numbers."

"Surely, you do not suppose that those miserable creatures could be spies? I'm told they practically kiss Elsiran soil when they arrive," Nirall replied.

"Never forget their witchcraft," said Calladeen. "This Earthsong they possess is dangerous. What is to stop them from bringing down a violent storm or a rockslide or a fire? We cannot afford to let our guard down."

Jack simmered just below a full boil. He'd never understood what Alariq saw in Calladeen. "Earthsong also healed me. On more than one occasion. And the number of refugees who even have their Songs is small. The True Father has drained many of his populace of their power. Is there a chance that there are spies among them? Yes. But does that mean we turn our backs on those seeking aid?" Jack shook his head. "A Lagrimari man is the only reason the coming attack is not a surprise. Instead of treating the refugees as enemy agents, we should be trying to learn from them, gaining additional intelligence, and working together to find a way to stop the True Father."

"That is a naive way of looking at things, Your Grace," Calladeen said haughtily. "The Lagrimari are not tacticians. Additional intelligence has never defeated them. Superior force, training, and discipline have done that for nearly five hundred years."

"Things are changing, Minister Calladeen. My time embedded with the enemy showed me that. We are on the cusp of something different."

"Perhaps your time with the enemy has changed *you*, Your Grace," Pugeros said. Every head turned to him. "The Lagrimari girl staying in the palace?"

Heads swiveled back to Jack, who gritted his teeth. "She is Elsiran-born. She has Elsiran kin, and in this city."

"Perhaps it would be better for her to reside with them instead of here. She may be as you say, but the appearance of the situation is less than ideal," said Pugeros.

"The *situation* is not up for discussion." Jack shot to his feet. "Order the voluntary evacuation of the borderlands. Stevenot, review my request for wartime funds and find the money. Both for the army *and* the refugees. No excuses. Minister Nirall, as there are many children in the camps, begin plans for educating them and teaching them our language. Gentleman, these are war refugees fleeing the most brutal dictator our world has ever seen. We are honorable Elsirans. Let's start behaving as such."

He slammed out of the room amidst a chorus of grumbles and stalked down the hall.

JACK SLIPPED INTO the side corridor and over to the unused back passageways. A steep staircase, coated in dust, took him up to the roof of the palace. He'd come here often as a child to escape the tense misery unfolding between his parents and to take in the spectacular view.

The palace sat at Rosira's highest point, backing up to the steep rise of jagged mountains separating the capital from the rest of the country. In the distance, the ocean sparkled in the afternoon light. Beyond the endless waves lay worlds he couldn't fathom. Then again, he was having enough trouble understanding his home country.

The formal jacket he'd worn to the Council meeting chafed at his neck; he pulled on the collar. How was he going to do this for the rest of his life?

He stood there regarding the city for so long that the sun began its evening journey home. A hand on his shoulder pulled him from his musings.

"Found my hiding place, did you, old man?" he said, turning around.

Usher smiled. "Not very difficult since it hasn't changed in fifteen years."

"What can I say, I'm a man of habit." Jack shrugged then sighed, leaning back against the railing. "Why am I called a prince if I can make no moves without the assent of the Council? And why do they oppose me at every turn?" He dropped his head into his hand.

"They will come around," Usher said, placing a comforting hand on his arm.

Jack snorted. "They treat me like a child. I'm four years older than Alariq was when he took office."

"And I'm sure they treated him the same."

"I doubt it. I'm almost certain he never had to threaten to use Prince's Right to get the Council to take action. Those old men are so stubborn and callous—"

Usher straightened. "I don't recall Alariq doing quite this much whining."

Jack frowned.

"If you're quite done with your tantrum, young sir, you have dinner with General Verados in an hour."

He had neither been whining nor having a tantrum, but the old man was right: he'd never seen Alariq moping about. Duty was duty, and there was little he could do now but square his shoulders and steel himself to step back into his role. Perhaps he could get some advice from the retired general on his strategy for dealing with Lagrimar.

He followed Usher to the far side of the roof, where the proper entrance was, though he missed a step, stumbling when he saw a massive shape covered in a tarp.

Usher followed his line of sight and sighed.

"I thought it was destroyed," Jack said through gritted teeth.

"Only the front of the craft sustained any damage. The day after the crash, technicians arrived from Yaly to repair it."

Jack approached the contraption and began pulling the tarp down.

"It's been fully inspected. You don't have to—"

"I just want to see it." With a final tug, the tarp fell away, revealing the airship his brother had died in.

The great balloon portion that when filled with gas, lifted the machine into the air lay on its side. Heavy, reinforced cables attached it to the carriage. The inside offered seating for four, plus the pilot's chair behind a great steering wheel.

Jack reached out for the polished wood of the carriage but drew his fingers away before they made contact. The windows sparkled deviously. Even the propeller attached to the front had been buffed to gleaming. From the outside, it was remarkable. It did not look like a coffin.

"What in all that is sacred possessed him to pilot this monstrosity?" A cold fear pummeled his gut.

"Alariq did not share your aversion to heights. He enjoyed every moment he spent in the air."

"I am not averse to heights. Are we not standing on the roof?"

Usher's eyebrows rose. "Yes, the roof of a building that is only three-stories high. Would you care to go to the clock tower and have this conversation?" He pointed to the tower below in the town square.

Jack's eyes widened, but he swatted away the fear. "I'll have you know I climbed a mountain three times, old man. Once with a bullet in me. Though I did manage to be pushed off a cliff by an avalanche for my trouble." He shivered at the memory. "There's nothing wrong with wanting to stay on solid ground. If men had been intended to fly we would come with wings. Have someone take this thing away from here. It won't see any use from me."

Usher nodded, holding his peace for once. Jack stalked down the stairs and back into the thick of his life.

———

JASMINDA STOOD AT the intersection of two hallways. How was it possible that every corridor in the entire palace looked exactly alike? After her disastrous attempt to visit her family, she'd returned to the palace where the driver had dropped her off at the side entrance next to the vehicle depot. She'd hoped to be able navigate back to her rooms, but before she'd made it very far, her stomach had rumbled. With no intention of attending any more official dinners and unsure of the meal schedule here, she'd changed course for the kitchens. However, her confidence in her ability to manage the often crisscrossing, often dead-end passageways of the palace had been optimistic at best. Swiveling her head back and forth at the T-shaped intersection, she searched for a clue.

"May I be of assistance?" a deep voice purred behind her.

Jasminda turned to find the unpleasant man who'd practically dragged Lizvette away from her the night before watching her from a doorway. Tall and broad shouldered, he had unusually dark hair and a precise goatee. But he stared at her as if she were an item in the display case of the butcher's shop.

She squared her shoulders and refused to be intimidated. "I don't think we've been properly introduced. I am Jasminda ul-Sarifor." She held out her hands, challenging him to greet her properly.

"Zavros Calladeen, Minister of Foreign Affairs." He ignored her outstretched palms but bowed deeply. The bow was more formal than the pressing of hands and indicated a higher level of respect, but she got the sense he found it distasteful to touch her.

"I was searching for the kitchens," she said.

"Are your servants inadequate?"

"No, no, my . . . the servants are fine. But I'm capable of feeding myself." Her chin shot up, daring him to contradict her.

"Well then allow me to escort you," he said, offering his elbow, though his expression made her think he meant to jab her with it.

"Oh, that's not necessary." She had no desire to spend another moment in his company.

"I must insist. It seems my cousin has taken quite a liking to you," he said, motioning to the hallway on the left with a sweep of his arm. "As, of course, has our prince." His long legs set a quick pace, and Jasminda hurried to catch up. "I would guess the palace is different than what you're used to."

"Yes, quite," she said, nearly out of breath.

"And what is it you're used to?"

"A small cabin. My family are goat farmers. Or, rather, we were. I was . . . am." She nearly jogged alongside him to keep up.

"I see," he said, raising an eyebrow. He led her down a flight of steps to a wide hallway. Even without Earthsong, she could sense an intense energy swirling around him like a cloud of dust. If she dared use her magic, she suspected she would find something dark lurking within him.

"And how do you find the royal palace?"

"Overwhelming."

"And our Prince . . . How do you find him?" Zavros stopped so suddenly, Jasminda just narrowly avoided bumping into him.

His pointed gaze indicated that he knew why Jasminda was in the palace and considered her little more than Jack's whore. Drawing herself up to her full height, she refused to look away, unwilling to be cowed by such a dreadful man.

"Prince Jaqros is everything honorable. We owe one another a life debt, you understand."

"Yes, I have heard." Zavros continued walking. "We Elsirans take our life debts seriously."

"Yes, I am an Elsiran."

"Half? Am I correct?"

"Excuse me?"

"You are half-Elsiran, are you not?"

"I was born in Elsira, as was my mother. My father was born in Lagrimar."

"And he managed to seduce and impregnate one of our Elsiran maids."

They were on yet another staircase, and Jasminda missed a step tripping on her long skirt. Zavros's hand shot out to steady her. His grip was firm, not painful, but not gentle, either.

"They fell in love."

"Interesting. Well, here we are," he said, pointing to the swinging doors of the kitchens at the foot of the stairs. "Please do help yourself to whatever you'd like. You are a guest of the Prince Regent, after all, and must be treated accordingly." His voice oozed like poisoned honey.

"Thank you, sir," she said through clenched teeth.

"It has been a pleasure, my lady. May She bless your dreams," he said with a sweeping bow, then turned and disappeared down the hallway.

Jasminda stood outside the kitchen, suddenly not hungry anymore.

"ARE YOU SURE you don't want me to find a way to even inconvenience her just a little? I'm sure the tax collectors could come up with something. If not them then the housing patrol. Apparently roof-color violations are on the rise."

Jasminda smiled. "No, not even so much as a parking violation. You promised."

Jack grumbled an unintelligible reply. For the past two days he'd been trying to convince her to allow him to retaliate against her grandmother in some way. His response had siphoned away some of the sting of the meeting. She had no doubt if she'd wanted the woman locked in a dungeon for hurting her feelings, Jack would have made it happen.

She hadn't mentioned Aunt Vanesse. That wasn't her secret to tell.

Her head lay on his chest, dipping and rising with his breath. She ran her hand across the ridges of his stomach. Regardless of when this ended, she was grateful for every stolen moment, every kiss and touch. Each time they made love, her heart expanded just a little more.

That he kept returning was a continual surprise. She kept at bay the dribble of dread seeping into the back of her mind, fear for the night he didn't show up. The time would come soon enough, and though she longed to prepare for it, to protect her heart from the inevitable pain, she could no more stop herself from falling for Jack than stop breathing on command.

She placed a kiss on his chest. He tilted her head back until he could reach her lips and kiss her passionately. She delighted in the taste of him, in his tongue seeking hers and warming her entire body.

"How much longer can you stay?"

His expression darkened for a moment, and he drew her even closer. "A little while. I should go before the morning servants start their rounds."

She understood his desire for discretion, agreed with it even, but her heart sank a bit each time it was confirmed. There were those who knew—Nadal for one. The girl had obtained the sylfimweed necessary to prevent pregnancy, though she had not yet seen the prince in Jasminda's chamber. Jack had mentioned that his valet, Usher, knew, and one other person who he didn't identify but said would keep the secret. Though after the confrontation with Calladeen, Jasminda didn't know how much of a secret it really was.

"I am sure that people suspect. Would it be better if I were somewhere else? I don't want to make things difficult for you."

"Jasminda, my darling, you make everything immeasurably better. The thought of being with you at night pulls me through my days."

She returned his smile, hiding her apprehension, not saying the one thing on her mind—*for how long?* When would their inevitable ending be?

"Would you do something for me? If you're not too busy?" His teasing voice made her chuckle. He knew she'd spent the last couple of days in the palace's Blue Library in a heaven of books.

"Certainly, Your Grace. Do you have any rogue goats needing herding?"

He squeezed her shoulder playfully. "None that I know of. However, there is another task for which you are uniquely suited." His face grew serious, and he sighed. "The refugees . . . There is some debate on how best to handle them. More seem to arrive every day."

"What is the debate? Is there some other option to caring for them?" Her tone was pitched high with disbelief.

"No." His voice brooked no argument. "There is not. But there are less than a handful in all of Elsira who speak any Lagrimari whatsoever, and none of them are even remotely proficient."

"Mother said Lagrimari was so difficult to learn, she thought the language must be spelled against outsiders. You are truly unique for your mastery of it." A knot of anxiety formed in the pit of her stomach. "You want me to speak with them."

"Yes. Public opinion is slowly swinging against the refugees, and the Council members are little better. They've agreed to help fund the camp and take some of the financial pressure off the Sisterhood, but they're insisting on having the army provide *security*." He gave a humorless laugh. "The language barrier is a problem, as well as the general attitude of the soldiers. I'm working on that, and I've ordered an education program for the refugees so they may learn Elsiran, but in the meantime . . ."

Jasminda drew the covers up around her shoulders, suddenly chilly. "What do you want me to say to them?"

"Just . . . talk to them. Learn their stories. Let me know what they need, what they want. Right now, most Elsirans barely view them as human. That has to change if there's to be any chance of them living happily in our land."

"Is there a chance of that?"

"Of them living here or living happily?"

"Happily. Ever after," she said softly. "There are five hundred years of reasons for our people to hate one another."

Even as she spoke, Jasminda was not certain who she had meant by "our people." She had not told Jack about meeting Calladeen, convincing herself it was nothing, simply an aristocrat looking down his nose at her. She expected nothing less. But there were other things she didn't mention. The whispers and glances following her about the palace. The scowls from the Royal Guardsmen, snickers from passing maids. She felt like a monster on display. The gruesome sideshow act everyone stared at. No one had been overtly rude—she had not heard anything specific—but the fear and distrust followed her.

Only with Jack was she comfortable, safe, happy. Could the refugees ever have that sort of security on Elsiran soil?

"Everyone has the right to seek happiness. I wish I could guarantee it, but I am only a prince."

She traced a pattern across his chest, then placed a kiss over his heart.

"Very well," she said. "I will go talk to them."

He took her hands in his and kissed them. "Thank you."

Jasminda nestled her body even closer to him as he dozed. She stayed awake for the next few hours, enjoying the feeling of their intimacy before duty and responsibility took him away from her.

The first light of dawn glowed pink through the windows. The early-morning sky was so different in her valley. With this new task heavy on her shoulders, she longed even more for the simplicity of the farm. For a Jack who was not a prince and would be happy with a quiet life. She would teach him to herd and plant, and they would spend evenings in front of the fire, reading and talking and making love.

In this imagined life, she would have her own family, a place to belong that could never be taken away. People around her who looked at her only with love. And her parents and brothers would live on in the tales she'd tell her children and then their children.

Jack awakened when the first rays of light hit the bed. She pretended to be asleep as he dressed, kissed her forehead, then slipped out the door. The bubble of Jasminda's dream popped. She was alone in a strange bed, in a strange city, about to go and meet more strange people.

She rolled into the warm spot Jack had vacated, plunging her nose to the mattress to capture his lingering scent. She stole a few more minutes in bed, grasping the threads of her impossible dream before facing what lay before her.

THE CAMP LOOMED larger than it had a few days before. Jasminda was not sure how many refugees were housed here, but little white tents filled her vision. The same driver as the day before pulled up to the entrance and let her out, then returned to the town car to wait out her visit.

She stood wide-eyed, surrounded by rifle-wielding soldiers and unsure where to begin. Tents were organized in wide and narrow lanes alternating in a grid, marked with letters and numbers. She walked along the wide center path, observing the mid-morning camp life. The subdued atmosphere hung thick and heavy. Women huddled in small groups outside their tents, mending clothes or doing laundry in small wash bins. Children sat quietly, often clutching ragged dolls. The raucous laughter and play she'd seen in the tiny mountain town was absent, the light in the children's eyes dim.

"So you return to us, eh?" a familiar voice said.

Jasminda turned to find Gerda standing behind her, hands on her hips. Jasminda offered a weak smile.

"Come, child," the old woman said before marching away down one of the narrow alleys. Jasminda followed. They turned corner after corner, passing identical white tents, moving deeper into the camp until she had no hope of finding the entrance again. Finally, Gerda stopped in front of a tent with a strange symbol painted on the outside.

"What does this mean?" Jasminda asked.

Gerda's eyes narrowed. "Can you not read Lagrimari, child?"

Jasminda's cheeks grew hot, and she shook her head. "My father had no books with him when he came here. We learned to read only in Elsiran. Is this how Lagrimari looks?"

"She's not one of us. She shouldn't be here."

Jasminda held back a groan. She spun to face Rozyl, who stood behind her.

"Slumming it, are we?" the woman spat.

Jasminda's jaw tightened. "No, I was sent here to help. To translate, if needed. There has been some trouble with the soldiers?"

The scarred woman's face contorted into a sneer. "It doesn't take a translator to know what these pigs' sons think of us."

"Rozyl, hush," Gerda said, and motioned toward the tent. "Let us go inside, beyond the reach of prying ears."

Jasminda scanned the area. The soldiers only manned the perimeter of the camp; she had seen none in the interior. What prying ears was Gerda afraid of?

"What is going on?" Jasminda asked.

"A meeting," Gerda said.

"I don't want to intrude."

Rozyl snorted in disbelief, and Jasminda tensed, restraining herself from turning on the woman and letting her temper reign.

"You are needed at this meeting, child," Gerda said, her gruff voice softening a bit.

When she pulled back the tent flap, Jasminda took a deep breath.

Casting a glance at a scowling Rozyl, she ducked into the tent. Gerda, Rozyl, and several others followed her in. It took a few moments for her eyes to adjust to the dim interior. With their arrival, the small space had grown quite crowded. Over a dozen people sat spiraled around the camp stove in the center. She took a place at the outside of the spiral, near the door.

Turwig, Lyngar, and the guards from the cave were among the cautious faces looking back at her. Gerda cleared her throat. "We are all here. Let us begin."

"I want to be sure that my objections are noted," Rozyl said. A few murmurs of assent rose in the close space. "I don't trust her—"

"We've taken your concerns under consideration, thank you," Turwig said, cutting her off. She pursed her lips and sat back. "But the decision has been made."

"What is this about?" Jasminda asked. Her question was lost amid the rising voices, some echoing Rozyl's concerns, others supporting Turwig. Each gibe and sentiment of distrust sliced into Jasminda like a knife. She stood, and silence descended.

"What is this about?" she repeated, forcing her voice to be strong when it threatened to quiver.

"Sit, please," Turwig said. He watched her closely, and she did as he'd asked, glad that the exit was so close. The desire to bolt, to get away from all the suspicion was strong, but curiosity begged she hear the old man out.

Turwig shared a glance with Gerda, then reached into the inner pocket of his threadbare jacket and pulled out a small bundle wrapped in cloth. He touched the bundle reverently then reached for Jasminda's hand and placed it in her grasp.

A deep, pulsing energy came from within the bundle. She nearly dropped it. Every person in the tent grew tense. "What is this?" she whispered.

"Open it," Turwig said.

Jasminda shook her head as her hand trembled. "I can barely stand to hold it. What is it?" Her stomach lurched as her breakfast threatened to come up. Whatever was inside this cloth was *wrong* somehow. Too powerful. It was like Earthsong had been trapped within a package that fit in her palm.

"Take it back."

"Open it," Gerda repeated gently. Jasminda didn't think the elders would give her something dangerous. On the contrary, every face staring back at her seemed expectant, almost hopeful. Even Rozyl's. That cemented her decision. Tears pricked the backs of her eyes, and she blinked rapidly to stay them. With a deep breath, she peeled away the layers of cloth.

Nestled inside was a stone, deep red in color and small enough that she could wrap her entire hand around it. It was smooth, though oddly shaped, like a gemstone had been sanded down to remove all its jagged edges. She held it up to her face, keeping the cloth between her skin and the stone, peering at the thing. Nearby, someone lit a lamp, bringing the stone into clearer view. Embedded within it were dark, swirling lines. Perhaps this was the fossil of an insect. She'd read about such things, though had never seen one before, but as the light brightened, it illuminated lines trapped inside which were too organized for a skeleton. A symbol was embedded beneath the surface. Recognition dawned, and she nearly dropped the stone a second time.

"It's the sigil of the Queen," she said. Everyone in the tent took a collective breath. With her other hand, she reached out a finger to trace the surface. A ripple of power went through her as her skin met the stone. It knocked her backward as blackness stole her vision.

WE RUN THROUGH the woods laughing. Yllis's fingers are intertwined with mine, and when he looks over, the love in his eyes makes my breath catch. My heart is so full.

Eero is behind us, thundering through the underbrush. I don't have to turn to sense my brother tripping over a root that Yllis and I had jumped over. It would be funny to let him fall, but it's not his fault he has no Song and cannot feel the forest around him the way we do. In the blink of an eye, I sing a spell to lift him back upright and set him on his feet. He stumbles a bit but rights himself, his emotions confused for a moment, before refocusing on the competition.

We clear the tree line, and Eero races ahead, beating us to the water's edge. He dives underneath and swims out a little ways, shouting, berating us for our slowness. Yllis and I splash into the waves, soaking each other, and I think this is the happiest I've ever been. The two people I care most for in this world are here, and it is the most beautiful day I could have dreamed.

Yllis said he would not let it rain on Eero's and my birthday, and he did not. I shall bring the clouds back myself tomorrow to keep things in balance, but for today, watching the smiles on his and Eero's faces as the sun shines down on us is the best present ever.

I wish . . .

JASMINDA OPENED HER eyes and winced at the burning sensation in her palm. Her empty palm. She sat up, and the people who had been leaning over her prone form quickly moved out of the way.

Clarity came back quickly. The tent, the elders, the stone . . . which had disappeared from her hand. She looked over quickly to see Turwig wrapping it up again. She rubbed her face as the chatter of a dozen voices quieted.

"It happened again," she said. There was no surprise on Turwig's and Gerda's faces. "You knew that would happen."

"We suspected, but were not sure," Gerda said.

"It was like in the cave."

Gerda nodded. "But not the Cavefolk this time." It wasn't a question. "Can you tell us what you saw?"

Jasminda related the brief vision she'd had. Once again she'd been someone else. Someone deliriously in love. She hadn't gotten a clear view of the brother, but she'd stared into the eyes her lover, a man who was both a stranger and the object of all her adoration. The visions were all encompassing, and it took a moment to adjust to being torn away and inhabiting her own body again. Whoever that girl was had been lucky.

She flexed her arms and legs, bringing feeling back into them. "What is that stone, and why does it cause visions?"

Everyone settled back down, and Turwig sat next to her, holding the wrapped stone. Her fingers itched to snatch it from him. She couldn't explain the strange possessive instinct that had arisen within her toward the thing, but she wanted it back.

"You must understand that this is our most precious treasure." He held up the wrapped stone. "It may be our last hope."

"You are all Keepers of the Promise?" Jasminda said, motioning toward the others present.

He nodded. "Throughout the war, the Keepers have fought against the True Father's tyranny, searching for a way to overcome his great power in order to awaken *Her*. We have always believed that killing the True Father was the only way to awaken the Queen. But the masked fiend is hard to kill."

"Almost impossible," Gerda said. "And there are those who believe he walks among us in secret, taking on the appearance of our trusted friends and confidantes."

So that was why they found it so hard to trust. "It's true that no one has ever seen his face?" Jasminda asked.

"No one has seen any part of him," Turwig replied. "He is always covered from head to toe and wears a jeweled mask to hide his face. The women of the harems are kept blindfolded when they are with him. And aside from the Cantor, only the Songless are allowed in his inner circle."

"The Cantor?" Jasminda frowned. "Who is that?"

"Every few generations, a powerful Earthsinger is spared the tribute in order to serve as the True Father's Cantor, someone who studies Earthsong, finds new ways to create the breaches. They develop new spells and increase the True Father's power."

Jasminda had never known how the breaches were created. She doubted anyone on this side of the Mantle knew. "And what about those who give tribute? They must be able to get close to him."

Turwig shook his head. "Tribute is given while unconscious. No one but the Cantor and the True Father knows how it is done. But we have chipped away, little by little, doing what we could, saving who we could. We've grown a network to hide as many as we can, so they may retain their Songs." He looked to Rozyl and some of the younger Keepers present.

"Like the one who disguised Jack?" Jasminda asked.

"Yes . . . Darvyn. The poor boy spent his entire life hiding from tribute-camp thugs, being shuffled from place to place. His power—" Turwig shook his head at some memory clouding his mind. "His power is blinding. Darvyn was the one who discovered this." Turwig motioned to the stone. "Years ago, when he was a small boy, we were secreting him away one night—there had been some betrayal at his previous residence, as was often the case. The boy was hidden in a wagon of straw pallets, but when we arrived at the checkpoint, he had disappeared.

"We doubled back, searching for him, but it was the middle of the night and the roads in Lagrimar are not somewhere you want to be caught after dark. I tracked him to the ruins of Tanagol, one of the first border villages destroyed early in the war."

Turwig's eyes softened as he became lost in the memory. "Imagine a child of four or five digging through centuries-old rubble, only to come out covered in dirt and muck with this treasure. He had felt the pull of the ancient spell within calling to him. Later, Darvyn began having the Dream of the Queen. She gave him certain instructions that we have been endeavoring to bring to pass for many years."

Understanding dawned on Jasminda. "She told you to bring the stone here." Turwig and Gerda nodded. "And did She tell you what it was? What it does?" She held her hand out for the stone, and to her surprise, Turwig gave it to her.

"No, She does not have control over the length or frequency of the dreams, so sometimes information is disjointed. We believe it is a caldera, an object that serves as a container for spells."

"I've never heard of anything like that," Jasminda said. "Are these common in Lagrimar?"

He shook his head. "Not at all. About a hundred years ago, a Keeper managed to get his hands on the journal of the Cantor. Everything we know about calderas comes from that book, and it's not much. Only the most powerful Earthsingers can create such objects, and it then holds parts of their Songs. It requires . . ."

She looked up from her perusal of the bundle in her hand. Part of her longed to touch it again, but another part was afraid. "It requires what?"

"A blood sacrifice. A death."

Jasminda's blood ran cold. "Cavefolk magic?"

"The diary didn't say, but once we saw what happened to you in the cave, well, we made an educated guess."

"And the visions . . . you all have had them, too?"

"Oh, no, child," Gerda spoke up. "Nothing at all happens when we touch the caldera."

Jasminda shuddered. "*No one* else has seen a vision when they touch it?"

"No one else could sing inside the mountain, either." Gerda's voice was calm, but there was an underlying tension to it.

"So, why me?"

"We don't know," Turwig said. "Perhaps because you're half-Elsiran. Perhaps some other reason. But I believe you are the only one that can unlock the mysteries of this stone."

Jasminda shook her head in disbelief. "What were the Queen's instructions? What did She say?"

"Her guidance has led us this far," Gerda said. "Though it has taken twenty years to find a way to get the caldera safely into Elsira. We had to trust that once we made it here, a way would be shown." She leaned forward, her intensity piercing. "You are that way." She placed her hand on top of Jasminda's closed fist and the caldera pulsed in response.

The importance of the trust these people were placing in her was not lost on her. "Who else knows about it?"

The elders shared a glance, looks of resignation appearing on their faces. Rozyl sighed. "The Cantor knows, which means the True Father knows—at least that the caldera exists—and he's searching for it. All along we had planned to use decoys to sneak it out. Though not quite this many." She waved her hand around, and Jasminda leaned forward.

"The refugees? They're all just decoys?" Her heart drummed as if ready to beat out of her chest.

Rozyl nodded grimly. "They don't know it. Only a handful outside this tent are Keepers, but word was spread of the cracks in the Mantle, and once our contacts did their jobs, the number of those packing up to escape Lagrimar grew and grew."

She pinned Jasminda with her gaze. "That's why it's so important that we trust the right people. If it falls into his hands, there is no hope. If he breaks out of Lagrimar, not just Elsira will fall but other lands will follow. The world could be his to control. We've got to end this."

For once, Jasminda agreed with Rozyl. "What do I do?" she said.

Uncertainty crossed more than one face. "Follow the visions," Turwig said. "Learn what the caldera wants to show you. It must lead to a way to awaken Her."

"And tell no one about it," Rozyl said. "The Cantor is very powerful, and her spies are clever. She could even have Elsirans working with her. We cannot take any more chances."

"I won't tell anyone."

"Not even that prince of yours." She pinned Jasminda with a hard look.

Jasminda froze. "He would never—"

"Can you risk the future of two countries on it?" Rozyl leaned forward. "The rest of the world? Palaces have eyes and ears. You must give us your word."

She knew without question she could trust Jack. But if what they said was true, there was nothing he could do to help anyway. The weight of the responsibility lay heavy on her shoulders. "I give you my word. I will tell no one and do all I can."

Turwig nodded and smiled at her, but she did not miss the anxiety in his eyes. She was truly the last chance for these people. For Elsira, as well. Cold dread took her over. She inhaled deeply, unwrapped the caldera, and lowered her palm.

THE FIRE CRACKLES before us, and I lean back into the strong hold of Yllis's arms around me. Eero sits just across from us, roasting tubers on a stick. His melancholy calls to me and I yearn to soothe it, but long ago he made me promise not to sing away his moods. I endeavor to respect his wishes, though it is difficult to see my twin so sad.

"What ails, Eero?" I say to him.

He continues to stare into the fire, his eyes faraway. I disengage from Yllis and move around to sit beside him. "We celebrate our birth today. Why are you downhearted?"

I nudge his shoulder, and his mouth quirks slightly in the beginnings of a smile.

"I do not aim to diminish any happiness of yours. I only wish . . ."

I remain patient as he forms his thoughts. Words are not always easy for him, but they eventually flow. I do not push.

"I wish I could sing, as you do. As Father did."

I reach out to him, placing my hand on his. "And I wish I shared Mother's talent at drawing the way you do. The pictures you create are unequaled. Everyone's talents lie in different directions."

"Yes, but to control the earth and the sky? It is magnificent." Wonder fills his voice. I feel ashamed for taking for granted the Song that swells within me, the feeling of oneness that I have with the life and energy of the world.

"We are different," I say. He looks pointedly at my hand, still on his arm, an example of the difference clearly displayed by the contrasting hues of our skin. Mine like our father and the other Songbearers with our dark hair and dark eyes, his the shade of Mother's and the other Silents, with eyes of vivid golden copper. "The blue of the day's sky and the black of the night's are different, but one is not better than the other. We need both. If I could give you part of my Song, I would, so you could feel what it is like. And perhaps you could give me some of your talent so that I could paint the murals that bring such delight to all who see them, and it will equal out."

He pulls away from my touch and stands, offering me his roasted tuber before turning to look at the water. "We will never be equals, Oola." My name on his lips has never sounded so hopeless.

My twin walks toward the water, and I move back to Yllis's arms.

"He offered for the daughter of the Head Cantor," Yllis says as I watch Eero's retreating form. "She turned him down for one of the Healers." A fissure forms in my heart.

"I did not know. He tells me little of his love life. Once upon a time, we were close as heartbeats." I shift to face Yllis. "Do you think there is a way?"

He leans his forehead to mine, his Song dancing at the edge of my perception, offering solace and comfort. I do not reach for it, but I am glad it is there.

"A way for what?" he says.

"To share my Song with him?"

A thoughtful look crosses his face. His studies with the Cantors are progressing; he is learning much about new spells, new ways to funnel and control the massive energy of Earthsong. "If there is a way, we will find it. I promise."

His lips slide to mine, the kiss is not all-consuming, it is simply a reminder that he is here for me and that any problem I face, he faces, as well. My worries flee. I would do anything for my twin, and if it is a Song he desires, I will do all I can to give it to him.

JASMINDA PRESSED HER face to the glass of the auto as it drove through the city and back up the winding roads leading to the palace. The caldera pulsed in her pocket, making her always aware of it.

When she'd awoken from the last vision, she'd tried to touch the caldera again. With the Mantle coming down soon, she wanted to learn as much as she could as quickly as possible, but there had been no effect. Unlike whatever had happened in the mountain cave, this caldera used the strength of her own Song, and after two visions, she was depleted.

She'd held back when telling the Keepers of the last vision. She would reveal everything eventually, but she needed time to wrap her mind around what she'd seen. The girl she'd been, Oola, was an Earthsinger with skin the color of Jasminda's own, and the girl had been born a twin to Eero, a Silent—as Oola called him—who resembled an Elsiran. These visions were windows into a world where Singers and Silents wed and apparently lived in peace with their children, normal and accepted. There had been no feeling of isolation in Oola's thoughts, no sense of being always mistrusted or feared for her magic. On the contrary, her brother was jealous of her power.

As soon as Jasminda's Song was restored she would try again. Unlocking the caldera's secrets was now her only goal.

CHAPTER SEVEN

THE NEWSPAPER CARTOON displayed a baby with a shotgun in one hand and a scepter in the other, a crown of bullets sitting askew on his head. On one side, grotesque caricatures of Lagrimari refugees gobbled food from huge bowls, while on the other, waifish Elsiran farmers split a single loaf of bread.

An editorial on the same page detailed Prince Jaqros's plan to starve his own people in favor of the refugees. It dredged up the swirling chaos surrounding his mother's emigration after his father's death. Those days had been dark ones. Jack's hands curled into fists at the memory.

The country had mourned their beloved prince, but for ten-year-old Jack, a sense of hope had finally begun to creep into his life. The man who had terrorized both him and his mother couldn't hurt them anymore. He'd thought his mother would feel the same relief he felt, but she slipped further and further away, becoming withdrawn and silent. One day she'd announced she was leaving. Not just on holiday, which would have been scandal enough during a time of mourning, but renouncing her citizenship and moving to Fremia.

She hadn't even sought him out to say good-bye. Had merely left him a letter of apology, saying if she had to see *his* picture again in the papers or hear all the gushing praise for a man who'd been the source of their own private misery, she would take her own life. So she'd fled, leaving Jack alone to withstand the national animosity left in her wake.

Today's newspaper article reported "no confidence that the offspring of a woman who many consider a traitor to her country could effectively rule." Tales of Jack's early missteps and indiscretions were laid out. Drunken brawls as a teenager. Being caught "cavorting" with the daughter of a Fremian official and almost inciting an international incident. His recent reckless undercover mission and subsequent disappearance. He was young and headstrong and prone to rash behavior.

Though the article did not specifically mention Jack's, mostly empty, threat of Prince's Right, it summarized constitutional law on the circumstances under which he could dissolve the Council and act alone. The article also took note that he had not yet relinquished his title of High Commander, strongly inferring that he had too much power.

Jack slammed the paper shut and tossed it to the ground. Usher stooped to pick it up, smoothing the folds and placing it neatly on the bureau.

"What happens if I abdicate?" he said, seriously considering the idea.

Usher sat next to Jack in the armchair in front of the fireplace, a finger to his lips in thought. "Your cousin Frederiq is a lovely boy, but a twelve-year-old Prince Regent would fare little better in the press, I'm afraid."

Jack groaned. "The Council would run that child ragged and rule unchecked. Sovereign only knows what manner of damage they'd cause if left entirely to their own devices." He rose and leaned against the mantelpiece. "I don't know what to—"

Before he even finished his sentence, his secretary burst into his office. "The Council has called an emergency meeting, Your Grace. They're threatening to vote without you."

"Vote on what?"

"I'm not sure, sir. They said it was urgent."

"Thank you, Netta." He straightened his suit coat and headed for the Council Room.

All of the men were already there, and expectant faces regarded him, some far too smug for his liking.

"What is this about?" Jack said, dropping heavily into his seat.

"Your Grace"—Stevenot's eyes were wide and round—"the people are demanding action."

"Action?"

"Yes, we've received a petition with well over two thousand names."

"And what do all of these people want?"

Calladeen leaned forward, hands clasped in front of him. "To eject the refugees from Elsira."

Pugeros passed around mimeographed copies of the treasury reports. "The numbers do not lie, gentlemen. The Principality simply cannot afford to continue providing food and care for the refugees. In a few more weeks, we will have run through our reserves entirely."

Jack reviewed the documents in front of him. "How is there no money?"

Pugeros widened his arms and lowered his head, the motion indicating that he was not to blame for the dire financial straits.

"Then we take out a loan." Jack turned to Stevenot. "And we work to educate the people on why ejecting political refugees is not only a callous move but is fundamentally un-Elsiran. We would send these women, children, and elders where, exactly? Back into the grip of a madman?"

"They could go to Udland. It is closest to the climate they're used to. Or perhaps Raun," Stevenot said.

"Udland is a wasteland of superstitious tribes. They would never allow outsiders entry. And Raun . . ." Jack shook his head. "You would send women and children to a nation of pirates?"

"Your Grace is surely not suggesting that we destroy what's left of our economy and plunge ourselves further into debt for a handful of savages?"

Jack slammed his hand on the table. "What of our honor?"

"Honor is not about doing what is right in a vacuum of consequences. Honor is doing the hard thing and letting history determine your legacy." Calladeen's voice was low and measured. He quoted words Alariq had said many times. Jack wanted to punch the man. "Besides, we have no knowledge that their safety is at risk if they are sent back to their home."

Jack's teeth ground together. "Why exactly do you think they risked their lives to leave?"

"I believe Prince Jaqros is right," Nirall spoke up. "The people are jumping to rash conclusions not borne of fact. Perhaps if His Grace were to give a speech? Take to the radio waves with a formal address and assure our people that we hear their concerns. That may go a long way toward assuaging them."

Jack considered. The idea of a speech made him antsy, but he had not formally addressed the people since gaining power. Maybe that was just what everyone needed, to be reassured he wasn't just the reserve prince, though that's how he felt every day. A strong statement could put things on the right track, acknowledging that though times were hard, Elsirans overcame.

He nodded, filled with gratitude for Nirall. The speech could change their minds. Even as he agreed to the plan, the faces looking back at him were less than convinced. Pugeros shuffled his papers, and Stevenot blinked his round, watery eyes rapidly. Calladeen seethed, glaring at his uncle.

"There is another matter, Your Grace," Stevenot said, some color returning to his features.

Jack kneaded the bridge of his nose, wary of whatever else the man had on his mind. "What is that?"

"High Commander of the Armed Forces."

"Is that a question?"

Stevenot swallowed. "The Prince Regent generally does not hold both titles at once."

"Minister, the eve of war is not a time to change the leadership structure of the military. I'm leaning on my top generals while I deal with things here, but it would be foolish to make a formal switch now. Besides the High General is only months from retiring, someone else must yet be groomed for the position."

Calladeen leaned forward, propping his chin on steepled fingers. "The option of a choosing a High Commander from outside of the military has been broached."

The air in the room changed as Jack met Calladeen's gaze. "And whom do you propose?"

No one spoke for a long moment, but Jack waited them out.

Nirall broke the silence. "Minister Calladeen focused on military science in university and even spent a year abroad observing the Fremian Warriors. He would be a suitable candidate for the interim."

Jack's eyebrows rose. "Observed and studied, but never fought, is that correct?" No one at the table would now look at him. "You gentlemen honestly believe our country is safer with the military led by an untrained novice who's never looked a man in the eye in battle and shot him where he stood?" He turned to Calladeen. "Or have you, Minister? Is there some secret life you've led of which I'm unaware?"

Calladeen's jaw tensed. "No," he gritted out.

"I trained for nine years before taking over the title I was born to. I lived side by side with the men whose lives would be affected by my decisions. I fought next to them in the last breach." He leaned forward, gripping the edge of the table so hard his knuckles cracked. "I have bathed in the blood of the men who gave their lives for this land, and I will not allow you to disrespect their memories with your ignorance or incompetence."

Outrage had his blood moving faster. He stood suddenly, the heavy wooden chair in which he sat screaming as it slid across the floor. "Is there anything else?"

Downcast eyes met him from every seat at the table. He stormed from the room, rubbing his chest where his wound had suddenly began to ache.

Or maybe that was just his heart.

IN THE DISTANCE, the clouds have not yet begun to form, but I feel them coming. A raw wind races across the mountain ridge, but I want to feel it so I do nothing to block its bite. The sensation of the air whipping against my skin grounds me.

Above my head, Eero turns circles in the air. I briefly wonder who taught him the trick, but no one needed to. He has been a quick study. He swoops before me, hovering just out of reach. I grab for him anyway, knowing it will make him smile, and he races away.

"You will burn yourself out," I call up to him, making sure my voice carries as his form becomes smaller and smaller. Within minutes, I sense him weakening. He has just enough Song left to land gracefully by my side, laughing, his face full of joy.

"A little more please," he says, holding out his hand.

"More? So you can waste it flying through the air like a deranged bird? There is a reason you do not see any other Songbearers tearing through the skies disturbing the clouds."

He snorts. "Because you are stodgy curmudgeons with no sense of adventure."

I roll my eyes. "No, because we respect the energy and do not squander it on frivolity. If you needed to fly to escape danger or forestall some terrible event, that would be one thing."

His resonant chuckle echoes off the mountain peaks behind us. "If you give me a little more, I will endeavor to seek out some poor soul in peril and give aid straightaway."

I turn away from him and cross my arms.

"My dearest, most beautiful and talented sister." He leans into me and makes his most pitiful face to engage my sympathy.

"Your only sister."

"Yes, and a more wonderful sister there could never be. I promise not to squander it. I shall give the Song the respect it deserves. Please?"

I want to hold my ground against him. But in the weeks since Yllis discovered the spell that allows gifting a portion of a Song from one to another, Eero has been happier than I have seen him since the loss of our parents. Perhaps happier than I have ever seen him.

We thought it best not to make the spell widely known, and so we are all sworn to secrecy. Eero and I come up into the mountains above town to let him practice so as not to be spotted. When I gift it to him, I give him just a little, but he has been using it up faster and faster, asking for more and more. Some part of me advises caution—having been born Silent, there is no telling how the power will affect him—but it brings him such joy.

With a sigh, I turn back to him and hold out my hands. The power is always there, humming inside me, a leashed beast waiting for release. I set a trickle free and sing it into my twin, deep into the core of him where it would last him quite a while if he didn't waste it.

"No more until tomorrow," I admonish. His eyes shine as he nods his understanding.

With a flick of his wrist, he pulls the moisture from the air until it forms a tiny dense cloud hovering above his palm.

"What are you going to do with that?" I ask, holding back a laugh.

His grin is mischievous, and he winks at me. "Just a bit thirsty is all." He opens his mouth and the little cloud becomes a stream of water that arcs, landing on his tongue.

I shake my head and turn back toward the ocean. "The storm will be here in a few hours," I say. "We had better head back down."

He squints into the distance unable to see what I see. "You cannot stop it?"

I shrug. "If we stopped every storm, nothing would ever grow." A greater unease pushes at me, but I brush it away. One storm at a time is all I can deal with.

JASMINDA OPENED HER eyes and sat up from where she'd sagged into the bench on the balcony of her room. The view of the ocean was beautiful, almost exactly the same as the one she'd seen in her vision. But the city of the vision had been only one-tenth its current size. Rows of small, wooden structures lining dirt roads stood where the clusters of magnificent stucco buildings with red-tiled roofs were today. She'd seen the Rosira of another time, a past where Earthsingers were called Songbearers and were vastly more powerful than they were now.

She knew without a doubt that if Oola had needed to cross a mountain during a snowstorm, she could have easily stopped the snowfall to do so safely. Or even flown across, if needed. Little Osar who had saved them from the avalanche was one of the most powerful Singers any of the Keepers had seen, except for perhaps Darvyn, and even the boy could not control the weather.

The glimpses she saw of the past made her long even more for that faraway time when life seemed calmer and easier.

"Miss?" Nadal called from inside.

"Out here," she replied, wrapping up the caldera and placing it in her dress pocket.

"Would you like lunch on the balcony, miss?" the maid said, already searching for a place to set down her tray.

"No, I'll eat inside. And can you arrange for a driver for this afternoon? I need to make another trip to the refugee camp."

"Certainly." Nadal nodded and breezed back through the door.

Jasminda tried to mesh the Rosira of her vision with the one that lay out before her. When had everything gone wrong? Why had the city and the country transformed into a place that feared magic and hated anyone who could perform it?

A foreboding cadence tapped out a rhythm in her head. It matched the gentle vibration of the caldera pulsing at her side.

SOMBER MEN IN dark suits with even darker expressions lined the streets. A few women were scattered among the group, as well, many waving hand-painted picket signs with slogans like WAGES NOT WITCHCRAFT! and FEED THE PEOPLE NOT THE REFUGEES!

Jack's motorcade wound its way back to the palace from the radio station. The speech he'd recorded would play tonight, but he'd lost any hope that it would make a difference. He did not begrudge the people their anger, if only they would focus it in the right direction. They wanted him to do something, but what did they expect? For him to pull food from the parched ground? Produce ships from thin air? Had they forgotten he was not an Earthsinger? They needed someone to blame for the misfortunes of late, and the Lagrimari refugees were simply convenient.

A smaller group of refugee supporters stood closer to the palace and lifted his spirits somewhat. Not everyone in his land was so callous. Then a woman with a sign reading WHY NOW? rapped on the window as the limo slowed for a sharp turn. Yes, why now? Why him?

When he reached the palace, he headed straight for his office, each step heavy. Perhaps he could take an unscheduled break and sneak off to see Jasminda. The thought brightened him. However, Nirall was waiting for him outside his office door, banishing all fantasies of sneaking away. The man's normally jovial face was grim. Jack forced out a warm greeting and led him inside where Usher was tidying up.

"You've seen today's paper, Your Grace?" Nirall asked.

That very paper was now in Usher's grip. Jack suspected the valet of trying to remove it before Jack saw it. He held out his hand; Usher frowned before relinquishing it.

The front-page article featured an interview with an eyewitness to the massacre at Baalingrove who told how Jack had threatened one of his own men with a pistol in order to save the lives of a group of murderous settlers. The term "*grol* sympathizer" was used by the anonymous interviewee. Jack seethed. The settlers hadn't done anything to deserve the farmers' attack. He needed to call Benn to find out how the inquiry into the massacre was progressing. He'd heard little about it during his week in Rosira, though it hadn't been far from his mind.

"What passes for journalism these days is offensive," he said, tossing the paper to the ground. Usher picked it up.

Nirall shook his graying head. "I have no doubt this was just a soldier with an axe to grind, Your Grace, but this refugee business has the people on edge."

"And they blame me? For seeking to punish those who would murder innocent men? For failing to turn away these threadbare women and children? Is that what the people are saying?"

"Your Grace, the people simply want to know that their Prince Regent and their Council hear their voices and have their best interests at heart. They're afraid helping the refugees is taking away vital resources from our own people."

"And the rest of the Council has their interests at heart?" Jack shook his head. "If we could get more of them to see reason . . ."

Jack closed his eyes, wearied of the task in front of him. Whenever he dropped his lids he saw Jasminda's face smiling back at him and the thought soothed him. The cares of the world disappeared every evening in her arms, but he would have to wait. With his plans of seeing her early now thwarted, he longed for nightfall and the comfort of her touch.

"What do you think Alariq would have done?"

Nirall exhaled slowly. "He would have examined all sides of the issue very carefully. Measured them twice to cut once."

A hint of a smile cracked Jack's bleak face. "He would have measured them no less than four times. That's why he was a good prince."

Nirall leaned in, resting his elbows on his knees. Round spectacles and a gray-streaked goatee in need of trimming gave him a professorial air. "Alariq was also very good at deflecting."

"How do you mean?"

"Sometimes, when people are up in arms about something, they need their attention to be redirected elsewhere."

Jack frowned. "What could redirect them?"

Licks of fire reflected in the man's spectacles, setting his eyes aglow. "The people have been displeased over the shortages for some time, but the royal wedding was going to be the perfect distraction. The right mix of glamour and austerity, of course, but an event to capture the public's imagination all the same."

With a sigh, Jack slumped further in his chair. "I'm sure that would have done the trick. It's too bad they could not have wed. I hope Lizvette's spirits are not too low."

"She's quite well. And she would still make a very fine princess." Nirall's gaze held Jack in its grip.

He was dumbstruck. Several moments passed before he could respond. "You can't be suggesting..."

Nirall reached for Jack's arm. "Our two families are still a good match. A strong princess will go a long way to improve your public perception. A wedding, an heir, it would be—"

"That is ludicrous!" Jack stood. "Lizvette loved my brother. How could I . . . It would be extraordinarily inappropriate, not to mention in very poor taste. I'm not sure how you could even think such a thing?"

Nirall stood and bowed his head. "I did not mean to offend you, Your Grace. I was simply trying to offer a potential solution."

Jack backed away. "The title Minister of Innovation fits you too well. But this is outlandish. I could never do such a thing to the memory of my brother, nor to Lizvette."

"You could honor him by maintaining his legacy. He chose my daughter for a reason, and you and she have always been friends. I do not believe the idea would be as unappealing to her as you think."

Jack held up a hand. "Please stop. I do not want to hear any more of this. I cannot."

"Forgive me, Your Grace. I won't speak of it again." Nirall bowed formally and took his leave.

Usher shut the door and came to stand by Jack's side.

"Has everyone gone mad, Usher?" When he did not respond, Jack looked over. "What? You can't think that lunacy makes sense?"

"Alariq was popular with the people. He had the luxury of waiting to marry. An unpopular man is aided by a well-loved wife."

"Don't spit platitudes at me, old man. How could she be well loved, jumping from one brother to the next?"

"Your grandmother did the very same thing to much regard when her first husband died. The people like continuity."

"The people are idiots."

Usher set a hand on Jack's shoulder. "I'm sure the feeling is mutual."

Jack scowled and shrugged off the contact. "I do not love her."

"Many things will be required of you in your new position, young sir. Unfortunately, falling in love is not one of them."

Jack's gaze fell upon the newspaper. He stormed over to the bureau, snatched up the offending sheets, and threw them into the fire.

THAT AFTERNOON A different driver met Jasminda at the outer doors of the palace. He looked to be in his early thirties and greeted her with an affable smile. As she settled in her seat, instead of the stony silence she'd received from the first driver, this one asked about her day and commented on the probability of rain.

"What's your name?" she asked, leaning forward in her seat. In the rearview mirror she noticed his eyes were a sparkling shade of green. She'd never seen eyes that color.

"I'm Nash, miss. Pleasure to meet you."

"Have you lived in Rosira all your life?"

He chuckled. "Oh no, miss. I'm Fremian. I've been here . . . going on three years now. I reached master level in the Hospitality Guild, and when I passed my Level Ones—that's the exam—I had my pick of positions. Most go to Yaly, but I've always liked living by the sea. I started in the resorts up north and let me tell you . . ."

Nash certainly wasn't short on conversation. He regaled her with stories during the trip and told how he came to Rosira following a young lady who had eventually relented and agreed to marry him. Nothing in his manner indicated any suspicion or distaste for Jasminda.

"Nash, I'm sorry to interrupt, but are there many Fremians in Elsira?"

"Not so many, miss. A few servants in the palace and at the premiere vacation spots, some professors at the university, too, but the immigration laws are strict. Down in Portside, you'll see folk from every corner of the globe working the ships, but they're prohibited from entering other parts of the city."

Nash's native Fremia was a land that valued knowledge and excellence above all else. They had the best schools and universities and offered elite training in everything from art, to science, to warfare and hospitality. Around the world, no one was better at what they did—no matter what it was—than a Fremian.

"And do your people have any . . . opinions on the Lagrimari?"

He gave her a knowing smile. "Fremia has always been neutral, miss. We stay out of the conflicts of other lands."

They reached the camp, and the town car slowed to a stop. Nash turned in his seat to face her. "It isn't like here. So many people from all over the world come to study back home, we're used to differences of all kinds. It must be hard living in a land with so much sameness that any deviation at all stands out."

She nodded but couldn't find her voice to respond. Nash sobered, then straightened his hat and exited to help her out of the vehicle.

"I shouldn't be too long," she said.

He tipped his hat to her. "Take as long as you like, miss."

The warm feeling she had from her conversation with Nash faded as she approached the camp. Apprehension about the minuscule progress she'd made with the caldera made her steps heavy.

She paused, noticing activity at the entrance. A familiar-looking boxy vehicle was parked right next to the tents. When a woman in blue robes emerged from the back, Jasminda's heart nearly stopped. Two Sisters wrestled with boxes at the back of the wagon, but she could not see their faces. The Sisters wrangled their load to the ground while soldiers stood several feet away, watching, not offering assistance of any kind. As much as Jasminda wanted to stay rooted to the spot, she could not.

"Do you need help?" she called out.

The women turned, startled. One was middle-aged with an austere face. The other was Aunt Vanesse. Jasminda's throat closed up to be once again face-to-face with her, but no recognition sparked in her aunt's eyes.

"That would be lovely," the older woman said, her musical voice at odds with her strict appearance. "You speak Elsiran quite well."

Jasminda peered into the back of the wagon and began unloading the heavy boxes. "It was my first tongue." Her back was turned, so she could only imagine the women's surprise.

She dropped her load and looked over. The older Sister's brow was furrowed, but Vanesse's expression was quite blank. Jasminda went to grab another box.

"How does that come to be?" the older Sister asked.

"My mother was Elsiran." With a great tug, she slid a crate forward into her arms then turned to stack it with the others. Brushing off her palms, she chanced a glance at her aunt, whose face had grown ashen.

"Jasminda ul-Sarifor," she said, holding out her hands. The older woman greeted her with a polite palm touch. Jasminda turned to Vanesse. After a moment's hesitation, she too offered the greeting, pressing her cool hands against Jasminda's.

"I'm going to see after that captain who promised the use of that dolly," the older Sister said. "I can't imagine where he's gotten to." She was off in a swish of blue fabric, leaving Jasminda alone with her aunt.

Vanesse stared at her mutely, recognition flaring in her eyes. Jasminda stared back. She was glad of the fine clothing Nadal had provided her with and resisted the urge to smooth out her navy-blue silk dress. Standing tall, Jasminda dared her aunt to deny her. The tension of the moment broke when Vanesse let out a gasp, almost like a sob, and rushed forward, wrapping her arms around her niece.

Jasminda was frozen in place as Vanesse squeezed tightly. "You look so much like her," her aunt whispered into her hair.

"No, I don't. But you do." She found the strength to wrap her arms around her aunt and hold on as the woman continued to squeeze.

When Vanesse pulled back, tears were streaming down her face. She raised her hands to cup Jasminda's cheeks. "No, I see her in you. Your chin, your forehead." She stroked each part as she mentioned it, and the tears continued. Jasminda felt them welling in her own eyes, as well.

"Why did you never respond?" Jasminda spoke softly, uncertain she wanted to know the answer.

Vanesse released Jasminda and wiped at her eyes, sniffling. "Come, let's sit." She motioned to a log in the grass a few metres from the wagon. They settled in next to one another, and Jasminda studied the burn scars marring her aunt's cheek and jaw.

Vanesse touched her face self-consciously and dipped her head. "Your grandmother did that."

Jasminda's jaw slackened as she struggled to comprehend a mother burning her own child. "Was it an accident?"

Vanesse let out a snort. "No. I was sixteen and she caught me with—" she looked over nervously at Jasminda "—someone she thought unsuitable." After coming upon her aunt's secret in the carriage house, Jasminda could imagine what sort of person her grandmother would find unsuitable.

"Emi had been gone for four years, sending us letter after letter. Mother would burn them, so I started going for walks to meet the postman so I could read them." Her voice hitched. "Mother had told everyone Emi died of a fever out in the Borderlands, but Emi had written letters to her friends telling what really happened. Mother was incensed. So when it looked like I was going to end up an embarrassment, as well—" Vanesse's gaze lengthened. She stared across the field towards the expanse of tents.

"When she came after me with the oil, I thought she wanted to kill me. She doused my bed and then lit the match before I even knew what was happening. Said she wanted to make sure no one at all would steal me away from her. No one would want me. I would never shame her the same way my sister did." Vanesse's hand fluttered near her face, never quite touching her scars.

Jasminda's breathing was shallow. A tear escaped as she took in her aunt's misery. "But the Sisterhood. How could she support you traveling the country with them to aid the settlers?"

Vanesse straightened and wiped her eyes again. "The Sisterhood is respectable. The Queen has shown us her blessing many times. Providing for the less fortunate is something that brings some honor to the family. The irony that Emi met your father while in the Sisterhood, is perhaps lost on Mother. Or maybe she just believes that I'm too ugly to be a temptation."

She dropped her head. "I'm sorry I haven't been able to be there for you. Mother is very . . ." She searched for a word, fear clouding her eyes.

"You're afraid of her," Jasminda said, growing cold as a guilty look of assent crossed her aunt's face. She could not fault the woman. How would she feel if she'd been burned by her own mother for falling out of line? Her grandmother must have a tenuous hold on her sanity to do such a thing.

"How did you come to be here? Where are you living?" Vanesse asked, changing the subject.

Jasminda told her of the events leading her to Rosira and of her visit to her grandmother's house. Vanesse listened to the story, her horrified expression growing with each twist and turn.

"You mustn't ever go back to that house," she said, desperation sharpening her features. Vanesse's fear was a noose around her neck. Any anger Jasminda had held toward the woman dissolved into pity. The family Jasminda had known was kind and loving. She'd never once feared either of her parents and couldn't imagine doing so.

"I don't plan to go back." The reassurance caused the haunted look in her aunt's eyes to vanish.

"Good, good." Vanesse rubbed Jasminda's hand between her own. "I hope that we can get to know one another. I would very much like that."

"Me, too." This was why she'd come to Rosira in the first place.

"There's a place we can meet where no one will see. Though you may have to invest in a good-sized cloak, or perhaps some face paint so you're not recognized."

Whatever else Vanesse said was lost to the rushing in Jasminda's ears. Her aunt could only get to know her in secret. Hidden corridors, cloaks, and face paint. Late-night rendezvous and secret trysts. Was there no one who would bring their acquaintance with her out into the light of day?

She pulled her hand out of Vanesse's grasp and stood on shaky legs. "I'm supposed to meet with some of the refugees now. I have to go."

Someone else's secret. Someone else's shame.

She left behind the question on Vanesse's face and the call of her name on the woman's lips.

JASMINDA WASN'T CERTAIN she'd be able to locate the tent where the Keepers had met the previous day. And even if she did, would any of them be there? They might have changed locations to maintain their secrecy. Especially if the camp really housed spies for the True Father. Though this was hard for her to believe—every face she saw seemed more downtrodden than the last. She fingered her silk dress, now self-conscious of the finery she was afforded because she happened to have been born on a certain side of the border.

A light rain began to fall as she wandered the lanes of the camp. Some of the tents had what she assumed were Lagrimari characters painted on them, but none matched the characters she'd seen on the Keepers tent.

Then she spotted Osar, playing with a group of children in the entrance to a tent. He grinned wide and waved, putting a smile on her face.

Around the corner, she found Rozyl chatting with three of the Keepers from the mountain. She dreaded asking the woman for anything, but she had little choice. The rain was falling harder now, and the thin fabric of her dress absorbed the water, chilling her. As she approached, a ripple of unease charged the air. The Keepers had their faces to the sky, as if they were listening to something.

"What's wrong?" Jasminda said, but her question fell on deaf ears.

She reached for Rozyl, brushing her hand to get the woman's attention. A violent press of Earthsong rose and slammed against her like a physical push. Rozyl turned, her surprise indicating she'd felt the force, as well, and hadn't caused it. Jasminda couldn't separate herself and was plunged directly into the flow of Rozyl's connection to Earthsong.

Jasminda cried out, suffocated by the maelstrom of energies of so many people around her. Pain, white and hot, lanced through her body, blinding her. Somehow she had linked to Rozyl's power, and it felt like being crushed into paste. Suddenly, a filter emerged between her and Rozyl's Song, like a window shade pulled down to hide the glare of the sun. It muted the volume of the energy, and the vise around her chest loosened.

She was still uncomfortable but could now pick out details in the Earthsong surrounding them. The nearby soldiers—tension rippling through them, fear and distrust pulsing like blood in their veins. The fear of the refugees, the hope and the hopelessness. Their heavy hearts and minds.

Finally, she was able to tear her hand from Rozyl's. She coughed and gasped, relieved to break the connection. Rozyl regarded her with disbelief.

"How did you link with me?" Rozyl said, looking at her like her hair were made of spiders.

Jasminda shook her head. She'd had no intention of linking with anyone.

"And why did you not shield yourself?"

"Shield?" So that must be how Earthsingers coexisted in large numbers. Again, Jasminda shook her head. "My father was the only other Earthsinger I knew. He did not teach me." She wondered what other lessons she had missed.

"Your Song is so weak."

Jasminda shrugged, her breathing slowly returning to normal. "My brothers could not sing at all."

"Half-breed. I don't know why it must be you," she said with disgust, and took off down one of the wider paths through the tents.

"I don't know what just happened, but I didn't ask for it, either. I didn't ask to be the only one the caldera will work for," Jasminda called out, racing after Rozyl's quick steps. The other woman ignored her, and soon they emerged at the camp's entrance where a crowd had grown. Rozyl disappeared into the throng of people.

Still shaking from the unexpected force of the link, Jasminda strained for a better view of what had captured everyone's attention. "What's happening?" she whispered to a woman cradling a sleeping baby.

"I think they're holding back the rations."

Jasminda moved to the front of the group to verify. Vanesse and two other Sisters stood near a line of soldiers arguing with the captain. At their feet were the crates of rice, potatoes, and vegetables sitting out in the rain.

"You cannot keep rations from these people. I won't allow it," the oldest Sister said.

Jasminda approached, mindful of why Jack had wanted her here in the first place. A few other refugees broke away from the crowd and drew nearer to the soldiers, as well.

"Is there a problem delivering the rations, Captain?" Jasminda said.

The man looked at her sharply, evidently surprised at her command of Elsiran. He glanced at her dress, obviously expensive even in its wet state and so different from the threadbare fabric covering the refugees. She'd not seen this man before, and he probably had no idea as to her identity, but he could plainly see she was different than the rest.

"This witchcraft will not be tolerated," the captain said.

Jasminda crossed her arms and stood her ground. "Exactly what witchcraft are you referring to?"

The man glowered at her, rain dripping off his nose. Jasminda looked around, searching for what could have angered the soldiers into withholding the rations. Finally, she looked down at her dress, clinging to her wet body. The rain had stopped where she stood, yet it still poured upon the captain standing less than a metre away. She looked to the sky—overcast—and then around at the camp. About a dozen metres of land were dry in the midst of the rain.

The explanation turned out to be simple. Several lines of laundry had been run between the tents near the entrance of the camp. Someone had cast a small spell, most likely to avoid having the clean laundry rained upon.

"It's just a spell for the laundry, Captain," she said, pointing to the lines of clothes.

The man's face hardened. "It's evil. The whole lot of you *grols* are evil." He spat, aiming at Jasminda's feet on the dry part of the ground. The Sisters raised their voices in protest.

A boy of about twelve or thirteen came to stand next to her. She did a double take, recognizing him as the child who'd aided the settlers in Baalingrove. On her other side, two old men she hadn't seen before regarded the confrontation warily.

Outrage overcame the pain of the words she'd heard so many times before. "You have no right to withhold the rations, Captain. You have orders to feed these people. Where is your honor?"

The captain's face contorted. "You'll not speak to me of honor, witch."

"Just leave the food here. We'll carry it in ourselves." She pointed and moved toward the nearest crate. The boy at her side approached, as well.

"Stay back, witch. Don't come any closer." The captain's hand hovered near the pistol strapped to his waist.

Jasminda stilled, but the boy kept moving, not understanding the captain's command. In the space of a heartbeat, the captain pulled his sidearm and pointed it at the boy. The entire line of soldiers drew their rifles on the gathered refugees. The Sisters, startled, took several steps back.

"No!" Jasminda screamed. In Lagrimari, she shouted, "Stop!"

The boy looked over at her, brows drawn. His eyes glittered, warm and golden brown, lighter than most Lagrimari's. His face still held the roundness of youth, but those enchanting eyes were hard.

The boy took another defiant step toward the food. Somewhere close-by, a woman screamed, "Timmyn!" He tensed, hearing his name, then took another step.

Time slowed as Jasminda shook her head and opened herself to Earthsong, struggling to work out the shield technique she'd witnessed Rozyl use during their unexpected link. It worked just enough so that the other energies weren't screaming in her head, drowning out her thoughts and severing her connection, but she was far from proficient. The soldiers' emotions were a whirlwind of fear and aggression. Too far gone to be soothed by Earthsong, even if she'd been strong enough to do so.

She reached out to Timmyn and found the well of pain to be deep. He was in a place beyond hearing, yet she still wished she had the power to push a message to him the way Osar could. *You don't have to prove anything*, she wanted to tell him. *We will not let you starve here. I know the prince, and he would never allow it.* Her helplessness crushed her as she felt his hurt.

When the shot rang out, Jasminda lost her connection to Earthsong. She grabbed at the air in front of her, too far away to catch him as Timmyn fell backward onto the ground. A deep-crimson stain ballooned across the fabric of his shirt. Jasminda looked up at the caption in horror. His face was an emotionless mask.

She fell to her knees. Her breath came in short, shallow bursts. Tears blurred her vision. She vaguely registered a group of refugees taking the boy away to be healed. Through the fog she heard Vanesse speaking somewhere close-by. Her words were just a jumble of sounds that didn't penetrate. Time ceased to exist. All she could hear was the crack of the gun and the thud of Timmyn's body hitting the earth, over and over again.

Wetness on her shoulder brought back her awareness. Nash stood over her, rain dripping from his jacket. He held out a hand. She took it and struggled to her feet. Her legs were stiff from kneeling for who knows how long.

The soldiers parted for them as Nash led her back to the town car. Jasminda looked over her shoulder. The rest of the crowd had long ago disappeared into their tents; all that remained was a ghost town.

CHAPTER EIGHT

BEDLAM STRIKES REFUGEE CAMP

(continued from page 1)
An ambassador from the palace to the refugee camp, Ms.
ul-Sarifor was a witness to the attack by the refugees
on Elsiran military personnel. While she did not take
part in the attempted mutiny, a witness reports that
her presence may have inflamed tensions and emboldened
the Lagrimari to pursue their assault.

According to sources within the palace, Ms. ul-Sarifor is
purported to be an Elsiran citizen of mixed heritage and
was specifically requested by the Prince Regent to
initiate diplomacy with the foreigners on our soil.

Jack crumpled the thin newsprint in his fist. He knew very well there had been no attempted mutiny. The evening papers had gone from printing gossip and long-ago scandals to outright lies. He regretted more than ever not being able to make it to Jasminda's rooms the night before. Palace business had kept him up late into the night, and he'd fallen asleep at his desk, surrounded by paperwork. He hadn't realized she'd been so close to the child's shooting.

News of the incident had enraged Jack the moment he'd heard. The captain had been arrested immediately, and while the boy had made a full recovery due to the camp's Earthsingers, Jack was resolved to court martial the offending officer. A decision that would no doubt be met with opposition.

The door to his office opened, and Usher stepped in. Faint music filtered in through the open door.

"You will have to at least make an appearance, young sir." Usher stood looking reprovingly at him.

"I don't know why they didn't cancel the bloody thing. Now is no time for a ball."

"Third Breach Day falls on the same day every year. They cannot cancel an entire ball because the Prince Regent is in a foul temper."

Jack stood, rolling down his shirtsleeves and buttoning them. "Don't I have the right to be in a temper when unarmed children are being shot? When this entire country seems to have fallen victim to lunacy? At what point, I ask you, am I permitted to be upset?"

Usher picked up Jack's discarded formal dinner jacket and held it out for him. He slipped his arms through and focused on working up some joviality for the ball he was being forced to attend. It wouldn't do for him to scowl his way through, giving more fodder for the papers. Only one thing would truly make him smile, though.

"Is she coming?" he asked, unable to keep the hope from his voice.

"Would it be wise for her to?"

Jack's shoulders slumped.

"She would prefer not to be at the center of any undue attention. Isn't that what you agreed to?"

"I know, I know. It's just . . ." He sighed and checked his appearance in the mirror. He looked tired, older than he had even a week ago. For a moment, he had an inkling of how this position could have turned his father into a brute. Jack could feel his edges hardening. The bit of himself that he'd always held back when he'd been in the army, that person he would have been if he'd been born to a baker or a farmer had always remained inside him, catching the odd glimpse of sunlight in stolen moments when he hadn't had to flex his muscles as the High Commander. But that hidden self was now being choked. The only times he could seem to breathe anymore were when he was with Jasminda, and even then they had to remain hidden, secret. He couldn't acknowledge anything true about himself, and he was afraid it was changing him.

He stalked down the hallways toward the cacophony of the ball. The ballroom had been decorated, somewhat garishly, in orange, the color of

Third Breach Day. Each of the seven breaches had a holiday attached to them, initially as a memorial for all that had been lost in the wars, but more recently it was just an excuse for a celebration. None were as lavish as the yearly Festival of the Founders where all work ceased for three days, but each Breach Day was commemorated by excessive decorations in the color of the holiday and a palace ball for the aristocracy.

Jack entered the corridor outside the rear of the ballroom where a dozen butlers were organizing trays of appetizers. The lead butler did a double take and rushed over, admonishing him, in the most respectful way, for being in the servants' hall. Jack brushed off the man's request to stop the band and make a formal announcement of the Prince Regent's arrival.

"I just want to watch for a bit," Jack said. "I promise you can announce me once this dance is finished. I'd hate to interrupt." The butler's obsequious expression barely hid his displeasure at this interruption to the normal order of things, but he backed off, allowing Jack to peek through the curtains separating the hall from the ballroom.

This was the vantage from where he'd watched these events when he was too young to attend and still longed to. The elegance, the glamor—long ago he'd found them fascinating. Now all he wanted to do was escape.

The band played one of the up-tempo, syncopated melodies that had become popular of late. Couples on the dance floor marched back and forth to the beat of the music. He wasn't the best at these modern dances but enjoyed them more than the tamer, boring classic steps.

A delicate fragrance reached his nostrils, and for a moment, his heart rose in his chest. But the light feminine scent wasn't Jasminda. He turned to find Lizvette standing next to him.

"How did I know I'd find you hiding back here?" she said, a smile on her lips. There was still tension around her eyes, but Jack knew that would take time to fade.

"What can I say? I'm terribly predictable."

She stepped to him, linking an arm through his and peering out at the crowded dance floor. "Perhaps *consistent* is a better word."

"Yes, I far prefer that. And I'm not hiding. I'm biding my time."

She chuckled and pulled him toward the doorway. "Come, Your Grace.

There is no time like the present. And yes, I would love to dance."

He barely masked his grimace and followed her out past the bewildered lead butler just as the band finished the current song. The man scampered up to the microphone on the bandstand and rushed through the recitation of Jack's titles at top speed as all present bowed.

Jack suppressed a groan as the band started in on a tame, traditional melody. He danced the long-practiced steps with Lizvette, holding her stiffly. Just beyond the dance floor, glass doors opened to the terrace and gardens beyond. A cool breeze filtered in, reminding him of his time in the mountains.

He could almost imagine he was holding Jasminda. They had never danced, though. Perhaps he would have a phonograph delivered to her rooms so he could hold her against him and feel her heartbeat as they moved in time to the music. The thought loosened the tension that was binding him. He would dance a few more songs then steal away to be with her.

"My father came to see you, did he not?"

Jack tuned back into the room, almost having forgotten it was Lizvette he held. "Ah, yes. He told you about that. I'm sorry he had to bother you with that business. Don't worry. The thought never crossed my mind."

She grew rigid beneath his fingertips. "Would it be so bad?" Sad eyes blinked up at him, and he missed a step, nearly bumping into a burly man dancing inelegantly beside him.

"What are you saying?" He was barely able to get the words out through his shock.

"I know the press has been harsh . . . with everything about your mother and this dreadful business with the Lagrimari. I just— Well, perhaps Father is right. Perhaps I can help."

Her face was open and hopeful. He couldn't sense any guile there, but her words were madness.

"What of Alariq? His memory?"

She lowered her head. "I will always hold Alariq's memory dear. He was truly one of a kind. But wouldn't he want you to be at your best advantage? I think he would want this."

Jack snorted. "My brother would not so much as let me borrow a pair of his shoes, much less his future wife."

"Alariq is dead." Her voice was clipped. "And I am not a pair of shoes." The eyes staring up at him were full of hurt.

"Of course not, Lizvette. I didn't mean to say— I only meant that — Wouldn't Alariq have wanted for you to find love again? Happiness? Not just sacrifice yourself to aid my popularity."

Her expression melted as she looked up at him. "Love?" She said the word like it was a curiosity, some foreign species of fruit that had appeared on her table. Her hand on his arm squeezed gently, then turned into almost a caress. Discomfort swirled within him. "Do you not think something could grow? Here?" She placed a hand on his heart.

The music stopped, and the other couples on the dance floor clapped. Jack drew away from Lizvette, from the unwelcome pressure of her hand on his chest, and turned to give polite applause, as well. He used the moment to gather his thoughts. She was in mourning, perhaps confused. He and Alariq were not much alike, but perhaps she was only grasping for the last threads of him left. He'd known her his whole life . . . at least he thought he knew her.

He bowed to her. "Thank you for the dance." Ignoring the question in her eyes, he rushed off the dance floor to stand near the doors leading to the terrace. The collar of his shirt constricted like a noose. He longed for fresh air to breathe.

"Your Grace," a voice called out behind him. He turned to find a cluster of men from the Merchants' Board regarding him expectantly.

He could see now how the conversation would go: A few minutes of pleasantries, how lovely the ballroom was decorated, how fine the musicians. Then, possibly a round of complaints when he inquired after their families— a son too enthralled by the weekly radio dramas for their liking or a daughter being courted by an unsuitable beau. Then, far too quickly, they would get around to what they really wanted to talk to him about. Some favor or request, with just a nudge so that he recalled how useful their support was and thinly veiled threats of the damage that would take place if that support were withdrawn. Nothing overt, but enough pressure exerted on any joint could eventually cause a break.

The men wrangled from him a promise to consider a proposal to reduce worker wages. He didn't tell them that as soon as the plan escaped their lips he did consider it . . . and found it untenable. No, he smiled and nodded, shook hands and wished them back to wherever they'd come from as quickly as possible. Just when he thought the Queen had finally smiled upon him and the conversation had reached its death throes, a rotund character called Dursall spoke up.

"Quite a shame what happened to that little *grol* boy yesterday."

Jack's jaw clenched at the epithet.

"Well, with so many of them there, something like that was bound to happen," a wine importer named Pindeet said.

"I don't know," said Dursall. "I don't suppose a *grol* is any more likely to commit violence than, say, an Udlander. If they were brought up in a proper environment, I'd think you could almost entirely erase their more barbaric tendencies." The gathered men nodded in agreement. "Speaking of which, what's this I read about an ambassador to the refugees? A Lagrimari woman raised in Elsira?"

Jack chose his words very carefully. "She is Elsiran. Born of a settler and a woman of the Sisterhood."

"Quite unusual," Dursall said. "But it proves my point. Perhaps it is in large part due to the gift of half her parentage, but from all accounts she is well spoken and well groomed. I daresay almost fit for polite society. How do you find her, Your Grace?"

Eight pairs of eyes were trained on him. He tasted each word on his tongue before allowing it to leave his mouth. "In truth, I don't know her that well. In the handful of times in which I've made her acquaintance, I've found her to be quite . . . acceptable." He swallowed.

The conversation continued for a few minutes but was impossible for him to follow. He regretted the words as soon as they'd left his mouth, but what was he to say? To mention that he was in a constant state of longing for her touch, that a day without seeing her was incomplete, that she was the most fearless and impressive woman he had ever encountered would have been more than these old hogs needed to know. Could it ever be enough that *he* knew? That he had these feelings very near to spilling over inside him with no outlet?

He was about to slip out to the terrace when an elderly woman dripping in diamonds, the wife of a former Council member, stopped him to complain about her neighbor's roof. Jack looked longingly at the doors to freedom before plastering on a smile.

SHE HAD ONLY wanted to watch, perhaps from a balcony where she would not be spotted, but the ballroom had only one floor. The best place to observe without being seen was from the shadows of the terrace. The billowing folds of the curtains hid her body, clad in the ball gown Nadal had insisted she put on, just in case she changed her mind about attending. The dress was midnight blue and let her fade into the night. She was a ghost and felt as diaphanous as one, as though her existence was mere myth. Jack's words to those men echoed in her head and seized her heart in an icy grip.

Last night had been the first night without him—the first of many she would surely experience. Soon she wouldn't even be able to watch him in secret. He would be only a memory.

A voice from behind startled her. "Not going in?" Calladeen's low timbre raised gooseflesh on her arms.

"No. A bit crowded for me," Jasminda said, keeping her back to the man.

"I can imagine."

She turned at his condescending tone. With a glare, she shouldered past him and dashed down the short staircase to the garden. A nearly full moon hung overhead, outshining the lanterns hung every metre along the gravel paths. Calladeen's slow footsteps clicked behind her on the steps. At the bottom, she turned to face him.

"What do you want?" she bit out.

"A young woman should not be walking the exterior of the palace unescorted. Even here there are unsavory characters around." He spread his arms to indicate the potential villains lurking about, but the only unsavory person here was him. "I'm sure our Prince Regent would never forgive me if harm were to befall you."

A blade of fear jabbed her, but she straightened her shoulders and stood tall. She had only to scream and palace guards would come running. Not to mention the open doors of the ballroom just above them. Calladeen would not dare make good on his subtle threat, if indeed that's what it was.

"I appreciate your concern for my welfare, but I am in no need of escort from you."

He quirked an eyebrow. "You have had a stimulating few days here, I'm told."

She remained silent. Surely he could not be so indelicate as to be discussing what she thought he was.

"The incident at the refugee camp? According to the paper, you were quite near the action."

She gripped the fabric of her dress in tight fists to stop the shaking of her hands as the images flooded her. "If by *stimulating*, you mean *horrifying*, then you are correct. That soldier had no honor . . . shooting a child."

He drew uncomfortably close to her, but Jasminda refused to step back. "And you feel the Prince Regent is acting honorably in subjecting the captain to a court martial that could result in his execution?"

"Of course. That man would have killed the boy for no reason if there had been no Earthsingers present. The prince is doing the right thing. *He* is honorable."

"It is a shame that honor is not the most important quality in a leader."

Jasminda blinked, choosing to take the bait. "What is a more important quality?"

"Decisiveness. The ability to do what needs to be done. Leadership is about making hard choices and not indulging one's every whim." He looked her up and down as she strained to remain poised under the inspection. "For example, bringing home a stray pet is not in line with effective leadership."

Jasminda's jaw tensed. "Say what you think you need to say to me."

His slow smile froze the blood in her veins. "Very well. You may be unsuitable, but you are by no means unintelligent. Let me be clear: you make him weaker. He was not strong to begin with, and Elsira's greatest tragedy was the loss of Alariq, a man truly fit to lead. However, given that we must make the best of what we have and there are no other princes coming out of the woodwork, Jaqros needs to be strong. He needs a princess the people can rally around, not some mongrel whore installed in the palace."

The *crack* rang out before she even thought about it. Her hand stung, and she stared at it as if it belonged to someone else. She had never slapped someone so hard before. She had never slapped anyone ever.

Calladeen's eyes narrowed. The fear snaking inside her enlarged as a cruel expression slid onto his face.

"Zavros." Jack stepped into view from behind Calladeen, and Jasminda gasped, her moment of alarm fleeing with sudden relief. He was all warrior, his face cut from stone. He stepped toe to toe with Calladeen, speaking in a low and deadly voice, forcing the taller man backward a step. "If you ever so much as look in her direction again, I will personally ensure your eligibility for the Order of Eunuchs. If you have a problem with me, you bring it to me. You do not speak to her. You do not look at her. As far as you are concerned, she does not exist."

Calladeen's sneer melted. His eyes widened in fear. The only movement in his body was the shudder of his throat as he swallowed.

"Now get out of my sight."

The man lowered into a hasty bow before fleeing up the stairs. Jack turned to Jasminda, reaching for her. She longed to fall into his arms but took a step back. His forehead crinkled in confusion.

"Are you all right?"

Shaking her head, she took another step away from him. Gratitude and self-preservation fought within her. "That will come back to haunt you."

He dropped his arms. "I don't care."

"Yes, you do." She drew her shaking arms around her, finally registering the cold of the night.

"Jasminda, you know I would not let anyone harm you. You're too important to me."

"Me? Important? I thought I was merely *acceptable*." She watched understanding dawn on his face. The misery that followed it tore at her, but his words had stung.

"You heard that? You know I didn't mean—"

"Shhh. Someone may overhear. Voices carry up there, don't they?" She motioned toward the terrace.

"Yours does when you're upset," he said, his eyes full of sadness.

Her steps were wobbly as she continued backing away from him. "Go back to your ball, Your Grace. Lizvette may want another dance, and you cannot disappoint your people." She turned then so he would not see the tears overflow their barriers. She knew she wasn't being fair, but nothing about this situation was fair, nothing about her life had ever been.

Leaving the music and the finery behind, she ran along the garden to the eastern entrance of the palace and enlisted the help of a passing servant to lead her back to her rooms. Once inside, she locked the door and dragged over a heavy armchair to prop in front of it. She would spend the night alone again. She had better start getting used to it.

"LADY OOLA, ARE you ready to begin?" My cousin Vaaryn stands in the center of the amphitheater that is the Assembly Room. Rows of benches spiral around him, filled with the other children of the Founders. He is aged and stooping, the eldest of the Thirds. Next to him, spine as rigid and unyielding as his face, sits my beloved Eero.

When I shudder, Yllis squeezes my hand. I stand, all the heavier for the weight pressing against my heart, and force myself to look upon my twin.

"Eero, son of Peedar, second-born to the ninth child of the Founders, what say you to the crimes of which you are accused?" My voice sounds strong, but inside I quiver from nerves. The closest relative of the accused must stand up for him in Assembly, but I do not want to be here, not as observer, judge, or as his Advocate.

"My only crime, *sister*"—the word is a sneer falling from his mouth—"was being born Silent in a world of Songbearers." He is not chained or bound in any way and crosses his arms in front of him defiantly.

I clear my throat and take a breath, still amazed at the cruel way he speaks to me now. "Your crime is the kidnapping of Sayya, Fourth descendent of the Founders. Do you deny this?"

He looks straight ahead, his gaze boring into the wall. "As a Third descendent, I see no reason to dignify this proceeding with a response."

I swallow. "As you well know, only Songbearers are counted in the line of descendents. The Silent are not—"

"Did you not gift me part of your Song, *sister*? Does that not make me a

Songbearer?" The accusation in his voice cuts me. There are so many feelings swirling inside—anger, pain, despair, even hatred. The person before me cannot be my beloved brother. He simply cannot be.

I step closer and feel Yllis rise beside me, lending his support, as always. "You are not a Songbearer, and it was my mistake to use that spell," I say. "I take responsibility for that. Because I love you and would do anything for you."

"Anything?" The venom in that one word burns.

"Anything but give you more of the power you abused. You forced me to cut you off by your actions."

"I was innovating, the way the Cantors do."

"You set things out of balance. Earthsong is not to be used for better prices in the marketplace or to cheat at cards. You cannot ruin a crop because a farmer insulted you." Tears well even as the anger rears its head. "And you cannot steal a girl away from her bed at night and attempt to force her to gift you her Song! She could not have done so if she wanted to. It is too advanced a spell."

I take a breath and step back, remembering my role as Advocate. "You have heard the accusation and evidence presented against you. And as you have not denied it, now is the time. Unburden your conscience."

He shook his head, and a smirk crossed his face. "You all think you can continue to subjugate us. That the Silent will continue living as second-class citizens for the rest of time. Sayya made me believe that she cared for me, but when I offered for her she could not bear to wed a Silent. And now my own sister forsakes me. This Assembly is a sham. If you want to judge me of a crime, then have my peers judge me. Why are there no Silent in the Assembly? Why must we make do with the scraps of life while Songbearers reap all the benefits?"

"What are you talking about, Eero?" I crouch down, near enough to look into his eyes, yet far enough so that he cannot reach out and strike me. The fact that I even think this is a possibility is sad proof of how much has changed over the past two seasons. Last summer he was the other half of my heart, but by the time the leaves fell from the trees, he had become my enemy.

"There are no Silent in the Assembly because only a Songbearer can read a man's heart, can know the truth buried within. How can a Silent judge? What scraps has life given you? We ate at the same table, all our lives. What inequities have you suffered, brother, that makes you hate us so?" My voice cracks on this last sentiment.

His eyes harden but still he does not look at me. His jaw is set, and his body may as well be made of stone. As his Advocate, I cannot use Earthsong to determine his state of mind, but as his twin I would never need to.

Yllis pulls on my shoulder gently, and I allow him to lead me back to my seat. Vaaryn struggles to his feet and calls upon Cadda, Sayya's mother and Advocate, to have the final word.

"It is so rare for us to hold one of us in judgment, crime in our land is so infrequent. The guidance of the Founders steers us toward mercy." Her voice is soothing and calm. "Though my daughter was troubled greatly by Eero's actions, she was not harmed. We ask for his captivity so that a Healer may give him the aid and comfort he so obviously needs."

Eero snorts and rolls his eyes.

Vaaryn stands before Eero, and suddenly my brother's expression freezes. He rises into the air, his arms locked to his sides, his legs still bent in the sitting position. For criminal proceedings, a random sampling of nine Assembly members serve as judges, communicating using Earthsong to make their decision. Eero floats for a few moments until Vaaryn speaks again.

"The Assembly agrees with the recommendation of Cadda. It is decided that Eero, son of Peedar, will be delivered to the Healers, who will tend to his mental instability until a time wherein he is determined to again be in his right mind."

"Be it so," the Assembly says in unison.

I do not want it to be so, but I cannot change reality. I watch my brother float away and wonder when I will see him again.

"WHAT IS THE meaning of this?" Pugeros said as he stalked sulkily into the Council Room. "Summoning us at this ungodly hour?"

The sun had not yet crested the horizon. The ministers were likely cranky, and perhaps a bit hungover from the ball the previous night, but Jack's exhaustion had nothing to do with alcohol. "We will begin once everyone arrives."

The grumbling around the table continued in the background, but he paid it little mind. Instead he focused on pushing the weariness back, tucking the hours of sleepless worry away to the far reaches of his mind. He didn't want to box those emotions up, but he needed the disquiet of this latest disaster to distract him from the pulsing ache that had started when he recognized Jasminda's heartbreak. But she was not his only woe. What had started as a pebble was now an avalanche, and he'd once again been swept away by its sheer force.

When the last minister arrived and took his seat, Jack took a deep breath. He opened the folder before him and pulled out a curling sheet of paper.

"I received this late last night. It appeared in my offices. And when I say *appeared*, I mean it popped into existence in midair right over my desk."

Gasps came from around the table. Jack had worked late after being denied entry to Jasminda's room. He'd risked being seen in the hallway outside her door for long minutes before finally returning to his offices. Not long after, the paper had hovered until Jack plucked it from the air, feeling the residual vibrations of Earthsong on the single sheet.

"It pertains to the True Father's terms for peace."

Another round of gasps and murmurs resonated.

Jack ran his fingers across the letter. He could recite it by heart now, had spent the early-morning hours thinking and worrying and reading it over and over again. He peered at every shocked face around the table, then repeated each word.

"*It has come to the attention of the beloved leadership of the Republic of Lagrimar that preparations for war are being made by the Principality of Elsira. While We assert Our right to pursue the protection of Our people against the ambition and reckless dominance of all outsiders, We acknowledge that a peaceful and permanent solution to the many years of strife between our lands would be advantageous.*

"*Our offer is peace in exchange for the immediate return of every Lagrimari within the borders of the Elsiran principality. Our people are Our greatest resource, and it is within Our right to negotiate for their safe return to home soil.*

"The entire power of Our crown is united behind this generous offer of peace. Once Our people are returned, a guarantee will be made to honor all current borders in perpetuity for the length of Our reign and to immediately cease and desist in any actions that may be deemed by the Principality of Elsira as acts of war.

"In witness whereof We have hereto set Our hand the eighth day of the tenth month this five hundred and twelfth year of Our reign."

Silence descended. Jack released the paper and let it fall back onto the table.

"The refugees," Minister Nirall said under his breath.

"Yes," Jack replied. "He's promising to abandon whatever scheme he has for the Mantle if we return them."

Calladeen leaned forward, not meeting Jack's eyes. "But why all of a sudden? Of what military value are they?"

Nirall shook his head. "Women, children, old men. Some of the children may have powerful witchcraft, but would that prompt the offer of permanent peace?"

"It seems the path forward is clear," Pugeros said. Every head in the room turned toward him. "We must return them," he said, wilting under the scrutiny.

"Return them?" Nirall asked, aghast.

"What is a handful of savages compared to peace?"

Jack ground his teeth together. "And what makes you think the True Father would keep this promise of peace? What confidence do we have in his word?"

"We have negotiated peace treaties before," Pugeros said.

"And they have all been broken. Whether in five years, fifty, or one hundred there is always another breach!" Jack slammed a hand on the table for emphasis. "He wants out of that Sovereign-forsaken desert he's been stuck in. That hasn't changed. What happens if we return the refugees and the Mantle falls anyway? He will be that much more powerful before he comes to invade us. We have no leverage here."

"It is a risk," Stevenot said thoughtfully.

"A great one," said Nirall, adjusting the spectacles on his face. "We will need time to consider the ramifications. Let us bring this to a vote tomorrow." He looked to Jack for confirmation. Jack gave his assent but stayed seated as the rest of the men filed out.

He did not move for a long time.

JASMINDA JUMPED AT the knock on the door. Nadal had just taken away her breakfast tray and the drumming did not have the rapid cadence of Jack's knock. She approached with caution, mindful of Calladeen's menacing tone the night before.

"Who's there?"

"Miss Jasminda, it's Usher."

She relaxed and opened the door, glad to see him. His gray head and kind face were welcome sights. Over the past week he'd delivered notes from Jack, assisted her in finding the library and helped in other small ways.

"Please, sit," she said, leading him to her favorite place in front of the fire.

"Thank you, miss." The smile in his eyes was edged with sorrow. "I overstep my bounds a great deal by coming here."

"Jack did not send you?" She hadn't recognized the bubble of hope blossoming within her until it suddenly deflated.

"Not precisely. But I have looked after him since he was born, and I know how his mind works."

He tapped his fingers on the armrest, clearly choosing his words carefully.

"Prince Edvard, Jack's father, was not an easy man. Alariq's mother was his true love and when she died, something in him changed. He remarried, but Jack and his mother were not well treated."

Usher sat back in his chair, clasping his hands before him. Jasminda hung on his every word and movement, eager for this glimpse into the boy Jack had been.

"It did not help that he was a peculiar child, given to flights of imagination. Did you know he painted? From a very young age he was able to create the most beautiful landscapes you've ever seen. It was quite a remarkable gift."

"Can I see them? Are they hanging in the palace somewhere?" She had been right when she first met Jack and thought him an artist. Something about his soul was far too bright to have been made for the military.

Usher lowered his head. "All of his paintings were destroyed. Burned by his father shortly before Jack was sent away to train. He did not paint again."

Jasminda sucked in a breath.

"Princess Rienne, his mother, slowly wilted, becoming more and more withdrawn, hiding away from society. When Jack would come home to visit, she would rally a bit, but he did not know how bad it had gotten until after Edvard's death. Even before then, the rumors and gossip flowed. Her bizarre behavior, skipping important functions, acting oddly when she did appear. By the time of Edvard's death, she was being openly vilified in the press, some going so far as to blame her for the prince's heart attack."

Usher rubbed the bridge of his nose, then locked his gaze on her. "When she left, she took a piece of that boy with her. He was only ten years old and blamed himself for not protecting his mother from his father, and from the rest of the country, as well. The press, the gossipmongers—in her absence, the brunt of their scrutiny fell on him, and it has followed him ever since."

Jasminda nodded, as the reason for Usher's visit became clear. "He wants to protect me."

"As much as he can, yes. He needs it."

Her throat ached for the boy he had been and the man he had become. She wiped away the single tear that trickled down her face. "Where is he?"

USHER LED HER through the bowels of the palace, down many steep staircases, each older than the last. Here, the original stone walls and floors had not been plastered over or carpeted. Kerosene lamps instead of electric shone dimly, lending an acrid tinge to the cool air, though to Jasminda's mind, torches would not have been out of place.

"This is the oldest part of the palace, Miss Jasminda. It is used exclusively by the Prince Regent, and none but his most trusted are allowed entry."

Something odd brushed against her senses. The energy of this place was almost overwhelming. She opened herself the tiniest bit to Earthsong, once again testing out the shielding technique. The crush of the city hovered in her periphery, but an even stronger force snapped her connection shut. She gasped and wobbled on her feet. Usher reached out to steady her.

"I'm all right, I just— There's something odd about this place."

Usher grew solemn. "Come and see."

The hallway in which they stood ended with a door. He pushed it open with some difficulty and motioned her through. Giving him a quizzical look, she stepped cautiously and found her feet sliding down almost immediately. The floor was like a bowl; the inside of the room a white sphere with the door hanging in the middle. Candles glowed eerily from little alcoves notched into curved walls made of no material she could fathom. Everything was smooth and white, but the shadows from the candles flickered gloomily.

Jack knelt on one knee at the bottom of the bowl, underneath a long, white capsule floating in midair. The smooth, seamless surface of the capsule was made of the same strange material as the walls. The object resembled an elongated egg, about six feet in length. It hovered courtesy of an ancient, intensely powerful spell that tingled the edges of her senses like static electricity.

Jack rose, facing her as she found her footing and gingerly stepped down the concave floor. Exhaustion wearied his features, but his expression brightened at the sight of her. She slid into his arms, and he held her so tightly she could scarcely breathe. But she did not complain. Finally, he released the embrace, stroked her face, and kissed her.

"I'm so sorry," he whispered.

"No, don't be. I should apologize. I cannot change the rules we both agreed upon." She was instantly lost in the depths of his eyes and wanted to stay there.

"I don't want there to be any rules for us. I just wish—" He squeezed her tight to his chest again, and she relaxed against him.

"Are we where I think we are?"

Jack lifted his head, looking up at the floating capsule. "The resting place of the Queen Who Sleeps."

She stared in awe. "But this chamber is sacred. I should not be here."

"Not even the Sisterhood may come down here—only the Prince

Regent and those closest to him." He took her hand and pulled her directly underneath the Queen's encased form, then led her to kneel with him. "We come to seek Her counsel and wisdom, to pray for the knowledge and strength to lead in Her stead."

She wrenched her gaze from the smooth surface of the Queen's tomb. Not tomb, for She slept only, and if the Promise was true, She would one day awaken. Jasminda looked at Jack, his expression heartbreaking.

She ran her fingers through his somewhat disheveled hair. "What is happening?"

He shook his head and grabbed both of her hands in his. Her heart caught in her chest as he told her of the letter from the True Father and the terrible demands.

"And the Council will take a vote?" she said, incredulous.

"Tomorrow." His voice was solemn.

Tears stung her eyes at the thought of all it had taken for the refugees to make it to Elsira in the first place. Only to be sent back . . . It was unthinkable, but she knew too well how little value a Lagrimari life held here.

"And there is a chance the Council will vote to send them back?"

"I can only hope that Nirall does not follow suit with the rest of them. As of now, he is the holdout. If all the ministers agree, my options are very limited. The Prince Regent cannot override a unanimous Council vote."

"There would be nothing you could do?"

He closed his eyes. "Only invoke Prince's Right."

"And Prince's Right would dissolve the Council?" She now wished she'd paid more attention to the Elsiran civics and history lessons her mother had given her.

Jack nodded slowly. "And label me a tyrant. I would be only the second Prince Regent in Elsira's history to do so."

"And what happened to the first?"

"He was beheaded in a coup."

Jasminda took a deep breath, her heart torn over his impossible choice. Deep within her Song, the spell surrounding the Queen's encasement pulsed. "And has She given any counsel?"

He shook his head. "She has not blessed my dreams. I do not think I hold Her favor. I pray mostly for Her awakening to save this land from me."

"Jack," she whispered, wrapping her arms around him and drawing him closer. "You are a good prince. You are selfless and fearless."

His head dropped. "I am constantly afraid."

She grabbed his chin and tilted his head up to face her. "But you rise above it."

He smiled grimly. "Even you are too good for me."

"Nonsense," she said and pressed her lips to his. He kissed her back greedily, holding her head firm in his grip. Gasping for air, she pulled back and rested her forehead on his. Her fingers found his head again, rubbing his scalp gently until he relaxed a fraction.

"What I can't figure out is why he wants the refugees back," he said. "Only a fraction of them have their Songs. Beyond using them to increase his power, of what value are they?"

Jasminda had made a promise, one she'd intended to keep, but this new threat changed the situation. This chamber was the most secure location in all of Rosira. She felt no betrayal when she reached into her pocket and retrieved the bundle.

"He wants this," she said, unwrapping the cloth, careful not to touch the stone. Jack inspected the caldera without reaching for it, a frown marring his face. "This is the reason the Keepers came. They needed to get this away from the True Father. He knows it's here, and he wants it."

"What is it?" His voice was cautious, his brow furrowed. It was as if on some level he could sense the caldera's power.

She told him of Darvyn's discovery of the stone and the Keepers' suspicion that the vision she'd had in the cave and her ability to sing there were linked to her ability to use the caldera and learn to wake the Queen.

"And it's been giving you visions?"

"Yes, though it's going more slowly than I'd like since it depletes my Song each time."

"Jasminda, this could be dangerous! There's no telling what it could be doing to you. You don't know anything about this kind of magic and neither does anyone else."

"But this a chance to get what you want. What the country needs. It's the only chance we have of awakening Her. If I can figure out a way— If I can help even a little, I must."

He leaned back, shaking his head. "No, no, you don't have to. You don't have to risk yourself. What if it hurts you? What if it kills you?"

She leaned back, gazing at him softly. "Then you are the only one who will miss me."

He froze.

Her jaw trembled at his stricken expression. "And if I die to awaken Her, then my life will have meant something to someone."

"You mean something to me already. You mean everything." He grabbed her free hand in both of his, dragging it onto his lap.

"I can't mean everything to you, my darling Jack. You should not let me."

"I cannot help it. It is far too late for that." He lowered his head, bringing his lips to her hand.

"I must keep trying," she said. They sat in silence, both staring at the caldera.

He kissed her hand again, then let it go.

The imprint of his lips burned hot against her skin. "Will you catch me if I fall?" Her voice was breathless.

Tear-filled eyes met hers. "You know I will. You never have to ask."

She swallowed the knot forming in her throat. With a single finger, she stroked the caldera and everything faded to black.

THE ASSEMBLY ROOM grows quiet as all eyes focus on me. Their expectant gazes draw me back to the present. My mind had been aloft, far from this room and out in the early-summer sunshine, feeling the waves gently lapping at my feet. That is how I wanted to spend my birthday, at the sea, as I always have before.

I straighten my shoulders and regard the room. Every face holds a tension it never has held before. And it is all my fault.

"All here are agreed?" I ask, my voice low. I speak out loud as has been the custom during Assembly for the past half a millennia. I will not give in to the paranoia of so many of my cousins gathered here, afraid of eavesdroppers.

We are agreed, murmur many Songs against my consciousness.

"Today is the first day of my twenty-first summer. I am the youngest Third. Vaaryn, you are two hundred years my elder. Your leadership has been unblemished. I am untested. Is this really wise?"

When Father, the last Second and the youngest son of the Founders, passed into the World After, Vaaryn assumed his responsibilities in the Assembly. The idea of leadership passing to me was unfathomable.

"Yes, dear cousin," Vaaryn says. "I am not much longer for this world. It is best that the youngest should lead us."

Most Thirds lived only a few years past their two-hundredth birthday. Fourths less than that, and Fifths barely made one hundred. The Silent were old at seventy.

"But it is because of me that we face war with the Silent. It is because of me—" I choke on the words as a sob rises to my throat. Yllis is there with an arm around me, steady and stable, my rock in the storm.

Yllis's mother, Deela, rises. "So it must be you to lead us through. We have lived in peace for hundreds of years with the guidance left by the Founders, but perhaps it has been too easy for us. We have never been challenged in this way before."

"Eero and those who follow him have poked at a sore that has been dormant for a long time," Yllis says. "The Silent have no voice in the Assembly. Their parentage is not claimed. If it was not Eero now, it would have been someone else in the future. It is not all because of us."

He wants to take more of the burden of Eero's fate away from me, absolve me of some guilt, but it is mine to hold. Yllis developed the complex spell, which allowed me to share my Song with my twin, but I was the one who used it. Who kept using it and ignored the truth for too long—giving Song to the Silent would cause them to go mad. The Silent were so for a reason.

"Very well," I say. "I accept."

It is as if the Assembly takes a collective breath. "Be it so."

And with three little words, I have been made Queen.

CHAPTER NINE

THE POUNDING OF rain against the window lulled Jasminda into a state between sleep and wakefulness. She sat in the palace's Blue Library, books spread around her, all of them on Elsiran history. Her mother had begun teaching them history, but after her death, Papa continued their lessons on more practical matters. Math and basic engineering, biology and horticulture—things that would be useful in maintaining the farm.

In the royal library, the options were limitless. Wanting to start at the beginning, she'd pulled down dozens of books from the shelves, growing more and more uneasy with each one she read through. Elsiran history before the war was treated like a fairy tale or a parable. Tales of the Founders were little more than children's stories written for adults. There were no dates, no names or locations—just stories of wonder and generosity from the esteemed Founders.

Even their eventual fates were never mentioned, only that leadership eventually passed to one of their descendants, the Queen Who Sleeps, who continued their wonderful work. Then, inevitably, each book would contain a short and very vague passage on her betrayal by the True Father and the spell he cast that placed her into an endless sleep. A sleep that could only be broken when he is sent to the World After. His true identity or where he came from were never touched upon. Nor were his motives.

It was as if history and myth had intertwined somehow, and vital facts had been lost or obscured. And now she was beginning to understand the truth through the visions. She wasn't sure if she could trust what she saw, but there was nothing in the recorded histories that could disprove what the caldera showed. And the emotions she felt when she was Oola, the Queen, were all too real. Every sorrow, every bit of angst and guilt and fear became hers, and lasted long after she came back to herself.

The time between the visions was shortening, as well. This morning she'd seen a brief vision of Yllis asking Oola to marry him. It was not the first time he'd asked, and she again denied him. Her emotions had been unstable —finding her brother and restoring peace to their land had been all she could think about—but her Song sensed Yllis's frustration and pain. The vision had ended abruptly, almost in the middle of a thought, and Jasminda hoped she would be strong enough to try the caldera again later that night.

She looked up from her spot on the floor and stifled a gasp to find Lizvette standing before her, willowy and elegant in a cream-colored gown.

"I didn't mean to shock you. Please forgive me," Lizvette said.

"No, I'm sorry. You haven't been standing there long, have you?"

"No." The generous way she smiled made Jasminda think that wasn't precisely the case.

Jasminda rose and tiptoed her way out of the prison of books she'd created, motioning to a set of chairs at one of the study tables. Lizvette perched in her seat, back straight, hands folded neatly in her lap. Jasminda copied her pose, but her body didn't take to it naturally.

"My maid told me you were often found here. I'd meant to visit earlier."

"Well, I thank you for thinking of me. I don't get many visitors."

Lizvette looked around. "I never come in here. It's so odd that I've lived in the palace all my life and rarely take advantage of its resources."

Jasminda shrugged. "It's easy to take things for granted. Hard to believe the things that seem permanent can ever be taken away." She sank in her seat like a deflating balloon.

"You have had a great many losses?" Lizvette's body was rigid, but her voice kind.

"I've lost everything. Everything I've ever had." Jasminda snapped her back straight again and refused to give in to the melancholy. "But I'm sure you don't want to hear about my sorrows."

"I cannot imagine what it must be like."

"You've had your share."

Lizvette's only response was a thinning of her lips. Jasminda opened herself to a trickle of Earthsong, becoming better at shielding each time she tried. Lizvette's emotions swirled in a storm of grief and longing. Surprised at their strength and depth, Jasminda lost her hold and the connection slammed shut. The other woman's placid, controlled face hid a maelstrom of pain.

Jasminda's heart went out to her. "Would it . . . help to talk about him?"

Lizvette's eyes widened, and her hands clenched in her lap.

"Prince Alariq?" Jasminda prompted. "It's said talking about our departed ones keeps them alive in our hearts."

Lizvette released her hands to the arms of the chair and took a deep breath. "Oh, Alariq. Yes. I mean, no, thank you. I—" She smoothed out the fabric of her pristine dress and smiled. "I came to see you to give you a warning. I'm afraid it might not be safe for you here in the palace. Things are becoming quite strained with public opinion regarding the refugees. Jack is doing his best, but he faces heavy opposition."

Jasminda's slippered foot tapped the floor as tension seeped into her limbs. "As long as your father votes against sending the refugees back, Jack will be fine, right?"

Lizvette brushed imaginary lint from her gown. Jasminda counted to three before the other woman met her eye.

"He's changed his mind?" Jasminda asked. "He cannot believe the True Father will keep his word of peace?"

Lizvette shook her head. "But the business owners, the aristocrats . . . the Council answers to them even more than to the Prince Regent. And they want the refugees gone. They are threatening not to sell food to the Principality if any of it is meant for the refugees."

"They would starve all the people over this?"

"And blame the prince."

Jasminda fell back in the chair. Lizvette's words hammered against the inside of her skull. The intolerance and cruelty of people should not surprise her anymore. She had seen so little of the world but much pain wherever she went. Too much pain.

"And you think someone will harm me?" Calladeen's vicious face popped into her mind.

Lizvette's long neck stretched impossibly longer. She stood and crossed to the shelves, holding the most recent newspapers. "Have you seen today's paper?"

When Jasminda shook her head, Lizvette brought it over, smoothing the pages on the table.

LAGRIMARI AMBASSADOR HAS PRINCE IN A TWIST

```
The royal ambassador to the Lagrimari refugee camp, a
Miss Jasminda ul-Sarifor, age and birthplace unknown,
is noted for her rare command of Elsiran, as well as
the Lagrimari tongue. But apparently His Grace the
Prince Regent has tongues around the palace wagging
with his reported admiration for the woman. Prince
Jaqros has turned down the social invitations of
several lovely young women in the Elsiran inner circle,
purportedly to further his relationship with the exotic
and interbred ul-Sarifor.

Her stay in the palace is said to be ongoing, and while
officials are tight-lipped as to her other assigned
duties, our eyes and ears remain open.
```

"The *Rosira Daily Witness* is not much more than an extended gossip column," Lizvette was saying, though the oceanic roar of blood rushing through Jasminda's ears made it difficult to hear. A bubble of despair burst in her chest as she read the headlines and scanned the other articles. She pushed the paper away, not wanting to read any more.

Lizvette's eyes were glassy, her face sorrowful. "The press has always bothered him. They've never cut him any slack. Ever since his mother's . . . emigration. And now it's worse than it was then." She clucked her tongue. "She was too young and possibly too delicate for the demands of palace life. It broke her."

Lizvette did not mention anything of Prince Edvard's treatment of her, but maybe that was not common knowledge.

Eyes the color of dying embers singed Jasminda. "He needs to be seen as strong. He needs to fill Alariq's shoes and be loved by his people and not hated. Do you understand?"

Jasminda nodded, fighting the approaching tears.

"Father says if he marries well, he can put these troubles behind him."

Cold fingers gripped Jasminda's heart. Lizvette's head lowered as she stared at the carpeting. A chilling knowledge bit Jasminda. She reached out for Earthsong again, this time prepared for the woman's hidden emotions. The longing pervading her Song was not a futile thing as it would be for a departed lover. It was vibrant, vigorous, and full of life.

"Are you in love with him?" Jasminda asked, her whole chest numb.

Lizvette blinked, momentarily taken aback at the question. A crack of vulnerability broke through her poised demeanor. In an instant, it was gone. She rose. "I only offer you advice. Please be careful. It would break him if anything happened to you."

She left the room in a cloud of soft perfume, completely extinguishing the dying cinders of hope still clinging to life inside Jasminda.

THE COUNCIL ROOM emptied, leaving Jack the sole occupant. Staring at the wood grain of the table. Sitting in the chair his brother had occupied. And his father. And his grandfather and great-uncle. A member of the Alliaseen family had been the Prince Regent since the loss of the Queen. The blood in his veins was noble, royal. That was supposed to mean he possessed the best qualities of an Elsiran.

Honor. Loyalty. Dependability.

Calladeen had said that honor was doing the hard thing and letting history determine your legacy.

Jack asked himself what Alariq would have done, what his father would have done. And they would have done exactly as he had.

They would have sent the refugees back.

Back to a life that was not a life. Back to die.

He could not save them, any of them.

His mother, gone without a word. His brother, determined to pilot that wretched airship, no matter how foolish. Jasminda, harassed by a member of his own Council. The press would soon follow.

He was unworthy of the crown, the responsibility, the power.

Even unworthy of the woman he loved.

When she'd walked away from him at the ball, the pain in her face seized him like nothing before. He could not deny he loved her. As Prince Regent, it should have been within his power to give her the world. Instead, she had to remain hidden, denied.

What would his legacy be? Would the pages of the history books be kind? Or would they only remember him for dooming hundreds of innocents? For the loss of an entire nation?

This illusion of peace would be short-lived.

The True Father would destroy the Mantle—if not tomorrow, then next month or next year. And what then? Being right would not save his people.

The knots in the wood of the table kept their silence, though they stared back at him in accusation. He did not blame them.

WAR.

Silent versus Songbearer.

Blood in the streets.

Silent outnumber Songbearers more than ten to one, and while Eero has not turned them all against us, he has managed to bring many more than I ever imagined over to his side.

I always thought he was able to wrap me around his finger because of my weakness for him, my love. But it is a talent of his. He is charming. When he talks, people listen. They believe and trust him. They follow him, taking up arms against their neighbors, rending our land in two.

Our Songs make us a fearsome foe, though Earthsong cannot be used to kill. Besides, none who have felt the energy of a million lives strumming in his or her veins can rejoice in sending any living creature to the World After.

Early on, we healed any Silent harmed in an attack. The Assembly believed this would bring them to our side. But it did not. I cannot understand if the Silent are jealous of our Songs or fearful of them. The truth likely lies in a combination of the two.

Swords clash. The Silent fight through the rain and ice, the mudslides and fire. They are pelted with rocks, tumbled with earthquakes, but they persist.

It is within the power of the Songbearers to entirely unmake the land from the fabric of its being, in the same way that our grandparents did the reverse, creating a beautiful landscape where once a desert stood. But we think of the future—a future of peace.

Eero knows my weaknesses. He knows me too well. I should never have been made Queen to lead the fight against him. I am the last person that should have been chosen.

Yllis studies with the Cantors day and night. His guilt is an anchor around his neck. It pulls him away from me. I have not allowed him to answer for his part in the scheme to help Eero sing. And I have not agreed to marry him. How could I with things the way they are? I thought I was protecting him by accepting all the blame, but that and my repeated refusals of his offers have changed things between us.

The hurt in his eyes when he looks upon me cuts deep. So deep I do not believe I have a heart any longer. My heart was never my own. It belonged more to the ones I loved than to me.

War.

It drags us under.

It tears us apart.

JACK PADDED INTO Jasminda's chamber well after midnight, glad to find her still awake. She sat by the fire, staring into the dancing flames. She startled as he drew near, before recognizing him, then her face transformed with joy.

"I'm sorry it's so late," he said, transferring her to his lap as he took her place on the chair. He rubbed circles into her back, noting the tightness in her muscles.

"It's all right." She collapsed against him. He exhaled the breath he'd been holding all day. His body relaxed, at home with her in his arms.

"How did it go?" Her voice was so small he strained to hear. "They voted to send them back, didn't they?"

A great hollow space opened in his chest. He could not bear to affirm it aloud.

"What will happen to me?" Her voice was empty as an echo.

He shifted her on his lap so he could peer into her eyes. Misery suffused the beauty of her face. "Jasminda—"

"Half-breed. Mongrel. That's what the papers say, right? I cannot stay here. And didn't the True Father's letter say every Lagrimari must be sent back?"

Jack's lungs compressed as if he was at the peak of a mountain sucking in air too thin to quench his need. "You are not Lagrimari."

"Am I not?" Her eyes were almost wild. "I may have been born in your land, share half your blood, but I'm not one of you. I'm not one of them, either. I don't belong anywhere, Jack."

"No," he said, voice steely. "No, you belong with me." He held her tighter, his chest vibrating with the racing of her heart.

"For how long? How long until you must find an acceptable princess? One that you need in order to regain the peoples' trust? We were only ever going to be temporary."

He crushed her to him and stroked her soft, springy hair. "Are you saying you want to leave?"

"No."

"Then—"

"But I cannot stay."

He shook his head rapidly, desperate to shake some solution into his brain. "If being prince is good for anything, then I should get to be with the woman I love." He pulled away and clutched her hands to his chest. "Do you hear me? I love you."

Saying it out loud took the edge off the panic building at the thought of her leaving. "You are strong and intelligent and fearless and beautiful. I had never even hoped a woman like you existed. I love you, Jasminda."

Tears traced her face. "I love you, too. You must know that. You are my whole heart, Jaqros Alliaseen. My whole heart. I never thought I would—"

She looked away, and he wiped her streaming cheeks.

"You are a good man, a good prince." She cupped his face in her hands and kissed him lightly. "You must be strong for your people."

Sad eyes surveyed him, and though the exhilaration of her declarations of love thrummed in his veins, a warning bell rang deep in his heart.

She kissed him again, so gently it made him anxious. He did not deserve such tenderness. He deepened the kiss, grabbing hold of her waist and stroking her side. The tightness she'd held melted away as her arms came around his neck.

Jack lifted her and carried her to the bed. She kneeled on the mattress as he stood devouring her mouth with needy kisses. She slid her palms down his chest and began working on the buttons of his shirt. Her expertise at removing men's clothing had grown, and she had the shirt hanging open and trousers pushed to his knees in record time.

As he was undoing the ties of her dress and sliding it over her head, a blade of awareness sliced into him. Jasminda was soft and pliable, her body receptive to his touch, but something was different. There was a distance present between them that had never been there before, even as she discarded her slip with a seductive smile and lay back, inviting him between her thighs.

Vowing to make this night, this lovemaking, more memorable than any other, he set upon her with a fervor, licking and stroking his way up her legs. He reached her core and lapped at her, stroking her entrance teasingly with his finger. She panted and cried out his name, begging for more, but he continued the foreplay, holding off giving her what she wanted. He brought her to the brink of climax, then eased her back down, ignoring her protests.

Satisfied when her limbs shook with need, he kissed his way up her belly. One hand glided to her breast, and with the other he plunged two fingers into her center, causing her to buck, her back arching as moans of pleasure escaped her. She was more than ready. All it took was a thumb flicked across the right spot and she went over, cresting the wave.

When her cries gentled, they kissed and she guided his erection into her. The indefinable sensation of sinking deep inside her was so much more than lust. The gentle rhythm of their lovemaking sped up to a pounding beat as he fought to chase away the nagging worry, guilt, and fear. She loved him. She would stand by him in this dark time.

He drove into her, spurred on by her nails digging into his buttocks and her mewls of pleasure. Losing himself in her skin, her scent, her cries, he could almost outrun the gloom of what was to come.

Afterward, she lay in his arms stroking his skin, not seeming to mind the sweat and stickiness after so much exertion. He held her tightly against him, as tight as he dared without crushing her. For even though she had been right with him the entire evening, a voice in the back of his head told him she was slipping away.

JASMINDA AWOKE ALONE. It was just as well. She would rather remember Jack as he was last night, holding her close, whispering how much he loved her. She had already said good-bye to him with her body. His words of love would strengthen her in the days and nights to come, through whatever the future brought.

She scoured her wardrobe until she found her own dress, the one she was wearing when she had arrived. It had been washed and pressed and was the only thing she truly owned here. She grabbed the serrated knife she'd managed to nick from her dinner tray and strapped it to her thigh using one of the garters supplied with the palace clothing. After stroking the fine fabrics one last time, she snuffed out the fledgling hope they could ever truly be hers. The dream of a life surrounded by beautiful things and beautiful people who loved and accepted her was a fantasy that would never come true. The impossibilities only strengthened her resolve to leave, no matter the fractures and fissures forming on her heart.

Jasminda would never be a princess. There was a residue of dirt under her fingernails that could never be scrubbed away. Lizvette, on the other hand, was born for it. She hoped one day Jack would come to realize that.

She pulled on her sturdy coat, buckled her boots, and took a final look around—the tapestries, the plush carpeting, the enormous bathroom, the soaking tub. Part of her wished she'd never come here at all. It was impossible to miss what you did not know. But she could not wish for a life without having met Jack, no matter the consequences.

The palace hallways were quiet. She made her way to the office nearest the vehicle depot and asked for Nash. Within a few minutes he appeared, a newspaper tucked under his arm. With a nervous glance to the paper, she wondered what today's story was. Expecting accusation from him, she was surprised to find Nash's green eyes twinkling at her, a warm smile on his face.

"Back to the camp again today, miss?" he said, tossing the paper in the wastebasket.

"No, I . . . I just need to get away from here." She looked around and the sad truth descended on her. "I just don't have anywhere to go." She blinked, thinking hard. Could she try her grandmother's house again and expect any less chilly of a reception? Unlikely. Vanesse had mentioned some secret place where people were discreet, but Jasminda didn't know the location. She just needed a quiet spot to continue her work with the caldera until it revealed whatever additional secrets it possessed.

"Can we just . . . drive for a little while? Away?"

Nash's face softened. "Of course."

He opened the door leading outside and ushered her through. She matched his long stride down a row featuring an impressive array of vehicles to the town car he'd driven before. Just as he opened the rear door, rapid approaching footsteps caused her to turn.

Four Royal Guardsmen marched up, stiff and imposing.

"Miss," one of the Guardsmen said as she backed toward the auto. "I need you to come with us."

She had never before been summoned by the Royal Guard. Usher had brought messages from Jack, but he'd never sent anyone else. She cast a glance at Nash, whose brow was furrowed, before turning and following the Guardsmen back into the palace.

They descended a staircase, then followed a hall leading to another staircase. She wondered if Jack was visiting the chamber of the Queen Who Sleeps again, though this did not appear to be the route she'd taken before.

At the end of a sparse hallway, a fifth Royal Guardsman stood before an elaborate brass gate that he unlocked as they approached, then ushered them through. Jasminda froze when the iron bars of the dungeon cells came into view.

"What is this about?" she asked, whirling around.

The door to a cell hung open, and the Guardsmen all stopped walking, blocking every direction except into the cell.

"I'm being arrested?" Her gaze darted around the small space, sparse but clean. "By whose order?"

The young, bland Guardsman did not look at her as he spoke. "Miss, by order of Prince Jaqros you are remanded here for your own protection."

"My protection? From what?"

"Please, miss," he said, pointing to the cell.

"Why am I here? Why won't you tell me?"

"Miss Jasminda," a familiar voice said. Usher stepped out from behind the row of Guardsmen. "I assure you, this was not his first choice."

"This is how he plans to stop me from leaving?" she whispered, shaking her head. "Treating me like a criminal?"

Usher's voice was low. "There has been a threat made against you. And he doesn't know who to trust. He's trying to protect you."

She shivered. Lizvette had hinted as much the night before, but an actual threat turned her blood cold. "Then perhaps I would be safer elsewhere. He should just let me go."

With no other options, she stepped inside the cell and shuddered as the door clanked shut behind her.

"He is not strong enough to do that." Usher stepped to the bars and slipped a thick, warm blanket through a gap. Jasminda accepted it, lay down on the thin cot, and cried.

THAT IS IMPOSSIBLE, Vaaryn says through his Song.

Then how would you explain it? replies Deela. Yllis's mother, Vaaryn, and I sit in the Great Hall of the Citadel. There are still loyal Silent working as servants here, but there are no doubt also spies for the other side, as well. No important conversation is held out loud any longer.

No Songbearer would gift Eero their Song. There are only two who even know the spell. Deela looks at me, and I shrink a bit more inside.

So you believe he has learned to steal Song from a bearer? Vaaryn's forehead wrinkles in disbelief. *That would be . . .*

A disaster, I finish. But it must be true. Eero is singing again. Through the window, the battle for the skies is clear. Only hours ago, the placid, clear day was interrupted by sudden, unnatural clouds. Songbearers on the front lines had to fend off tornadoes, hurricanes, snow, and ice all afternoon.

Who has he stolen from? Deela says.

I shake my head. We are still accounting for all of the Songbearers in the city.

Will all the Silent want Songs now? Vaaryn wonders.

I frown, considering. *I do not think he will want to share. My brother was never generous.*

How do they still follow him? Do they not find him a hypocrite? Especially when his demands are for a separate land for the Silent. Deela's face is so like Yllis's, even moreso when working out a difficult problem. *He has split us apart and wants to make it official, by creating a land just for them, yet he steals the Song of a Songbearer.*

His gift is winning the hearts and minds of others, I say. *Logic is not always required for that. And as for his demands, perhaps we should give him what he wants.*

Vaaryn's rheumy eyes go wide.

Hear me out. If we take the abandoned land east of the mountains, we could reform it and rebuild, just as our grandparents did this land, I say. *We could leave the west to the Silent and rebuild to the east.*

I let them mull over my suggestion for a while. The thought of leaving my home sickens me, but this war must end.

We must bring this to the Assembly, Deela says.

I nod, certain I can convince them.

At least once he is separated from the Songbearers, he will not be able to steal what the Silent do not possess. Deela seems reassured by this.

Eero has already stolen so much from the Silent—their peace, their stability, their future—but I keep these thoughts to myself as we take our leave.

Yllis finds me before sunset as I pace the floors of the Citadel, awaiting updates from those on the front lines. He is rumpled and creased, his hair is lopsided, but he is as beautiful to me as ever.

"You must come with me," he says. I startle at hearing his voice aloud, but I am so grateful he has spoken. He leads me to his office in the laboratory of the Cantors.

"I think I have found a way —"

"Do you think it wise to speak?" Though I love to hear his voice, I too have been seized by the paranoia affecting the other Songbearers.

"You too, Oola?" He pins me with a withering glare, one I must grow used to seeing from him. What once was soft and cherished between us is now all hard edges. "No Silent are allowed within the walls of the Cantors."

"Very well. You think you have found a way to do what?"

He points down to his leather-bound notebook. Tight handwriting fills every page obscuring the color of the original paper.

"I have studied everything we have on the ancient ways of the Cavefolk. They were Silent but managed to harness a vast power different than Earthsong—from a different source. Just as powerful but not as limited. Cantors have long used the Cavefolk techniques, but only with Earthsong. They have never attempted any of the more robust spells because they all require one key ingredient." His finger stops below one word, written boldly, traced over and over.

Blood.

I meet Yllis's eyes, which gleam in the lamplight.

"With blood magic, we can create a spell to silence any Song," he says.

"Blood magic?" I shake my head and step away. "We cannot."

He steps toward me, his eyes on fire. "We must."

"No, there is another way." I tell him of the plan I shared with the others. "What he wants is his own land. The war will end once we give him this."

Yllis stares at me for a long while and shivers run up my spine. "You were always blind when it came to him."

"What do you mean?"

For a moment, the hard shell he's constructed around himself cracks, and I see a glimpse of the man I fell in love with. Yllis moves closer to me, placing his hands on my shoulders. "He wants what he has always wanted: power."

I shiver. Both from the truth of his words and his close proximity.

"So this spell . . . how does it work?"

"It is a binding spell to prevent connection with Earthsong."

"And we will need someone's blood?"

His eyes darken, and he nods. "Let me worry about that. Link with me, and I will teach you the spell."

His hand is the same as I remember. Warm and big, it swallows mine. I hardly get to relish the feeling of his skin when I'm thrown into his link, and he teaches me the spell. The feel of it sours my tongue, but I commit it to memory.

———

THE YOUNG MAID standing in Jack's office sniffled and wrung her hands. "No, Your Grace. I would never let anyone else in Miss Jasminda's rooms. Never." Red-rimmed eyes overflowed with tears. "I always saw to her myself, just as Usher asked."

Jack sighed and paused his pacing. "And you have no idea how anyone would have gotten hold of this?" He pointed to the low table where the blue gown Jasminda wore to the ball a few nights before lay. It had been found, slashed and partially burned, outside the doors to the Prince Regent's office suite.

"No, Your Grace." The girl shook her head violently, took another look at the gown, and burst into a fresh round of sobs.

"All right, all right, Nadal," Jack said, motioning for Usher to comfort her. "I believe you. But you haven't heard anything from the other servants?"

She leaned into Usher and quieted a bit. "Some of them have been cool toward me since I wouldn't gossip about Miss Jasminda with them. I haven't heard anything."

Jack dropped roughly onto the couch, nervous energy rattling through him. He answered the question in Usher's gaze with a nod, and the man led Nadal away, returning a few minutes later alone.

"She's going to hate me," Jack said as he rubbed his burning eyes, wishing he could rub away the weariness and the heartache. "She has every right to. But she's in the safest place in the palace. Almost anyone could have sneaked into her rooms. Any person in this palace could mean her harm."

Usher clucked his tongue, and Jack looked up. "What?"

"You should go to her, young sir."

"Was she really leaving?" He sank down, every bone in his body feeling twice its weight.

"It appears so."

Jack groaned, closing the lid on the emotions that threatened to spill out at the thought of Jasminda's absence. Then a horrifying thought struck him. "Mother often talked of wanting to leave. I would hear them arguing . . . He would never let her . . ." He scrubbed a hand over his face. "I'm just like him, aren't I? I will never be able to escape the shadow of his cruelty."

He stood and walked to the terrace doors, looking out at the city stretching before him and beyond, to the endless blue waves. Usher came to stand by him.

"You are nothing like him."

Jack rested his forehead against the cool glass. Outside, the perfect serenity of the day was so at odds with the whirlwind inside him.

"Then why do I feel like the villain here?"

The buses with the refugees were well on their way toward the border. By this time tomorrow, they would all be back across the mountain. Only the Queen knew what their fates would be, but Jack could guess. He chuckled mirthlessly.

"What have I done, Usher? The woman I love in the dungeons. Allowing the refugees to be sent back. What does this make me?"

"It makes you a prince."

"And what is that worth when I can't save anyone?"

The darkness in his heart was in danger of overtaking him. He rubbed his chest as if he could massage the broken organ from the outside. "You're right. I should go to her. Either she'll forgive me or she won't. Besides, I don't want her staying in the palace any longer than necessary. You've gotten in touch with Benn's wife?"

"Yes, she's happy to let Jasminda stay with her down in Portside. The family will keep watch for trouble."

Jack nodded. "All right. She should be safe there while I ferret out whoever's responsible." He cast another glance at the ruined dress, and anger beat a rhythm inside his chest. "I can't fail her, too," he rasped, nearly choking on the words.

Usher clapped him on the shoulder and squeezed. Some days the only thing keeping him upright was the man's presence.

He gave Usher a sidelong glance. "How do you stand me, old man?"

"I don't really have a choice, now do I?" Usher said with a droll smile.

JACK RUSHED DOWN to the dungeon, feeling even more guilty for keeping Jasminda locked away a moment longer than necessary. As he entered the outer chamber, the guards snapped to attention.

"Captain," Jack said, acknowledging the guard. "It's time to let her out."

The captain's eyes widened. "L-let her out, Your Grace?"

"Yes, open the cell. I'll take her with me."

The captain's gaze darted to his fellow guard, rigid beside him, then back to Jack. "B-begging your pardon, Your Grace, but she's already been let out."

Jack stilled, every muscle in his body tensing in alarm. "I gave explicit orders that the young woman was to be held here until I ordered her released."

"Yes, Your Grace."

"Then by whose authority was she released?" Jack roared.

"Yours, Your Grace." The captain held out a folded letter, stamped with the official seal of the Prince Regent. Jack snatched it from his hands and read the contents, instructions to release Jasminda to the custody of the letter's bearer.

He motioned for the guard to open the door to the cells, and he strode through, needing to see for himself that Jasminda was really gone. A blanket lay neatly folded on the cot inside an empty cell.

He spun back to face the captain. "Who brought this note?"

"A servant, Your Grace. A maid. I didn't know her."

"And you thought I'd send a maid to retrieve someone from custody?"

"The letter bears your seal, Your Grace."

Jack turned away, trying to tamp down the rage boiling in his bloodstream. At its edge was a cold fear he didn't want to inspect too closely. Whoever had stolen Jasminda's dress and destroyed it had wanted to send a message to Jack. They must have taken her, as well. Would they really harm her? All to punish him?

Only one person he knew had clashed swords with Jasminda recently. At the very ball where she'd worn that dress.

His breathing came in short spurts as he exploded from the dungeon, racing up the stairs three at a time.

"Where is Minister Calladeen?" he growled to the young man at the main Royal Guard station.

"He's in his offices, Your Grace."

A red haze swallowed Jack. His whole body quivered as he stalked down the hall and slammed his way into the offices of the Minister of Foreign Affairs. A startled young secretary yipped in alarm as Jack stormed into the inner office.

Calladeen stood, eyes wide, as Jack exploded into the room.

"What did you do?" Jack demanded.

"I don't know what you're talking about."

Jack marched across the room until he was nearly nose to nose with the man. "Where is she?" he yelled. Calladeen shrank back, leaning almost comically away.

"Where is who, Your Grace?"

"Don't play games with me, man. Where is Jasminda?"

Calladeen placed two hands up in a motion of surrender and stepped away from the wall of anger radiating from Jack's body. Jack clenched and unclenched his fists, waiting for the moment when he could release his frustration in a flurry of violence.

"Your Grace, I swear by our Sovereign, I do not know."

Jack's glare was ruthless, and the man seemed genuinely afraid. Jack held up the letter. "You did not forge this message from me ordering her release?"

Calladeen tentatively plucked the letter from Jack's hand and read it over, a frown pulling down his mouth. "No, I did not. But I do recognize the handwriting."

Jack had paid little attention to the curling script of the letter. "Whose is it?"

Calladeen's sharp face grew pensive. "Lizvette's."

CHAPTER TEN

THE CARAVAN OF buses rolled across the country as the sun-kissed day darkened into a tempestuous, thundery night. Rain pelted the metal of the bus's roof so hard it sounded like hail. Jasminda sat near the front, handcuffed to a bar running under the window.

On the bench across from her sat Osar, squeezed together with a woman and two smaller children. All the mothers held their children close, blanketed in fear and sadness. The refugees had taken a risk in trusting their Elsiran neighbors, and they had lost.

Jasminda felt her own loss acutely, the loss of Jack and now her freedom. The cold metal bit into her skin when she jangled the chain connecting the cuffs. The soldier sitting in front of her craned his neck, glaring at her. She narrowed her eyes at him, hardening her stare until he turned back around.

She'd thought being locked in the dungeon would be the worst this day would hold. She was wrong.

Her hours in the dungeon had been spent mulling over the latest vision from the caldera and counting the stone blocks in the wall, waiting for Jack to appear and explain himself. Then the clank of keys approaching had made her sit upright.

A maid appeared outside her cell with two Guardsmen in tow. The cell door opened, and the maid motioned Jasminda forward. She stood, shocked the Guardsmen allowed the maid to lead her away.

"Did Jack send you?" Jasminda asked as the woman passed her a hooded cloak, large enough to cover Jasminda's face. "Where are we going?"

"There's a car waiting for you, miss."

"To take me where?"

"We must hurry," she said, leading her through the servants' passages at a rapid pace. With a sliver of Earthsong, Jasminda tested the woman's emotions. Uncertainty and caution pulsed powerfully within her. Jasminda couldn't imagine that Jack would have allowed her to be released to just anyone, though it was odd that he'd sent a servant she didn't know instead of Nadal or Usher. They soon arrived at an outer door where Lizvette waited with an unfamiliar driver and vehicle.

Jasminda froze. "Jack didn't send you, did he?"

"It isn't safe here for you," Lizvette said, scanning the area as if a ruffian would spring from the bushes at any moment.

"Who wants to hurt me?"

"Please believe me. This is for the best."

Lizvette wouldn't meet her eyes but nodded at the driver before stepping back. "Do not harm her."

The driver, a burly man with an icy gaze, approached, and fear spurred Jasminda into action. She spun away and ran, but the man reached out a long arm and grabbed her. She kicked and flailed, but her shout was muffled by his large hand over her mouth. A pair of handcuffs clinked as the metal slid across her skin.

He manhandled her into the backseat where another man, who she hadn't noticed before, waited. In the brief moment when the driver removed his hand from her mouth, she gasped for air to scream but a gag was stuffed between her lips and tied around the back of her head. She continued thrashing, but the second man held her in a crushing grip. The driver took his seat and slammed the door. Jasminda struggled to look out the window, seeing only Lizvette's retreating form.

She writhed and twisted, but the fellow holding her had arms of iron. Deciding to save her strength, she relaxed her body and the man's grip lessened somewhat. Stealthily, she inched her skirt up to reach for the serrated knife strapped to her leg. Removing the blade, she twisted again preparing to slam it into her captor's thigh. The driver's gaze flicked to her in the rearview mirror, and he wrenched the steering wheel, swerving the car and knocking the knife from her grip.

Her captor growled and smashed her head against the window, momentarily blacking out her vision. She stilled as her wits returned and rested her head against glass to cool the pounding.

Lizvette's betrayal shouldn't have been as shocking as it was. The woman's coy warnings the day before had been for what? To simply mask her own desire to do Jasminda harm?

As they wound their way through the city, another possibility emerged as to Lizvette's true intentions. Maybe she simply wanted Jasminda out of the way. Then the auto made a turn onto a dirt road that led only one place.

The camp was in chaos when they arrived, stopping just past a line of waiting buses. The man holding her, whose face she still hadn't seen, pulled her from the auto. She stumbled before finding her footing. Dismay and anger bubbled within as she was pushed along.

Dozens of Sisters stood before her, arms locked together, attempting to form a human barrier between the soldiers and the refugees. The Sisters repeated a prayer over and over, asking the Queen Who Sleeps for protection.

Starting at the end of the line, the soldiers pried the Sisters' hands and arms apart as the women's prayer grew louder. Behind the Sisters, many of the refugees were lining up solemnly in rows, waiting to board the buses, resigned to their fate. But some would not go quietly. As the soldiers broke through the resistance of the Sisters, a handful of refugees screamed and wailed, planting themselves on the ground and refusing to move.

Soldiers handcuffed those who protested and held them under armed guard before forcibly placing them on the buses. The man holding Jasminda transferred her to a young soldier who dragged her over to the group of restrained refugees and pushed her to the ground. Four men trained their rifles on the group.

She angled her head down until she could pull the gag from her mouth, then sucked in deep breaths, surveying the turmoil around her.

A white-haired general barked orders, instructing his men to ensure every Lagrimari made it across the border. No exceptions.

"What if they won't go?" a lieutenant asked.

"Shoot them."

Jasminda shivered. Those couldn't have been Jack's orders, but it didn't seem to matter.

Screams and cries filled the air. The protesting Sisters were being gathered, some handcuffed, as well, although they were treated far more gently than the refugees. Among them was Aunt Vanesse, who spotted Jasminda and broke away from the others to rush to her side. She was distraught, her neat topknot had slipped out and her robes were covered in splotches of mud.

"Oy!" Vanesse hailed one of the officers and pointed to Jasminda. "She is not a Lagrimari; she is an Elsiran citizen."

The lieutenant looked at Jasminda askance and raised his eyebrows. "Do you have proof of that, Sister?"

"You have my word as an Elsiran. This girl's mother was my sister," Vanesse pleaded.

The lieutenant shrugged. "Even if that were true, we're under orders." He looked Jasminda up and down again. "How Elsiran can she be if she looks that much like a *grol*?" He shrugged and walked away.

Vanesse screamed at the man, and Jasminda reached for her hand, clasping it in her bound ones. Vanesse fell to her knees, sobbing, but a strange calm had fallen over Jasminda. In the midst of all this chaos, one truth was clear.

"We both know I don't really belong here."

"No. You're all I have left of Emi. I will find someone who will listen. You don't belong over there, either." Vanesse shuddered. "We can find a place for you. I promise." She squeezed Jasminda's hands.

Jasminda smiled through her own welling tears. "Do *you* even have a place here? A way to be who you really are? With the person you love?"

Vanesse reared back as if slapped. Her mouth hung open. "What do you know of that?"

"I know that I love someone I can never be with. Not openly. And I thought stolen moments would be enough, but they're not. I don't want to be a secret, hidden away never allowed to see the light of day. I don't want to be a liability. I want to be a treasure."

Recognition lit within Vanesse. She nodded slowly and wiped at her eyes. "I'm not giving up, but for now, you should take this." She pulled a worn envelope from the pocket of her robes. "Emi sent it to me a long time ago, but I think it belongs to you."

Jasminda recognized her mother's delicate handwriting. Her fingers shook as she opened it. Inside was a photograph, the same image of her family that had sat atop the mantle at home.

"This burned in the fire," she whispered in awe, tracing the outlines of her parents and brothers. "I thought I'd never—"

Vanesse placed her palm on Jasminda's cheek, then leaned forward to kiss her forehead. "You *are* a treasure. I'm sorry that you've never felt that way." She stood, smoothing out her robes, her expression faraway.

"If you can get a message to the prince . . ." Jasminda said. There was little chance that Vanesse could get through to Jack in time. An unknown woman, even one of the Sisterhood, was unlikely to receive an audience with the Prince Regent.

Vanesse's brow furrowed, but she nodded. "I will pray for us to meet again." And then she was gone.

Within a half hour, Jasminda was herded toward a bus with the others. A soldier pushed her roughly into a seat and locked her handcuffs around the bar, securing her in place.

Rozyl tripped up the steps, a soldier at her back. The two locked eyes. "I guess you're one of us now," the Keeper said, her lip curling up. The soldier shoved her toward the back of the bus.

Jasminda pressed her head against the window and slumped in her seat, her mind racing. She had no intention of being dragged into Lagrimar, especially with the caldera heavy in her pocket. Besides the obvious lack of appeal of living in a land she knew nothing about, she could not allow the stone to fall into the hands of the Lagrimari. Even if she could not figure out all of its secrets, she must keep it concealed. That meant finding a way to escape as soon as she could.

The picture in her hand burned with almost as many memories as the caldera. Seeing the faces of her family again gave her hope. She stared at the picture until the bus pulled forward and the long journey began.

A sudden jerk brought her back to the present. Through the windshield, the headlamps illuminated only a few feet ahead of them. The rest was inky blackness, rain tapping a staccato beat on the roof. The driver took to the radio, inquiring as to whether they would be stopping due to the hazardous conditions. The only response was static.

Flash floods pooled in the dips of the road, and crackles of lightning raced across the sky, illuminating the scenery in quick flashes. Lush, fertile farmland stretched on around them. The driver shouted a curse and twisted the steering wheel violently. Jasminda slid in her seat, banging her shoulder against the window. Headlights flew past the hulking form of a cow in the middle of the road, and the bus careened in an attempt to miss it. Water sloshed around the tires as the massive vehicle tilted, the driver unable to wrestle back control.

They teetered that way for agonizing seconds, everyone frozen in shock. Then the bus was falling, pushed off the road and onto its right side. It slid down the muddy incline and flipped again. Jasminda squeezed her eyes, holding her body rigid as the impact of the crash shook her body.

LIZVETTE'S ONLY MOVEMENT came from the rise and fall of her chest as she breathed. She didn't move so much as an eyelid in order to blink. She sat rigid in the chair, hands clasped neatly in her lap.

Jack, on the other hand, was all motion, pacing the floor of the sitting room in the Niralls' residence suite. Two Guardsmen stood at the door. Jack did not trust himself to speak yet, so they all waited in silence.

Then a knock sounded and a terrified maid was led in by the same Guardsman from the dungeon.

"Is this the woman who delivered this note, Captain?" Jack asked.

"Yes, Your Grace."

"And you . . ." He rounded on the maid who shrank into the Guard still holding her arm. He gentled his voice and posture; there was no need to give the poor woman a heart attack. "Who gave you this letter?" He held up the forged paper.

The maid's eyes darted back and forth between Lizvette and Jack.

"It's all right, Cora," Lizvette said. "You can tell him."

"Miss Lizvette gave it to me, Your Grace."

"Thank you," said Jack. "You may go back to work. All of you." He made a motion with his hand and the room cleared, leaving him alone with Lizvette. He did not face her, could hardly bear to look at her.

"Where is she?" he ground out.

"On a bus with the other refugees."

He dropped his head into his hand. "Why?"

"It was the best place for her."

Jack spun to look at her. "And that was your decision?" His supposedly healed wound throbbed angrily, as though the grief and pain were trying to claw their way out through his chest. He wrenched open the door and ordered the Guardsman outside to radio the refugee caravan and pull Jasminda off the bus.

"And was it you who destroyed her dress?" he said, resuming his pacing.

Her head shot up, brows furrowed. "Her dress?"

"Her ball gown, ripped and burned and left in front of my office today."

Lizvette blinked slowly and took a deep breath. "That wasn't me."

"Do you know who it was?"

She notched her chin up higher and stared straight ahead.

Jack made an exasperated sound and crouched before her, careful to maintain his distance. "Tell me."

A single tear trailed down her cheek. Her jaw quivered. "I think it was Father," she whispered.

"Nirall?" Jack reared back on his heels, almost falling. He braced himself with a hand on the floor and shook his head. "I don't understand."

Her hands were squeezed together so hard, the tips of her fingernails had lost all color. She shook her head and another tear escaped her eye. Those were more tears than Jack had ever seen her shed in her entire life. She had always been a stoic child, never screaming or crying, not even when injured. Everything kept bottled up inside, even now.

Her whole body vibrated as if the strength it took her to remain composed had run out and pure chaos reigned underneath her placid exterior. She was at war with herself. Jack could see it plainly. Her distress stole a measure of rancor from his anger.

"Vette, we have known each other all our lives. You must tell me."

Her jaw quivered, but she nodded, darting a glance at the closed door.

"He wanted me to be the princess. I suppose it would make up somewhat for me being born a girl. Alariq was kind, but he never held my heart."

She looked at him pointedly, and his stomach sank in understanding. He opened his mouth, unsure of what to say, but she continued. "When Alariq died, Father didn't miss a beat. He was determined to be the grandfather of the next Prince Regent, no matter what it took. Jasminda was an obstacle, but one that worked in his favor. If you would not choose me of your own free will, then he would give you a push."

"What kind of push?"

"Feeding information to the press. Giving them fodder for the fire. Presenting me as the solution."

"And you went along with this, Vette? Why?"

She swallowed and brushed away the wetness from her cheeks. "I never wanted to hurt you, and I certainly never wanted to see her harmed. But Jack, you are the Prince Regent of Elsira. You must marry well. Your wife is not just for you; she will be the princess of the land. Did you really think there was a future with her? It's for the best that she leave now with the others."

Jack shot to his feet as the ache in his chest seemed to spread to his whole body. His hands pulled at the short ends of his hair, searching for a release from his frustration. "Lizvette, there is no future for me without her."

"So she should have stayed here, hidden away for the rest of time so you could sneak into her chambers? And then what? What about when you need an heir? She's to be content being your mistress while you sire the next prince with someone else?"

"You had no right! Not to decide her fate. Did she get on that bus willingly?"

Lizvette turned her face to the fire. "I gave explicit instructions that she was not to be harmed."

Jack leaned against his desk, imagining Jasminda fighting tooth and nail against whatever hired thugs Lizvette had acquired.

"Did you think of what it must have been like for her?" Lizvette looked down to her folded hands. "If one day, someone ever loves me, I would hope they would scream it from the rooftops." Her smile was brittle.

Jack fell onto the couch and slumped down. Lizvette was right. In a perfect world, he would have shouted his love for Jasminda from every window in the palace . . . but the world was far from perfect.

A knock sounded at the door, and a Guardsman entered.

"Your Grace, radio communication with the refugee caravan is down due to the thunderstorm. We're unable to contact them."

"Then send a telegram to the Eastern Base and keep trying the caravan. I want to make sure she doesn't step one foot inside Lagrimar."

"Yes, sir." The Guardsman spun on his heel, readying to leave.

"Wait." Weariness lay over Jack like a blanket. He looked at Lizvette and sighed. "Take her to the Guard's offices for questioning. The charge is kidnapping. And arrest Minister Nirall, as well."

Lizvette stood and brushed her dress off, her sad eyes relaying an apology. Jack's head fell to his hands as the weight of the crown grew even heavier.

THE NOISE OF the crash reverberated through the bus, screams and wails, crunching metal and glass. Then all movement ceased, and they were held in a bubble of stillness for a pregnant moment. Jasminda may have lost consciousness, she was not certain, but after a timeless period of insensibility, the world came back piece by piece.

First, the cold rain seeping into her clothing. Burning metal tinged with blood and fuel assaulted her nose. Crying, moaning, agonizing sounds of suffering. The tinny taste of blood on her tongue. Osar's eyes, inches from her own, peering at her. The warmth of Earthsong cradling her in calm, knitting her wounds.

Jasminda jerked to life, flexing her arms and legs. The bus had landed on its right side. Those in the window seats, like herself, would have sustained the worst injuries. She was sore, but whatever injuries she'd had, Osar had healed. Her hands were now free; the bar she'd been chained to was cracked and the chain broken, leaving only the heavy silver bracelets on her wrists.

She levered herself up and held out her arms for Osar. He fell against her, and she squeezed him close. The uninjured helped the injured from the wreckage. As they clambered out, they found the two buses directly behind them in the caravan had also crashed, unable to avoid the accident.

Chaos reigned on the ground as the last of the refugees were rescued from the wrecked buses. Faces peered out the windows of the other buses farther back in the convoy. On the ground, severe injuries were being tended to by the children, using Earthsong. Soldiers stood grouped together, huddled around maps and radio transmitters or tending their own injured.

Jasminda set a young girl she'd been carrying down on the sodden ground, then straightened. In the east, the muted glow of dawn emerged behind the mountains. Perhaps a two-day's walk to the southeast lay her mountain. Buried hope bloomed in her heart.

An old barn loomed a hundred metres away. If Jasminda were to go now, during this confusion, she could escape and could keep the caldera safe. She would head to her valley where odds were that no one would find her.

She searched the crowd for Turwig and Gerda but couldn't find them. Osar was healing a woman she didn't recognize. Most of the other Earthsingers were resting. Hopefully not many more needed healing, and the healers' magic would not be exhausted, but there were too many people around—injured and uninjured—for Jasminda to search through. She would have no chance to say her good-byes. This may be her only opportunity to escape.

She kept low to the ground so as not to bring attention to herself and backed away from the throng. At the bottom of the hill, a stream overflowed its banks. Trees dotted the ground, offering cover as she made her way to the barn. Most of the refugees were focused on their family members or the injured. Her retreat went unnoticed until a sharp face shot in her direction, as if drawn by a magnet.

Rozyl crouched on the ground in conversation with two other women. Jasminda froze, just steps from cover. She glanced at the nearest group of soldiers, arguing among themselves, not paying attention to the scattered refugees. Rozyl followed her gaze, then turned back to Jasminda. The two locked eyes for a long moment before the other woman dropped her head, silently giving consent.

Jasminda darted behind the tree, hiding just as the soldiers dispersed.

The men took up places around the perimeter of the refugees and herded them into a tighter group. Visually marking her path, she searched for the fastest way to move from her current position to new cover.

A scream tore through the air, rippling chills across her skin. One soldier broke through a cluster of refugees, dragging a child with him. Her breath caught at Osar's wriggling form being dragged by his collar.

The soldier holding Osar tugged him along until they reached the lieutenant in charge. A line of refugees trailed behind them.

"This one bewitched me!" the soldier shouted in Elsiran.

One bedraggled woman wailed in Lagrimari, "Leave him alone! Leave the boy alone!" She was working herself into a frenzy. Others tried to calm her, but she brushed off their aid. Jasminda recognized her as Timmyn's mother. The poor thing had already seen her son shot, the threat of violence to another child must have pushed her over the edge.

"What is the problem, Sergeant?" the lieutenant asked.

"Sir, this vermin spawn performed his enchantment on me. I . . . I felt a strangeness befall me. Some unnatural thing." The sergeant shook Osar in anger, and Timmyn's mother lunged toward them.

Another soldier pulled his weapon, training it on her. "Keep back!"

She screamed for them to let the boy go.

"What is she saying? Where's the one that can translate?" the lieutenant barked. To Osar he said, "What have you done, boy? What vileness have you brought upon us?"

Gerda approached, her presence calming many of the refugees, though Timmyn's mother grew even more hysterical. "All the boy's done is heal your soldier," Gerda said.

The lieutenant drew his own pistol, not understanding her words. "Get back. All of you get back!"

Other soldiers mobilized, drawing their firearms on the refugees. From behind her tree, Jasminda watched in horror. Rozyl stood at the edge of the group, her stance defiant. She darted a glance to where Jasminda hid before snapping back to the soldiers.

Cold logic told her there was no better time to go. The attention of the soldiers was fixed on the refugees. There would not be another opportunity.

But the image of Timmyn, flat on the ground, blood pooling on his shirt, would not leave Jasminda. If someone was shot this time . . . Were there any Earthsingers not drained from helping the others?

Her brain knew the caldera was more important than the lives of a few refugees, but could she stand by and watch a potential massacre just to keep it safe? The mother screamed again, thrusting Jasminda from her daze.

She rose and started back toward the others.

Escape would have to wait.

CHAPTER ELEVEN

"THERE IS TOO much interference, sir." The communications officer flipped a switch, testing yet another connection.

"What kind of interference?" Jack said, peering over the man's shoulder.

"It's very unusual, but we're not able to contact any unit east of the Old Wall." Static could be heard from the man's headset.

"So the entire northeastern sector of the country is radio silent?"

"Yes, sir. No telephones, two-ways, or cable communication is operational. They're just silent."

Jack rubbed the back of his neck. "It's almost as if this were intentional."

The officer looked up startled. "Well, yes, sir. It could be."

Jack did the math in his head. The caravan was too far along for vehicles to catch up with it, and there was no way for him to contact anyone who could get Jasminda to safety. Panic threatened, but he beat it back through force of will.

Dusk had fallen, bringing with it rain from the east that pelted the city mercilessly.

He banged his fist on the table, and the young officer jumped.

"Blast it! I would need wings to get to her now," Jack murmured, then stopped short. His gaze rose to the ceiling.

The airship.

Alariq's pride and joy. And the cause of his death.

It was risky, too risky to even be contemplating, but what was the alternative? Jasminda trapped in Lagrimar? Forced to work in the mines or the harems or worse. She could be killed. He could not save the hundreds of refugees, much as he wanted to, but the life of one woman, the woman most precious to him, could he not even save her?

The airship was the only way to get to the border fast enough—maybe even beat the caravan that had left hours earlier. However, it was this precise situation, flying in a thunderstorm, that had killed his brother. Jack had called Alariq foolish ... Who was the fool now?

He stalked out of the communications room and into the small office the army maintained in the palace.

"The airship that was on the roof—is it still there, Sergeant?" he asked the soldier on duty.

"Yes, sir. It's scheduled to be moved next week."

"Never mind that. I need a pilot. Immediately."

"Sir, the army doesn't have any ships or pilots. The airship was a gift to Prince Alariq from—"

"Yes, I know all that. But there must be someone in this city who can pilot a bloody airship. Find the ambassador to Yaly. It's their invention, he must know someone."

The sergeant rushed to stand, confused but determined.

"Your Grace," a Guardsman appeared in the doorway. Jack whirled around to face him.

"What is it?"

"There's a woman here from the Sisterhood. She's been raising quite a ruckus for some time now, saying she needs to speak with you."

Jack sighed. "I can't imagine a worse time."

"Your Grace, she's saying it has to do with Miss Jasminda. I thought you might want to speak with her."

Jack peered more closely at the Guardsman. He was the same fellow who'd escorted Lizvette to questioning. Tension gripped Jack, and he nodded. "Take me to her."

They'd kept the woman in the main lobby of the palace, and Jack could hear her voice from two corridors away.

"I will not stand down, and you would do well to keep out of my way, sir. I refuse to leave this palace until I have seen Prince Jaqros!"

"Sister," Jack said as he approached. The woman startled and spun around, gracing him with the tiniest curtsey possible before rushing to his side. A Guardsman reached out to stop her approach, but Jack brushed him off. "What can I do for you?"

"You can stop a great miscarriage of justice, Your Grace. My niece, a citizen of Elsira, despite all appearances to the contrary, was chained and forcibly placed on a bus headed to Lagrimar with the refugees. She does not belong there and I—"

"You are Aunt Vanesse," Jack said. The woman stopped, looking stunned. He should have recognized her at once, but his mind was scattered in a million directions. How many Sisters had burn scars on their faces? "Jasminda told me about you."

She looked confused, but the determination in her eyes burned bright.

"Please, come with me," he said, leading her toward his office. "I have been trying to rectify that situation, believe me. But I've been stymied at every turn."

Jack stopped at his secretary's desk. "Netta, I want you to check in with the palace regiment every five minutes for an update on their search for an airship pilot."

Netta nodded and picked up the phone.

"An airship pilot?" Vanesse said, squinting at him.

"Yes. I fear that is the only way to get to her before the caravan reaches the border. My brother had the only airship in Rosira and pilots are in short supply."

"Your Grace, I have a . . . a friend, who can drive just about anything. She's competed in the Yaly Classic Air Race the past two years flying speed crafts. If there's anyone who can pilot it, she can."

Jack stared, speechless, before breaking into a grin. He picked up the startled woman and spun her around, only putting her down when her small fist began beating against his back.

"ARE YOU SURE this is wise?" Usher said, following Jack up the stairs and onto the roof. Rain attacked the building; wind gusts blew sideways into the covered awning they stood under, soaking them.

"No, I'm pretty sure this is the least wise thing I could ever do. But I can't lose her, Usher. I can't."

"I understand your feelings are strong, young sir, but this country lost a prince to that very airship not three weeks past."

"Duty has taken everything from me. Everything I've ever loved I've lost —and that hasn't been much. I've sacrificed my life for this country again and again and what does it give me in return? Nothing but heartache. I will not allow Jasminda to be another casualty."

Usher's face was grim. Jack didn't want to argue with him. He didn't have the strength for it. But to his surprise, Usher merely nodded. "Come back with her quickly, then."

"Thank you, old man." They embraced, and Jack raced over to the airship.

A lump formed in his throat as he grew closer. He'd never been in anything like it before. They were common in other places—the Fremian army had an entire fleet—but Elsira was not a country that took well to change, adopting new technology only when absolutely necessary.

He climbed into the cabin where Vanesse's friend Clove already sat in the pilot's seat, checking over the instruments. At first glance, the woman was unassuming. She barely came up to his shoulder and her heart-shaped face seemed made to smile. Strawberry-blond hair curled around her head, and he couldn't place her age. Vanesse was in her early thirties, but Clove could be ten years younger or older—it was hard to say.

"Everything look all right to you?" Jack asked, taking his place on one of the plush seats, dripping water all over it. Across from him sat Vanesse who had removed her robes and wore a smart-looking pantsuit, similar to the one Clove wore. She appeared perfectly dry.

"This is beautifully made, Your Grace. It's an honor to be able to fly it. Just a few more calculations, and we'll be ready to go."

Jack nodded, tamping down his impatience. "How bad is the storm?"

She turned in her seat to face him. "I'm not going to lie and say it's a stroll through a straw garden. This will probably be the toughest flight I've ever made. But I'm game. When it's time to face the fiddler, best do it with your dancing shoes on." She smiled at Vanesse, who beamed back at her. Though Jasminda and her aunt didn't really resemble one another, something about Vanesse's smile made Jack's heart lurch. He recognized adoration when he saw it and sensed there was more to these two women's relationship than friendship.

Usher remained under the awning, watching them solemnly, but gave a supportive nod when Jack caught his eye.

Then the engine whirred to life. "Are you ready, Your Grace?" Clove shouted.

He closed his eyes and said a silent prayer to the Queen Who Sleeps that he live long enough to save the woman he loved. "The only way to the other side is through it!"

"That's the spirit!" Clove said as the ship lurched into the air.

THE REFUGEES TRAVELED on foot, abandoning the wrecked buses. The rain ended shortly before dawn and the cool morning air left Jasminda's clothes damp and chilled. Guards from the buses formed a perimeter around the group, weapons in hand.

Tension between the guards and the refugees still crackled, though once Jasminda had translated that Osar was only trying to heal the soldier, things had calmed somewhat. The Elsirans, so fearful of magic, had been uninterested in being aided by an Earthsinger, and Jasminda had warned the children off their natural, helpful instincts.

The paved road ended at the Eastern Base at the bottom of the foothills. The border loomed just beyond, deceptive in its ordinariness. Her last time here, she had not even registered the proximity of the base to Lagrimar proper. There was no visible line, no wall, just the grass of the foothills giving way to a stretch of rocky dirt about a thousand metres wide. The hills on either side veered up sharply, transforming into jagged mountains towering overhead. This small stretch of flatland was not only the sole break in the mountain range separating the two countries but it was the location of all seven Mantle breaches.

The only other visible indication that one country ended and another began were the hundreds of Elsiran troops and vehicles gathered with weapons drawn pointing toward an equal number of Lagrimari troops on the other side. Bullets could not pierce the Mantle until it was breached, but the

Elsirans showed no signs of backing down from their standoff.

The sun shone overhead, lighting the bleak landscape of sandy soil and sparse, tough vegetation. The refugees had been quiet since leaving the buses, but now at the end of their journey, their silence was a shroud. Osar stood on one side of Jasminda, Rozyl on the other. The only words the woman had spoken had been to ask whether Jasminda had the caldera on her. After she'd affirmed it, Rozyl had not left her side.

Jasminda's fingers itched for her lost shotgun. Rozyl's hands curled into fists, probably wanting the same thing. Across the border, rows of Lagrimari stood at attention. At the front of the line, an older man with a world-weary face stepped forward.

"By order of His Majesty the True Father of the Republic of Lagrimar, I, Brigadier Joren ol-Tarikor do hereby declare this a day of peace. My brothers and sisters, I welcome you home."

He held both hands over his head and paused dramatically before clapping them together. An earsplitting crack rent the air. The ground shuddered, rolling and shaking, throwing everyone off-balance. From the direction of the army base, an alarm sounded.

"Breach!" shouted an Elsrian.

"Breach!"

"Breach!"

The word was repeated, the message passed along, as the Elsiran soldiers tensed almost in unison.

The armies were evenly matched in numbers, though the Lagrimari weaponry was visibly old. The men bore muzzle-loaded, single-shot rifles that were at least fifty years out-of-date. Many had bayonets or swords, as well. Jasminda eyed the Elsiran soldiers nearest her, noting the far more advanced automatic rifles with coils of ammunition at the ready. Tanks were spaced evenly along the border with smaller armored four-wheelers bearing giant rifles and larger weapons that looked like cannons or grenade launchers. The Lagrimari had no vehicles, but the barrels of huge wheeled cannons sat on the front lines. Elsira's superior economic power and technology was unquestionable. But the Lagrimari had one advantage the Elsirans couldn't buy.

The wind grew from a gentle breeze to a gale within the blink of an eye. Jasminda's hair whipped back, the force of the wind stinging her eyes. It died down after a few breaths. But thick clouds exploded into existence over those on the Elsiran side. They swirled and raged unnaturally, then shuddered as deadly sharp icicles shot down. The ice stopped in midair a hand's breadth from their heads, then crackled and fell apart, dusting the Elsirans and refugees in a layer of snow.

The army's Earthsingers were taunting them.

Movement at the top of the lower foothills drew Jasminda's attention. Lines of additional Lagrimari troops came into view from behind the hilltops on either side of the flatland of the breach area. They marched over the hills, descending across the border between the lands.

"They've done it," she whispered. "They've destroyed the whole thing. The Mantle is gone."

Within minutes, the number of Lagrimari soldiers more than doubled. According to Jack, almost all of Elsira's fighting force had been gathered here.

Technology versus superior numbers and magic.

Jasminda fought against the building despair.

The brigadier marched forward, leading his men across the invisible barrier that no longer existed. An Elsiran general marched forward to meet him.

"There is no need for losing life this day. I will address my brethren," Brigadier Joren said in broken Elsiran. The general stood aside as Joren approached.

"Please, listen close," he said in Lagrimari. This seemed to be a cue for all the refugees to sit down. Jasminda settled on the muddy ground with the others. "I am happy to welcome you back to the open arms of the Fatherland. Your presence will help us usher in a great peace. But before your return, there is something His Majesty requires of you. One of you holds an artifact that has great significance to our blessed leader. A stone, smaller than my palm." He raised his hand over his head. The Elsiran troops nearest him followed his movement with their rifles, but he paid them no mind.

"The stone must be returned before your homecoming may begin."

Jasminda's chest tightened. Though it must have been her imagination, the caldera in her pocket seemed to hum to life. She flexed her fingers, eager for a weapon of any kind, a way to fight through the terror and escape.

Brigadier Joren paced the length of the tightly gathered crowd of refugees. "To underscore the importance of compliance with any and all beneficent requests of His Majesty's, I will return one of you to the World After every minute the artifact is not within my possession."

He pulled his pistol from the holster at his hip and pulled back the hammer. The Elsiran soldiers tensed almost as one. The general closest to Joren pulled his sidearm, as well.

Brigadier Joren chuckled. "I will harm no Elsiran. This is between me and my countrymen," he said in Elsiran. The general nodded but continued pointing his own pistol at the man.

The brigadier produced a pocket watch, and though Jasminda was at least a dozen metres away, she could feel each tick of the clock like a beat inside her chest.

The minute that passed felt like the longest of her life, until it ended and Joren grabbed a random refugee from the crowd. Gray hair, a stooped stature . . .

Gerda.

Jasminda barely stifled a gasp. When Joren lifted his pistol to the old woman's head, Jasminda hurtled into motion. Her body acted without thought, but she struggled against an immovable object while trying to get closer to the woman. She looked down to find hands wrapped around her waist, squeezing painfully and holding her in place. Wrenching her neck around, she stared into Rozyl's hard eyes. They were wet with unshed tears, but Rozyl's face was implacable. Jasminda turned back to the front. Through the crowd, Gerda met her gaze and gave an almost imperceptible shake of her head. Jasminda squeezed her eyes shut.

The shot rang out.

"No!" Jasminda's scream echoed in the wake of the gunshot, reverberating off the mountain peaks. Many things could be healed with Earthsong, but a close-range shot to the head was not one of them.

Rozyl didn't let go, tightening her embrace and forcing Jasminda's head down.

"Someone has something to say? The location of the artifact perhaps?" Brigadier Joren's voice was self-satisfied. Nausea swept over Jasminda. Her empty stomach heaved, but nothing came out. The Elsiran general looked horrified, but made no moves to stop the executions.

The clock continued to tick, and Jasminda couldn't watch another person die. She couldn't be responsible for the death of one more innocent.

This time Brigadier Joren pulled a young girl from the crowd, out of the arms of her shrieking mother. Jasminda slackened her body, and Rozyl's hold weakened slightly. Taking advantage, Jasminda broke out of the woman's arms and shot to her feet.

The brigadier's gaze landed on her, and Jasminda opened her mouth to confess. Before she'd taken a breath, Rozyl shot up beside her.

Turwig was next, moving faster than a man of his age rightly should. One by one, the other Keepers she'd met in the cave and at the camp stood, and even Lyngar, a man she'd suspected of having no emotions whatsoever, had tears in his eyes as he looked at Gerda's lifeless form sprawled on the ground.

Brigadier Joren was not impressed at the show of solidarity. "The artifact. Where is it?"

"I have it," Rozyl called out, her voice strong and clear.

"I have it," Lyngar said.

The statement was repeated by every Keeper standing.

"I have it," Timmyn said, taking to his feet. Other refugees, children and mothers, the young and the elderly all stood, proclaiming to have the caldera. Most of them had no idea what they were even admitting to, but Jasminda was moved all the same. She had thought she'd known misery and heartache since the loss of her family, but she had nothing on these people. She'd also thought she truly understood love, but the actions of the other refugees humbled her.

Her hands shook, and she stuffed them into her pockets, brushing against the photo of her family. Fingering the smooth paper, she felt her family now extend to everyone here. They were all in this together. These people that she never thought she'd fit in with were acting as one with her. Standing together in the face of almost certain death. Tears streamed down her cheeks, and she swiped them away.

Osar grabbed her hand. Without even thinking about it, she reached for Rozyl's hand, as well. When their skin met, like before, Jasminda was thrown forcefully into a connection with Rozyl's Song. She instinctively slammed down a shield. Rozyl startled. Through her energy, Jasminda sensed the Songs of the others crowded around her vividly, in sharp contrast to the bleak, emptiness of the many Songless.

The caldera pulsed again, vibrating through the layers of fabric, warming Jasminda's skin. The spell Yllis had taught Oola in the vision tickled her memory.

A blood sacrifice.

Gerda's blood bathed the ground beneath her body.

A powerful Song.

Rozyl's Song was intense, stronger by far than Jasminda's own father's. She knew from linking with Osar before how strong he was, as well. Many of the other children, as well as the Keepers, held Songs of varying strengths.

"Osar," she whispered. "Can you send a message to everyone to link with me?"

His big eyes shone as he nodded. Like a ripple spreading through a pond, every refugee took the hand of the ones next to them. Jasminda felt each link expand the pool of power she had access to by orders of magnitude.

She felt every heartbeat inside her body, every breath. Insects burrowed deep under the ground came into crisp focus. Every blink of every eye of each of the thousands of soldiers surrounding her was loud as a camera's shutter. The brutal rainstorm drifted off to the west. Access to every living being within a million metres was at her fingertips. Power raced through her. Every Song linked with her was at her control.

She centered her attention on the ground beneath their feet and reached for the memory of Oola's spell. Through the link she could almost taste Gerda's blood mixed with the dirt and sand. She twisted the energy of Earthsong, mixing it with the woman's lifeblood.

The power swelled within her as she wove the threads of the differing energies together. The spell came to her as if channeled from another mind— in a way it had been. The complex fabric of intermingling energies was nothing she could explain, but she sang the spell as if possessed.

When she was done, she looked up, breathing heavily, coming back into the knowledge of her surroundings. Below her feet, the ground had become glassy and smooth. Dark as midnight, it extended all around them, like fast-spreading molasses. Soon, the earth beneath the soldiers, both Elsiran and Lagrimari, was transformed to the polished rock surface of the caldera. Just as in the caves.

Shouts of alarm rang out around them as the soldiers took in the transformation. Jasminda's vision, blurred from the heavy strain of working magic far beyond her experience, came back into focus. Then the shots began. She did not know which side fired first, but a hail of gunfire whizzed around her, heralding the beginning of the war.

The refugees shrank back as a group, scurrying to move out of the line of fire as the bullets flew. Jasminda's feet were leaden, but she was dragged along with the others, still hand in hand, as they moved backward to allow Elsiran troops to fill in the gap they created.

Some refugees fell, struck by bullets as they made their retreat. The others ran toward the squat buildings of the Eastern Base, taking cover behind them. Here, the ground was hard and shiny, as well. The massive caldera extended far beyond the base as far as she could see.

Jasminda placed a palm on the ground and caught a subtle trace of the wrongness she'd felt in the cave. She recognized it now as the residue of magic that required death. There was something unnatural about it that made a shiver go up her spine.

What had she done?

She peered around the corner of the building to view the fighting. The Elsirans were pushing forward against the overwhelming number of Lagrimari. Tanks and weaponry felled many a Lagrimari where he stood. She sighed and slumped against the wall, all energy draining away.

"They're not using Earthsong," said Rozyl, watching the fighting unfold.

"They can't," Jasminda breathed. "This land is like the cave now. No one can sing." She let out a hollow chuckle, then winced and grabbed her stomach in sudden pain. Looking down, she scrunched her brow in confusion. Her palm came away coated in blood.

"You've been shot," Rozyl cried, kneeling before her. "I'm no good at healing. Osar!" she called, looking around for the boy.

Jasminda shook her head, then placed her hand over Rozyl's. "No one can sing but me."

Recognition sparked in Rozyl's eyes. "Then sing. Link with me."

"Making this—" she tapped the hard ground beneath her "—even with the link . . . it took almost everything I had. I can't link again or heal myself." The last vestiges of her Song's energy were dwindling.

"Then we'll get you off this bloody thing. How far does it go?" Rozyl looked around wildly.

"Too far," Jasminda whispered, struggling to breathe. The pain was a haze. It seemed far away but she was losing control of her body. Her arms were so heavy. "Rozyl, my pocket. I can use the last of my Song to read the caldera one more time."

Rozyl sat stubbornly motionless, her face a mix of betrayal and hurt.

"Please." Jasminda opened her palm, her fingers fluttering. "This is the last chance."

With a resigned expression, Rozyl reached into Jasminda's pocket, pulling out the photograph and the bundled caldera. Jasminda smiled at the photo but reached for the caldera. Rozyl unwrapped the stone carefully, then placed it in Jasminda's hand.

THIS IS GOOD-BYE. The last time I will see my brother.

We have given him everything he wanted. We stand at the border of what will now become two lands, two peoples. Songbearer and Silent, separated for all time.

Once Yllis's barrier spell falls into place, there will be no crossing—those were the terms of the treaty. That stipulation was put in by our side. Many Songbearers have grown weary of the fighting. It is against our nature. Some feel if they never see another Silent, it will be for the best.

Already I miss the way things were, but this was my decision and I must stand by it.

"Will you embrace me one last time, sister?"

The odd, smooth bracelets adorning his wrists hold the magic of Yllis's binding spell. The blood magic that ensures Eero doesn't use whatever stolen Song may be left inside him. He can cause no further harm before the Mantle is erected.

His eyes shine, and I see the boy I once knew within them. One last time could not hurt.

I step closer. My arms wrap around him. We came into this world together, and I thought we would stay that way forever.

A sharp pain pierces my side. I pull back from him and stare at the dagger sticking out from between my ribs. I gasp up at him in horror, but Eero's face is a mask.

I reach for Earthsong, trying to knit the wound, but something is wrong. My Song is weakening, slipping out of my grasp like a wisp of smoke. I breathe in, and in some more, but the breath never makes it to my lungs. Eero whispers a string of foreign words, and I fall to the ground.

Everything goes black.

Voices call my name.

One voice.

Yllis.

"Oola! Oola! Please come back to me. My love, please."

He is mine again after being so cold for so long.

He begs and pleads, apologizes and bargains.

I try to go to him but am locked in place. My breath is gone, and I am separated from my body.

Three archways loom before me. The widest leads back to my body. Another leads to the World After.

But the third calls to me, though narrow and ominous. I step through it, sealing my fate.

The World Between is a smoke filled antechamber full of endless images of the living. Neither here nor there, it is vast and lonely, only grazed by the living in their dreams. Some believe all dreams take place here.

For me, it is a nightmare.

From here I bear witness to my body on the ground. Eero smashing the bespelled bracelets. He is full of my Song, stolen from my last breaths.

Yllis gives a great cry. He gathers a swell of Earthsong and sings the spell to create the barrier between the lands. Eero steps away from his Silent followers, over to the band of astonished Songbearers. Yllis is too focused on his spell to notice. The barrier slams into place leaving him holding my body on one side with the throng of Silent and Eero, bursting with my Song, on the other with the rest of the Songbearers.

This was his plan all along.

He never wanted to be shut up along side the Silent forever. He merely wanted to have an inexhaustible supply of Songbearers to steal from.

Eero stands at the barrier, expression smug. "Worry not, Yllis. She is not dead. She will awaken at any moment and live quite a fine life without her Song. She will know what it is like to be me."

Two archways still stand behind me, the one leading to the Living World pulsing brighter than the sun. Calling to me. Pleading with me. I am being given a choice.

Eero's look of triumph changes to a frown. "She will awaken," he says, a tremor invading his voice.

Yllis growls and pulls my body closer.

Eero tries to move forward, but the barrier stops him. He beats against the invisible wall with a fist. "Oola! Oola!" he screams.

Both archways dim and begin to fade. I must make my choice quickly.

If I go back to the Living World, I can resume a life without my heart. The World After holds no appeal, though Mother and Father are there. How can I face them with what I have done to Eero?

Here, in the World Between, I may watch. That will be my punishment.

Justice finally served for my crimes.

I will watch.

The archways fade and disappear.

I watch Yllis bear my body back to the city and cut a chamber into the mountains to house me. Above the chamber, the Silent construct a magnificent palace.

Yllis chooses a loyal Silent to rule. A young man of character and honor, Abdeen Alliaseen, to lead the people in the absence of their queen.

Yllis makes Alliaseen promise to ensure that history is kind to me and bears no recollection of my fault in the start of the war. He spends weeks, months, years locked in his laboratory, scouring the libraries of the Cantors, searching for something. Doing what he does best, studying magic.

I watch on the day he finds what he has been seeking. He chants words in the ancient tongue of the Cavefolk, words I don't understand. He takes the pendant bearing my father's sigil, the one I always wore around my neck and cuts himself, spilling his blood over it. He calls for Alliaseen, who, when asked, spills his own blood on the sigil without hesitation, binding the spell. The blood congeals and the magic grows, encasing the pendant in a blood-red stone.

Blood magic will do what Earthsong cannot.

Blood magic may be broken only by those who bear the blood.

Yllis journeys back to the barrier he created and crosses it, using another bit of magic.

He gathers those unafraid of standing against a now impossibly powerful Eero. Those who want to learn to fight. Songbearers are peaceful by nature, but these men and women have been broken. They become something new. He crafts the words of a promise to me, one these new soldiers vow to keep.

I watch as my beloved Yllis wages war on my beloved brother, and I watch when Yllis is slain. Eero is too strong, and the stolen Songs have twisted his mind and made him far more ruthless than even the broken Songbearers.

Yllis dies with the stone in his hand.

His final spell traps his Song in the stone.

The Keepers of the Promise are supposed to take the stone, cross the border, and present it to the prince, whose touch will unlock the magic. But the Keepers he commanded to hold back and stay safe, rush in seeking revenge. None survive the battle.

The stone sits where it lies. Yllis's gift to me, his whispered spell to bring me back to my body and gift me his own Song, lies under the rubble of the fallen city as his body turns to bones.

The archways are long gone now.

If they were here, perhaps I would pass into the World After to be with him. To thank him for trying to save me.

But being with Yllis is not punishment enough.

So I watch.

For a very long time.

Sometimes, a dream will find me and pierce the loneliness.

But more often, it is endless agony. Standing by watching while the centuries pass.

And now, Jasminda, you have heard my story. Judge me for my faults if you must. But you bear the only evidence of Yllis's love for me. His Song is in your hands.

Release it.

Release me.

It is time for me to end this.

JACK GRIPPED THE edge of the seat as the airship descended from the clouds. The battle taking place below belonged to his worst fears. Judging by the sheer extent of the fighting, the Mantle had already been destroyed. As the ship flew closer to the ground, he marveled at the strange change in the soil for a moment, and then focused on the troop advancement. His men were beating back an impressive number of Lagrimari. He found it odd that no environmental disasters had been unleashed as in the Seventh Breach.

The ship set down safely just beyond the Eastern Base.

"That was some bloody fine piloting, Clove," he said, clapping the woman on the back. He opened the carriage door and tore across the ground before she even had a chance to respond.

Flying through the vicious storm had been just as difficult as he'd imagined. They'd been bandied about by the wind and rain, and nearly struck by lightning twice. But Clove was unflappable, gripping the steering wheel with bloodless hands and navigating them safely through.

Now the only thing on his mind was finding Jasminda.

They'd set down about one hundred metres from the fighting, but he didn't see any refugees near the battle or beyond it. Could they have already been taken away? Were they even now beyond sight, well on their way into Lagrimar? He spun in a circle, desperately hoping he was not too late.

A small figure emerged in the corner of his eye. Jack whipped around to find Osar standing next to the base mess hall, beckoning him forward. Jack took off at a run, vaguely aware of Vanesse and Clove scurrying after him.

Small clusters of refugees hid behind the outer buildings of the base. He searched their faces anxiously, running over and falling to his knees when he finally found her. Jasminda's head rested on Rozyl's shoulder. She appeared to be sound asleep.

So absorbed was he in his gratitude over locating her, several moments passed before he registered the blood covering her midsection. He met Rozyl's eyes with horror. She shook her head.

He turned to Osar who looked on solemnly. "Can't you do something?"

"This—" Rozyl tapped her knuckle to the hardened ground "—is like the cave. No one can sing." Rozyl touched Jasminda's head gently. "It will probably win your side this war."

Jack ignored the last bit. The war could be dealt with once Jasminda was better. "Then we have to move her." He reached forward and hauled Jasminda into his arms. Her breathing was shallow. He took off running in a random direction, determined to find a way out of this cursed, bespelled rock.

Jasminda's eyes fluttered open, and his pace slowed.

"Jack," she said, a smile splitting her face.

"I'm here. I'm going to get you off this blasted thing so they can heal you up, all right?"

"Jack." She grazed the knuckles of her closed fist against his lips. "I need you."

"I need you, too. You're the only thing I need. I don't have to be prince. I'll give it up. You just . . . you just need to say with me."

"Stop."

"What?"

"Stop moving."

"I can't. I have to—"

"Please."

Tears clouded his vision, and he fell to his knees with her in his arms.

She turned her closed fist palm up and unfurled her fingers to show him the caldera. "I need you to help me bring Her back."

Jack searched her face, his eyes full of questions.

"Your hand." She was so weak. If this was what she wanted, he would do it. He pressed a kiss to her lips, then closed his hand over the caldera.

Searing pain shot through his entire body, as if being pulled apart one cell at a time. He might have screamed out loud, he wasn't sure, but the burning agony was like nothing he'd ever felt. His blood was on fire, it burned bright and hot. Then it was gone.

Breath returned to his lungs. He was once again kneeling on the glossy surface of the unnatural ground, holding his love in his arms as she slipped further and further away.

A brittle cracking pulled his attention upward. The perfect, smooth surface of the Queen's encasement, hovered here, out in the open, nearly a thousand kilometres from the palace. The shell was cracked open like an egg.

Below it, a figure floated, wrapped in ivory fabric. Her skin shone gloriously, her dark, curling hair swirled around her head, blown by a nonexistent breeze. She moved like liquid, spinning and stretching. She righted herself and hovered before Jack, her dark eyes piercing him with intensity.

He swallowed and lowered his head in deference.

The Queen had awoken.

CHAPTER TWELVE

JASMINDA WAS DROWNING in Earthsong. Normally, her Song was the placid surface of a well. Now, instead of being calm and still, the well was a raging river, with white-capped waves shuttling over its banks. The swell pulled her under with its sheer force, leaving her sputtering, coughing, gasping for breath.

A warm solid hand rubbed her back in gentle circles. She focused on the feeling, the comfort, and leaned into a familiar embrace. Hands stroked her head, her face. Lips brushed her forehead. She wanted those lips someplace else so she rose to meet them.

Jack.

His kiss was like air to her. She breathed him in and held him there inside her, never wanting to exhale. His arms tightened around her, and he pulled his lips away. She whimpered, wanting to keep kissing him. On his chuckle, she opened her eyes.

His smile undid her. She stared at him, drinking in the beauty of his features.

"You died again," he whispered.

"I did?"

His expression shuddered, and he glanced down at her clothes. She followed his gaze down to her dress, covered with blood.

"You have to stop doing that. I don't think my nerves can take it." He pressed her back to him wrapping his arms around her as she became aware of her surroundings.

Shell-shocked refugees emerged from their hiding places, staring in awe at a point behind her. She pulled away from Jack, craned her neck around, and nearly fell backward.

Floating above them was Queen Oola, ethereal and beautiful, fierce and overpowering. Jasminda gaped at the Queen's familiar face. Looking at the woman was like looking into a mirror.

Something hard jabbed Jasminda's closed fist. She uncurled her fingers to reveal the bronze pendant bearing the Queen's sigil attached to a thin metal chain. The caldera surrounding the pendant was gone, burned away by the awakening spell.

A hush of quiet descended. No bullets hissed, no canons roared. Though she could not pull her attention away from the Queen to the battlefield, the fighting must have stopped upon Her arrival.

The refugees begin to kneel. Jasminda climbed off Jack and kneeled, as well, bowing her head.

"Jaqros Alliaseen. Jasminda ul-Sarifor." The Queen's voice rang out, rich and thick as raw honey. "Rise."

Jasminda darted a glance at Jack, and both of them stood on wobbly legs. Power surged along her skin as she and Jack were lifted into the air and drifted over the heads of the awe-struck crowd. The spell released her less than a metre away from the Queen, her legs even wobblier than before.

Queen Oola floated down until She was almost at eye level. The pendant in Jasminda's hand seemed to transfix Her. Jasminda held it out in offering. The chain lifted into the air and settled around Her neck, where it belonged.

"I owe you a gratitude for awakening me. In return, you must bow before no one."

Though she had not initiated it, Jasminda's connection to Earthsong flared to life. The slow trickle of her weak power enlarged, and she was engorged with a rush of Earthsong. She struggled to catch her breath as the sensation shot through her. It was like being in the link all over again: everything around her sharpened into focus. She gasped as pure energy pulsed inside her.

Jack caught hold of her hand to steady her. She gripped him hard.

"Your Majesty," she said, inclining her head. "Why me?"

Queen Oola drew closer, Her dark gaze peering deep inside Jasminda as if seeing her very soul.

The power surging within her made it hard to concentrate, but Jasminda stared at the pendant resting against Queen Oola's chest to bring her thoughts into focus. "Why was I the only one affected by the caldera? Why could no one else see the visions?"

Queen Oola's expression did not change, but Her eyes lightened and a breeze lifted Her hair. *Blood magic may be broken only by those who bear the blood.*

"Whose blood? Mine? I'm sorry, but I don't under—"

"Prince Jaqros," the Queen interrupted, rising.

Jasminda wanted to push for answers, but Queen Oola had effectively ended her inquiry. She looked around. Every eye in every direction was glued to the Queen.

"You are the rightful ruler of this land," Oola said, turning to Jack.

He deepened his bow. "I rule only in your stead, Your Majesty."

"You are loyal and true, as is your beloved." She swept Her gaze to Jasminda, who still vibrated with her new, incredibly powerful Song and a head full of questions. "I will abdicate my throne to you."

Gasps sounded. Jasminda's own heartbeat pulsed rapidly. She held on to Jack even tighter.

"My gift to Jasminda is the strength of Song she will need to be queen. Use it well. My wish is for you to unite the people as they once were. And rule. Well."

She surged over the heads of the troops, toward the place where the two lands met. "This border is no more," Her voice carried, strong and clear. "Singer and Silent will live as one. Be it so."

"Be it so," said Jasminda under her breath. She could barely think for the questions swirling around in her head. Could it really be true? She and Jack together as king and queen?

Oola rose higher into the air, surveying the land and the people. A disturbance among the Lagrimari caught Her attention, and She hovered staring at the sea of soldiers. Jasminda craned to see what caused the lines of Lagrimari to part. From this distance, all she could make out was the movement of a bright, reflective object, glinting in the sun. She pulled Jack forward, passing through the sea of stunned Elsirans to get a closer look. Every sense was on alert.

They reached the front of the crowd, and Jasminda jerked to a stop, causing Jack to plow into her back.

"What is it?"

She could only stare as dread cooled her skin.

Sunlight glittered off the jewel-encrusted mask covering the face of a man walking across the battlefield. No holes for eyes, nose, or mouth were visible—just a covering of multicolored precious stones obscuring his entire head. A heavy tunic lined with even more jewels flowed nearly to his ankles. He walked across the caldera-covered ground as if laying claim to the land. As if he had already conquered everything he surveyed.

Jasminda tapped into the maelstrom of emotions surrounding her and struggled to parse them out. The strongest by far were from Oola—pain, shame, anger, heartbreak, and finally, relief. Oddly, Jasminda could sense nothing from the man in front of her, who could be none other than the True Father. *Eero.* His emotions were a vast emptiness. Were he not standing directly on the caldera she would have thought he was blocking her Song somehow, but perhaps he had no feelings left after centuries of tyranny.

Oola lowered herself before Her twin until Her feet hovered over the ground. She reached for him and ran a finger across the grotesque mask. Jasminda once again pushed forward, drawn toward the two as if by an invisible chain. Having spent so much time inside Oola's head, worry blossomed within her at the Queen's reaction.

"You have returned," Eero said. His voice was nothing like that of his younger self. Hollow and raspy, it was the sound of death. Both Oola and Jasminda flinched.

"I have come back for you," Oola said.

They spoke quietly, just for the two of them, but Jasminda made out their words.

"You came back to take from me what is mine," Eero grated.

Oola dropped Her hand. Jasminda was now close enough to see the tears welling in the Queen's eyes. Her worry grew.

"I came back to right my wrong." One tear broke free and streamed down Oola's cheek. "What have you done, brother?"

Eero raised his hands to his mask and pulled it off his face. A silent shudder went through those on both sides. None alive had seen beneath the mask he'd first donned centuries ago. Subjugation and misery had altered the collective memory, and the Lagrimari had forgotten their leader was not an Earthsinger like them. They'd forgotten why he preyed on them and stole their power.

The jeweled mask fell from his gloved fingertips. Beneath it, Eero's face was unchanged from the young man Jasminda had seen in Oola's memories. The shock of the crowd was oppressive. It slammed into Jasminda, forcing her to throw up a shield against the assault.

"Will you embrace me one last time, sister?" Eero's words echoed those he'd spoken before betraying his twin all those years ago.

Oola's emotions sharply changed. Guilt came to the forefront, her resolve to right her wrong was slipping away under the weight of the familiarity and love she still felt for her brother. His amber eyes held a warmth that did not correspond to the emptiness inside him. Oola could not sense it, she had always been blinded to him, just as Yllis had said, and even now, *even now*, as Jasminda observed, she continued to be so.

Jasminda needed a way to get through to Oola, to make her see her brother for what he really was.

Your Majesty. Jasminda thought a message, the way Osar and the Earthsingers of old had. She did not know if it would work, she had little control over the vast power now bursting beneath her skin, but she had to try. *He is not the boy you knew any longer. You must not allow him to sway you.* If the message had gone through, if Oola had heard her plea, she gave no acknowledgment. Instead, her self-condemnation seemed to grow.

Jasminda trembled. History could not repeat itself again. "We have to help her," she whispered to Jack.

"Help *Her*?"

Jasminda never took her eyes off Oola. They'd thought her a goddess, but she was a woman, a woman with a broken heart who had nothing left in this world. A woman caught in a vortex of pain.

"She can't do it. Even after everything . . ." Jasminda wrung her hands. She too knew heartbreak. She too knew loss. But somehow Oola had allowed those emotions to overtake her resolve, and now she faltered when she needed to act.

"We have to stop him before he harms her."

Jack's expression was incredulous, but he nodded. The True Father was now bound from using Earthsong by the caldera, and if Oola's feet touched the ground, she'd also become powerless. But in the final vision Jasminda had seen through Oola's eyes, Eero had even then been bound by Yllis's blood spell. The bracelets on Eero's wrists had been calderas. But those bracelets had not stopped him from stealing his sister's Song. To do that he must have used pure blood magic, Jasminda surmised. And blood magic had allowed him to destroy the calderas.

If the True Father were to access his power now, there was no telling the amount of damage he could do.

Jasminda strained to remember the words Eero had spoken after he'd stabbed his sister, words Oola had not understood for they had been in the tongue of the Cavefolk. The words invoked the blood spell, and if Eero used it, so could Jasminda.

She stooped next to a fallen soldier and pulled the knife from his belt. Jack's gaze was questioning, but he made no move to stop her. She squeezed the knife's handle and moved closer to the standoff between the twins with Jack on her heels.

Oola's face was clouded in misery as Jasminda circled around Eero and approached him from behind. His shoulders stiffened, but he did not turn. Instead, he took a step closer to his sister and wiped the tears from her face, then wrapped his arms around her waist.

With a yell, Jasminda ran forward and plunged the knife into his back, then whispered the string of words that would bring him to the brink of death and release his Song.

The stolen Songs inside him catapulted at her, their attack violent. She kept a hand on the knife but her knees buckled under the onslaught. The Songs were tainted; they battered ruthlessly. Her connection to Earthsong flared as her own Song fought back. Like a virus infecting her, the stolen Songs wore away at her shield, dragging her under. They were oily, slick with a layer of malevolence from their former host. Jasminda took them on, having no other option, but feared she would not survive the struggle.

Her knees hit the ground, and blackness swept over her vision.

Suddenly, another Song brushed against her consciousness. Oola was trying to link with her. Jasminda gladly gave up control of her Song, and the practiced strength of Oola's immense power took over. The queen funneled the stolen Songs away from Jasminda. Her hand, still clutching the knife impaled in Eero's back, was covered by Oola's. Blood ran down Jasminda's arm.

Using the same spell Yllis had discovered to trap his Song in her pendant, Oola manipulated the energy to force the stolen Songs into the knife before pulling the blade from Eero's back. The sickly taste of blood magic fled Jasminda's tongue as the Songs were imprisoned.

Oola pulled both their hands away, and the knife clattered to the ground, the blood on it spreading, hardening, transforming into the red stone of a caldera.

Jasminda fell back, gasping for breath, as Oola released their link. Jack was there behind her, propping her up, his arms buoys in the whirling sea, keeping her afloat.

Eero crumpled to his knees screaming, his brittle shell pierced at last. Jasminda slammed her shield into place as the man's emotions sprang free of their bonds. She did not want to experience the suppressed feelings that five hundred years of ruthless brutality had forged.

Oola's tear-stained face stared blankly at her brother's weeping body. Her attention moved to Jasminda, eyes heavy, but grateful. "It is done," she whispered, then shot into the air, soon becoming a dot against the sky.

"YOUR MAJESTY." A phalanx of uniformed men approached, each bearing stripes marking them as generals. Jasminda pried herself from Jack's arms, intending to give him space to deal with the endless duties that must await him in light of all that had just happened.

"One moment, if you please," Jack said, holding up a finger. He extended his hand to Jasminda who grabbed it without thinking. He pulled her forward, away from the men and towed her along, moving swiftly through the multitude of people, all of them in various stages of confusion or awe.

"Where are we going?" she asked, darting a glance behind her at the frowning generals.

"I have no idea. Somewhere without all these blasted people." He quickened his pace.

They were nearly at a run when they reached the outer buildings of the base. Jack led them into a structure she quickly recognized as the storage room they'd slept in on her first visit. It was only days ago but it felt like another life.

He pulled the door closed then turned to rest his forehead on hers and brought their joined hands between them. A single overhead bulb barely illuminated the space, but his face was so familiar to her it did not matter.

"I'm sorry I put you in the dungeon," he whispered, his breath warming her mouth.

"I'm sorry I tried to run away. So there, we're even. No more apologies." She could not keep the smile off her face, even as the exhaustion of the past hours took hold.

He captured her lips with his, and her fatigue melted away. She wrapped her arms around him, drawing him close, feeling energized by this stolen moment.

Beyond the walls of the storage space, voices called out searching for Jack.

"You have much to do now, Prince Jaqros. Or should I call you king?"

"Only if I may call you queen." He took a step back and bent to one knee. "Jasminda ul-Sarifor, will you marry me?"

Her heart stuttered at the sight of him before her. He brought her hands to his lips. "Will you love me? Honor and protect me? Rule with me? Be my queen? Repair the damage of the two lands with me? Grow old with me? Have children with me? Make this world a better place with me?"

Tears pricked her eyes and her whole body trembled. Her answer stuck in her throat, but she pushed it out.

"Of course, Jack. Of course."

She fell against him, and they both toppled to the ground.

The generals had to wait quite a while before their prince returned.

———

THE QUEEN HAS ARISEN
"Week-long Celebration Scheduled Across the Land"
"Elsira Enters New Age of Hope"

The shortest Breach War in history ended only hours after its commencement, and the faith of thousands of Elsirans was renewed when our beloved Queen awakened from her five centuries of slumber. Details are still coming in at this time, and we still do not know what prompted this miraculous resurrection, but a source from within the Sisterhood stated that magic was almost certainly involved. . .

QUEEN OF DECEPTION?
"Reactions To Her Appearance Shock Many"

[Continued from page A1]
One witness to the awakening, speaking on the grounds of anonymity, shared his displeasure with the revelation of the Queen's physical appearance. "To think, we'd been praying to a *grol* this whole time. I just can't believe it." Others call such statements blasphemy. Syllenne Nidos, High Priestess of the Sisterhood, decried the "false believers," saying, "Those whose faith was built on any assumption of the Queen's appearance must search their hearts and remember all of the blessings She has provided to so many. We must work together to heal the years of false thinking, both about magic and those who bear it."

Temple attendance has surged in the days following the Queen's awakening, though so has defection from the religion that many are now calling a cult. Attendance is rising at gatherings of Dominionists, a tradition which originated in Yaly and boasts a growing membership worldwide.

JACK AND JAS: THE PEOPLES' WEDDING
"Union Blessed by Queen Oola"

THE GIRL WALKING down the aisle toward him looked like a mirage. Jack blinked rapidly, not sure if the joy flowing through his body was making him see things. He'd never witnessed anything more beautiful than Jasminda, radiant in traditional Lagrimari green, drawing closer to him to promise her love for all time.

Usher stood beside him, the sentimental old man sniveling like an infant. Perhaps Jack shouldn't be so hard on him since tears were flowing freely down his own face, as well. On Jack's other side stood Queen Oola, who was presiding over the ceremony. Her presence officially passed on the duties of leadership to her chosen successors.

The ceremony took place on the site of the old refugee camp. In the crowd, a mix of Elsiran and Lagrimari faces observed the union. A peaceful gathering of former enemies—merely a herald of things to come.

The True Father sat in the dungeon; Lizvette was under house arrest in her rooms, facing the possibility of exile; and her father, Nirall, had not been seen since the day of the breach. An arrest warrant had been issued for several counts of treason, but Jack did not expect the man to turn up anytime soon.

Without a doubt, the days ahead would be difficult; the collective wounds on both sides were deep. But, with Jasminda by his side as queen, Jack was certain no task was too daunting.

In moments, she would be his bride. And after the wedding, they would travel back to her valley to allow her to once again see her family's land. When they arrived, he hoped she'd be surprised by the house he'd had built for her over the ruins of her cabin. Perhaps that would be their vacation home, where she could spend time closer to the memories of those she'd lost. The goats had already been rounded up and safely transported back to the palace, where they would be well taken care of.

She stepped up to the raised stage and grasped hold of his hands. His heart swelled to near bursting. She cast a nervous glance back at the people in the audience for the nuptials. Jack lightly squeezed her fingers. Jasminda straightened, throwing her shoulders back and lifting her chin. There she was, his warrior bride. He wondered if she had a blade strapped to her even now.

He couldn't wait to find out.

EPILOGUE

THE NEW KING and queen embrace before me, the love between them a living, breathing entity. I numb the sliver of jealousy slicing my heart. I cannot begrudge these children their happiness.

Every head in the gathered crowd turns to follow Jaqros and Jasminda as they retreat down the aisle. Every head but one. Dark eyes glare at me, not in awe or reverence like the others, but in accusation. I nod in acknowledgement.

Darvyn. Are you ready to accept my offer?

His eyes bore into me coldly. He clenches his jaw so hard I think he may break a tooth. *What exactly is your offer . . . Your Majesty?* He adds my title as an afterthought. His impertinence is actually refreshing.

You may be of service to our new queen. I still owe her a debt, one even she does not know of but that you can help me to repay.

He scowls. *I am nothing if not your pawn. What would I need to do this time?*

Her father and brothers. You can retrieve them for me.

And why should I do you this favor?

I smile, baring all my teeth. *Kyara.*

I only have to say her name and his whole demeanor changes. All bravado falls away, and raw pain flashes across his features.

Do this for me and her life will be spared.

I call the wind to me and rise into the air, already certain of his decision.

THANK YOU

Thank you so much for taking the time to read this book! Reviews mean the world to authors, and they help readers find new books, so please do leave a review at your retailer, blog, or favorite book site. And if you enjoyed the book don't keep it to yourself. Recommend it and share the love! ☺

ACKNOWLEDGMENTS

I am truly fortunate to have such a supportive family, both here and in the other room. I can't thank my parents enough for their consistent encouragement and Paul for the story triage.

I owe a great debt to the writers and teachers at The Muse Writers Center in Norfolk, VA, the Hurston/Wright Fiction Workshop, and my VONA/Voices family: Junot Díaz, the Kwisatz Haderach and the Fiction Vixens.

Endless thanks to Danielle Rose Poiesz for bringing order to the chaos and to Marjorie Liu for helping me figure out where to begin.

Without the generosity of my critique partners and beta readers, this book would be significantly less coherent. Thanks to Lauren Dee, for her eagle eyes, and to James T. Egan for creating a cover that still makes my jaw drop.

To my sistren, Nakeesha Seneb and Kara Stevens, we did it!

And to Jared, thank you for believing in me and for your gentle, daily ~~harassment~~ encouragement.

ABOUT THE AUTHOR

Leslye Penelope has been writing since she could hold a pen and loves getting lost in the worlds in her head. She's a romance junkie who self-medicates with happily-ever-afters and steaming mugs of green tea. She lives in Maryland with her husband, an eighty-pound lap dog, and an attack cat. Visit her online at http://www.lpenelope.com.

CPSIA information can be obtained at www.ICGtesting.com
Printed in the USA
LVOW09s1059170116

471043LV00007B/754/P